Praise for *Dangerous Straits*

"Chris Norbury's Matt Lanier thriller series gets better with each story.... This is a story of unlikely allies and lethal enemies that brims with tension as Lanier navigates the poverty-stricken urban areas of Minneapolis. The pacing in this gripping thriller is fast-paced, keeping the reader riveted to the page." — **Gregory L. Renz, author of *Beneath the Flames* and *Beyond the Flames.***

"This installment of the Matt Laniermystery-thriller series is well worth the wait. Norbury sets the hook on page one and keeps the line emotionally taut to the very end!"—**Laurie Buchanan, author of the Sean McPherson crime thrillers.**

"Again, Chris Norbury is a masterful storyteller as he pulls the reader through unexpected twists and turns as he builds to an exceptional conclusion of the trilogy!"—**Valerie Biel, author of the *Circle of Nine* series.**

"... a thriller that packs a wallop.... The breakneck action and suspense will keep the pages turning."—**Brian Lutterman, author of *Incel* and the Pen Wilkinson thrillers.**

Books by Chris Norbury

Straight River (Matt Lanier #1)
Castle Danger (Matt Lanier #2)
Dangerous Straits (Matt Lanier #3)

For Middle-Grade and Older Readers

Little Mountain, Big Trouble

DANGEROUS STRAITS

CHRIS NORBURY

CSN
Press

To my friend, Thea. Her perseverance in overcoming all the obstacles life has thrown in her path is inspirational—similar to the way my fictional character, Matt Lanier, battled the obstacles I threw in his path.

To all those who seek the truth and promote logical, fact-based thinking.

And as always, to Sandra, who makes this all possible.

Chapter 1

If long-dead Ludwig could've heard this street music version of Chuck Berry's rock 'n'-roll classic, "Roll Over Beethoven," he might've clutched the sides of his coffin and refused the command. Nevertheless, the small crowd was digging the sound. Despite the two-man band's unpolished voices and thrift-store instruments, they generated a solid groove and enough energy to get toes tapping and heads bobbing. A pair of well-dressed women seemed ready to bust some moves, and their two toddlers bounced up and down, clapping awkwardly.

Matt Lanier had played the song on guitar a hundred times, so his musician's brain was on autopilot. That allowed him to do some people watching behind an impassive "performer's smile." But when he spotted a bald man standing in the audience, his autopilot switched off, and sight-reading mode switched on. Six-two, two-fifty, broad shoulders, no discernible neck, menacing countenance. Uncanny resemblance. Panic-inducing. A twin?

Although *that* man couldn't possibly be *the* man, brutal memories of their last encounter sent Matt's head spinning. His fingers suddenly felt like sausages, and he stumbled on the chords. Hypo, his drummer and lead singer, shot him a puzzled glance but kept playing. Matt silently cursed, refocused, and concentrated on forming each note. An interminable minute later, they ended the song with a rapidly strummed D9 chord over a drum roll and cymbal crash.

He looked up—but away from Baldy—to acknowledge the enthusiastic applause. Unfortunately, his gaze landed on two Minneapolis police officers standing behind the crowd. After seeing the bald man, the cop sighting put him over the edge. His adrenaline rush triggered flight mode. Nodding toward the police, he said to Hypo, "I'm outta here."

Hypo glanced at the cops. His shoulders slumped. "Aww, Jazzman, not *again*." He gestured toward all the people standing in a loose semicircle around them. "Lunchtime business crowd. Serious coin. We can make us a killin' here—at least double what we get anywhere else."

Hypo was right. Lots of paper cash had been tossed into Matt's open guitar case over the past hour. A few more bills were being added now: primarily singles but at least one five. Almost everyone who'd donated tossed in several coins at a minimum.

Matt, known to everyone as Jazzman since he arrived in Minneapolis a few months ago, shook his head. "The money don't matter, Hypo. You know the deal. I get nervous; we find a new gig."

"*Nervous?*" Hypo shot him a frowning glare. "Dat ain't nerves, man. More like panic on crack. Make yo' ugly white face look like an albino's."

Hypo had seen him like this before. After asking what was wrong the first time—and receiving stone-cold silence and an expression that warned: *never ask me again, or you'll suffer severe pain*—Hypo had learned not to press the matter. Instead, he smiled and waved at the crowd. "Show's over, folks. Thank you kindly."

Their stage was a set of steps in Peavey Plaza outside Orchestra Hall. Today was their debut outdoor performance after they'd perfected their set list in the skyways of downtown Minneapolis in March. The balmy April weather had lured office workers, shoppers, and downtown residents eager to enjoy the outdoors after a long winter. Now they could do so without risk of frostbite, a broken bone from slipping on the remnant winter ice, or a slush bath from a passing bus. It was the Minnesota-human version of emerging from hibernation.

Hypo grumbled something unintelligible, then began packing his drum set—five-gallon bucket, two-gallon bucket, five-quart ice cream pail, and a cymbal scrounged from a discarded child's toy drum set that was barely thicker than heavy-duty aluminum foil. His drumsticks looked as if they'd been carved into shape by starving mice. He flipped the largest bucket over, nested the other two inside the first, and slid his drumsticks inside. Then he removed the cymbal from its stand, wedged the stand into the nest of plastic cylinders, and laid the cymbal on top like a makeshift lid.

Matt scooped up the paper money, shuffled the bills into a foldable order, and shoved the thick wad into his pants pocket. He gave the coins to Hypo. After encasing his guitar, he shouldered it by the makeshift strap he'd made from a length of rope, then picked up his battery-operated mini amplifier.

"Thanks for comin', sistas," Hypo said to two women Matt vaguely recognized from another gig he and Hypo had recently played.

"See ya next time, Lefty," Hypo said to an older man, bent and frail, dressed in blue jeans that had the shine of months-old street grime. Lefty smiled and waved from his perch on a nearby half-wall.

The duet walked away from the police, using the dispersing crowd as a visual buffer. Matt repeatedly glanced over his shoulder until they'd turned the corner and were out of sight.

Limping alongside him, Hypo sipped from the silver flask he always kept in his pocket. "I know you got serious issues in your head," he said, "but for a pair of shitty musicians, we was cleanin' up. Almost had that crowd writin' checks to us."

"Speak for yourself, Buddy Rich," Matt said, half kidding.

Hypo was a decent amateur musician. He kept a steady, unflashy beat and could reel off a solid drum break. He might have been wedding-band good on a standard drum kit. With proper training, his clear, strong tenor voice could've earned him a living as a singer. He sang melody and harmony equally well. Because Matt was a baritone and his voice didn't project as much as a tenor's voice, Hypo usually sang lead. Unfortunately, his phrasing and singing diction were only average, which doomed him to be a decent semi-pro at best. His biggest asset with street crowds was an effortless, good-natured banter between tunes. He could always persuade the listeners to chuck a few more coins or a bill or two into Matt's open guitar case. The man would've made an excellent used-car salesman.

"Where you wanna set up now?" Hypo asked.

Matt shrugged. "Not in the mood anymore."

"Aww, come on, man. Let's do another hour somewhere." Hypo had switched on his whiny voice, the one that clenched Matt's teeth with its metallic edginess. "I gotta pay my rent this week. My monthly don't come till the day after rent's due, so I'm a little tight."

They were approaching Loring Park from West Grant Street. The grassy areas were still wet and cold, so all the benches were occupied. The duo could have set up and played there, but the lunch hour was over, which meant paying listeners would be scarce.

Distracted by the sight of a woman and child sitting on a bench twenty yards away, Matt stopped and said, "Tell you what. Take my share."

Hypo pulled up and gave him the fake double-take expression Matt knew was the prelude to a torrent of feigned gratitude. "You sure? Don't wanna be takin' food outta your mouth. But I sure appreciate it, brotha."

Matt waved him off. "I haven't donated any plasma lately. Maybe I'll go down to the center and give a couple times this week. I'll check out the day labor place too. Should be some landscaping or yard work I can get now that the snow's gone."

"*Maybe* don't help you today, Jazzman. You got enough for now?"

Even though *enough* was a relative term, Matt nodded. He'd be able to eat modestly for a few days. Making sure they weren't being watched by any would-be muggers, he reached into his pocket for the wad of paper currency he'd stashed earlier. After peeling off a five, he slapped the remainder into Hypo's hand.

"Thought you were givin' me all your share," Hypo said.

"Changed my mind." Then Matt remembered the hand-scrawled note on a scrap of paper someone had tossed into the cash pile. He gave it to Hypo. "Okay, now we're square."

Hypo read the note aloud. "Don't quit your day job." Frowning, he crumpled the note and tossed it into a nearby trash can. "Muthafuckin' comedian."

Matt slung his guitar case over his shoulder and grabbed his amp. "See you later, partner."

He waved goodbye to Hypo and walked toward the woman and child—a girl—on the bench. They had sallow skin, haggard expressions, and eyes devoid of alertness. The woman's hair was brown and shoulder length. The girl's hair was shorter, curly, and dishwater blonde. Both looked in need of a shower. They wore nondescript blue jeans and T-shirts under nylon jackets. Their clothes were frayed, torn, and stained. The girl, maybe five years old, played listlessly with a small teddy bear. The woman's expression turned wary, and she sat up straighter.

Matt smiled. "Hi."

She studied him, tight-lipped, greeting him with only a slight lift of her chin.

He extended the five-dollar bill in his hand. "Buy some lunch for the kid, okay?"

Her eyes grew wider as the bill got closer. Years ago, she might have been pretty, before whatever terrible shit happened that led to her sitting here with her presumed daughter on a pleasant weekday afternoon in April. Drugs, parental or spousal abuse, prostitution, lack of education. The cause didn't matter. Now she looked twenty years older than her actual age, which he estimated to be in the mid-twenties.

"What you want for it? Head? Hand job? Talk dirty to you?" The distrust in her voice was unmistakable. "Whatever you want gotta be quick because that Uncle Abe only pays for a few minutes of my time."

Matt fought down the urge to scream that not all men were slimeballs. She noticed his tension and shied backward a few inches. He put as much calm into his voice as he could muster and said, "Buy some lunch for your daughter. That's all."

She relaxed and snatched the bill from his hand, then stood and said to her daughter, "Up, baby. Time for lunch."

The child stood, clutching her bear, staring blankly at Matt. *She's almost past hope too,* he thought. But he smiled when she noticed his guitar case and eyed it as if it were an object from outer space. *Still a little bit of wonder in her mind.*

The woman grabbed her daughter's hand, and they trudged toward the neighborhood convenience store. There was a fifty-fifty chance she'd buy any healthy food, like milk or fruit. At least they'd stave off hunger for a few more hours.

From behind him, Hypo said, "Man, you one sorry white-ass sucker for a sob story."

Matt formed a *Mona Lisa* smile and walked past him, heading downtown.

Seconds later, Hypo exclaimed, "Hey, sista. Hold on."

Turning, Matt watched Hypo limp toward the mother and child, his bucket rhythmically slapping against his thigh, until he caught up to them. The woman stopped but clasped her daughter at the sight of the wiry stranger approaching them. Her eyes widened when she noticed his prosthetic foot and the two missing fingers on one hand. Hypo thrust some cash into the woman's hand and said something Matt couldn't hear. When she took the money, Matt chuckled and shook his head. *Sorry* black-ass *sucker for a sob story.*

He resumed his walk to the plasma donation center on Washington Avenue, moving east on Grant Street until it veered northeast and became Second Avenue. After a few blocks, he turned left toward Marquette Avenue but entered an alley between the two avenues to cruise the back-door areas of restaurants between Ninth and Fifth Streets. Many times before, he'd scored tasty leftovers of food that were prepared but not served to anyone and couldn't be saved for the dinner crowd. America's wasteful obsession with throwing out food because it wasn't either perfect or up-to-the-minute fresh was disgraceful. But it was a godsend to hungry people who struggled to eat every day. It helped that many kitchen workers were only a missed paycheck away from landing on the street themselves. They showed remarkable compassion for the street folks who were regular dumpster divers. Sometimes, all it took was a knock at the back door for a sympathetic dishwasher or line cook to "find" a burger that had been "dropped" on the floor, a piece of toast that was "burned," or the dregs of a soup pot that held less than a whole serving.

Between Tenth and Fourth Streets, Matt scored a bagel, two slices of cold pepperoni pizza, and a cardboard cup of tomato bisque. As he sipped the soup, he wistfully recalled the days when he could afford to come to that restaurant and buy not only the bisque, but also a complete lunch or dinner when he performed at Orchestra Hall with the Minnesota Orchestra.

Simultaneously refueled and dejected, he resumed his trek until he arrived at City Hall. Made of rose granite and topped with a green copper roof, the building stood out like an old, short, dumpy member of a tall, lean basketball team of modern skyscrapers. If not for the clock tower soaring over 300 feet into the air, the squat building would be invisible in the downtown skyline.

Matt had a few blocks to go, but when he saw the parked police cars and several uniformed officers entering and exiting the law enforcement side of the building, his gut clenched, and a wave of panic flooded through his veins. He thought he'd be able to run this gamut, having seen police on the streets almost daily and realizing they barely noticed him. But with this many cops—especially the higher-ups mixed in with the front-line officers—a flush of sweat chilled his forehead. Sergeants, lieutenants, and plainclothes detectives were much more likely to be on the lookout for fugitives, even those brazen enough to walk past their headquarters.

Although Matt looked nothing like the photo of him that every law enforcement officer in the state had probably seen, irrational fear overwhelmed him. Certainly, one of these cops would see through his "disguise": a long, scruffy beard, faded and torn blue jeans, a work shirt frayed at the collar, and a grimy Twins cap pulled low on his forehead. If that sharp-eyed cop sounded the alarm, twenty others would instantly descend upon the man wanted for allegedly killing one of their own. Despite being broke, living in the wild and in homeless shelters, doing odd jobs, and now playing music on the street for spare change, he'd survived and lived to fight another day for the chance to reclaim his real identity. The trouble was, another day had become another week had become another month and was rapidly approaching another year. Calming his trembling body with a shaky breath, Matt turned and retreated.

Chapter 2

The free clinic on Franklin Avenue was a forlorn structure befitting the neighborhood. Downtown gentrification had yet to reach this far south, nor had it spread northward from über-trendy Uptown. The standard look of the buildings was peeling paint, cracked windows covered with permalayers of grime, and crumbling concrete stoops. More trash lay on the sidewalks and in the gutters than was typical in other parts of the city. Subtle hints of rotten garbage, sewer gas, and general decay tainted the air.

Matt had walked straight to the clinic from City Hall. Seeing the bald man at Peavey Plaza brought back the headaches and anxiety he'd suffered from ever since he arrived in Minneapolis. Even though the bald man wasn't Witt—because Witt was dead—the resemblance was close enough to trigger nightmarish memories.

The medical staff provided essential services for the local indigent population who couldn't afford health insurance and would wait as long as needed for free medical treatment. When Matt entered the cramped waiting area, his spirits fell. All the chairs were occupied. A few men leaned against what little wall space was available. A quick scan of the room yielded a half dozen mothers with children in tow. They'd take twice as long to be helped as the adults, who got to the point and knew going in what meds or treatments they wanted. Most hoped to score any pain relief strong enough to numb whatever ailment was causing them the greatest distress that day.

Opioid addiction and abuse were common in the neighborhood. Therefore, many patients tried to convince the medical staff that their intense suffering was because of something unmeasurable, such as back pain or whiplash from a fall or a fender bender. The better actors had perfected their moaning and looks of suffering to levels worthy of an Academy Award. Quite annoying when several waiting room habitués were vying for the title of "Most Deserving of the Hard Stuff."

To their credit, the medical staff was stingy about dispensing opioids. They quickly learned who the worst abusers were and gently steered them toward treatment. Unfortunately, homeless folks and the working poor couldn't afford the kind of rehabilitation facilities that boasted high success rates. They might get into a program run by the county, but most did the revolving-door act of sobering up for a month or so, then succumbing to temptation and getting hooked again.

Because of the warm weather and poor ventilation, the crowded waiting room smelled of unwashed bodies and dirty diapers. Thankfully, the clinic director had instituted a number system for busy times. People checked in at the desk and were given a numbered plastic poker chip that would be called when it was their turn to see a professional. Matt got his chip, multiplied the number of waiting parties by ten minutes, and went to a nearby coffee shop for a doughnut and a cup of coffee. Lattes, espressos, and cappuccinos were not in his budget. Hell, neither was coffee, but he allowed himself an occasional cup to reminisce about better days when he lingered in trendy coffee shops, sipping lattes, and enjoying pastries for breakfast.

The coffee was weak, and the doughnut was dry and flavorless, but they satisfied Matt's appetite. He nursed his coffee and loitered for two hours before taking the subtle, non-verbal hint from the owner that he'd overstayed the welcome he'd rented with his three-dollar purchase. He left and ambled to a nearby pocket park to sit in the shade before returning to the clinic five minutes before he was called to see the doctor.

Fifteen minutes later, he left with a plastic vial full of Tylenol 3—a combination of acetaminophen and codeine. He'd had the drug prescribed to him before. It was only marginally better than any over-the-counter pain reliever. Still, it would dull the pain to a bearable degree. But in the depths of his heart and mind, he knew that pills only treated the symptoms. They never addressed the cause of his pain. And with all that had transpired in the past year, curing his pain was impossible.

Matt trudged east on Franklin, turning a few blocks later down a residential street lined with old brownstone duplexes and once-stately three-story Tudors and Victorians. Most of the mansions had been subdivided into multiple units, typically a small bedroom with a retrofitted bath and equipped with a rudimentary kitchenette—hotplate, microwave, mini-refrigerator, and maybe a sink for dishes. Some people he'd met on the street had told him about those units and how the rent was sky-high for a place that barely qualified as an efficiency apartment.

Because Matt had no income other than from what he earned playing music on the street for spare change, the occasional day labor job, and donating plasma, he was relegated to living in a homeless shelter for men. Located in one of those three-story Victorians, its ten bedrooms had been split into twenty. Each floor had a bathroom to be used by the six or seven residents per floor. When he reached his building, he walked up to his third-floor hovel and flopped onto the single bed with the saggy mattress. After kicking off his boots, Matt popped two of the Tylenol 3s into his mouth and washed them down with the tepid water from the bottle sitting on his only other piece of furniture, a two-drawer nightstand. Heaving a long, tired sigh, he lay down and stared at the brown water stains on the ceiling.

It was only late afternoon, but he was more mentally than physically tired. He wanted to sleep but didn't expect it to come quickly. Instead, the memories projected themselves onto the grimy ceiling. Somewhere down that painful memory lane, Matt drifted off to sleep, and the nightmare clicked on like a horror movie in his subconscious.

He walks down the street toward his car on that rainy April afternoon in the Riverside neighborhood. A chilly drizzle is falling. The air smells of spring—fresh, earthy, energetic. Head down, he reaches the corner and starts to cross the street. Hears an engine revving, a car approaching. Zach Perez yells from behind him, "Look out!" Matt looks up, sees the Mercedes-Benz barreling toward him. He freezes. The driver's face comes into focus. Ugly. Snarling. Twisted smile. Pure evil. Charlie Witt. Looming above Witt is Leland Smythe, the untouchable puppet master, far above the scene, urging Witt onward.

This time, Zach can't push Matt to safety. Matt's legs sink into the now-liquid asphalt, which instantly hardens to concrete. Witt speeds up. His face looms in Matt's vision as large as if it were on an IMAX movie screen. Matt screams. Braces for impact. The car hits him square on, knocks him flat onto his back. The pain is excruciating. Witt stops, backs up. Matt springs back to vertical, like a kid's inflatable punching bag. Witt runs him over again. Matt screams again. Feels the agony again. Feels his body shatter again. The scene repeats a third time, then a fourth. Each impact racks Matt's body. His bones must be crushed to shards by now. Each time he returns to an upright position, he desperately tries to free his legs and run. But he can't. And Witt never stops. And Smythe floats above it all.

Chapter 3

The Duluth public library on Superior Street was almost empty of patrons. The building—designed to resemble a Great Lakes cargo ship, a Laker—featured a long row of windows that curved around what would've been deck level on a real Laker. The windows were angled downward to overlook the streets below. It was a bright, comfortable place to read or study on a sunny day. But on this chilly April night, with recently plowed snow still lining the streets and a bitter east wind blowing in off ice-encrusted Lake Superior, the spacious facility exuded a bleak, lonely feeling.

Ben Nowitzki sat back from the study carrel he occupied and checked his watch. Closing time. He yawned and stretched, then tossed the copies he'd made of several old newspaper and magazine articles into a manila folder marked *SMYTHE*. This data was too old to have been available via computer and needed to be scanned and copied from microfiches.

Ever since his fateful encounter with Matt Lanier two months ago, Ben had become obsessed with learning more about Leland Smythe, a Twin Cities millionaire real estate developer. Smythe's connection to Lanier was simple, yet complex. The simple part? Smythe wanted Lanier dead. The complex part? Smythe had hired Ben for the hit job.

However, Ben hadn't known Smythe's true identity until after he'd tried and failed to kill Lanier. Somehow, Lanier had outwitted him, then overpowered him. But to Ben's amazement, Lanier had spared his life. That's when Lanier informed him that the man Ben had known only as "Mr. Jones" was actually Leland Smythe, a wealthy, unscrupulous Twin Cities real estate developer. Although Smythe had painted Lanier as a cold-blooded killer of as many as six people, there was something about

Lanier that belied Smythe's claim. Sparing Ben's life for starters. What cold-blooded killer doesn't kill someone who tried to kill him? What cold-blooded killer rescues an injured man in the wilderness and drags him ten miles to safety? What cold-blooded killer saves a woman and her son from a bastard of a husband? Ben's desire for the truth had gradually overpowered his desire for a lucrative payday.

He wasn't proud of the fact that he'd fallen so far from grace in less than five years. He'd been a fast-rising Minneapolis Police Department officer who became one of the youngest detectives in department history. However, accepting a bribe to look the other way on an arrest cost him his badge. He'd taken the bribe and the hit job only because of his salient weakness—valuing money above morals. After he'd been fired, he slunk back to his hometown of Duluth and hung out his private investigator shingle. Although his investigative skills remained sharp, he struggled to earn a living because of his tarnished reputation. Smythe's six-figure contract on Lanier seemed like the best way to keep his business afloat for at least two more years, so he'd jumped at the offer.

On the drive home, Ben weighed the pros and cons of his plan. Smythe wasn't aware that Ben knew his identity. Putting aside any obligation he felt toward Lanier, he might be able to leverage that knowledge for some serious cash. The big negative for pursuing a double-dip into Smythe's money was Lanier's insistence that Smythe was ruthless, powerful, and showed little regard for human life, especially the lives of his enemies.

By the time he arrived at his duplex in the West End, Ben had decided on a strategy that allowed him the most options as it unfolded. If he played his cards right, the giant payday he'd dreamed of would come soon ... possibly within weeks. But first, he needed to know if Lanier was still alive, and if so, where he was hiding.

Tracking Lanier back to the Minneapolis-St. Paul area was Ben's prime lead. During their last encounter in Castle Danger, on Minnesota's North Shore of Lake Superior, Lanier had virtually guaranteed he was intent on revenge when he said: *Tell Smythe I'm coming after him.*

Maybe that statement was boastful anger, but Ben heard enough sincerity in Lanier's voice to be confident Lanier at least wanted to try to stop Smythe—legally or not. After all, Smythe had destroyed the man's life. Why should Lanier worry about dying or going to jail for crimes he claimed not to have committed? He might as well have a legitimate reason to fear imprisonment or death.

Minneapolis was the logical place to start a search. Lanier had recently owned a condominium there and been a member of the Minnesota Orchestra until he went on the run. Additionally, he'd performed around the area with his jazz trio and as a first-call bassist when big-name jazz singers and performers came to town and needed a backup band.

Of course, Lanier might be anywhere else in the world too—within reason. With little money, and fearful of revealing his identity to anyone, Lanier wasn't likely to travel to a strange place to be a fugitive. Easier to hide in a familiar area. A relative or friend might shelter him for a while, but Lanier had no close relatives, and his friends would be reluctant to hide someone with a price on his head and a bullseye on his back.

Lanier would be too easily noticed in predominantly minority neighborhoods like the North Side—primarily black—and the East Lake Street neighborhoods populated by many Hispanics, Southeast Asians, and Somalis. So Ben focused his search on the South Loop—roughly bordered by Loring Park on the west, Franklin Avenue on the south, Interstate 35 on the east, and downtown Minneapolis on the north. Also possible was the Cedar-Riverside neighborhood, which extended parallel with Franklin Avenue toward the Mississippi. Still a sizeable geographic area but manageable in Ben's estimation.

His first step would be to comb the free clinics and homeless shelters, then hit the streets. As long shots went, it wasn't as foolish as a bet on the hundred-to-one horse in the Kentucky Derby. And if he got no hits on his "wanted poster" or from checking the shelters and clinics after a week or two, he'd figure out a new plan of attack.

What gave him hope was that he'd tracked down Lanier on the North Shore in less than a week using the same reasoning he was employing with this search. Lanier wasn't a hardened criminal or crafty fugitive. He made mistakes, and his biggest mistake was he kept things simple. Easy to understand why. If Ben had been an experienced hit man and hadn't tried for the doubled fee for making Lanier's death seem accidental, Lanier would have died in Castle Danger.

Ben reserved a room in a budget motel in Northeast Minneapolis—his old neighborhood when he worked for the Minneapolis PD. Then he packed a suitcase and assorted investigative gear, weapons, and ammunition, prepped his research data and laptop, went out to his car, and drove to the Twin Cities.

Chapter 4

Matt woke to a sharp knock on his door that he first mistook for a series of rifle shots. Jerking upright, he reflexively looked for cover. Seeing his window and feeling the warm breeze brought him to his senses. It was light outside, so he assumed he'd slept for an hour or two.

When Matt opened the door, Hypo was standing in the hall, looking royally steamed. "Man, where you been?" he asked. "We were gonna play at Peavey again today, but you were a damn no-show. What's up with that?"

"Huh?" Matt asked, still groggy. "Whaddya mean, again? We played there a few hours ago." Then he checked his watch. One o'clock. "Oh, Jeez, man, I'm sorry. I fell asleep yesterday afternoon and just woke up."

Hypo reeled backward as if he'd been shoved. "Say what? You been sleepin' a whole damn day? What da hell you do yesterday get you so tired? Screw a set of hot triplets twice each?"

"Nah, nothing like that. Got some pain meds at the clinic yesterday, then came here. Guess I was more tired than I thought." Regaining his awareness, he noticed he was soaked with sweat. He walked to his bed and felt the sheets. They were as damp as his clothes. He remembered hearing deep thumps as he slept that sounded like cannons or dynamite explosions. Those must have been from the guy in the adjacent room pounding on the wall for Matt to stop screaming. He remembered waking for a few seconds, but he was so mentally drained, he fell back into his near coma, and the endless horror movie started again.

Now fully awake, he realized his mouth was sandpaper dry. Made sense. Most of the water that had been in his body yesterday was now on the sheets and his clothes. "I need a drink of water. Hang on."

He went to the bathroom down the hall, relieved himself of what little urine his bladder held, and gulped four tall glasses of tap water. The combined body odors and bathroom-related smells of a half dozen men who weren't big on hygiene and healthy food were unbearable unless the window was opened to let fresh air in and dilute the stench. As usual, he held his breath as much as possible and breathed through his mouth.

Glancing in the mirror, Matt barely recognized himself. Not because of his long hair and shaggy beard. No, he didn't recognize the man behind the eyes. The spark and fire of a confident professional were gone. There were wrinkles on his forehead and around his eyes that hadn't been there a year ago. His neutral expression, the one he displayed when he posed for passport or driver's license photos, had taken on a hang-dog edge. He massaged his face with both hands, splashed cold water on his face and neck, toweled off, and returned to his room.

Hypo was sitting on the floor with his back against the wall under the window, sipping from his flask. His prosthetic left leg protruded from under his pant cuff. The prosthesis was one of those twenty-first-century high-tech models made of titanium and custom-fitted to precise specifications.

"What kinda joint this be, not even a rickety ol' chair for an honored guest?" he said with mock disdain. "Make a cripple sit on the damn cold floor. Shameful." He shot a sly grin at Matt. "I wasn't about to sit in your puddle of sweat."

"If I had a better musical partner," Matt said, "I could afford a rickety ol' chair."

Hypo's expression changed to a questioning look—the look a bartender gives a patron who might be unfit to drive home. "You all right, brotha? Not like you to blow off a gig. Plus, you look like shit that been pissed on, then puked on, then smeared into the sidewalk."

Matt waved him off. "I'm good. Took two T-threes to get a jump-start on my headache. Probably should've started with one."

"I noticed you ain't been doin' too well lately. Sorta mopey, not all there. And not just cuz of yesterday's gig, either. It's like somethin' on your mind takin' over your body, draggin' you down." Hypo narrowed his brows and softened his tone. "You sure everything's okay?"

Matt sat on his bed and slumped against the wall, unable to pretend any longer. "No, man, nothing's okay anymore. And I can't deal with it. Thought I could, but ..."

Hypo studied him for a while, then said, "I know a cat might be able to help. I had some issues back in the day with this." He held up his right hand, the one missing two fingers, to hint at the severity of those issues. "Actually, I know two cats. I'll take you to the first one. He might tell you to talk to number two if he don't think he's the man for the job."

The crack in Matt's defensive wall widened as he fought his reluctance to share his secrets with anyone. His present state might not qualify as hitting rock bottom, but it felt damn close. Tamping down his eagerness, he said, "When can we see this guy?"

Hypo pocketed his flask, sat forward, and extended his left hand. "You help me up; I take you outta this shithole right now. Then we'll go see da man with da plan that'll help you screw your head back on straight."

As he helped Hypo to his feet, Matt looked at him in disbelief. This strange, funny man with a past more secretive than Matt's had become such a good friend, a trusted friend, in the space of a few months. The power of music had flexed its muscle again.

In his first week as a street musician, Matt performed as a solo guitarist. Hypo had been listening with the small crowd in a downtown skyway one day. After he'd complimented Matt's playing and tossed a dollar into his guitar case, they began to chat. When Hypo mentioned he sang in his church choir when he was a kid, Matt said, "Want to sing a song with me?"

Hypo's eyebrows shot upward. He glanced at the other listeners. "You serious, man?"

Matt nodded. "Sure. Why not?" He gestured to the five listeners standing nearby. "This look like Orchestra Hall to you? No pressure."

Hypo pondered for a few seconds, his eyes upraised. "You know 'Amazing Grace?'"

"Of course. Why that tune?"

"My mama's favorite. She dragged my scrawny ass to church every week, always wipin' smudges off my face with a tissue wetted with her damn spit. Every time the preacher said somethin' in the sermon 'bout a particular sin I committed, she'd remind me of my unworthiness with her elbow in my ribs and a loud 'amen' in my ear. Pretty soon, I figured singing in the choir was a helluva lot better than gettin' broke ribs and *amened* to death."

Matt chuckled. "My mom was pretty fast with the wet tissue trick too." He checked his guitar to make sure it was still in tune, then asked, "What key?"

"Let's do it in *A*."

Matt strummed a four-bar intro to set the key, and Hypo started singing.

Despite being untrained except for his church choir experience, Hypo's voice was powerful and in tune, with an earthy edge. He emoted without seeming to try. Maybe it came out from all his previous sorrows, the way past emotions poured out through the instruments of so many musicians. Best of all, he listened to Matt's guitar lines—rudimentary though they were because of his two damaged fingers—and responded and communicated with his voice. He had above-average improvisation skills and wasn't afraid to take liberties with a melody.

At the song's end, Matt wasn't sure whether the tear in Hypo's eye was genuine or not. However, an old woman shuffled forward, pulling a two-wheeled, wire-framed shopping basket, and gave Hypo a hug. Her cheeks were also damp from tears. She said the song took her back to better days with her recently deceased husband. He used to sing it to her whenever she got discouraged or sick or angry. It was his way of reminding her that God had a better plan for them both and that "This too shall pass."

Matt choked up when she said her husband had suffered from Alzheimer's disease for five years but remembered "Amazing Grace" well enough to sing to her until his final days. So, when she dropped a twenty-dollar bill in Matt's guitar case and gave him a hug as well, a musical partnership between two strangers—a fugitive guitar player with an injured hand and a one-legged, eight-fingered singer—was born.

Chapter 5

After a leisurely half-hour stroll from Matt's place, the duo reached Bubba's or Moe's or Smitty's or whatever the bar was called. Matt didn't notice any sign on the storefront. It was the kind of place that served basic booze at affordable prices to working stiffs who couldn't care less about microbrews or designer wines. The place reeked of stale beer and some other vaguely unpleasant smells but was well lit. The bar was long and rectangular, made of polished mahogany. The half dozen tables were topped with Formica. The chairs were upholstered with decades-old Naugahyde that was frayed but otherwise clean. Matt's impression was of a budget bar whose owner at least took minimal pride in his establishment.

Hypo pointed to a dark-haired man sitting at the end of the bar, wearing black jeans and a navy-blue fleece pullover sweater. "Yo, Hawk. This the cat I told you 'bout."

Hawk looked up from his drink with a tilt of his head and nodded. Hypo led Matt to the end of the bar. "I figure he got some sort of legal name, but he call himself Jazzman."

Matt and Hawk exchanged polite but curt greetings, looking each other up and down. Hawk was of average height, thick but not obese, with skin darker than white but lighter than Hypo. His face seemed ruggedly pleasant, with a large nose, firm chin, and intelligent-looking eyes. What initially looked like dark hair from afar was actually jet black sprinkled with gray.

Hawk studied Matt for a long, silent moment. There was no background music to lessen Matt's discomfort. Hawk's penetrating gaze made Matt feel as though he were standing naked in front of the man. Yet, he couldn't look away. Since confiding in Hypo earlier, Matt's doubt about revealing even a small part of himself to anyone had grown with each step he'd taken toward this bar.

After he'd finished his scrutiny, Hawk faced Hypo and said, "I can help him."

Matt did a double take. "Excuse me?" He stiffened. "I can't believe you have a clue about my problems after staring at me for one minute. Sounds more like you're pulling a scam to con me out of the few dollars I have left."

Hawk looked at him with bemusement and shrugged. "Suit yourself."

As Hawk turned back toward his drink, Hypo said, "Easy, J-man. You got it all wrong."

Matt glared at Hypo. "What's the deal? You get a referral fee for sending patsies like me to this guy? Ten percent of whatever he cons out of us?"

He turned to leave, now positive that trying to get help had been a terrible idea. He walked toward the exit with a downthrust of his arm.

"Hey, stupid! Dig this." Hypo's angry edge stopped Matt in his tracks. "Da man here got chops for helpin' people like you and me ten times better than Charlie Parker's got chops for playin' bebop. You a royal-flush fool to walk outta this bar without at least talkin' to him for five damn minutes."

Matt's face burned hot. Was he afraid of what this impassive stranger might tell him? Afraid to admit he was standing on the edge of the abyss of giving up on life altogether? He'd never suspected Hypo to be less than an upfront cat, but now he was torn between trust and doubt. Such a familiar theme in the past year. Who do you trust?

"Besides, what else your sorry ass got to do this afternoon? Go back to your stinkin' lousy crib and enjoy another eighteen-hour nightmare?"

Matt slumped to the brink of collapsing. He never wanted to sleep again if he had to relive past events whose memories were triggered by seeing that bald man at Peavey Plaza. He turned, stabilized his shaking hand on the bar, and walked back to the two men.

Before Matt could apologize, Hawk said, "You wouldn't be the first who left immediately. Many came back. However, the ones who never walked away are those who turned their lives around the most. Better thank Hypo for talking some sense into you."

Matt glanced at Hypo, who gave him an impish grin and said, "You luckier than you can imagine that I like you, J-man. I see lotta dudes on the street who're messed up. But they assholes or violent bastards. Don't deserve anyone's help, so I let 'em die slow street deaths. But you different, you got somethin' inside worth savin'. Took me a month of knowin' you to realize that. My man Hawk here, he figure it out in a minute." Hypo snapped his fingers to punctuate *minute*. "That's how good he is."

Without being aware of moving, Matt sat on a bar stool, looked at Hawk, and locked onto his gaze. The man exuded an aura of peace and calm that gave Matt a slight bit of hope, like a seed waiting to be planted, watered, and nurtured.

"Sorry. I freaked out a bit. I've been closed off to everyone for a long time. I wasn't ready to hear I needed help. I'll give this a try."

A wisp of a smile grew on Hawk's lips, but his eyes remained impassive. "Do. Or do not. There is no try."

Matt's doubts resurfaced. "What the hell? You start by quoting Yoda from *Star Wars*?" He shot Hypo a withering glare, then focused on Hawk. "Pop psychology?"

Hawk shrugged. "I enjoyed the movies. It seemed appropriate, pop psychology or not. Would you prefer an apt phrase that's musically related?"

Matt refocused on Hypo, who gave him an annoyed look.

Hawk recited part of a song lyric that didn't register with Matt because his mind was still reeling with doubt about Hawk's casual methods. He focused his memory, and a vague recollection of those words came to him. He looked back at Hawk, who had a slight look of disappointment on his face.

"It loses impact without the music and rhythmic beat," Hawk said. "But surely a talented musician such as yourself remembers a popular line from one of the most beloved musical poets of the Sixties."

Finally, Matt made the connection to the first line of a classic Beatles tune. "John Lennon. 'I am the Walrus.' *Magical Mystery Tour*."

Hawk smiled and leaned forward, elbows on the bar, hands clasped. "So, what does that line mean to you in the context of this meeting?"

Matt stared at the floor as he thought, figuring he'd humor this old guy one more time before leaving. Then a grain of understanding came to him. He looked up. "Something like ... you and I—and maybe Hypo—all have something in common."

"Well, cuckoo for Cocoa Puffs or whatever the hell the next line of that song is," Hypo said. "You ain't as stupid as I was startin' to believe, Jazzman."

Hawk's appreciative nod confirmed Matt's interpretation. He stood and gestured to a table in one corner of the room. "Let's have some coffee and talk further. My treat."

After they were seated and the coffees were delivered, Matt asked, "What's with the references to old movies and music?"

"I grew up fascinated by the Sixties and Seventies," Hawk said. "A time of significant social upheaval. I was stimulated by all I saw and heard. It spurred me into a life of curiosity and inquiry. And I learned valuable lessons about human nature. Surprisingly, song lyrics during that era made some incredibly perceptive social commentary. Lots of so-called words to live by."

Matt thought of all the great lyrics he'd learned and performed with his teenaged rock band, the Czechmates, growing up in Straight River, Minnesota. Simple phrases like "All you need is love," "Give peace a chance," and "Born to be wild," while trite and simplistic, might form a decent basis for an impressionable teenager's philosophy of life.

"Nevertheless," Hawk said, "I don't pretend I can help you by spouting platitudes based on movies or song lyrics. Your problems go so deep that some men could never mine the depths of that pain and burn it away like coal. But instead of helping them dig a hole in which to bury themselves, I counsel men—and now, unfortunately, some women—to climb out of the hole, throw away the shovel, and start building a tower from where they can see their greater selves and understand why the pain remains."

"Sounds all neat and tidy and wrapped up with a bow," Matt said.

Hawk cracked one side of his mouth into a wry smile. "That's the 10,000-feet version. Overcoming post-traumatic stress disorder is a tough battle. Many never—"

"Whoa, whoa, whoa," Matt said. "You think I have PTSD?"

Hawk shrugged. "I see war inside you."

"I was never in a war. Never even served in the military."

"I didn't say you were a combat soldier. I see war in many people who've never touched any sort of weapon. But your eyes told me of much violence in your life. War, for lack of a better word. Some call the look in your eyes 'the thousand-yard stare.'"

Matt sat back, reeling at the amount of information Hawk had gleaned in a few minutes.

"Man's good, bro," Hypo said. "You ain't nothin' he ain't seen a hundred times before."

Hawk said, "I was in the Army for twenty years. Experienced some bad stuff myself. Most of the people I've helped were in the military and served overseas. Too many theaters to name: Viet Nam, the Gulf Wars, Afghanistan. Business is too good these days."

"Which reminds me," Matt said. "What's this going to cost?"

Hawk gave him a serene smile. "Just your time and commitment to be open and honest and willing to listen."

Matt looked at Hypo for confirmation and received an emphatic nod.

"No catch, dude. Hawk does this cuz he good at it. Most of his clients can't pay him anyway. No sense tryin' to suck coins outta empty vending machines."

"So you think I have PTSD?" Matt asked again.

Hawk nodded. "Trauma doesn't have to be war-induced. People who live through horrific natural disasters, car crashes, terrorist bombings, domestic horrors like sexual or physical abuse are traumatized. Anytime anyone experiences violence firsthand, there exists a potential for PTSD. But soldiers are the ones in whom it manifests most often."

"I see," Matt said. Memories of *his* wars swirled in his brain. A hit-and-run attempt, an explosion, several gun battles. Five enemies killed. Two friends, his ex-wife, and a cop were also dead because of him. He reached for his forehead, closed his eyes, and massaged the sudden ache that spread from temple to temple.

"So, Jazzman, you in?" Hypo said, rousing Matt from his thoughts.

Matt started, focused on Hypo, then faced Hawk. "Yeah. I'm in."

Hawk nodded and smiled. "I'm glad. For starters, would you care to share your real name with us?"

Matt stiffened and fought the urge to leave. Through tight lips, he said, "How about I wait until after we talk a little more?"

Hawk and Hypo exchanged glances.

"Normally," Hawk said, "I'd suggest seeing a professional first to confirm what I already know about you. But since you're withholding your real name, I assume you have a strong reason to stay out of the medical system as much as possible."

Matt gave him a hesitant nod.

"If you change your mind, I have a good friend who's a psychiatrist. She can help you with PTSD and prescribe some meds that might work better for your headaches and nerves. I merely counsel my clients."

"Thanks," Matt said, "I'll consider it." He looked at the two men. "So, when do we start?"

"Whenever you decide," Hawk said and handed him a business card. "I carry my cell phone with me at all times. Call anytime."

Matt waggled the card in his hand. A wave of positive energy washed over him. The seed of hope had sprouted. "Thanks. How about now?"

Hawk nodded. "I like your attitude."

Hypo grinned and said, "I got things to do." He stood and walked toward the door. "Think I'll split and let you two start the healing."

Chapter 6

At the third homeless shelter he visited on his first day in Minneapolis, Ben hit pay dirt. He was sitting with Pastor Jeanne Hanks in her office. She ran a soup kitchen along with the shelter in the basement of her church.

"Yes, I've seen that man in here several times," Hanks said after she'd studied the photo Ben handed to her. "He's much hairier now. Has a beard. But his facial structure is the same."

"Of course," Ben said. "This isn't a recent photo."

Hanks eyed Ben with suspicion. She was short and stocky, with shoulder-length dishwater-blonde hair, and she had an intelligent-looking countenance. "Why are you looking for him?"

"I'm a friend from Duluth," he lied. "I last saw him a few months ago. He was quite despondent. Got into drugs a bit too deep. Had money and job troubles. He mentioned going to Minneapolis to change his luck. I had a few vacation days I needed to use up before they expired, and I decided that finding him was more important than a vacation."

He sensed Pastor Hanks possessed an innate streetwise intuition that smelled bullshit quickly. But she said, "That's very Christian of you."

"When did you last see him?"

"A week ago. He came in for our evening free-will meal. He was toting a guitar case and a small amplifier." She smiled. "You don't see many of those in the hands of our guests."

He returned the smile, mainly to cover the buzzing sensation he felt when she mentioned the guitar. He gripped the arms of the chair he was sitting in to remind himself not to bolt out of the room and start his search. Instead, he forced a concerned expression onto his face. "Sounds like Matt.

He loves that guitar too much, I guess. Did he mention if he was staying anywhere, had a job, anything like that?"

Hanks, sitting in her chair behind her office desk, gazed at the ceiling and pursed her lips. "Not that I recall. I try to chat with everyone who comes through the serving line, but we were busy that night."

"I see." Ben pulled a business card from his pocket showing his cell phone number and undercover name, David Parker. Handing it to her, he said, "If you see him again, please call. I'd ask you to have him call me, but I know he's too embarrassed about his situation. I hope I can confront him and persuade him to let me help."

Hanks seemed puzzled. Ben hoped she was overworked and stressed enough not to press him for a better explanation. He stood, eager to get back on Lanier's trail. "Thank you for your time, Pastor Jeanne. May I make a donation to your facility?"

Her eyes brightened. Nothing worked better than cash to deflect doubt or suspicion away from creative truth-bending. "Yes, of course, Mr. Parker." She stood and accepted the twenty he produced from his wallet. "Bless you."

"Happy to help," Ben said and turned to leave.

Pastor Jeanne said, "I almost forgot. If you work the streets around here, look for a man who calls himself Hypo. He has a prosthetic foot and only three fingers on one hand. He's sort of a street ambassador. Makes it a point to get to know as many street folks as possible. I understand he and another man help homeless veterans. If anyone on the street has seen your friend, odds are good that Hypo has."

"Hypo," Ben said, wondering about the unusual name. "Thanks." He left and made a mental note to stop back at Pastor Jeanne's church every day at free mealtime to check for Lanier. Then he hit the streets with copies of Lanier's photo, working his prime areas in grids and charting the foot traffic to further narrow down where Lanier might hang out. He put out the word, asking where the popular spots for street musicians were located. If Lanier had a guitar, chances were decent that he might be playing somewhere in public to earn a few bucks.

Almost everyone Ben approached looked intently at the picture. Eagerly sometimes, as if it were an appealing break from the drudgery of hanging around doing nothing, waiting for some miracle to change their life for the better, but ending the day with even less hope than they'd had the previous day. Ben studied each pair of eyes to see if a viewer showed the slightest hint of recognition. Ninety-nine percent of the time, he noticed nothing remarkable.

As Pastor Jeanne had suggested, everyone on the street knew Hypo. At least that was Ben's impression after he started asking about the man with the fake leg and missing fingers. It was a rare day when Hypo wasn't making his rounds. Ben soon learned he was also a street musician who liked to brag about his musical talent. He was always telling his friends to come down to one street corner or another, a skyway, or an atrium in an office tower to hear him sing. That was enough to convince Ben that Hypo at least had seen Lanier, maybe knew him. When Ben showed interest in hearing some good street music, one homeless man told him Hypo would be performing in the skyway outside the Target Center before a Timberwolves game in a few days. The big time, according to the man. And Hypo's musical partner would be some guitar-playing white dude called Jazzman.

Unfortunately, two more days passed before Ben ran into the disabled street ambassador. But his patience paid off in spades. Late afternoon on his third day of searching, Ben rounded a corner and saw a group of four men standing in a loose circle. They were listening to a Bluetooth speaker playing a hip-hop song and singing along in rough harmony. They stopped when he walked up and gave him looks ranging from wary to mistrustful to outright contemptible.

"Hi guys," Ben said and held out Lanier's photo. "Anyone seen my friend here? I want to make sure he's okay. Give him a few bucks until he gets back on his feet."

The group broke their circle to view the photo. Ben studied each man's eyes as they passed the photo from man to man. Four replied with blank stares and head shakes. But the fifth man's eyes showed a hint of surprised recognition. He had a prosthetic left foot and appeared to have two fingers missing from his right hand. Ben didn't get a good look because he stuffed his hand in his pocket as Ben approached his group.

"You've seen him?" Ben said, feigning eager concern. "Twenty bucks if you can tell me where."

"Nah," the man said. "Just look like a cat I used to know. But he dead now, so unless you God, he can't use any kinda help you wanna give him."

"Are you Hypo?"

The man turned and walked away with his buddies. Ben watched them leave until they rounded the corner. As they did, the one-legged man looked back at him with a penetrating stare, as if he were memorizing Ben's face.

One of a handful of men who'd been listening to the singers said, "Hypo don't trust strangers looking for people because a lot of folks on the street don't want to be found. Matter of fact, *most* of us don't trust strangers."

"So that was Hypo?" Ben asked.

"Yeah," the man said. "Who're you?"

Ben stared him down with a hard, blank look. "Just a guy looking for his friend, trying to help him out with a few bucks. Thanks for the info."

As Ben walked away and headed for his car, he allowed himself a mental fist pump. After the encounter with Hypo and his spark of recognition of Lanier's image, chances were almost guaranteed that "Jazzman" was Lanier. His next step would be to stake out the Target Center skyways before the Timberwolves' next home game, while Lanier and Hypo played their gig. Then he'd follow Lanier to wherever he called home. *Probably a cardboard refrigerator box under a bridge.* A kill there would be quick and easy.

Visions of the enormous payday leaped into his mind. However, right after those images flashed through his brain, he realized he also wanted to know Lanier's complete story. Was he a serial killer or simply an innocent musician who was in the wrong place at the wrong time and uncovered a conspiracy headed by the wrong man?

Chapter 7

Back at his motel room after several long days pounding the Minneapolis pavement, Ben grabbed a beer from the mini-fridge and sat in the rickety desk chair, trying to concentrate. Before completing his search for Lanier and earning the hit man fee, he first needed to contact Mr. Jones, a.k.a. Smythe, to find out if he was still willing to pay. They'd parted on uncertain terms. Jones claimed that because Ben had found Lanier in Castle Danger but hadn't killed him, he wouldn't pay the $100,000 originally agreed upon. Glad merely to be alive, Ben decided his initial $20,000 down payment from Jones was sufficient for his one week of work and brush with death. Jones's last warning echoed in his mind. If word ever got out that anyone other than the police was actively looking for Lanier, he would assume Ben had leaked the secret, which meant Ben would be dead within twenty-four hours. Two months had passed. During that time, Ben laid low until the buzz subsided about the two men Lanier had most certainly killed in Castle Danger.

Ben looked up the last phone number Jones had given him and tapped it into his phone, unsure if it still worked. A secondary concern was the elapsed time since his unsuccessful attempt to kill Lanier. Smythe might have hired another hit man in the interim. Lanier might already be dead. But if he was alive, where was the harm in asking for a chance to earn the remaining $80,000?

The phone rang ten times before he heard a click, followed by a computerized voice that said, "Leave a message."

"Mr. Jones, this is Nowitzki. I think I can satisfy the contract terms we discussed back in January. Please call if your offer is still valid."

After clicking off, he settled onto the bed to binge-watch two weeks' worth of *Jeopardy!* episodes on his laptop's streaming TV service. He was excited because this batch was the latest Tournament of Champions. One of his bucket list goals was to try out and qualify for the popular game show. He knew he was fast enough, sharp enough, and had stored enough trivia in his memory to qualify and win the damn thing.

An hour later, Jones called. With two beers in him, Ben was slightly buzzed. He worried he'd stumble, say the wrong words, and blow his chance. After a head-clearing breath, he focused his mind on his task and said, "Nowitzki."

Jones's voice was edged with ire. "What makes you think you can belatedly fulfill the contract we had that is now null and void?"

Sheesh. The guy doesn't mince words, does he? Ben forced down the defensiveness that welled up. "I have a lead on the subject of that contract."

Jones was silent for a disconcerting length of time before asking, "What kind of lead?"

"I know his whereabouts. I believe I can find him and satisfy our original deal."

"But you've already failed. Why will this time be different? And please do not use names or other specifics or details. I doubt you're bright enough, but I can't be sure you aren't recording this conversation."

Ben futilely shot Jones a contemptuous glare through his cell phone. The man had a way of asserting his presumed superiority with every utterance. "Because I'm prepared for him now. He caught me off guard the first time, which is the only reason he escaped."

"The *only* reason?"

"Yes."

"Where is he?"

"If I tell you, you might send your own man to do the job. I want first crack at him."

Another long pause. "What do you propose?"

"Give me two weeks. If I succeed within that time, you pay me the balance of our original deal—eighty grand. If I fulfill the bonus portion of the contract, you pay me that too." The six-figure bonus payout would be Ben's if he made Lanier's death look like an accident.

"And if you don't succeed?"

"I'll go home and forget we ever did business together. I kept silent the past two months, so you know my word is good."

"What happens if you get caught in the act?" Jones asked. "After your first try, I'd say the possibility exists you might blunder again."

Much to Ben's chagrin, Jones made a valid point. He barely knew Lanier. Perhaps the guy *wasn't* a novice fugitive. Perhaps he *was* a trained killer who had gone easy on him during their first encounter. Perhaps in a big city, with many potential witnesses, and security cameras recording activity in thousands of locations, he'd make one miscue and blow the job.

Ben cleared his throat. "I'll cover every contingency before I make my move. If I get caught, I'll claim mistaken identity with another guy. I plan to watch our subject for a day or two, learn his movements, and catch him in a spot where I can execute my plan. I double my payday with a little extra preparation. But, if necessary, I can live without the bonus payment."

A third long pause ensued. "Mr. Nowitzki, I'm a patient man because I know sometimes plans don't go perfectly. My big-picture strategy is back on track, and I don't anticipate this man harming my employees or my operation anymore. However, he still poses a threat. I put another man on the case, but he's not a skilled investigator. So, I'll give you a second chance. If you fulfill the baseline of our original contract, I'll pay the balance we originally agreed upon. If you take the extra step, I'll pay half the bonus. That is my final offer."

Ben tightened his grip on the phone. *The asshole plays hardball.* But he couldn't argue with Jones's logic. If the roles were reversed, Ben would be reluctant to pay full price for a job that took two attempts. Sighing, he said, "It's a deal. Two weeks from today."

"Very well then, Mr. Nowitzki. Good luck. Based on your first attempt, you'll need it."

Chapter 8

Late afternoon the next day, Matt and Hypo set up in the skyway connecting Target Center to the enormous parking ramps that served that arena. The Timberwolves were on a winning streak and hosting the Milwaukee Bucks. Thanks to the sizable percentage of Bucks fans who lived near Minneapolis, the stands would be packed. Even though pedestrian traffic was sporadic three hours before tipoff, they were in a prime location—the end of the skyway closest to Target Center. The acoustics were good enough that people would hear the music as they made the long walk across the skyway and might stop to enjoy the end of the song. Matt knew from experience that listeners who stayed to hear the end of a tune almost always gave them a buck or two. That's when he and Hypo turned on the charm and acknowledged anyone who smiled, clapped, or tapped their toes. Additionally, the early birds often stopped to listen for a few minutes. And because the fans had yet to buy fifteen-dollar burgers and ten-dollar beers at the game, they'd be more likely to leave a tip.

Hypo was borderline brazen about asking for donations. "Hey, brotha, this fine drum set cost big bucks to maintain," he'd say as he pointed to his buckets or waved his battered drumsticks. His favorite comment to the best-looking women in the audience—"It's hard work singing my heart out for you, mama. Gotta buy food to keep my energy up."—often earned an extra dollar or two.

Another sales technique was to solicit requests from those who stayed to hear another song. Matt possessed an encyclopedic memory for any popular song in the last hundred years—other than the recent pop hits he'd missed during his time as a wilderness fugitive. Similarly, Hypo had an amazing ability to recall song lyrics. Between them, they could fake their way through almost any tune well enough to justify their one-dollar-minimum request fee. If they both knew the song well—or it was already in their repertoire—they could usually coax another few bucks from the requester and also persuade other listeners to donate.

As Matt tuned his guitar—a beat-up old Martin DX acoustic-electric he'd found in a pawnshop for fifty dollars—a pall of melancholy overcame him. He felt better after he'd met Hawk and talked to him, but his issues were too deep-seated to go away with a few relaxation techniques and an hour-long chat. He'd gotten a decent night's sleep thanks to Hawk's suggestion of thinking about the positive parts of his former life. He'd had only one short, disturbing nightmare that woke him in a sweat. But after reminiscing about a memorable day when he was a boy growing up on the family farm, he drifted back to sleep. He didn't wake until he was roused by the noises of the other men on his floor preparing for the day.

He watched Hypo arrange his buckets and cymbal, then stared up and down the corridor. Like Hypo, was he doomed to this life until he became another casualty of homelessness and poverty? Matt struggled to play more than basic chords and a few easy riffs on his guitar. Unless he could get his injured fingers fixed well enough to play his double bass at a world-class level again, street music might be the best he could do. He stared out the skyway window, wondering as he did every day what he could have done differently in the past year to prevent the death and destruction he'd experienced. All the answers boiled down to an action he was incapable of doing: ignoring friends and family in their time of need.

A gentle kick in the foot from Hypo snapped Matt back to the present. "Hey, Jazzman, you gonna tune your damn guitar all night, or are we gonna play?" Hypo pinged his cymbal to emphasize the question. "You been tunin' it for five minutes, and we both know it goes outta tune every five seconds."

"Sorry, just thinking," Matt said, glancing apologetically at his partner as he strummed one last E major chord. Close enough for street music. But any guitar chord of his or note of Hypo's that wasn't perfectly pitched grated on him like a mosquito buzzing in his ear that he couldn't swat away. Although Hypo knew Matt possessed exceptional talent, he didn't know Matt was once in the top echelon of Twin Cities jazz and classical bassists, which put him in the world-class category. Matt also knew little about his drummer and lead singer. He'd wanted to ask how he'd lost his foot and two fingers but was afraid he'd have to confide parts of his past to Hypo—details such as how an obviously talented musician ended up playing guitar for tip money with two injured fingers. Matt had quickly learned most street denizens were hiding checkered, tormented pasts and weren't eager to share details with anyone.

Even though Hypo acted and talked like a typical poor person hanging in the streets of a large urban area—assuming such an individual existed—there was much more to the man than he'd revealed. His eyes seemed to take in every detail of a setting. A few idle conversations had shown him to be more attuned to politics and world affairs than might be expected. Behind his eyes lurked obvious intelligence and self-confidence. Which caused Matt to wonder: *What does he see behind* my *eyes?*

Pedestrian traffic was still light. There was no rush to start playing, but it was a suitable time to warm up or try a new tune in the repertoire.

"Whattaya wanna open with?" Matt asked.

"How 'bout 'Happy' by Pharrell?" Hypo said.

"Sounds good. We'll run through it now, then repeat it every thirty minutes as the crowds pick up. Get 'em in a dancing, spending mood."

"Word, bro. Set 'em up for the return trip. You okay stayin' until postgame traffic?"

"Sure. If we have a decent pregame haul, we can grab some Jimmy John's during the game, chill awhile, then resume playing near the end of the game when people start leaving."

Matt ghosted the chord progression to "Happy" to refresh it in his memory, settled on a tempo, and began a guitar intro. Hypo always preferred him to start, the amateur deferring to the pro. Matt cued him with a nod, and Hypo started in with his drum riff. They ran through "Happy," then brushed up on a few other tunes in their set list.

Matt tailored their music to the situation. A predominantly white, professional, and prosperous audience such as the people who comprised the majority of a Timberwolves crowd called for more folk music, pop-rock, easy listening, Americana, and jazz standards. Yes, there were plenty of minorities in the Timberwolves' fan base. But the fans who streamed through the skyway from the parking ramps *were* predominantly white. Conversely, on a warm, dry day on the street in front of the arena, the duet played tunes more recognizable to the younger, more "melting-pot" crowd. That's where Hypo's taste rose to the forefront. Although he liked jazz almost as much as Matt did, his repertoire of hip-hop and R&B was a good fit for the fans who parked in the cheaper surface lots or arrived via bus or light rail. Matt usually figured out the chord progressions and rhythmic vibe by himself after hearing a song a few times on the radio or someone's portable media player or getting coached by Hypo.

When the skyway traffic from the ramp picked up to a steady trickle, Matt counted out a beat, and the duet dug into their performance-level version of "Happy." By the time a group of six had walked from the ramp entrance to the musicians, the two men chaperoning four kids were walking with a rhythmic bounce. A boy of about six flashed some respectable dance moves. The other two boys and a girl, each about ten, sang along. The group stopped to hear the end of the song. When it was over, one dad tossed five dollars into the tip case. A positive omen?

"Thank you kindly, sir," Hypo said. He flashed a sincere smile that was part of his shtick. "Those kids sure do recognize great music by two world-famous musicians."

The adults laughed, the kids waved, and the group sauntered toward the arena.

They played for another thirty minutes as T-Wolves fans flowed past. But a few people stayed. Ones who looked as if they couldn't even afford a ticket to a high-school basketball game. More street people. Hypo chatted with them between songs and knew most of their names. He'd recently mentioned he'd been on the streets for about two years and did what he could to help others endure another day of hopelessness. At a minimum, he'd offer them a friendly smile, nonjudgmental compassion, maybe a dollar or two. Whatever he thought would help. Hypo survived on a modest disability pension from his unnamed previous employer, so he was better off than most. Much more so than the homeless drug addicts, traumatized veterans, or single mothers with children fleeing abusive husbands or boyfriends who had no family to turn to in their time of need.

Matt glanced from face to face at the sad-looking group. Did he look as beaten and downtrodden as they did? A few more months of street life might put him past the point of no return. Then again, with the cops and Smythe chasing him, he might not live long enough to find out.

Chapter 9

Matt heard the thugs long before he saw them. Five fans came from one of the arena's exit doors and headed for the skyway. They were loud, boisterous, and—to Matt's trained ear and experience playing dive bars in college—obviously drunk. Matt and Hypo stood with their backs to the arena, packing their instruments after a successful gig. One hundred apiece after subtracting their fast-food dinner expense. They'd played for thirty minutes after the overtime game ended with a T-Wolves win, so that group was possibly the last group from inside the arena.

"Hey, putz!" said one of the drunks. "Play 'Freebird.'"

Matt sighed and whispered, "And here we go."

Requesting "Freebird" anywhere other than a Lynyrd Skynyrd concert was one of the lamest, most annoying music jokes of the past fifty years. Glancing over his shoulder, Matt shrugged. "Sorry, buddy. We're done for the night."

"Nonononono, you didn't understand," the drunk said, waving his forefinger at Matt. "That wasn't a request. I'm *tellin'* you. Play. Fucking. 'Freebird.'"

Hypo looked concerned but not nervous. The corridors were empty in both directions, so help from the police or passersby wasn't likely. Drawing himself up to his full height, Matt stepped forward and locked eyes with the guy—about 250 pounds of white blubber on a short sumo-wrestler's body. "I'm sorry, sir, but if we don't leave by eleven, the police will arrest us." He pointed to his empty wrist as if he were wearing his watch. "Almost eleven."

It was total bullshit. But to shut the guy up, it was worth a shot.

The drunk teetered back and forth, trying to focus on Matt and what he'd said. "Play the damn song, asshole, or my friends are gonna be *reeeally* disappointed."

He jerked his thumb toward his posse. Two were nasty-looking biker-gang-sized white men. The other two were black men who looked as if they'd played some high-level basketball at power forward. All five appeared to be in their twenties and were in various states of inebriation. The group was obviously in a good mood because their sports-fan apparel showed they had cheered for the victorious home team.

The foursome crowded closer, invading Hypo's personal space and mumbling agreement with their leader's assessment of their mood. To his credit, Hypo assumed a ready-to-rumble stance and expression even though he was six inches shorter and fifty pounds lighter than the smallest antagonist.

Sounding far too confident, Hypo said to Matt, "I can take down three of these mofos if you can handle fat boy and his babysitter."

Sumo Drunk guffawed and snorted. "*You?* Me and my friends munch on dickwads like you for appetizers."

With pleading eyes, Matt sent Hypo an urgent, yet silent, message to stand down. Then he said, "No fighting. Doesn't work for a man in my situation."

"You sure, bro?" Hypo asked. "I'm serious. I can take three of them down in about twenty seconds. You hold off the other two for that long. I'll take care of them right after."

Matt waved him down with both hands. "No fighting means no cops. *Please.*"

Hypo shrugged. "Okay, J-man. But I got yo back if they get nasty." He turned to Sumo Drunk. "If I were you, brotha, I'd go home, save yourself a trip to the emergency room."

Sumo Drunk lurched backward in mock surprise, then unleashed a contemptuous, "Hah!"

Matt was about to reason with the drunken lout, but before he could get a word out, the man lunged for Matt's guitar case and tried to jerk it from his hand. Matt reflexively pulled it free, causing Sumo Drunk to stagger backward into his buddies. They steadied him and sprang into action. One of the power forwards leaped at Matt and put him in a choke hold. The other ripped the guitar case from his hand. The biker dudes grabbed Hypo an instant before he could come to Matt's aid. Hypo tensed but stayed passive. Sumo Drunk took the guitar case from his buddy, flipped open the latches, and dumped the guitar onto the floor. It landed with a *twang* that echoed through the silent skyway. With his right foot, clad in a red Chuck Taylor Converse All-Star, Sumo Drunk stomped the neck where it joined the body.

The crunch of splintered wood made Matt flinch with visceral pain and anguish. It wasn't because they destroyed a cheap guitar. The instrument wasn't much above the level of trash, anyway. It was the principle. He respected all musical instruments because, in the proper hands, any instrument, even this one, had a transcendental ability to entertain, inspire, and soothe the soul. To add further insult, one of the power forwards kicked a hole in his amplifier.

Whether it was the choke hold or the wrecked guitar or the resemblance of Sumo Drunk to Witt, something snapped in Matt's head. A fierce pain welled up deep in his brain. He groaned. The scene got blurry. Sweat burst from his pores. Deafening explosions rattled his brain. He covered his ears to no avail. A guttural wail burst out from deep inside. *"Noooooooooo!"* His legs gave way, and he crumpled to the floor as another nightmare started.

A quiet spring evening on the farm. Faithful old Jack, the black Labrador Retriever, waiting for him as usual. They walk toward the house. Jack whines and paces. A warning. Matt calls 911. Officer Sandvik arrives. Checks the exterior of the house. Steps inside, flashlight on. Matt decides his fear is groundless. Sandvik looks around, flips the light switch. House blows to pieces. Matt flies through the air, lands hard. His entire body flares up in pain. He's dizzy, can't see through the smoke, flames, and flying debris. Everything goes black. Then he's awake. Same situation. This time he's inside the house when it explodes. He's in the bowels of Hell as he watches his body disintegrate into a million pieces. Smythe floats above the scene again, untouchable, laughing, looking like the Devil himself. He presses the button on a device that looks like a remote control, and the nightmare replays itself again. And again. And again. Explosion after explosion after explosion. Matt screams, tries to lunge at Smythe and grab the remote, but Matt has no physical body. All he can do is watch.

"Jazzman ... Jazzman ...?" A pause. "You okay, brotha?" Hypo's voice. The nightmare was over.

Matt was on the floor in the fetal position. The skyway carpet smelled faintly of carpet cleaner. Drained of energy, confused, and damp with sweat, Matt opened his eyes and looked up.

Hypo stood over him, glancing around nervously.

"Where'd they go?" Matt asked. He raised his still-pounding head and looked around.

"Assholes left when you freaked out, man." Hypo knelt and touched Matt's shoulder. "You 'bout scared the shit out of me. Cryin', screamin', flailin' your arms. Thought sure the cops would come. But they busy with some sorta commotion down on the street."

Through parched lips, Matt said thickly, "You okay?"

"I'm good."

"Did they get our money?"

Hypo shook his head. "They were about to, but you went ballistic just in time. I gotta remember that next time I get mugged."

Matt returned Hypo's weak grin. If he hadn't been afraid of getting arrested, he might have indeed gone ballistic and vented some rage on their attackers.

"Muthafuckers trashed my drum kit, too."

Matt glanced at the cracked shards of plastic that used to be a drum kit.

"No big loss," Hypo said. "Just need to dumpster dive for a few more buckets. Maybe Hawk's gonna paint his crib. If he does, I'll talk him into buyin' a five-gallon bucket of whatever color and then givin' me the empty."

Matt rose to a sitting position. "Let's get out of here. I'm wiped."

"Want me to call the police?"

"No," he said. "I doubt they'd find the Neanderthals. And if they did, Sumo Drunk would say, 'Hey man, we were joking. We're peace-loving gentlemen. Wouldn't hurt a fly.'"

Hypo chuckled at Matt's exaggerated impression of a drunken fat slob with an attitude. Then he shrugged. "Guess we go home, dude. Nothin' to be done. Street war same as real war. Biggest army usually wins."

"You sure you didn't get hurt?"

"Nah. I been in way worse than this. Seriously, I coulda taken three of them myself, but *you* against two is beggin' for a nice long hospital stay. Especially since you don't look like no fighter to me, PTSD or not."

Matt huffed out a resigned chuckle and nudged his toe against his broken guitar. "What do we do now that my guitar is scrap wood?"

"Oh, that." Hypo pondered for a second, then nodded at his mangled drum kit. "This gig's just pin money for me. At least I got a disability check comin' in every month. Not much, but it pays for a roof, food, and heat in the winter." He gestured at the broken mess of wood and strings. "Far as I know, that's all you got."

Matt had spent the last of what little he'd saved from working in Castle Danger two months ago. He'd scraped by since then, spending his first month in the Twin Cities, taking advantage of free meals at churches and sleeping in any free shelters he could find. The sponsoring groups discouraged permanent residency, so Matt had found the place near Franklin Avenue that charged an amount he could afford on his paltry income. However, unable to repair or replace his guitar, he was in the direst straits he'd ever been in. He had enough money left to last about a week on his own. What disturbed him more was the apprehension that he might suffer through another eighteen-hour nightmare tonight.

"Can I ask you a question?" Hypo said.

"Ask away."

After taking a sip from his hip flask, Hypo said, "You got any enemies you know about? Piss someone off recently?"

Matt tensed, sensing trouble in Hypo's hesitant tone. "Why?"

Hypo shrugged, but his lips were tight against his teeth. "Might be coincidence, but ..."

"Spill it."

"Dude was makin' the rounds on the street, flashin' your photo."

"*What?*" Matt's blood went icy.

"Wasn't recent. Looked like one o' them posed photos workin' folks put on their resumes."

That sounded like a publicity photo for his trio or the Minnesota Orchestra. Matt glanced around, looking for anyone who might be watching them. "What did he look like?"

"White, 'bout your size, short dark hair, wearin' khakis, collared shirt, rolled-up sleeves. Luggin' a suede leather jacket. Coarse features but not ugly. Carried himself like a cop. You know how it is with them."

"You say anything?"

"Hell, no! I look like a stool pigeon? He offered cash too. Twenty if we pointed him in your direction. But after I said *no*, he stared at me long and hard. I thought I gave him a poker face. Shit, man, I'm sorry. Musta cracked jus' a hair."

Matt massaged his face. "Jesus Christ."

"Reason I ask, I'm wonderin' if the cat followed me here, then sent in his buddies to fuck with us. Timing was right."

Matt visualized the faces of their attackers. He hadn't recognized any of them. But that didn't mean Smythe, or the cops, weren't back on his trail. However, neither possibility made sense. Smythe wanted him dead. The cops would've arrested him. Harassing two musicians scraping by for a few bucks didn't fit into either narrative. "I don't know," he said. "I'm pretty sure this wasn't related to the guy flashing my photo around, but people are looking for me."

"Sorry to hear that, my man. I been there before. Turned out *real* bad."

Nearly getting mugged was bad enough, but when paired with a PTSD nightmare, this day immediately sunk into the cesspool of horrible days.

Matt wondered where he could run to now. And if he did, what was the point? Ever since he'd first escaped to the Boundary Waters, his nightmare existence would only end one of two ways: victory or death. Running might postpone death, but it wouldn't bring victory. And he wasn't ready to die. That meant he needed to activate his plan for escaping fugitive status tomorrow.

Chapter 10

With no reason to rise early the next day, Matt slept in. Or rather, tried. He gave up because of the frequent nightmares. Then he took a long shower, thinking it might be the last one he'd get for a while if he left the men's shelter. If someone working for either Smythe or the cops had been flashing his photo around on the street, Matt wanted to be as mobile as possible. It was warm enough that sleeping outside wasn't suicidal. He'd endured much colder temps in the woods in northeast Minnesota last winter. Freedom was now his number one priority.

He was in his bedroom loading his gear into his large backpack as he waited for his laundry load to dry in the basement laundry room when Hypo walked in through his open door. His musical partner sported a wide grin—surprising for a man who'd almost been robbed and beaten up less than twelve hours ago.

"Jazzman, my brotha, how ya doin'?" he asked, far too cheerfully.

Matt regarded him suspiciously. "You get laid last night?"

Hypo waved him off with a *pfft*. "Hell, no. Jus' happy and feelin' good because me and Hawk got your back."

"I'm gonna need some explanation." Matt sat on his bed and looked at his friend expectantly.

"Remember me tellin' you the other day my landlord been givin' me shit about late rent?"

"Yeah, so?"

"I'm done with that dump. Asked Hawk to let me know if he hears about a place I can afford, which, as you know, ain't much."

"Keep talking," Matt said with growing impatience.

"Hawk says his landlord raised his rent. He told me gettin' a roommate would help him manage the increase. He knows I struggle a bit, so he's gonna cut me a deal."

"A deal?"

"This where it get interesting. His spare room got two single beds. Not very big. But bigger than this damn closet." He waved his hand around Matt's room. "Bein' the man he is, Hawk said if you interested, he let you share the room with me."

Matt perked up. Staying with Hawk would be safer and more comfortable than living on the street, especially with someone on his trail.

Hypo continued. "I figure we get along good on the street. We can survive sharin' a crib."

Matt shook his head in disbelief. "That's quite generous, but I hardly know the man. I don't want to be a burden. Besides, I can't afford it."

Hypo scowled and crossed his arms. "You jus' don't get it, do you?"

"Get what?"

Hypo took a huge breath and exhaled slowly. As he did, his persona changed. Matt intuited rather than saw the transformation.

"Hawk isn't looking to make money," Hypo said. "You stumbling into our lives was meant to be, whether you believe it or not. 'Everything happens for a reason,' he says. This reason is he can help you better and faster if you live with him. Talking to a street creature once a week for an hour never yields positive results. His goal is to turn around men and women who suffer from PTSD. Help them escape this hell. *Your* hell. He cares more than you'll ever know about his people, and it turns his stomach when some of them drop through the cracks. But he keeps trying because it's the right thing to do. Because that's what he knows in his heart is his one true purpose in life. I've been there myself, but I can't help you anywhere near as much as Hawk can. He's a brilliant counselor. The best I've ever known. And I talked to a lot of shrinks in my day."

Mouth agape, Matt said, "Why are you talking differently?"

"You mean, why am I talking with clear diction, proper grammar, with no street in my tone or attitude or choice of words? As if I'm a middle-class white guy like you?"

Matt nodded. "Exactly."

Hypo looked away, seemingly reluctant to explain. When he turned back, he locked eyes with Matt. "Okay. Confession time. I'm not who I appear to be."

Fully curious now, Matt said, "Then who the hell *are* you?"

Hypo pointed at the hallway through the open bedroom door. "Lots of ears on this floor. Thin walls. I'll tell you later. But I need to know if you're in or not."

Considering what had happened last night, Matt would be stupid to refuse such a generous offer. Yet, he struggled to process the fact that Hypo had fooled him for months about his dual personas. Could he trust someone like that with anything? Did he have a better option? He slapped his thighs and said, "Let's give it a shot."

"Good," said Hypo. "Finish packing, and I'll take you over there. But this isn't charity. He expects you to pay rent. A percentage of whatever you can. I told him you can earn more performing than anything else. But until you get a guitar, you can do some chores."

"Hey, I'm glad to pay my fair share." Matt stood and resumed loading his pack. "As soon as my laundry is dry, we're outta here."

Chapter 11

Hawk's apartment was in a fourplex a few blocks south of Franklin and not far from the men's shelter. The neighborhood had more trees and evoked a less desperate feeling, but it was still in one of the poorer parts of Minneapolis. As he and Hypo walked there, Matt surreptitiously glanced over his shoulder every few minutes to make sure someone wasn't following him. Hypo noticed but kept quiet.

The place was small and tidy, with wood floors in the living room and dining area. The furniture was utilitarian. The sparse décor showed a Native American influence: a framed oil painting of a warrior in full headdress; a pencil sketch of a Great Plains teepee village from the nineteenth century; a large buckskin draped over the back of the sofa. An open doorway led to the kitchen. A hallway ran back toward the bedrooms and bathroom.

After inviting them in, Hawk said to Matt, "Drop your gear in the first bedroom, then come back and we'll talk. Want some tea or coffee?"

"Either is fine with me," Matt replied and walked to the bedroom. Definitely on the small side but still twice the size of his previous room. Two single beds occupied the space on either side of a double-hung window. A nightstand stood between the beds. A four-drawer dresser occupied the wall opposite the window. A closet was on the shared wall between the room and the bathroom. The room—the entire apartment—smelled faintly of herbs.

Matt laid his backpack on the bed to the left of the window, shrugged off his jacket, and returned to the kitchen. Hawk and Hypo were seated at the square table. A teakettle was heating on the gas stove.

"I can't thank you enough," Matt said to Hawk. "I'm still amazed you came into my life at such a crucial time."

"Things happen," Hawk said. "Maybe for a reason, maybe not. Perhaps we intuitively guide ourselves into relationships that allow us to take advantage of what might be available. The fact that you connected with Hypo, of all people, shows me you have an intuition about character." Hawk glanced at his friend. "He's brought many tormented souls to my attention."

The teakettle spewed a strident *high C*, prompting Hawk to rise and turn off the burner. "You boys okay with Earl Grey?"

His guests nodded, and he poured water into the mugs. After setting them on the table, he brought out milk, sugar cubes, and a small dish of lemon wedges. Each man doctored his tea and began idly dunking the tea bag up and down in the water.

Hawk broke the silence. "My first rule of therapy is total honesty." Focusing on Matt, he said, "But rest assured, whatever you tell me won't leave this room." Seeing no reaction, he continued. "Hypo is essentially an overqualified assistant. I assure you he'll be even more tight-lipped than me. As my good faith offering, I'll share a bit of my sordid past with you."

Hawk summarized his life and career: His real name was Norman Peltier. He was an enrolled member of the Mille Lacs Band of Ojibwe. After growing up on the Mille Lacs Reservation near Garrison, Minnesota, young Norman enlisted in the army. He excelled in basic training and quickly achieved the rank of Private First Class. A month later, he was thrown into the breach of Desert Storm. After that, Operation Enduring Freedom in Afghanistan. Then two tours in the big one—Operation Iraqi Freedom. He was wounded twice by shrapnel, witnessed limbs blown off several comrades from roadside IEDs, and rescued two wounded platoon members under heavy enemy fire. His payback for that service included two Purple Hearts, a Silver Star, and several promotions. After his last combat tour, Staff Sergeant Peltier was shipped stateside. He finished his career at a training post at Fort Sill in Oklahoma with the rank of Master Sergeant. The nickname "Hawk" evolved in the service because Sergeant Peltier's buddies noticed his quiet, powerful demeanor—like a hawk surveying the territory from a high perch. He also watched over his men with hawklike vision. When spurred to action to protect his charges, he became fierce and ruthless against any threat—also like a hawk.

When Hawk finished and took a sip of his tea, all Matt could say was, "Wow." Inwardly, he wondered how the man had handled the stress, the months-on-end pressure cooker of being in a combat zone, knowing an attack and death might come at any time. Hawk's calm exterior seemed impervious to any kind of stress or mental pressure.

"One thing Hawk and I have in common is our minority status," Hypo said, "which helped us learn to cope better than most. We immediately figured out why you'd be more closed up. Privileged white kids like you never saw too much day-to-day tragedy growing up like we did. So when the shit hit the fan big-time for you, there was no way you'd be prepared to handle it. The middle-class white kids we both saw overseas in the service usually got the worst cases of PTSD. Not a racist thing, just an observation."

Matt had somehow struggled through his current trauma. But with nothing to compare it to except getting belt-lashed by his father several times as a young teen, he had no idea if he was salvageable. Facing Hypo, he said, "Okay then, what's your story?"

Hypo shot a knowing grin to Hawk—a *this oughta be fun* look.

"My real name's Kenneth Carrillo. Kenny or KC for short. The abridged version is I worked my way up from the mean streets of Chicago. Englewood, to be precise. That's about as bad as it got for kids of color. I did the gang thing, dropped out of school, got shot at but never hit, had a few close calls with knife wounds, knew some homies who got killed, but never saw the worst street shit." He spaced his thumb and forefinger a quarter inch apart. "I was this far from getting caught in a drug deal and going to jail. When my mama heard about that, she about killed me herself. She grew up the same way, had brothers and cousins and boyfriends die or go to prison for life. Something snapped in her, and she said, 'No more. The cycle of death and despair in *my* family ends here.' She made me promise to quit the gang, get my diploma, get out of town. So I did, and I moved on to what I hoped would be a better life." He stared at the floor. "Those words were the last she spoke before she died."

A weight of sadness pressed down on Matt. He recalled his mother's dying wish to him. It was simpler and far less urgent: "Make me proud." Matt believed he had fulfilled her wish—until a year ago. Since then, he'd undone everything he had accomplished that would have made Arlene Lanier proud of her eldest son.

Matt broke the silence. "You sure had me fooled with the street act."

Hypo glanced up at him through raised eyebrows. "One of my talents. I'm as good an actor as anybody in Hollywood. That's why my last employers hired me. I'm a chameleon and can fit into any situation you can name."

"Who was your last employer?"

A wry grin formed on Hypo's lips. "The Central Intelligence Agency."

After figuratively scraping his jaw off the floor, Matt said, "Doing what?"

"Notice my skin color?"

Matt studied Hypo's face. His color was not too dark, not too light, the color of someone with multiple heritages—light-skinned black, Hispanic, Middle Eastern, even southern European. His facial features didn't suggest a particular race or ethnicity. He was a brown-skinned everyman. Matt's brain clicked onto an answer. "You were a spy?"

Hypo nodded. "Three years. Deep undercover in Afghanistan. I was one of the early infiltrators tasked with locating Osama bin Laden."

The force of that name shoved Matt against the back of his chair. "Seriously?"

"I was one of the first operatives in-country. I played the son of a rich Afghan businessman who'd been educated in the States and made important connections there. Then I returned to Afghanistan to use my education to plunder the Afghan populace in the guise of reforming the government. I put out feelers to connect with bin Laden's money men. The goal was to talk to him about financing his fight against the U.S. But I made one mistake."

He paused for effect. The obvious question was on Matt's lips, but he kept silent.

"I met a woman," Hypo said. "Turns out she was an advance scout for bin Laden. Anytime a man with money showed an interest in helping him, she was sent in to seduce the guy and find out if he was legit. She was one fine looker." He whistled, low and appreciative. "Smart too. More than she let on. I'd been trained well, and we started this romantic little fencing match. I thought she could get me closer to bin Laden, but somehow, I blew my cover. Remember back in World War Two, when the soldiers were trained to ask trick questions to possible German spies who talked with American accents? Things like lesser-known ballplayers' names or smaller towns that most Americans would know what state they are in, but a spy might not?"

"Yeah," Matt said.

"Well, she caught me in some sort of trap. I replayed our conversations in my mind a hundred times and still can't remember what I said or did that screwed me. Best I can figure, I mispronounced a word no Afghan would ever mispronounce. Stupid, huh?"

"I guess so," Matt said.

"They arrested me the next day and sent me to some hellhole prison. Let me stew for a while, then started torturing me."

A lump rose in Matt's throat. He'd read about how brutal some Middle Eastern regimes were regarding torture.

"One thing about radical Muslims: they're damn creative. Sadistic bastards too." Hypo raised his right hand, the one missing two fingers. "I'll spare you the details, but that's how I lost these and my foot." He looked away and massaged his face with both hands.

Matt swallowed with difficulty because his mouth had gone dry. He thought of his trauma, which seemed trivial now compared to being dismembered by men who were in complete control of your fate. Choking back the urge to vomit, he croaked out, "Holy shit."

Hawk impassively sipped his tea. Had he heard this story so many times that it didn't bother him? Or was it not the worst PTSD story he'd heard?

Matt refocused on Hypo. "How'd you get out of Afghanistan?"

"Prisoner exchange. Afghans knew I wouldn't be able to resume spying again with two fingers and a foot missing. Might as well put a big red bullseye on my back if I tried to work anywhere in the Middle East. They figured they'd trade for someone they could reuse, but the joke was on them. CIA sent them a guy they'd turned into a double agent. He's the hero. He helped us find bin Laden a year or two sooner than we dared to hope. In fact, some CIA honchos say they couldn't have found bin Laden without him."

"Wow," Matt said. "And if not for one minor mistake, you might've been the hero."

Hypo waved him off. "I doubt it. I just laid the groundwork. All I found out was that bin Laden was probably in Pakistan, not Afghanistan."

Hawk finally spoke. "Tell him how you got your nickname."

"Prison sanitation was nonexistent," Hypo said, "and I got gangrene. They took me to a clinic that wasn't much better. Made me think of a Civil War field hospital. The interrogators didn't want me to die. They had a lot more questions because I hadn't told them anything true except my name, rank, and serial number."

"The CIA's like the military that way?" Matt asked.

"I joined the Army first. They found out I was smart and a quick thinker, so they transferred me to Military Intelligence. I have an ear for languages, so I learned Arabic, then Pashto, for translating documents. Eventually, my commanding officer noticed I spoke both languages like a native. He called his superiors and suggested I be loaned to the CIA. Less than a year later, I was in Afghanistan." He took a sip of his tea. "Got anything to eat, Hawk? I'm starved."

Hawk did an eye roll and said, "He may be small, but he eats like an NFL lineman." Feigning annoyance, he rummaged through his cupboards for some edibles. He produced packages of chocolate chip cookies and tortilla chips and placed them on the table. They all grabbed a few of each and munched quietly for a minute.

After swallowing the rest of a cookie, Hypo said, "Anyway, the docs patched up my hand well enough. But they screwed up on my foot, and the gangrene got worse. Moved up my calf. The bastards hardly ever used gloves or masks when they were around me. I figure they saved them for Muslim patients. What the hell do they care if an American spy croaks? They amputated my leg below the knee. I thought I might be okay until I got a post-op infection. Unfortunately, this infection went to my kidney. I started peeing blood. *That* was a fun week. Damn docs told me it would clear up by itself. But my fever spiked to near 105. I was thinking, *I'm gonna die*. They eventually discovered one of my kidneys had shut down, so they took it out. Of course, that incision got infected. I was laid up an extra two weeks after all the fun I'd had before with those butchers."

"Let me guess," Matt said. "*Hypo* is short for *hypochondriac*."

Hypo touched his nose. "Thanks to those Neanderthalic medical imposters, I'm deathly afraid of hospitals, clinics, doctors, even ugly nurses. I forgot to mention the interrogator who lopped off my body parts wore a white doctor's coat when he did it. Fucking sadist. When I got back from Afghanistan, the other patients in the VA Hospital started calling me *Hypo* after I told them my story." He shrugged. "I guess it stuck."

Astonished, Matt shook his head. "I always assumed *Hypo* was short for *hypodermic*."

"Oh, sure," Hypo said with mock disdain, reverting to his street voice. "Typical white honky assumes da black dude da one shootin' up wit smack every day."

Matt returned the mock disdain. "Hey, listen, I grew up naïve in a small farm town that had about six non-whites. All I knew about drug addicts was from movies and the news media."

Hypo flashed a toothy grin. "Just yanking your chain, my friend," he said without the street tone. "Actually, it helps us if people assume I'm just another poor brotha. I can get closer to more people who might need Hawk's help. They talk to me easier than if I walked, talked, and acted like I normally do."

Matt's estimation of both men rose another notch. These two were fighting a good and noble fight for veterans and others battling PTSD who couldn't or wouldn't seek help from the Veterans Administration or local health services. But something nagged at him. This world of theirs—dealing with homeless or poor street people, many with mental and physical issues that compounded their poverty—was *not* his world. He wanted more than anything to return to his old life as a musician. He was grateful for Hawk's help and Hypo's friendship, but the urgency to find a way out had intensified ever since he'd seen the bald man at Peavey Plaza.

"Time to spill your guts," Hawk said to Matt.

"Okay," Matt said, wiping his palms on his pants. He craved a shot of Jim Beam Black to brace himself, but didn't figure Hawk would offer one. "My name is Matthew Lanier. I grew up in Straight River, Minnesota. I'm wanted by the police for killing a police officer by blowing up my father's farmhouse. Although I was supposed to be inside the house and was severely injured in the blast, the Straight River Police Chief framed me. He and the thug who blew the house worked for the man who's been trying to kill me for more than a year, Leland Smythe."

Matt glanced at each man, looking for a reaction of recognition. Neither spoke, but Hypo's eyes widened.

"Smythe's a real estate tycoon," Matt said. "He leads a conspiracy of rich, powerful people who are stealing farmland. I uncovered a complicated scheme while helping my old neighbor keep her farm. Smythe's group is extorting, blackmailing, or committing murder to get farmers to sell their farms to them at fire-sale prices. They'll eventually sell the land to the federal government at a huge profit for a massive interstate highway expansion project along I-35 from Duluth to Laredo, Texas. Extrapolated to all the farms along I-35 from here to Mexico, dozens more innocent people may die. Hundreds, maybe thousands, could get screwed out of their family farms. If Smythe pulls this off, he stands to make hundreds of millions. Maybe much more."

Again, Matt checked expressions. Hypo now seemed intrigued. Hawk's expression was of concentrated thinking.

"Uhhh," Matt said, "this is where people usually question my sanity or ask how much I've had to drink or what I've been smoking."

Hypo said, "One thing Hawk taught me is to keep quiet until the patient is finished. No judgment, no disbelief, no dismissiveness. This is your truth, Matthew."

Hawk said, "I sense you've experienced more personal trauma, Matthew, so please continue."

Matt took a deep breath. "Okay." He told them about watching his childhood best friend, Dave Swanson, die from multiple gunshot wounds. About killing the man who'd killed Swanson—Charlie Witt—at point-blank range. About another childhood friend, Clay Gebhardt, who died later the same day after helping Matt. About killing his ex-wife, Diane Blake—and Steven Crossley, a Smythe ally—in another gun battle. "I never wanted to kill anyone," he said, his voice cracking. "I never fired the first shot. Every incident was self-defense."

Hawk said, "You okay, Matthew? You're sweating and trembling."

Matt had broken out into a cold sweat, but he wasn't trembling. He was shivering—either from cold or shock. Since it was seventy degrees in Hawk's kitchen, that left shock. He ran his hands through his hair, noticing the shakiness of his fingers as they combed the long strands.

He said, "Yeah, I'm okay. Just getting to the hardest part."

Hawk leaned over and patted his shoulder. "Take your time."

Hypo put a hand on Matt's knee. "It's cool, brother Matthew. First time talking about it is always the hardest."

Matt nodded at each man, forcing a wan smile. "By the way, call me Matt. The only people who called me Matthew were my mom and my teachers when they got mad."

Hypo and Hawk nodded.

"Okay, here goes," Matt said. "Diane was the love of my life. She'd been dating Crossley recently but had just broken up with him. We were rekindling our relationship. She helped me uncover information about Crossley that connected him with Smythe." Matt put his elbows on his knees and stared at the floor, then massaged his damaged fingers. His voice barely above a whisper, he said, "I'd called her earlier and told her to drive up to meet me in Duluth so I could protect her. Crossley must've tapped her phone or eavesdropped or followed her. He set me up because he was driving her car. At the last instant, I realized she *wasn't* driving. I didn't know she was in the passenger seat. Crossley started shooting. I dove to safety, then returned fire. The whole incident took about two minutes."

Matt looked up, slumped back in his chair, and studied his friends' expressions. Both seemed unmoved, but each had a distant look in their eyes. *Reliving their own personal horrors?*

"Well," Hawk said, breaking the silence that engulfed the room. "That qualifies as one of the more unique PTSD stories I've ever heard."

Hypo nodded.

Matt's initial thought was, *they think I'm a nut who's making this up*. He was preparing to defend himself when Hawk continued.

"But the horrors you described, while quite serious, are nothing out of the usual from what I've heard from my dozens of clients over the years."

Matt sat up, feeling a sense of validation and brotherhood.

"Violence of any sort doesn't care about the location, the circumstances, or the people involved," Hawk said. "Nor does it care about the characters' backstories or personal situations. You suffered violent, traumatic injuries. You watched friends and loved ones suffer violent, traumatic deaths. You inflicted violent, traumatic deaths on people. That's what we all have in common: one or more of those experiences."

"Yeah," Hypo said. "The how or the who or the why doesn't matter. Nasty shit happened. Violent shit. That's the common denominator. We're here for you, Matt. Hawk can definitely help you get your head on straight."

Matt looked at Hawk, who cocked an eyebrow toward Hypo but gave Matt a reassuring nod. "Nothing is guaranteed, but my success rate is better than most. I'll listen and give you some advice and tools to help you cope. But your attitude and determination are what's most important if you want to get out from under the weight of guilt and anxiety."

"That's it exactly," Matt said, almost shouting. "I feel like I'm carrying a two-hundred-pound pack on my back. And I never get enough rest to carry it the next day because my sleep is so full of nightmares."

Hawk let loose a short sigh and clapped his hands together. "Well then, let's see if we can remove some of the weight from that backpack."

Matt forced a tight smile, wondering if this near stranger was as talented as Hypo claimed.

Chapter 12

Fifteen miles northwest of Hawk's fourplex, in the corner office of the top floor of a suburban Minneapolis office tower, Leland Smythe barked orders into a burner phone. It was one of many burners he used to guarantee conversations like the one he was having now couldn't be traced.

"Bankruptcy might seem harsh," he said, "but it's good business. Much faster than foreclosure. We've wasted enough time and effort on this farmer. Get this done by tomorrow or I'll find another banker."

Smythe picked up a second phone and made another call. He grilled the man for five minutes, growing increasingly impatient. Displeased with what he heard, Smythe said, "If your farmer doesn't agree to sell by tomorrow afternoon, call me immediately."

The pace of deals was recovering after a hiccup last year, caused by a nosy musician named Lanier, who was too smart for his own good. The musician killed Steven Crossley, Smythe's key political liaison. Crossley had been the Minnesota Governor's chief of staff, and it had taken Smythe months to find and set up a new governmental connection. But with his new handpicked chief of staff successfully installed at the Capitol, he was certain his crowning legacy would be orchestrating the most monumental real estate deal in modern American history.

His extensive team was actually ahead of the timetable he'd developed when Millennium Four, or M4 for short, was a radical idea sketched out on a cocktail napkin at his country club's bar while enjoying a drink with Crossley. Barring another disruption, M4's ultimate goal would become a reality within five years.

Yes, purchasing farmland adjacent to Interstate 35, the aorta of the United States ground transportation system, seemed both financially and politically impossible. Yes, obtaining that land at bargain prices through blackmail, extortion, coercion, and the occasional murder added much more risk. But M4's goal wasn't to buy all the farmland needed for this project, just enough to make Smythe a mega-millionaire—maybe even a billionaire—when he sold all M4 properties to the Feds for an outrageous profit. Thanks to his Congressional contacts, the sales would be buried in whatever massive bill Congress passed authorizing the acquisition of all the land not owned by groups such as M4. Soon after that, construction would begin on the first North American Superhighway.

A superhighway would be needed because Millennium Four anticipated the likelihood of a three-sided economic world war. The players would be economies controlled by China, economies controlled by an expanding Muslim influence, and economies in the Western Hemisphere and allied countries led by the United States. M4 operatives—influential politicians and businessmen—would appeal to U.S. patriotism and insist that America remained the greatest country in the world no matter the cost. Once the citizens had been whipped into a nationalistic frenzy, they'd clamor for fast, decisive action. A superhighway linking North and South America would be the first step in strengthening the economy of the entire hemisphere.

Smythe turned his attention to the man sitting quietly on a leather easy chair in the conversation area of his office. He was thick and muscular, built like a heavyweight wrestler. He wore dark-colored clothing, favoring tight T-shirts that emphasized his rock-hard physique. The man's footwear was soft-soled shoes with steel toes, handy for stealth when needed and driving home his point with those who caused any sort of trouble for his boss.

"Mr. Volkov, I need you down in Ellendale tomorrow. It might be a two-man job. I'll let you know first thing in the morning."

Ivan Volkov's eyes widened. "How do you want it done?"

Midwest farm folks rarely encountered Russians in their daily lives, so the shock value alone was enough to focus their attention after Volkov's first visit. His Russian accent was noticeable enough to inject another layer of suspicion and fear into the minds of those who found themselves on Smythe's bad side. It was usually a warning to shape up fast or face unpleasant consequences.

Smythe appreciated Volkov's ability to speak *sans* accent when a situation called for it. He could play a regular Midwest guy on reconnaissance trips to area farm towns to discover which farmers were contemplating selling their land or open to an option-to-buy deal. And he was more intelligent and cunning than the last primary enforcer Smythe had employed: the sadistic but unimaginative Witt. Sending him up against Lanier several times only resulted in Witt's brutal death, proof that he was no match for intelligence and quick thinking.

After mulling Volkov's question, Smythe said, "We've not used the accidental silo fall of late. One more death shouldn't skew the statistics enough to raise a red flag with the authorities."

Volkov's eager smile revealed his crooked brown teeth. That, combined with a low forehead, acne-scarred complexion, and a nose deformed by multiple breaks, made him look unpleasant from the neck up—a stark contrast to his hard-muscled physique. In a matter-of-fact tone, as though he was taking a diner's order in a restaurant, Volkov said, "One silo accident coming up."

Later that night, Ben sat in his car parked down the block from the apartment where Lanier and Hypo had walked to earlier that day. He'd staked out Lanier's men's shelter the night before and early that morning, after spotting him in the Target Center Skyway where Lanier and Hypo performed before and after the basketball game. He was initially puzzled when the two men entered the modest fourplex, definitely an upgrade from a homeless shelter. Unless Hypo was slumming on the street for fun and could actually afford a decent apartment, Ben assumed Lanier was temporarily crashing with a friend of Hypo's.

Going with the assumption that Lanier would live in the place for a few days, Ben checked his watch, decided Lanier was in for the night, and returned to his motel room. He'd resume his surveillance early tomorrow.

He figured he'd need only a few more days of tracking Lanier to analyze his movements, then lay an ambush. Lanier would never know what hit him. Then it would be a simple matter of waiting until Lanier's body was discovered and identified and his death was made public. Soon after that, he would collect his contract money from Smythe and get the hell out of town with the biggest payday of his life.

Chapter 13

Matt was lying in bed in Hawk's guest room the next morning. Sunshine lit the majestic treetops. A cool breeze wafted in through the screened window. Thanks to no nightmares last night for the first time in weeks, he felt more energized than he'd felt in months. But it was dark energy. Desperate energy. He wanted a normal life. But that would be possible only if he took desperate measures. Failure to do so meant he might as well turn himself in at the police station and be convicted for the crime he didn't commit but couldn't prove—killing the cop.

The most sensible solution to his problem was getting a new identity. And with it a new driver's license, Social Security number, and birth certificate. All fake. All illegal and difficult to obtain. To get them, he needed cash. Lots of cash. And he needed it *now*. Playing guitar on the street for ones and fives wasn't the answer.

After dressing, Matt went to the kitchen for breakfast. Hawk had left a note saying he'd gone out for the morning and for Matt to help himself to any food in the kitchen. He fixed two scrambled eggs, a piece of toast, a slice of lunch meat, and a cup of coffee from the half-full, still-hot pot.

That was another reason he needed to act now. He intended to repay Hawk for his hospitality, all the food he'd be eating, and at least a token payment for his counseling. After Hypo left last night, Matt and Hawk ate dinner, then talked for hours in the living room about PTSD and other topics. Hawk's mind was sharp and inquisitive. He knew a lot about American history, geology, horticulture, and botany. A community garden at the end of the block kept him in touch with like-minded neighbors. On top of that, he had lots of potted plants and flowers around the interior of his apartment. He even had a small, fresh herb garden in his kitchen window.

When Matt asked why horticulture and botany, Hawk replied, "Plants are living things just like animals. Yet they can't communicate with us like many animals can, especially pets. I always wondered why. I've often speculated that some plants might be trying to talk to us. So I like to hang around growing things in case my rosebush ever decides to tell me why it evolved to be so thorny."

"Interesting theory," Matt said.

"More importantly, plants clean the air, produce oxygen, and provide a bit of aromatherapy. Plus, I love fresh vegetables. We always had a garden when I was growing up. Can't let summer go by without fresh tomatoes, berries, greens, and sweet corn."

"Amen to that."

Matt's trust in Hawk had grown last night, along with his respect for the man. But this morning, he had plans that were better put into motion with no one eavesdropping. Hypo was right: Hawk seemed to see everything, notice everything, sense the slightest change in a situation. Matt wasn't sure he could conceal his plan in the man's presence. But he'd have to try.

Done with breakfast, he cleaned up the kitchen and scribbled a note to his host saying he'd be gone all day. Then he headed for the downtown Minneapolis Public Library. The crisp, fresh April day lightened his mood. He felt as though he was walking on a thick carpet rather than concrete. He was finally taking charge. He fell into a steady rhythm and tapped out a basic rock beat on his thighs. As he tapped, a song came to him. Rapid-fire sixteenth-note guitar picking to the walking tempo—actually more of a strut. Thumping bass drum. Light touches of a synthesized keyboard. Kelly Clarkson's sultry voice singing the first few verses of "Stronger (What Doesn't Kill You)." Momentum building with every measure. Then the wailing chorus to the now-throbbing dance beat as she belts out the climactic line. That was it. Matt felt stronger. Lighter and stronger than he'd felt since leaving Castle Danger two months ago in the dark of night through a raging blizzard.

At the library, Matt paid a scruffy-looking woman at one of the public computer terminals five bucks to let him use hers so he could remain anonymous. The woman readily agreed to the deal, since she could simply request another terminal.

Matt looked for newspaper articles that mentioned him concerning all the deaths connected with Smythe. Of course, there'd been a flurry of front-page stories immediately after each incident, but the statewide manhunt for him died down to nothing a few months after he'd bugged out to the Boundary Waters.

His online search for "Leland Smythe" was a different matter. Although Smythe's real estate empire received regular media coverage, his personal and social life was barely mentioned, other than appearances at a few charity events. Nor did Matt find any sign that an enterprising investigative journalist had been digging into Smythe's nefarious activities.

Searching for Smythe's conspiracy, Millennium Four, also revealed little new information. A few mentions had been made on the blogs of infamous conspiracy theorists who routinely had been discredited regarding most of their earlier claims. Either no one cared about the massive land grab still in motion, or Smythe and his M4 minions had quashed or discredited all investigations into their clandestine operation.

Although he didn't really want to know the answer, Matt typed in "typical costs of hand surgery." He had a glimmer of hope when he saw one entry on the search page that gave a range of $2,000 to more than $25,000. He feared his cost to find a virtuoso surgeon with the skill to restore world-class-musician dexterity to his fingers might be a multiple of the high estimate. Of course, there was no guarantee any surgical repair could achieve a perfect result. Although depressing to contemplate, it sealed his resolve that he had to go big. He needed that new identity and all that came with it *now*, not *someday*. Because *someday* might be too late.

Matt's last check was of the latest *Star Tribune* Sunday Arts & Entertainment section for the calendar of music events coming up that week. He jotted down some club names and addresses on a piece of scratch paper next to the computer terminal and returned to Hawk's place.

It's now or never, Matty.

Chapter 14

That night, although he could ill afford the ten-dollar cover charge and two-drink minimum, Matt paid the woman at the hostess stand inside the Diamond Lounge and took a seat at the old wooden bar. Located in the Warehouse District in downtown Minneapolis, the Diamond was a second-tier club that was too small to book most national names. Instead, it featured local and regional performers. The interior was warehouse chic—industrial tables and chairs, warm, indirect lighting, brick walls. The place had a modest dance floor used mainly when a hip-hop or alternative rock group performed. The spacious room smelled faintly of beer and wine and gin and fried food, and more strongly of perfumes and aftershaves. For the musicians, the pay barely exceeded union scale, but the acoustics were excellent. Some walls were adorned with sound baffles for acoustic purposes, and the lofty ceilings were crisscrossed with sound-deadening fabric. For customers, the drinks were cheap, and the food was elevated pub grub.

Matt sipped the screwdriver he'd ordered and acted like a typical customer there to listen to decent jazz and get buzzed. The band was a local group that had been around for years but never quite hit it big. He knew all the members but wasn't about to rekindle any friendships. His sole purpose was to talk to one of the club's regular customers. "Regular" only in the sense of *frequent* because she was one of the biggest drug dealers in the Upper Midwest.

Queenie Delacroix had been a decent jazz and blues singer in Chicago whose real name was Linda Pierce. Barely scraping by, singing in local clubs, and waiting tables in local restaurants, she caught the eye of an older black man, Kareem "King" Coleman, and they began a relationship.

Unbeknownst to her, Coleman headed a large gang in Minneapolis. He'd traveled to Chicago to recruit more lieutenants so he could make a play to become the dominant drug dealer in the Twin Cities. Lured by the cash Coleman flashed around and his promise to promote her career in Minneapolis, Linda Pierce changed her name to Queenie Delacroix at his suggestion and eventually became his trophy wife. Good for his drug business. Not so good for her singing career. She didn't mind because the money flowed, and life was easy and exciting.

After a rival gang murdered Coleman in a drive-by shooting, Queenie moved decisively to take control of his business, consolidate power, and exact revenge on the responsible organization. It was a Midwestern version of Michael Corleone's housecleaning in *The Godfather*. She'd learned at Coleman's side for years and discovered she possessed a knack for business. That and her forceful, charismatic personality earned respect from her troops as well as the competition.

She'd been arrested and charged several times for drug-related offenses like trafficking, assault, even conspiracy to commit murder. Predictably, her sleazy, big-buck attorney either got the charges dropped or got her acquitted. And because the gang wars in the area had died down since her ascendance, local law enforcement and politicians weren't eager to harass her. Fewer gang wars and murders benefitted not only the citizenry's peace and safety, but also the re-election prospects of the pols.

Matt spotted Queenie sitting with a man and a woman in the far corner of the club. He finished his drink and headed for their table. To a rational mind, his strategy was senseless. He was counting on the impact of a maximum first impression.

The couple noticed Matt first, eyeing him suspiciously as he approached. The man had an earnest-looking face on top of a well-toned body. He was handsome in an intellectual way. The woman was a knockout. Runway-model quality with high cheekbones and all those other modeling prerequisites. While not as dark-skinned as the man, she was darker than Hypo. They were fashionably dressed—nothing extravagant but definitely showing their nightclub-chic fashion taste. The man nursed a dark-colored drink. She sipped white wine.

The conversation stopped when Matt reached the vacant side of the table and said, "Ms. Delacroix?"

Queenie Delacroix looked up from her cocktail, her narrowed eyes disdainfully sizing him up. "Yes?"

"I just spent twenty bucks that I can't afford to get in here and talk to you. You're one of the largest employers in the Midwest for your kind of business, the kind of business that pays extremely well. I need a job like that. I need it now, and I want you to hire me."

Bemusement overcame Queenie's face. She leaned back and laughed. Pushing fifty, she tried to fool people into thinking she was in her thirties with thick makeup and a tanning-booth tan. She was big-woman voluptuous, like Jennifer Lopez minus the intense workouts. Her shoulder-length, bottle-blonde hair hinted at wavy curls. Warm eyes offset a hard-edged mouth. She wore a red V-neck silk blouse over dark slacks. Surprisingly, the only jewelry she wore was gold hoop earrings and a gold wedding band.

"Mister," Queenie said, "I've heard a lot of pickup lines in my day but never one that pathetic." Her alto voice carried subtle power but lacked the warmth of a singer like Ella Fitzgerald. That shortcoming had probably stalled her career at the level of "respectable lounge singer.

Matt steeled himself, drawing upon his improvisation skills to find the right words at the right time. "Glad I've made an impression," he said and drew a deep breath. "I'll be brief. I know you run a high-risk business. To show you I'm serious, I'm willing to make the *ultimate* sacrifice to do the job."

Queenie shook her head. "Son, I don't know if you're doing a PSA for the Marine Corps recruiting office or campaigning for mayor. Either way, get the hell out of my face."

Improvise! Matt sat in the fourth chair and folded his arms. "Let's talk."

The man slid his chair back and unbuttoned his suit coat. *Getting ready to pull a gun?*

Queenie's face hardened. "You don't hear so well, buddy. I said, 'Get lost.'"

"What she said," echoed the man. He tried to look tough, but his earnest face managed only pissed off. The runway model shifted in her chair and furtively glanced at her companions.

Matt leaned toward Queenie and fixed his gaze on hers. "I'm looking for the kind of job you can't find someone foolish enough or brave enough to do. The kind of job that'll make your life a whole lot easier."

"What makes you think I'm hiring?" Queenie asked.

He lowered his voice. "I've been shot at, blown up, run over, set on fire, and chased all over the state. I've killed men. But I'm not an assassin. I'm a survivor. Right now, I don't care if I live or die. That makes me the exact sort of employee you want. A volunteer with nothing to lose who's not afraid of dying for a paycheck."

Queenie digested his statement in motionless silence.

"Come on, Ms. Delacroix. I'm a musician. Most of the cats I played with used mood-altering substances. Twenty percent were into the hard stuff. I heard stories. How you took over after your husband was murdered. How you survived and rose to the top in the Twin Cities. You're the CEO of a business bigger than some Wall Street corporations. The people who run those companies always want more. Which means *you* want more." Matt thumbed his chest. "I'm the man who can get you to the next level."

Queenie looked around the room, saw no one was paying her table any attention, and refocused on Matt. Then she said, "Victor, you and Cara finish your drinks at the bar. I'll wave if I need you."

The couple shot nasty glares at Matt as they left. Maybe they were trying to make their own deal with Queenie before he'd elbowed them out of the way. Or maybe they were thrill-seekers who'd brag to their millennial friends tomorrow about how they'd hung out with Queenie Delacroix at the Diamond.

Queenie pasted an insincere smile on her face and folded her arms across her ample chest. "You got the balls of a gorilla, my friend. How about you start by telling me your name?"

"Call me Jazzman."

"Jazzman?"

"If I'm anonymous, we're both much safer."

"*You* maybe," Queenie said with a huff. "Everybody already knows me."

"Another reason to hire me. I'm as anonymous as they come. No way anyone can connect us through back history. As long as Victor and Cara don't talk about this, you're in the clear."

"But you can implicate me if you get caught."

"If I go to jail, I'll be dead before the ink's dry on my arrest papers. Ratting you out won't matter if I don't live long enough to testify in court."

She raised her thick, black, painted eyebrows into two unnatural-looking arches. Smirking, she said, "You gonna do something noble like swallow a cyanide capsule?"

Matt shook his head. "I have a man on my tail who wants me dead. He's got the cops in his pocket too. Once he finds out I've been arrested, he'll pay a jailhouse snitch to give me a twenty-one-shiv salute. His only cost will be a few bucks to bribe a judge to turn that two-to-ten the snitch is doing into time served and an immediate parole."

For the first time in their conversation, Queenie seemed impressed. "Those gorilla balls of yours have some weight to them. But that doesn't make you any less an undercover cop who's itching for a big score. You have any proof you're not working a sting?"

He'd never considered the question because he'd estimated the odds of him getting anywhere near this far in the discussion were a hundred to one. Slumping back into his chair, he looked down and said, "No."

In a bar across the street from the Diamond Lounge, Ben Nowitzki sat at a window table facing the entrance to the Diamond so he could see Lanier when he came out. He nursed a Grain Belt Nordeast and wondered how a man with a great life had fallen so far, so fast. From a world-class musician to a street denizen struggling to survive. No surprise considering the man's immediate past history: on the run from Smythe and the police for nine months; a brief respite in Castle Danger working for Allyson Clifford but still living under the radar; then fleeing to Minneapolis after he'd probably killed two more men to save Clifford and her son.

If he'd been in Lanier's shoes, Ben would've surrendered to the cops. Guilty or not, three squares and a cot in Stillwater state prison were better than scrambling for food and shelter every day. The guy was broke, homeless, probably traumatized, and had incurred some injuries. Still, at their last meeting, he'd mentioned that he intended to stop Smythe *by himself*. More stupid crazy. Except Lanier was *not* stupid.

That's what bothered Ben. If the police and newspaper reports were accurate, Lanier had been directly or indirectly responsible for at least *eight* violent deaths in less than a year. A total most serial killers would envy. Why? Was he delusional? Did he have a vigilante complex? Had he constructed a devious alibi to hide his psychopathic ways? If all those deaths were justifiable homicides, why had he always disappeared after each incident?

As for the Castle Danger deaths, Lanier was the only person who could have killed those two men. But those homicides also might've been justifiable. Thanks to a blizzard raging that evening, the authorities couldn't have saved Allyson Clifford in time. In addition, her scumbag husband, Donnie Vossler, would've escaped with their son. Ben vividly remembered Lanier's shattered snowmobile helmet after he'd returned to Allyson's house. If the helmet hadn't deflected Vossler's bullet, Lanier would've been killed.

After more than an hour of waiting, Ben spotted Lanier leaving the Diamond. He paid his bar tab and stepped outside, expecting to follow Lanier on foot as he'd done coming from the fourplex to the Warehouse District. Since Lanier walked almost everywhere, Ben wondered why he'd gone into the club and spent precious hard-earned cash on the cover charge and standard two-drink minimum. *Take the damn bus or light rail once in a while, dude.* Another incongruity. Did he go to the club to listen to the music? Or was there another reason?

Ben settled in a half-block behind Lanier and matched his leisurely pace through downtown, heading south. The cool, moist April air was refreshing after the stuffy bar. But with more time to think as he walked, he wondered if the money he'd get for this job would assuage the doubts that would nag him for the rest of his life if he killed a man who didn't deserve to die.

Chapter 15

After striking out with Queenie Delacroix, Matt returned to Hawk's place and flopped onto his bed fully clothed. Hypo hadn't moved in yet, so Matt had the small bedroom to himself. Although his energy level was zero, he wasn't tired. Guilt hung over him for being so desperate for money that he was willing to commit a crime. Failure weighed him down because he'd blown this chance to get the job that could change his life and put him on a path to normal.

As he stared at the ceiling in the dark, his thoughts drifted to another woman—Allyson Clifford. Barely three months ago, she had saved him from freezing to death on the doorstep of her restaurant, the Halcyon Bar & Grill in Castle Danger, Minnesota. A day later, she hired him as a temporary cook when her chef abruptly quit. Beautiful, intelligent, and charming, she was everything a man could want in a woman. She was also a terrific mother to her son, Josh, to whom Matt had grown quite attached in short order. His brief experience as a father figure to Josh often had felt as emotionally rewarding as making music.

But then Donnie Vossler had shown up. Allyson's husband, Josh's father, and one of the sleaziest scumbags Matt had ever met. Five years earlier, Allyson had taken Josh and gone on the run to escape Vossler's criminal abuse, ending up in Castle Danger and starting a new life. But Vossler found them and came to take back his son by any means possible. Persuaded by her to protect Josh at all costs, Matt was nearly killed twice, once by Vossler and also by Nowitzki, who'd tracked him to Castle Danger on Smythe's orders. With the help of an accomplice, Vossler kidnapped Allyson and Josh, intending to kill her and return to California with his son.

Because of a blizzard that made the roads impassable in the entire region, law enforcement's help was nonexistent. After Matt survived the attempts on his life and saved Allyson from a drug overdose administered by Vossler, he did the only thing possible under the circumstances to save Josh—he chased Vossler and his accomplice, who were escaping with Josh, and killed them both.

Since that fateful night, thoughts of becoming a family with the Cliffords forced themselves daily into Matt's conscious *and* subconscious mind. Dozens of times, he dreamed of surprising her at the Halcyon, where she'd leap into his arms, smother him with kisses, and pledge her eternal love. Yet as he lay there, one step removed from living a nightmare, he realized his dream was a pipe dream, as were his other goals: stop Smythe, get the murder charge dropped, repair his left hand, resume his music career. Now those dreams were wispy memories, vapors so tenuous the vibrations of passing street traffic shook them out of the air like dust falling to the floor. What kept him going, kept the dreams alive, was his last conversation with Allyson.

After rescuing Josh, Matt returned to her house and prepared to run again. Admitting to anyone besides Allyson that he'd just killed two men in self-defense with no witnesses might cost him his freedom. If that happened, dealing with the law could lead to his arrest for allegedly murdering the cop in Straight River. But when she called from the medical clinic where she was being monitored after the drug overdose and thanked him for saving her and Josh, he had a disturbing revelation. He'd *enjoyed* killing Vossler. Pulling the shotgun trigger and blowing a hole in the bastard's chest overwhelmed him with feelings of power and righteousness. He'd played the role of God: judge, jury, and executioner. Worse, he felt no remorse. What Vossler had done to Allyson, and how he might have abused Josh in the future, deserved a death sentence. He hadn't fully grasped that feeling until that moment.

How could his dreams of forming a family with Allyson and Josh come true when he believed he possessed the heart and mind of a killer? When the inevitable lover's quarrel happened, would he go ballistic on Allyson? What if Josh misbehaved? Matt had suffered the sting of his father's belt on his backside many times and vowed he would never raise a hand to a child, a woman, *anyone*. Violence should always be the last resort, and only in self-defense. But after making the leap to feeling no remorse in killing certain humans, could he dare hope to revert to his peaceful ways?

That's why he'd abruptly left before she returned home. He couldn't face her if she saw him as a violent, murderous man. He wanted to prove that he was a genuine pacifist in normal times. The only way to do so was to stop Smythe and disprove the police reports that portrayed him as a serial killer. He fell asleep wrestling with the twisted logic of believing the best way to absolve himself of a crime was to commit another crime.

Chapter 16

When Matt appeared in the kitchen for breakfast the next morning, Hawk wore a cheery grin along with his standard uniform: jeans, work shirt, well-worn hiking boots. "Good morning, my friend," he said. "Are you enjoying the accommodations at Chez Norman?"

Although Hawk's place was a significant improvement from the homeless shelter, Matt's sleep had been riddled with nightmares again. But he felt vaguely cheerful, even optimistic. Safer? More relaxed? He replied, "Best I've had in months."

"High praise indeed from the homeless wanderer. Coffee?"

"Black, please."

Hawk poured a cup, handed it to Matt, then returned to the chair above which the *Star Tribune* lay open on the table. Eyeing Matt with a concerned look, he said, "I heard you get in rather late last night. Did you find another guitar and play a midnight street gig?"

A night owl by nature, Matt struggled to clear his mind this early in the day. He sat down opposite his host and stalled by taking a slow sip of coffee. Choosing his words carefully, he said, "I was … looking for a job."

"A musician job? Like an audition?"

Matt looked away and massaged his two injured fingers. "I guess you could call it that."

Hawk's expression was placid. He worked his facial muscles as if he were chewing on an idea. "Hmm. Maybe we should have another session today. Get you to examine those inner demons in detail." His face brightened. "Say, why don't you help me in my garden while we talk? I find that simple chores like gardening are a powerful healer."

"Sounds good," Matt said. "I still remember how to shovel manure and dig holes."

After breakfast, they went outside to the small but dense garden. It reminded Matt of the tiny allotment gardens he'd seen in Germany. Every square inch of plots no larger than twenty feet by twenty feet was filled with flowers, plants, and vegetables. The riot of colors and textures at their summer peaks was amazingly intense. Of course, at this time of year in Minnesota, all Hawk had to show for his efforts were tulips, crocuses, and early greening vegetables like chives. Based on the footprint of this garden and how much was given over to perennials, it likely would be as lush as a tropical forest by July.

The men went to work adding compost to the soil, then transplanting a few hostas. Chatting idly at first while they worked, Matt gradually opened up. He shared the deeper, darker feelings about his encounters with Smythe and his minions. As Hawk had predicted, Matt's internal pressure eased with every detail he shared. Hawk said little other than to ask clarifying questions or change the course of the discussion to another topic. He occasionally shared a tip on how he counseled a veteran with a similar issue by drawing parallels to Matt's situation.

Two hours later, Matt was convinced he suffered from PTSD and was far from alone. Hell, probably half of the homeless men wandering the Minneapolis streets were either vets with PTSD or men who'd been involved with brutal gang activities.

When they broke for lunch, Matt whipped up a chicken salad loaded with chopped vegetables he'd perfected over the years. Hawk was impressed and ate heartily. He also complimented Matt on his outstanding work ethic. "I never met a musician who lacked the discipline and drive to do everything right and to the best of his ability."

"It's in my DNA," Matt said.

"You saved me two days' worth of garden work. Thanks." Hawk cocked an eyebrow and smiled. "That earned you an extra week of free rent."

"I appreciate it, Hawk. If I get my life on track, I'll pay you back with interest for everything you've done."

Hawk waved him off. "Giving me this chicken salad recipe would be a start."

"Sure." Matt wrote the recipe on a piece of paper and handed it to him.

They spent another hour discussing Matt's traumas. After suggesting a few more relaxation techniques and stretches to ease headaches, Hawk said, "Permit me an observation. I've noticed your self-discipline and drive to do things right doesn't stop with your music, my friend. It's useful in *all* parts of your life. Please be careful how you use those traits."

A sharp pang of guilt and shame pierced Matt like an arrow. Hawk *knew* he was hiding something. With a straight face and flat tone, Matt said, "I will."

Chapter 17

Matt shivered as he stood across the street from the Diamond Lounge a few minutes before closing time. A storm front with a brisk wind had blown through earlier and dropped the temperature about fifteen degrees. On the positive side, the rain had cleared the air of the unpleasant smells of downtown—sewer gas, garbage, and lingering odors generated by people using dark alleyways and the doorways of abandoned buildings as public toilets.

This was his fourth consecutive night waiting for Queenie Delacroix. A conversation with the regular bartender at the Diamond on the first day of Matt's stakeout revealed that Queenie regularly held court there. She probably did some business under cover of the music and loud conversation. He'd decided to demonstrate his determination by being outside the club every night until she broke down and gave him a job.

Tonight, he'd fended off several come-ons from street prostitutes, both male and female. A beat cop ordered him to move along after passing him for the third time in fifteen minutes. Matt quickstepped around the block, grateful for the activity so he could stop shivering. After checking to see that the cop wasn't nearby, he resumed his post, hoping he hadn't missed Queenie's exit.

He was tired, hungry, and annoyed by the well-to-dos leaving a bar or club. They consistently flung insults at him, probably to vent some deep-seated prejudice against poor and homeless people. "Get a job," "Go home to your cardboard box," or "Shouldn't you be dumpster diving right now?" Based on this small sampling, the level of disdain for the less fortunate was appalling and depressing.

As Delacroix left the club on that first night, Matt bounded across the street to meet her. "Ms. Delacroix, remember me?"

She glanced up with a blank look, which was quickly replaced by vague recognition. "Get lost," she said, then got into her car and drove away.

The second night, he approached her again. "I won't give up, Ms. Delacroix."

She passed him in silence.

On the third night, two men accompanied her. One was Victor, the man at Queenie's table during their first meeting. Matt's first instinct was that Victor might try to take him to the alley behind the Diamond and teach him a lesson. Unafraid because of the crowds of people still on the street, he said, "I'm not a stalker, Ms. Delacroix. I'm looking for a job."

Queenie stopped and faced him full on. "Mister, what's the word for *no* in your world? You obviously didn't understand English the first time we met."

He fumbled for a reply, but she walked away before he could open his mouth.

On this, the fourth night, she cracked.

"Ms. Delacroix," Matt said with forced enthusiasm and a phony smile. Even he was tiring of this Don Quixote quest. Why the hell did he believe she would change her mind if he couldn't prove he wasn't an undercover cop? She kept walking, but this time, he followed her. "I'm more desperate every day."

"You startin' to annoy me, boy." Her tone was harsh, her language more "tough hood" than refined.

"All I ask for is a chance. One small job as a test, then you can decide. If you say no, I'll never bother you again. Promise."

That halted Queenie in her tracks. Matt stopped with her. She gestured to one of the men in her group of three men and two women. Victor slid toward her. They whispered back and forth. Then Victor stepped between Matt and the group as Queenie walked away. Matt tried to walk around him, but Victor thrust out his arm.

"Hold on, man. She's leaving. You're not."

Matt tensed, ready for Victor to flash a gun or a knife or sucker punch him or call the cops. But as he analyzed Victor's expression, he realized Victor didn't intend to harm him.

"She told me you don't smell like a cop, not even an undercover narc. She's got a job in mind."

Resisting the urge to grab Victor by the lapels and shake that information out of him, Matt said, "Like what?"

"Got some questions."

"What do you need to know?"

"Show me where you live first. Then we go from there."

"You up for a long walk?"

Victor scoffed. "Hell, no. I'll drive. Want to waste as little time as possible with you. Queenie told me if I get one negative vibe about what you're showing and telling, I can tell you to fuck off, and you're history. Understand?"

"Of course."

Victor led the way to his car, a dark-blue Cadillac sedan. Other than Matt giving directions, they traveled in silence. As he pulled up in front of Hawk's fourplex, Victor said, "What kind of deal you got here? This looks damn spendy for a dude who looks as poor as you."

"A friend of a friend. He rents one of the units. Before that, I was at a men's homeless shelter not too far from here."

"Which one?"

Matt recited the name and address.

Victor nodded. "I heard of that place. One of my men has a brother who did too much meth, fucked himself up, lost his job, yada yada. Ended up there until he OD'd."

"Drugs aren't my problem," Matt said.

"Queenie noticed. Normally guys like you looking to score some work from Her Royal Highness are stupid-ass crackheads. They believe if they do a solid for Queenie, she'll give them a lifetime stash of whatever they want."

"How could she tell I don't do drugs?"

"Beats me. She just knows. Has this sixth sense. I don't like it much because she screwed up a few times when she trusted the wrong people. Fortunately, it wasn't anything big. But the times she was right paid off huge more than once. The biggest was when she suspected she was being set up for a coup. Turns out, one of her lieutenants thought he'd take a run at her. She must've sensed he was plotting something. As you can guess, she turned the tables because her lieutenant is gone, and she's still the Queen."

"Gone where?"

"Don't be stupid, white boy. If you can't figure it out, I might pull the plug right now."

Matt instantly regretted his gaffe. Here he was thinking *corporate takeover*—legal maneuvers, espionage, blackmail. Assassination to take over a drug lord's turf never popped onto his radar. Maybe he wasn't cut out to be any sort of criminal. This was the big-time, not open mic auditions at a comedy club.

"Sorry. Didn't mean to overstep. What else do you want to know?"

"Where'd you live before the shelter?"

"Up North for a year. Different places."

Victor nodded. "Who's the dude you crashin' with?"

"A guy named Hawk. He's sort of a street psychologist."

"You makin' any money now?"

"No. And I've only got a few bucks left. I do some work around the place—garden stuff, cooking, cleaning. But it's not enough to cover what normal rent would be. I'm a charity case for this guy."

"Charity? How?"

A rush of heat flooded Matt's skin. *How much to tell this stranger?* "I've got some ... issues. He's counseling me. Does it with lots of guys. Sort of his calling in life, so he doesn't charge me or anyone else. Figures getting at least a few of us closer to a normal life is payment enough."

Victor cracked a smile and nodded. "Ahh, one of those bleedin' hearts. A Mr. Do-gooder so he can stand looking at himself in the mirror."

"You're wrong. He went through the same trouble as me and the others."

"What kind of trouble?"

After a long hesitation, Matt said, "PTSD."

Victor's expression didn't change. "That's rough, man. My old man fought in Nam. He came back a different guy according to my mama."

Matt sensed Victor's opinion of him was softening ever so slightly.

"How'd you make money before moving in with this cat?"

"Street musician."

"You any good?"

A loaded question. Was Victor gauging Matt's confidence to do whatever job Queenie might have for him? Prying for details about his identity? Checking for an inflated ego? Matt raised his left hand and wiggled his damaged fingers. "Not as good as I used to be."

"What's your ax?"

"String bass *was* my living. Right now, just mediocre guitar."

"What genres?"

Matt was impressed that Victor even knew the term *genre*. "Typical white boy growing up on the farm," he said. "My dad loved country western. Mom liked Top 40 stuff and classical. But of course, it was rock 'n' roll for me until I got into the school orchestra. I led a jazz-rock-country band in high school. We played weddings, school dances, anything that paid a few bucks. Learned hundreds of songs from all genres. I've had serious classical training, but my first love now is jazz."

"You sayin' that to impress the black dude next to you?"

"No, man, I'm serious. I'm not a fan of the postmodern noise they *call* jazz today, but I dug Ornette Coleman back in the day. Ron Carter was my idol on the bass. I also loved Oscar Pettiford because he was a local cat. I played a lot of big band gigs. Did lots of trio work."

"Well, dude, you talkin' the talk for sure. That's what my old man loved: jazz from the sixties and seventies. He was into cats like Herbie Hancock, Wayne Shorter, Freddie Hubbard."

"Your old man has excellent taste."

"*Had.*"

"Oh. Right. Sorry. Mine's gone too." Matt had a fleeting thought that Victor's father might have been Queenie's husband, King Coleman. A flush of panic welled up. Was Victor setting him up for a quick hit and disposal of his body in a back-alley dumpster? Just another TV news teaser headline: *Vagrant found dead in trash. Details at ten.* "Anything else you want to know?"

Victor turned and locked his gaze on Matt. His eyes had a fiery glow Matt hadn't noticed before. "Are you working for any sort of law-enforcement agency?"

Without hesitating, Matt stared deep into Victor's eyes, as if daring him to blink first. The dead vagrant scenario leaped back to mind. "No. I'm a regular guy who stumbled across something he wasn't supposed to stumble across that put him on the street. Now I want my old life back."

Victor studied him for a few seconds, then stared out the windshield. He chewed on his lower lip, then rubbed his jaw. "Get out of the car."

Matt felt as if a trapdoor had opened below, and he was free-falling to his death. He'd come close, or so it seemed. What had he said that soured the deal? *Damn!* He'd been honest, straightforward, no bluffing or bragging or tough-guy attitude. Maybe that was it. He didn't come off as tough enough or confident enough. Holding back the desperation in his voice, he said, "Is there anything I can do to change your mind?"

"Get out of the car. I gotta make a call in private. Go across the street so you can't hear me."

Matt strode to the sidewalk and turned, looking toward Victor but not *at* him. The wait dragged on endlessly. Victor talked on his phone for several minutes, then clicked off and lowered his window. Matt stood silently, hesitant to act. Then Victor motioned for him to come closer, and Matt walked to within six feet of the car. To Matt's extreme surprise and shock, Victor pulled a pistol and pointed it at Matt's head. Matt froze and breathed what he assumed would be his last breath.

Chapter 18

The first night Lanier returned to the Diamond Lounge, Ben followed him, hid in the shadows a safe distance away, and watched his prey. He thought it strange that Lanier stood around for hours waiting until a woman exited the club, then approached her and spoke to her, only to have her ignore him and leave. Ben was puzzled when Lanier repeated the same routine the second night—apparently with the same woman. He couldn't get a good look at her other than to see she was white and full-figured. On the third night—with the same woman—her body language radiated annoyance or anger, which was intriguing. Was Lanier harassing her? Stalking her? Ben assumed nothing had been resolved because the result was the same—Lanier trudging home, slouching, head down. Ben decided history would repeat itself tomorrow, but now he wanted details. He would also arrange his hit around this schedule, assuming Lanier stuck to the same routine.

Tonight, the fourth night, Ben slipped into the bar he'd sat in the first time he followed Lanier. He again found a window seat with a clear view of the entrance to the Diamond. After ordering a beer, he grabbed a small DSLR camera from his coat pocket. He'd preset the zoom lens, F-stop, and shutter speed to capture quality long-range images in low light.

Lanier played the same game as he had the first three nights: loiter without being noticed by cops, get harassed by some passersby, and watch others either rush past, veer into the street to walk around him, or reverse course and find a different route to their destinations.

An hour into Ben's surveillance, the woman exited the Diamond accompanied by three men and two women. Sure enough, Lanier approached her. Ben grabbed his camera, focused on the group, and snapped pictures using the *burst* setting, which generated a dozen images in mere seconds. When he refocused and got a single close-up shot of the mystery woman, he finally recognized her.

"Well, I'll be damned," he muttered and lowered the camera. "Why the hell is Lanier talking to Queenie Delacroix four nights in a row? Is he stupid enough to try to buy drugs from *her*?"

As a rookie Minneapolis cop, Ben had heard of Queenie's storied past from the veterans, who grudgingly praised her for her Teflon skin. He'd left Minneapolis five years ago, so seeing Queenie still alive and kicking was confirmation that the illegal drug trade was still lucrative.

After scanning his photos to verify it *was* Queenie Delacroix in the shots, Ben looked up in time to see Lanier walking with a black man from her group. He tossed some cash on the table to cover his tab and rushed outside. He was half a block behind Lanier and walking fast, trying to draw closer. As he rounded the corner, he saw Lanier and the other man get into a dark sedan and drive away, with Lanier in the passenger seat. Ben's car was a block away. He'd never be able to reach it in time to follow. *Shit.* He'd lost his man but gained some helpful knowledge. The only logical option was to return to Lanier's place and hope he'd eventually show up.

As he drove, Ben's roiling gut suggested Lanier messing with a drug queen might not end well. That meant his lucrative payday might vanish. He turned from East Franklin onto the street where the fourplex was located, then slammed to a stop when he saw an astonishing sight in the middle of the block. Lanier stood in the street ten feet from the same car he'd been riding in. The driver held a pistol leveled at Lanier's head. The driver's hand moved several times as he pulled the trigger. Lanier didn't fall, didn't duck, didn't run; he just stood there. Ben heard no sounds of gunfire. Not even the muffled pop of a suppressor. He saw no flash. Saw no smoke from the barrel. The man pulled the gun back inside the car and drove away. As Lanier entered the fourplex, Ben gaped at the scene. *What the hell just went down?*

Despite the clock ticking on his two-week deal with Smythe, confusion flooded Ben's mind. He needed time to think, investigate, and figure out exactly who Matt Lanier was. So instead of staking out the fourplex until morning, he returned to his motel room, retrieved a Grain Belt Nordeast from the mini fridge, and sprawled on his bed. He wished he had a bottle of something stronger.

What he'd seen tonight made him realize he'd been dragging his heels about assassinating Lanier ever since identifying him outside Target Center a week ago. On any of the first four nights he'd been tracking Lanier, he could have driven up alongside him, fired a suppressed round or two into his brain, and sped off into the darkness.

Yet Ben had *not* pulled the trigger. Hadn't even considered it. He needed to figure out why, and he needed to do it before his contract expired in a few days. At stake was a six-figure payday. The most logical reason for his hesitation was that he didn't know the whole story. He thought he understood Lanier based on police reports, newspaper articles, and what Smythe had told him. But those sources gave him no information about the inner man.

Lanier's being a PhD-level case study in contradictions further muddled Ben's thinking. Accused cop killer, brilliant musician. A reputation for ruthlessness. Yet he'd spared Ben's life in Castle Danger. A possible serial killer with as many as eight likely victims, yet he stood outside a second-rate club for four consecutive nights waiting to talk to Queenie about … something. Who does that besides obsessive fanboys and fangirls wanting autographs from celebrities?

And now tonight's finale. Lanier couldn't have known the gun was unloaded. Why would he and the driver stage that little drama if he did? Any sane man who had a stranger aim a gun at him from point-blank range would've either run, ducked, pulled his own gun, pleaded for mercy, or at least flinched. But this strange, unpredictable man stood there as stoic as a marble sculpture in a museum. Did he freeze in panic? Was he resigned to dying? Wishing to be dead? After Queenie's man drove away, Lanier turned and entered his building as nonchalantly as if he'd been out for a late-night stroll. Was he strung out?

Ben chugged the rest of his beer and got ready for bed. He needed a few hours of sleep before going on a brief road trip first thing in the morning.

Chapter 19

As Matt lay on his bed in Hawk's apartment, Victor's parting words echoed in his head. *Queenie told me to find out if you were telling the truth about not caring if you live or die.* Matt was still stunned and bewildered by his lack of reaction to the gun pointed at his head. He'd felt an adrenaline surge, then tried to duck, to run. But for some reason, his body wouldn't move. By then, Victor had pulled the trigger six times.

Matt rolled over and faced Hypo's bed. "You awake?"

Hypo, who'd moved in yesterday, spoke in a sleepy monotone. "Course I'm awake. Even when I'm sleeping, I'm awake."

"Why's that?"

"In my previous line of work, the only operatives who slept well are dead."

"Oh. Right." Matt couldn't imagine life as a spy, operating in a foreign country, speaking a non-native language, acting like a regular guy going about his life, but actually working to find the most wanted man in the world in the early 2000s. The pressure must have been unbearable, looking over his shoulder every waking minute.

Since going on the run last year, Matt had slept well on many nights, especially after the canoeing season had ended in the Boundary Waters. From then on, the risk of being discovered by Forest Service rangers was minimal. He'd also slept well in Castle Danger until Vossler showed up. He chalked it up to his gift of getting a fast read on people, particularly those who were up to no good, like Vossler. But Victor had fooled him. He'd been unreadable. He'd also been fooled during his initial encounter with Ben Nowitzki in the Halcyon. Nowitzki had dined there and asked to meet the chef, Matt, to pay his compliments. Matt took him for a grateful diner and had no clue Nowitzki intended to kill him.

That brought him back to the present and another question for Hypo. "The guy who was showing a mugshot of me last week. Did you get a good look at him?"

"Already told you," Hypo mumbled. "I took him for some sort of cop right away. Mainly by his body language, the way he walked, making eye contact with everyone in my group."

Matt tried to conjure up an image of Nowitzki. He'd only seen him clearly in Allyson's house the night Matt saved her and Josh. He remembered Nowitzki as having coarse features. Probably Slavic heritage based on the surname. Dark hair. Piercing eyes. Large nose. Shorter and heavier than Matt. And the voice ... "What did he sound like?"

Hypo emitted a sound that was part groan, part curse word. "I don't know. Like a white guy. Middle class. With a hint of Iron-Range twang."

"I mean his tone quality. I hear a voice; I compare it to an instrument. Brass, woodwind, violin, things like that."

"Aww, man, you makin' me use my brain at two in the morning," Hypo said, whining in his street voice. "What that gotta do with any little thing?"

"Please, think about it. Give me your first impression recollection."

"If I do, you let me saw wood till morning?"

"Promise," Matt said.

Hypo rolled onto his back, thought for several seconds, and said, "He sounded like a tight guitar string. No, a tight piano string."

Matt nearly sat up with excitement. "Baritone range?"

"Yeah, lower than my voice, but not opera-villain low."

As soon as Hypo mentioned a *tight string*, Matt knew they were talking about the same man. Nowitzki *had* sounded tight, stressed from almost making the kill, only to have Matt turn the tables and tie him up in Allyson's kitchen. Would Matt kill him? Take him hostage? Summon the sheriff?

"Thanks. G'night, Hypo."

"You welcome, honky." Hypo rolled away with a flourish, fluffed his pillow, and emitted an exaggerated sigh.

Now, Matt had to assume Nowitzki had found him and was waiting for the opportune time to strike. Starting tomorrow, he'd have to be alert for a setup or ambush. He recalled Nowitzki relating the terms of his contract with Smythe: Make Lanier's death look like an accident and earn double the six-figure hit fee. On the bright side, staging a hit to look like an accident in a major metropolitan area would be nearly impossible compared with the relative ease of pulling it off in remote Castle Danger. The logical assumption then was that Nowitzki would settle for a straight assassination. That narrowed the options, but Matt couldn't anticipate what those options might be. Drive-by shooting? Sniper shot from a secluded upstairs window? A hit-and-run with a stolen vehicle that Nowitzki would quickly abandon for a getaway car? Matt concluded that the sooner he got his quick-score payday and bought a new identity, the sooner he'd be safe from Smythe's wrath.

He returned to Victor's evaluation of their brief scenario on the street outside Hawk's place. He hoped Victor would tell Queenie that Jazzman was indeed not afraid to die, which would imply that the job Queenie was considering for him involved a high degree of danger. But a life-or-death task might require him to take a life. Matt had *reluctantly* killed many people in self-defense. Except for Diane—whose death was unintentional—his victims were all criminals who deserved their fates. Tonight, he was *willing* to kill again, possibly a premeditated act against an innocent person. On the other hand, the victim might deserve to die as much as Witt had deserved to die. In that case, he might be able to live with himself for committing murder.

A simple, elegant lyric started up in Matt's musical memory, followed soon by the melody. Linda Ronstadt's vulnerable, mournful alto voice floating above Nelson Riddle's lush orchestration of Thelonious Monk's classic jazz ballad, "Round Midnight." Matt had performed the tune hundreds of times and listened to dozens of different recordings. Tonight, Linda's interpretation encapsulated his mood far better than any other version—frustration, hopelessness, quiet desperation.

Finally sleepy, Matt closed his eyes. A red line zoomed into his imagination. A trickle. As the line got larger and nearer, the trickle became a stream, wider, deeper. A stream of blood. Images of those he'd killed floated past like corpses bobbing on red waves. He squeezed his eyes tighter, trying to erase the images. Unsuccessful, he looked out the window and focused on the ambient light of the street. His heart pounded. His head ached. He felt sick. No matter what song he forced into his mind, he would not sleep well 'round *this* midnight.

Big Island. Crystal Lake. The Boundary Waters. April. Traces of snow on the ground. Paper-thin ice along the shore. Total solitude. Watching, waiting, preparing. The distant crash of a canoe against a rock—a heaven-sent warning. His trap isn't fully set. Too late to run. Barely time to hide. Witt and Flannery paddle toward his island. They search his campsite, then start up the hill toward him from separate trails. He aims his rifle over the barricade. Scans the wooded hillside for movement. Each man trips over one of his warning signals—tin pots full of rocks tied to a fishing line. They scramble to their feet, see him, begin firing. No more doubt—they intend to kill him. Petrified with fear, he must return fire. He wounds Flannery. Witt takes cover. A temporary standoff.

But now Swanny and Clay are paddling toward the island. He'd never told them where he was going, so they must be enemies. Painful anguish wracks his body. He must kill his friends. He waits for a clear shot. Steady. Breathe. Aim low. But Witt shoots first! Why? Confusion, then clarity. If his friends can escape Witt's bullets, it's three against two. Swanny paddles like a maniac high on speed. Clay provides covering fire. Shot after shot echoes across the lake. They reach the safety of Matt's side of the island.

Matt and Swanny capture the wounded Flannery. Then everything goes wrong. Swanny is crazed, thinks Witt raped his wife, wants bloody vengeance. He tears off down the trail toward Witt. Rapid-fire gunshots seconds before Matt can catch up to his best friend. Witt stands above Swanny, ready to deal the death blow. Matt yells. Clay, who has also taken a bullet, limps into the scene, fires at Witt. Witt dives for cover, takes aim at Matt, shoots, and misses. Matt shoots and hits. Shoots again. Four more blasts. He repeatedly pulls the trigger even after the magazine is empty. Witt bleeds from numerous bullet holes. His face is a bloody pulp.

Matt floats out of his body. Beholds the cold-blooded killer he has become: the man who took visceral pleasure in ending Witt's life. In his ethereal state, can he somehow offset the killer in him by breathing life back into Swanny? But the blood never stops flowing from Swanny's wounds. Searing pain courses through every nerve in Matt's body. He's tasted victory, yet won nothing other than staying alive for another day. He paddles Clay and Flannery back to civilization, to a hospital, alive. Hours later, both are dead. Smythe is responsible, but how? He's hundreds of miles away, yet he knows what happened. In Matt's nightmare, Smythe's image, not Witt's, is in his gunsight. He fires hundreds of shots, but Smythe won't die. He floats up to the top of a tall dead pine tree and perches like a giant vulture pleased with the carnage. Matt's plan to prove his innocence and Smythe's guilt fails in the worst conceivable way: dead friends, no witnesses, no proof.

Chapter 20

"We need to talk," Hawk said when Matt entered the kitchen for breakfast. His voice—normally as soothing as open-fingered cello notes—was in drill-sergeant mode. Matt had heard that tone once before when Hawk cornered some kids in his garden who'd attempted to vandalize his freshly planted annuals. He'd chewed them out as if they'd been first-day Army recruits who couldn't figure out how to stand at attention.

Apprehension tightened Matt's body. He swallowed hard. "Talk about what?"

"What went down with the guy in the car last night?"

Matt flinched, almost spilling coffee on his hand as he poured a cup. "You saw that?"

"I sleep with open windows most of the year, and I was reading in bed. Got up to pee, noticed the car pull up, watched to see who it was. Imagine my surprise. So, what's going on?"

Matt silently cursed. Unsure if Hawk had heard anything, he stalled. "It's personal."

Hawk set down his coffee cup, folded his arms, and leaned back in his chair. His pupils were two black bullets aimed at Matt's eyes. "Not when you're my guest and my client."

Deep down, he knew Hawk had a right to know, especially if events went south and Queenie decided Matt wasn't even worth cannon fodder but wanted to shut him up permanently. He slumped in his chair, sipped his coffee, then looked at his host, still motionless and hard-eyed.

"I need to get out of this rut. I'm at my breaking point. My best way out is to start over as a new person, in a new town, with a new identity and an honest job. If I can't be the real me and make my living playing music, I want the next best thing. Being on the run for a year has worn me out. One of these days, the nightmares will get so bad that the only way I can stop them is to step in front of a speeding bus or do the suicide-by-cop thing."

His nervous, anxious energy strained for release. He wanted to yell, unload a primal scream, but Hawk's impassivity challenged him to control his own emotions. He drew a breath, focused, and leaned closer.

"You ever get so down and depressed that you'll do anything to get a sliver of peace?" Matt asked. "I want to live, but I also want to get some of the weight off my shoulders, relax for more than five minutes, *enjoy* being alive. You and Hypo figured out how to survive after your traumas. My story was nowhere near as bad, but we all took parallel paths. I'm where you were at your lowest point, and I don't know any other way to handle it."

They suspended the conversation when Hypo entered the kitchen, fresh from a shower. He was using crutches so his stump could fully dry and get some air. Matt had learned that little tidbit of personal hygiene early in their acquaintance. Chafing, blisters, or open sores could develop if a prosthesis was left on for too long. Even an amputated limb needed regular fresh air. Hypo wore gray sweatpants and an unbuttoned red shirt. A few lighter-colored scars marked his otherwise taut, blemish-free torso. He'd bragged to Matt that he did one hundred pushups, sit-ups, and squats every morning. His current mission was to persuade Hawk to hang a chin-up bar from the living room ceiling.

"Wazzup, my brothas?" Hypo said in his street voice as he poured himself a cup of coffee and joined them at the table.

Hawk seemed annoyed at the interruption but maintained his drill sergeant persona. "Matt's about to explain why he was talking to a man who fired an empty pistol at him last night."

"Say what?" Hypo said, gaping at Matt. "You strayin' off the path of goodness and light?"

Matt's lowered head was all the answer his friends needed to confirm their suspicions.

"There's a better way to fix your life than getting involved with people who point guns at you, loaded or not," Hawk said. "Why don't you start by telling us what went down last night."

Hypo nodded his assent. "Yeah, spill it."

Cornered and outnumbered, Matt forced himself to remain seated. "I was talking to this guy about a job that pays better than a street musician."

"A job?" Hawk asked.

"My guitar's broken. I need a gig that pays a steady wage so I can get back on my feet. I can't mooch off you forever. This cat's a bit crazy. Thinks he's some sort of tough guy. He pulled the gun on me as a joke. Wanted to see how I'd react. That was too much. If he offers, I'll tell him to take his job and shove it." He pretended to make eye contact with each man as he spoke, but the connection was fleeting. Lying made him uncomfortable, and this was a big lie. But lying was the only way he could prevent his friends from talking him out of doing a job for Queenie—*if* she made an offer.

"You can stay here as long as you want," Hawk said. "At least until you gain some control of your PTSD symptoms."

"Yeah," Hypo said. "Get your head on straight first, then go from there. Any job you get might not last if you have a meltdown at work like you did the other night after the game."

"I appreciate your concern," Matt said. "I'll keep looking. Maybe I can wash dishes or mop floors somewhere in the neighborhood. But it's tough to find a cash-only job under the table that's legal and not dangerous."

Hypo said, "I'll spread the word. My street folks are good about finding borderline honest jobs. But don't give up on the music either. We can look for a guitar at a pawnshop I know."

"Thanks. I don't see any other options unless a long-lost aunt or uncle dies tomorrow and leaves me a big inheritance. But I'm pretty sure any relatives who might've been considering that changed their minds in a flash when they first saw my name splashed across the papers as an accused cop killer."

Chapter 21

B en's preliminary homework included researching Lanier's hometown of Straight River. He initially assumed the stereotypes of a small farming community were true—safe, low crime, closely knit, wary of strangers. Then he read about the spate of seven suspicious or violent deaths within a month, starting with Lanier's father and a neighbor. Two of the dead men connected with Lanier's claim about Smythe's conspiracy were boyhood friends. In addition, a local realtor, a police officer, and the police chief had also died. Excluding Lanier's father's death, all killings occurred after Lanier had come home to settle his father's estate. No way in hell that was a coincidence, which made it easy to believe Lanier was a mass murderer.

That was the picture Smythe—posing as Mr. Jones—had painted when he hired Ben: Get rid of a menace to society but do it secretly. The reason had seemed so plausible, and the contract offer so tempting, that Ben hadn't bothered to look for another side of the story. Today was the day he'd start looking.

His first stop was the farm of Betty Myrick, the old, widowed neighbor. She graciously invited him into her small but immaculate farmhouse after he'd shown her his private investigator's license and asked if he could talk to her about Lanier. It took two cups of tea, a half-dozen delicious oatmeal-raisin cookies, and ninety minutes to hear Lanier's life story as Betty Myrick knew it. The salient theme? He was one of the finest young men she'd ever known. No doubt she had a long personal-history bias. But when Betty told him Lanier had performed a near-miracle by proving her husband's death was because of a heart attack and not suicide, Ben took it as a sign of Lanier's true character. Because of the suicide rider in an insurance policy on her husband, Betty would've been unable to get the insurance money and keep her farm. A huge point in Lanier's favor.

"How'd he manage to get the autopsy changed?" Ben asked. "And why was it incorrect in the first place?"

"He never told me how," Betty said. "Insisted it was safer that I didn't know. As far as the *why* goes, it's because Helmer would've never committed suicide. He wasn't the most moral man in the world. Goodness knows he drank, smoked, swore around the other men. You know how it is; boys will be boys."

Ben stifled a smile. "Of course. I'm guilty of those sins too."

She nodded as if not surprised. "Helmer had the fear of God in him from childhood. Suicide was at the top of his sin list. Yes, he was old. Yes, his health was poor. Yes, farming is stressful. We struggled most years to pay our bills. But Helmer wasn't a quitter. Even if he had a horrible terminal disease that would cause us to suffer for months or years, he would never take his own life. Many times he'd say, 'Betty, if'n I ever get da notion to end it all myself, git yerself a bag o' rocks, whup me upside my head with 'em, and knock some gol' durn sense into me.'"

Her impression of a gruff, old, first-generation Norwegian immigrant farmer was so believable that Ben wondered if Betty hadn't channeled her late husband's spirit. He nodded. "Sounds like the words of a man with strong beliefs."

Betty glanced at the church directory photo of Helmer that sat atop the china hutch. "The last time Matt saw me, he said Helmer's cause of death was corrected to a heart attack, which was logical. He'd had a bad heart for years. I called both the new police chief and the coroner and asked why it had been changed. They both said it was a clerical error. I decided to let well enough alone. Helmer is dead. I still own the farm."

"Mrs. Myrick, who was the coroner?"

"A nice doctor named Anne Vincent."

"Is she still the coroner?" Ben asked as he jotted down the name in his notebook.

"She retired last year. Not sure if she's still in town. The hospital might know."

As the conversation proceeded, Betty was also adamant that Lanier had no reason to blow up his father's farmhouse and kill a police officer. She'd talked to Matt in the hospital the day after the blast and again a few weeks later. During both meetings, neither his words nor his body language suggested he was guilty of murder. Even though she was well into her eighties, her mind seemed sharp, and the details she shared were quite specific. If Lanier ever went to trial for his alleged crimes, the widow Myrick would make an ideal character witness for the defense.

After thanking Betty for her time and insights, Ben returned to his car. Could Lanier have conspired with Betty to scam the insurance company and split the money? If so, why? So Betty could save face about how her husband died? And who actually declared that Lanier had *proved* the correct cause of death? Right now, it was only Betty's belief.

He called Directory Assistance, got Dr. Vincent's phone number, and dialed. No answer. He didn't leave a message.

His next stop, on the other side of the Lanier farm, was to interview Amy Swanson. Her late husband, Dave, had been Lanier's best friend growing up and another casualty from last spring's events. Amy received Ben more coolly than Betty Myrick had. Still, she let him in when he said he wanted to verify all the positive statements Betty had made about Lanier.

Petite, farm-wife attractive, with short brown hair, Amy looked to be in her mid-thirties. Alert, wary eyes contrasted with pleasant features, a soft voice, and a shy smile. Her skin showed some weathering from the outdoors. She had that vague look of sadness Ben often noticed with people who'd prematurely lost a loved one, especially a spouse.

She offered him water instead of tea, no food, and confined the interview to the living room. In contrast, Betty had almost dragged him into the kitchen and would've offered lunch if he'd shown up two hours later.

"I'm sure this still hurts, Mrs. Swanson," Ben said as they settled into opposing positions on the sofa and love seat. "But I'd appreciate some background on the relationship between Matt and your husband. I understand it dates back to their childhoods?" The uplifted tone of his last word was intended to encourage her to elaborate.

Amy fidgeted with her fingertips before speaking. "And you want to know this again for what reason? You weren't one-hundred-percent clear about why you're here."

He spread his hands, palms up, and shrugged. "Private investigators investigate. You're not obligated to answer my questions. I just want to know what sort of person Matt Lanier is."

"Why?"

She was going to be a tough interview. Ben didn't explain himself any more than necessary because his visit might be a front-page story in the local newspaper the next day. He didn't want the publicity on the off chance Smythe regularly read small-town newspapers. "I'm sorry. I'm not at liberty to give you details."

"Let me see your credentials again, please."

Ben pulled out his license and handed it to her. She studied it as if she were memorizing every detail, then sat back and crossed her legs and arms. A classic defensive shell. Why? Some personal trauma related to Lanier and her husband? Was she keeping a secret?

When she didn't ask him to leave, he said, "I've read the police reports about what happened in the Boundary Waters. Matt's the sole surviving witness. He's the only one who knows the truth. I simply want your general impression of him. It might help me figure out the truth too. I understand you first met a few days before his farmhouse blew up."

She stared out the window and sighed. "Dave said Matt was the smartest guy he'd ever known. After meeting him, I had no reason to disagree. He was quite charming too. Dave mentioned Matt a lot before I met him. Maybe I was biased. But I'm a schoolteacher, and I've learned to size up my new students quickly. I can usually tell who the obedient students will be, the teacher's pets, the troublemakers, the class clowns. You know how it is?"

Ben nodded.

"Matt would've been one of the model students. He has a stubborn streak, for sure. But he must be extremely disciplined to have achieved what he did in music. My gosh, playing for the Minnesota Orchestra. Recording with jazz groups. Those aren't hallmarks of a serial killer or any sort of violent person."

"How did your husband get involved with Matt last year?"

Amy bowed her head and fidgeted with her fingers again. "Dave was a wonderful husband, but he wasn't perfect. Too concerned about money and maintaining a prosperous image. Not that we made big bucks, but he always wanted to give the impression he had a magic touch with the farm. He also trusted people too much. Rarely questioned their motives. He said he was going to help Matt in the Boundary Waters because he'd accepted money from an anonymous source who was trying to kill Matt. Someone named Leland Smythe."

"Really?" He pulled out his notebook and began to write.

She nodded. "Dave originally thought Wayne Hibbert was sending him the money. He was a sleazeball realtor who abruptly switched to doing farm deals a few years ago. Personally, I doubt Hibbert had enough money or brains to hire a spy. Dave said Matt told him Hibbert was working for some secret corporation owned by that Smythe guy."

"A spy?"

"Smythe wanted to know what the other farmers were doing. Who's buying, selling, in financial trouble, sick, dying, that sort of thing. He was sending Dave hundreds of dollars for the information. But as soon as Matt told Dave that Smythe was trying to kill him, Dave immediately tried to help Matt. Then Dave told me Smythe had blackmailed him into doing things like pressuring the Myricks and Matt's father to sell and spreading rumors to the other farmers. I intended to ask for more details when Dave came home, but ..."

Ben waited for her to continue. She stared at the wall, a distant look in her eyes. After silently finishing her sentence: ... *he never made it home,* he cleared his throat. "Did you see Matt often? Talk on the phone? Any type of contact?"

Amy stiffened as if he was suggesting she'd had a more intimate relationship with Lanier. Her wary eyes looked him up and down. "I passed the phone off to Dave once or twice when Matt was here settling his father's estate. He left town a few weeks after we met."

"So, no other conversations?" He was about to write this interview off as a dead end.

"Well, there was one last time. After Dave died, Matt came here to tell me in person. He looked like hell. Had a glazed look in his eyes, like he was in shock, like he'd been overcome by an evil spirit. That scared me something fierce. He told me not to tell anyone about Smythe or Witt—the goon who beat us up to find out where Matt was hiding—especially the police, because it would put me in danger. I've never told anyone."

Ben leaned forward, curious. "Why'd you tell me?"

She looked at him, her eyes flicking side to side as if she wasn't sure herself. "A year has passed. My life's meaningless without my husband. This Smythe guy, if that's his real name, if he's even a real person—maybe Dave made it up to appease me—can't do any more to ruin my life besides kill me. And if he does, Dave and I will be together in heaven."

According to Ben's research, Witt was one of the two men who died on Big Island in Crystal Lake in the Boundary Waters last April. Dave Swanson had been the other one. Both had died from gunshot wounds inflicted by different weapons. He asked, "What can you tell me about Witt?"

Amy re-crossed her arms and legs. Her expression went far away again. "A big, ugly, scary man if I ever saw one." She shuddered and hugged herself tighter. "He tied us up in our barn, beat up Dave to get him to divulge where Matt was hiding after he left town. But Dave didn't know." She sniffed derisively. "So, Witt started in on me."

Ben remembered the newspaper article about the Swansons getting attacked by an unidentified assailant in their barn. He was pretty sure he knew what had happened. Sometimes he hated prying into the lives of people who'd been emotionally scarred or suffered such trauma. Hearing her personal recollection brought brutal reality into focus.

She exhaled long and slow. "Witt didn't rape me, but he might as well have. Dave bought Witt's act and went crazy with rage. He blurted out a location off the top of his head, hoping Witt would believe him and stop attacking me." She focused on Ben, who glanced up through lowered brows. Her voice softened. "Dave guessed correctly. Now I'm a widow."

Chapter 22

When Matt and Hypo returned from the pawnshop without a guitar, Hawk looked up from the book he was reading in his living room and said, "Couldn't find a replacement?"

Matt frowned. "Nothing in my price range that I'd expect music fans to listen to for more than thirty seconds."

"We can try another place tomorrow if you want," Hypo said. "A place in the suburbs if we can borrow Hawk's wheels."

"Sure," Hawk said. He turned to Matt. "I think you got a fan letter."

"A what?" Matt said.

"The envelope was addressed to *Jazzman*, so I assumed a lovestruck female fan of yours sent it." Normally, that line would be teasing. But Hawk's voice and expression were full-on somber. "It's on your bed."

Matt stared at Hawk, wondering about the conflict between the man's words and the emotion he projected.

"Curiously," Hawk continued, "the letter had no stamp or return address. Someone snuck in and dropped it off at my apartment door while I was pruning the shrubs outside. A bit cloak-and-dagger if you ask me."

Matt glanced at Hypo. "I'm pretty sure I don't have any groupies—yet."

"None that I ever noticed," Hypo said. "Of course, you aren't much competition for this package." He smiled and thrust both thumbs at his chest.

With his curiosity piqued, Matt hurried to his room. A letter-sized envelope sat on his pillow. Sure enough, it was addressed to *Jazzman*. Then his throat tightened. Beside Hawk and Hypo, the only other people with whom he'd shared that moniker and who mattered were Pastor Jeanne from the soup kitchen ... and Queenie Delacroix.

He opened the envelope, read the message, and sagged onto his bed. Resting his elbows on his knees, he held the note in both hands and reread the words several times. As he did, he heard the muffled, animated voices of Hawk and Hypo talking in the living room. When the discussion became heated, Hypo said what sounded like, "But he's our friend, man! A fellow warrior."

Matt fluttered the paper back and forth, listening to the crinkly noise it made. He rubbed his thumb and forefinger together on each side of the page, felt its grainy but smooth texture. Turning it over, he examined the back, then picked up the envelope and reread his nickname. After one last read, he tore the letter into small pieces and flushed them down the toilet. He returned to his room, flopped onto the bed, and stared at the ceiling. Regardless of his decision about the letter, tonight would become a turning point for whatever remained of his life.

Chapter 23

Smythe sat in his oversized executive chair in his large office inside his spacious house built on a sizeable piece of land in the big-money suburb of Orono. Although the location wasn't convenient to either downtown Minneapolis or St. Paul, he had a reasonable commute to Smythe Properties in Plymouth. His two-story house had exponentially more space than a bachelor needed: five bedrooms and bathrooms; gourmet kitchen; sixteen-seat dining room; two decks; private balcony off his master suite; swimming pool, sauna, jacuzzi; fitness center in the basement. The estate provided a home-field advantage when he threw parties to curry favor with politicians and the movers and shakers of the real estate world.

He sipped an after-dinner cognac as he studied the latest transactions his Millennium Four operatives had recently closed. Acquisitions were accelerating thanks to his new technique. Instead of buying a parcel of farmland adjacent to Interstate 35, or buying the entire farm in some cases, Smythe's latest tactic was purchasing options on the desired land. Since an option was merely a right to purchase property before a specific date, ownership didn't change hands until a deal was made. Smythe could control much more land without the necessity of recording ownership with the county. That reduced the paper trail, which was the only serious risk his operation faced. Since the local realtors dealt with one of the many faceless shell corporations Smythe's legal team set up, they'd never know Smythe was the ultimate owner.

With a final check of his spreadsheet, Smythe took a sip of cognac and called Ivan Volkov. "I got your text," he said. "May I presume your assignment was successful?"

"News hit the local paper today," Volkov said. "No one doubts the silo accident story. Helped a lot that a thunderstorm went through shortly after I was there. Everyone *knows* the old guy slipped on the wet steel and took a header."

"You took care to avoid inflicting any injuries?" If he'd learned one thing from dealing with the musician, it was to stay vigilant and careful. Accidents had to be unequivocal in the eyes of the local authorities.

"Of course, as you demanded. He did a perfect swan dive into the center of his soybean pile." Volkov chuckled at his wittiness.

"The man's dead, Mr. Volkov." Smythe injected anger into his voice. "There's nothing funny about it. This is a business operation. Please maintain your composure."

"Right," Volkov said, sounding contrite. "Sorry."

"The Albert Lea area is next." Smythe returned to his all-business tone. "Something different, though. There's at least one established gang in the area, so let's cause some trouble with the farms along I-35 and blame a gang. Can you manage it?"

"Of course," Volkov said. "I'm thinking some drive-by shootings of outbuildings, maybe a few farmhouse windows, then leave some gang graffiti as a calling card. One post on social media, and everyone in town will be on edge. That'll lay the groundwork for some fast transactions by nervous farmers who want out at any price."

Smythe nodded, smiled, and stared out his window at the fading orange glow of the sunset. "Make it happen."

Chapter 24

Returning to Minneapolis on I-35, Ben whizzed past the rolling brown hills, looking for hints of green sprouts from early planting in the fields but seeing none. Pockets of snow still dotted the north sides of barns and silos. Snow in April was common most years in Minnesota. The greening up of farm country was still weeks away. He called Dr. Vincent twice during the drive and got the same results—no answer. Again, he left no message.

He turned off I-35W at East Hennepin Avenue and headed to his motel on Central Avenue Northeast. His plan was to grab a bite to eat, do some online research, and then stake out Lanier's place. But first, he called Vincent again. As before, he got her voice mail and hung up.

After walking to the corner coffee shop for a sandwich, he returned to his room and fired up his laptop. He started by searching the news archives of the *Straight River Press*. A long shot, but he might get lucky and find some articles about the young Matt Lanier. Perhaps he'd even find a local-boy-hits-the-big-time human-interest story from when Lanier first gained fame as a musician.

While he waited for a web page to load, Ben called Dr. Vincent one last time. When the voice mail recorder clicked on, he considered leaving a message but hung up instead. He always preferred the element of surprise when interviewing someone during a case, so they wouldn't have time to prepare lies or fake alibis.

Staring at his computer, he got a nagging feeling that there was a missing piece to his investigation puzzle. Had he visited Straight River too late in the game? He was about to step out of his motel room and head for his stakeout of Lanier when his phone rang. He answered with a terse, "Hello?"

"Who the *hell* are you, and why do you keep calling me?" The female voice was simultaneously wary and irate. She spoke so loudly that Ben held the phone away from his ear.

"Who is this?" Ben said, then immediately realized who had called. He returned to his room and closed the door. "Dr. Vincent, I can explain."

"Keep it up, and I'll report your number to the authorities."

"I'm sorry my calls seemed like harassment. But it's an urgent matter."

After some hesitation, Vincent said, "First, your name?"

"I can't tell you, but I'm a private investigator."

"Strike three! Goodbye."

"No, no, no, please! I'm calling about Matthew Lanier."

Several seconds went by. *Come on, come on, don't hang up.*

"Matt Lanier?" She sounded surprised, and the edge dropped from her voice.

"Do you know him?"

"Barely. I performed the autopsy on his father, Raymond Lanier. We met briefly at the hospital. I explained that his father died of asphyxiation after falling into the corn in his silo. He also asked about the death of his neighbor, Helmer Myrick."

"I see. I have some questions about those autopsies and what happened after those two deaths." Ben sat at the desk, opened his notebook, and took out a pen.

Vincent said, "You mean the farmhouse explosion and the incidents Up North, right?"

"Yes."

"What do you want to know?"

"Why did you change Myrick's cause of death from suicide to a heart attack?"

"Myocardial infarction," she corrected. "I changed it because that was the actual cause of death."

"Was there some sort of clerical error?"

The ensuing icy silence sent a shiver down Ben's spine.

Vincent sighed. "No."

"What then?"

Another long pause. "I was blackmailed."

Ben stiffened. This day was providing one surprise after another. "Blackmailed by who?"

After a third, longer pause, Vincent said, "I guess it doesn't matter because the blackmailer's dead. And I'm retired now, so my career is no longer in jeopardy. Worst of all, my husband passed away a few months ago. He's the only other person I didn't want to hurt with my secret."

"I'm sorry for your loss," he interjected.

"Thank you," Vincent said unemotionally. "We planned to have so much fun in retirement. Travel, new adventures, see more of the grandchildren. But he died a few months after *he* retired. So much for old history and me caring about my reputation."

"You were about to name the blackmailer?" he asked.

"Straight River's dear departed police chief, Michael Flannery."

"The same Flannery who tracked Lanier to the Boundary Waters and was later killed in the Ely hospital by an unknown assailant?"

"Yep, *that* bastard." Her words dripped with bitterness.

"Tell me, Dr. Vincent, do you believe Chief Flannery was a crooked cop?"

"Not at first. He came in highly regarded as a law-and-order type who ran a tight ship, by the book, all those clichés that apply to strait-laced cops. Some folks in town were annoyed that he cracked down on speeders far more than his predecessor. Lots of complaints about him trying to build up the police coffers with traffic violation fines. He personally gave me a ticket when I was going to the hospital to deliver a baby. Boy, was I pissed. Thought I'd be too late. But I arrived in time, and there were no complications. So no, I never thought he was crooked until the blackmail incidents."

"I see. How did he get the blackmail information?"

"Had to have been from someone else," Vincent said. "My transgression happened decades ago. I believe someone with major political and legal connections that go way back told him what I'd done. I'd never met Flannery or even heard of him before he came to Straight River three years ago. Then a few months after he gets appointed Chief, he drops the bomb on me and says, 'From now on, if I need a favor, do it, keep quiet, and don't ask questions.'"

"That's quite an assertion."

"Believe it or don't. I'd swear to it in court. There's no way he could've dug up the dirt he threw at me to get me to falsify those autopsies."

"There were *multiple* bogus autopsies?"

"Only two. The second was Raymond Lanier's."

"How was that falsified?"

"Flannery told me to omit any references to Lanier's skull. It was fractured above his left temple. The fracture couldn't have been due to Lanier slipping and bumping his head. Someone very strong slammed him into the silo hatch."

"Holy sh—" Ben caught himself, not wanting to appear crude and insensitive.

"What I never figured out is why Flannery sent me a text directing me to correct Myrick's autopsy mere hours before he died after the Boundary Waters shootout."

"You're kidding," he said, genuinely surprised. That information wasn't in any police reports or other sources he had studied.

"I was surprised too," Vincent said. "He didn't seem like the type of person who'd admit his mistakes or atone for his sins."

"Three more questions."

"Ask away."

"What do you know about the deaths involving Lanier in the Boundary Waters and Duluth?"

"Only what I read in the papers. Hard to believe Lanier killed all those people."

"Ever heard of someone named Leland Smythe?"

"No. Why?"

"How about an organization called Millennium Four?"

"No. Why?" She'd answered all three questions with no hesitation or change in her tone. Anne Vincent wasn't lying.

"Following a lead," Ben said. "It's not crucial." Actually, if she was being truthful, those were the *most* crucial questions he'd asked. He thanked her for her time and willingness to talk and ended the call.

Confused and depressed now, he wished he could unhear their conversation. It cast doubt on his entire working thesis of Lanier as a serial killer. Killing to avenge his father's death—an emotional act—didn't jibe with a serial killer's cold, emotionless calculation. And if Flannery had a personal stake in falsifying *both* causes of death, what was *his* angle?

Ben wasn't a big drinker by nature. But tonight, he headed for an old neighborhood haunt from his police days to drink Grain Belt Nordeast until he was drunk enough to make sense of the situation. *Damn you, Lanier.*

Chapter 25

Queenie and Victor had discussed every detail of her plan and prepared for several scenarios. However, they were still taking a big chance on the wild card—the enigmatic, borderline-crazy Jazzman. Although he was one seriously fucked-up dude, he hadn't come close to setting off Queenie's narc radar. If Jazzman was telling the truth about having killed in the past and being unafraid to risk his life for a few bucks, he seemed capable of doing the job. She finally agreed to use him after Victor reiterated his belief in the genuineness of Jazzman's reaction to his point-blank shooting test—a reaction impossible to fake. The 800-pound risk in the room was that Jazzman was indeed a double-crossing narc setting them up for a sting complete with a SWAT team lying in wait. If that scene went down, he would've pulled off a performance ranking with De Niro's best.

And if he failed? Queenie smiled. There'd be zero fallout. It was as close to a perfect plan as she'd ever devised. *That's* why she'd ruled her queendom for all these years. She saw possibilities and opportunities others couldn't see with a flashlight and a magnifying glass.

Queenie sat at her usual corner table in the Diamond Lounge with her back to the wall. Victor and Cara sat to her right. Extra men were stationed near the door and outside as a show of power to the man who had just entered, a rival drug lord named Tyrone Taylor.

Of average height and weight, and wearing a gray suit over an open-collared purple silk shirt, Taylor—also known as Double Tap or Double T—compensated for his lack of size with multiple gold chains and bejeweled rings. Stereotypical, yes, but somehow the bling looked good on him.

Accompanying him was a nervous-looking young woman—Keisha or Kenisha—with cocoa skin, a generous booty, and hair that was far too blonde for someone with her jet-black roots. One of Taylor's lieutenants—Hondo or Honcho—also sat at the table. The names wouldn't matter after tonight. Taylor had brought two other men. One sat at the bar, facing them. The other guarded the door.

Queenie and Taylor were meeting on the pretense of a progress report on the consolidation of their respective drug empires. Queenie controlled most of the territory west of the Mississippi River and south of Minneapolis within a radius of about 150 miles. Taylor controlled St. Paul and the metropolitan area east of the Mississippi. The balance of power favored Queenie about three to one. She courted Taylor as if the deal would be fifty-fifty, even though his revenue would add much less than that to her bottom line.

What Queenie coveted most was Taylor's pipeline to Chicago. He barely tapped his potential with that vast supply, while Queenie sometimes struggled to keep up with demand. If she could secure Chicago's drug pipeline for herself, growth prospects would be excellent. So good that she envisioned controlling the entire Upper Midwest and Plains states west of the Mississippi within three years.

The key to that expanded pipeline was fentanyl. The powerful, dangerous opioid was the "next big thing" in the illegal drug trade. Queenie was missing out because her suppliers in Kansas City, St. Louis, and Denver couldn't supply her consistently with the good stuff. Fentanyl was so potent that a few too many *micrograms* could be lethal. The drug needed to be pure to be anything close to safe. Queenie wanted to know exactly what she was selling to her customers so they wouldn't OD. If a junkie died after voluntarily taking another hit, that was his business. But word spread fast if a dealer was supplying an inconsistent product. And in the drug trade, reputation was more important than price. Even one death from an accidental overdose attributed to lax quality control would send Queenie's customers scrambling for a more reliable product—like the stuff Taylor was getting from Chicago.

Unfortunately for Taylor, Queenie ran a lean business model. There was no room for two bosses. She'd baited her trap with hints of an equal partnership, so the dollar signs lighting up Double Tap's eyes blinded him to the fact that Queenie was the only royalty in her court. Waiting to move him out of the company *after* the merger was risky because she sensed that he'd eventually try a coup of his own. Getting rid of him through *normal* channels was an open invitation to the cops to investigate her yet again. Option three: He'd get his pink slip tonight.

The band was generating a hip-hop groove that had about half the patrons gyrating on the dance floor, which lessened the chance of someone eavesdropping on Queenie's chat with Taylor. Once her guests had been seated, pleasantries exchanged, and drink orders delivered, Queenie started the negotiations. "So, Tyrone, have you checked with your people in Chicago?"

Taylor took a sip of his Chivas and soda, set his glass down, leaned back, and draped his arm around Keisha's shoulder. "Damn straight, Q. It's all set. They love the idea of more business in the Twin Cities. Police been cracking down out East, so business is a little slow for my suppliers. If we give 'em enough business here, they might tell the entire East Coast to go fuck itself."

He laughed heartily, as if he were a significant player discussing some Podunk small-timers who fancied themselves as hotshots.

Queenie hid her smirk with a sip of white wine. She signaled the server to bring another round. She wanted to get at least three drinks into Taylor, so his inhibitions would be low and his reflexes slow. With luck, she'd get his bodyguard buzzed too. Taylor ran that sort of organization—too much partying, not enough emphasis on running the business. Another reason he wasn't a good fit for Queenie's organization.

She had instructed the bartender to cut her wine with two-thirds water and leave the gin out of Victor's gin and tonics. Taylor's drinks would be spiked with Everclear. This colorless, tasteless, high-proof alcohol would turn three drinks into the equivalent of six. At the end of the night, Queenie would've drunk the equivalent of one glass of wine, Victor would be stone-cold sober, and Taylor would be as vulnerable and clueless as a freshman frat boy at his first kegger.

Victor's job was to schmooze the bodyguard and try to get him to match each of Victor's non-alcoholic drinks with one containing alcohol. Should the plan not go according to script at the crucial moment, Queenie's team would maintain the mental advantage and could react faster. Unfortunately, Victor worried so much about Jazzman's role that Queenie knew he craved at least one shot of booze to take the edge off. Going out in the alley for a joint was out of the question tonight too. If the shit hit the fan, he'd need to be ready for war.

When Victor's cell phone rang, he pulled it out of his pocket and said, "Yeah?" He listened, then said, "Right. Thanks." After ending the call, he gave Queenie a thumbs-up below the tabletop so she alone would see it.

She gave him a slight nod and intensified the smile she'd been aiming at Double Tap Taylor. Step one had been successful.

Chapter 26

The music volume from four different clubs waxed and waned as Matt headed to the Diamond Lounge. The cacophony included hard rock, country, hip-hop, and—surprisingly—Dixieland jazz. Adding to the din were drunken revelry, honking horns, and revving vehicles that seemed to lack mufflers. The enticing aromas of garlic, barbecued meat, freshly baked bread, and spices like curry and chiles wafted sporadically through the air, polluted by hints of cigarette and marijuana smoke. The Warehouse District certainly lived up to its well-earned reputation as the focal point of Minneapolis nightlife. But tonight, Matt would not join the revelry or listen to music. The short, cryptic note on his bed that afternoon had instructed him otherwise:

Outside the Diamond 10:30 p.m. pass V's car on sidewalk be ready for anything. $5K.

Victor's Cadillac was parked in its usual space across the street from the Diamond. Matt checked his watch to ensure he was on time, then crossed the street. As he reached the rear fender of Victor's car, the front passenger door opened. An arm reached out, placed a handled paper bag on the sidewalk next to the car, and closed the door. Matt kept walking, picked up the bag, and continued at his same casual pace. To the casual observer, he was just some shabby-looking guy carrying a paper bag he may or may not have possessed ten seconds earlier.

Resisting the urge to look around to see if he was being followed, Matt stopped in an empty doorway and peered into the bag. On top sat another note. He unfolded it and read:

bus station men's room third stall from far wall.

Under the note was a gray bundle. Matt felt it—material. Clothing. He headed for the bus terminal, presumably to change into the new clothing.

Arriving at the bus station men's room after the half-mile walk, he entered the third stall in the men's room, locked the door, and removed his shoes, pants, and shirt. The place smelled marginally better than the bathroom at his last homeless shelter thanks to proper air circulation in the large room. Matt hesitated, listening for suspicious sounds, then put on the jogging suit. It fit him well. The bag also held a pair of athletic shoes—cross-trainers. Another note was stuffed inside one shoe. He opened it and read:

TP dispenser

Puzzled, he examined the toilet paper dispenser—a typical public-toilet device that held two rolls side by side, with one roll hanging in reserve behind a sliding plastic cover. He unrolled several feet of paper from the exposed roll but saw nothing. So he groped above the roll and under the dispenser cover. Sure enough, he found a small white envelope. The note inside said:

SW end 3rd Av bridge lamppost chain-link fence 11:30

After memorizing the text, Matt shredded the paper, flushed it, and put on the cross-trainers. The fit was tight, but he figured he would need them only for tonight. At the bottom of the bag lay a terrycloth headband. *Nice touch of authenticity, Queenie.* He didn't put it on because he doubted he'd perspire enough tonight to need it.

Matt placed his old clothes in the bag, extracted some coins from his jeans pocket, and put the bag in an empty station locker. He wasn't sure when or if he'd be able to retrieve his clothes, but they comprised almost half his current wardrobe, and he didn't want to throw them away. A check of his watch showed he had plenty of time to get to the Mississippi River. He recalled Victor's instructions in the notes, verifying that he'd done everything right and knew where to go. His musician's mind for memorization came in handy in non-musical situations too.

He slipped out of the bus station, shooting furtive glances from side to side. Queenie might still suspect he was a narc who'd set up an elaborate sting to nail her. In that case, she might have sent someone to follow him, watching to see if he placed a phone call or talked to anyone on the street. Tonight might also be a preliminary test to determine if he was bright enough to follow directions. He saw no one who seemed to be watching him, but how could he tell in the low light and shadows of the night?

Matt jogged down Tenth Street toward Nicollet Avenue, humming "Gonna Fly Now," the theme song from the movie *Rocky*. Foot traffic became lighter than the always-buzzing Hennepin Avenue and Warehouse District. After two blocks, his lungs burned with each breath. Although he'd maintained the muscle tone developed while living a strenuous life in the Boundary Waters, Matt's aerobic capacity had suffered since his arrival in Minneapolis. He walked a lot, but without running shoes or access to any aerobic training machines, his lungs were not those of a regular runner.

He slowed to a walk and glanced in all directions. No one appeared to be following him, although there were plenty of pedestrians on Nicollet this night. He passed several homeless people who sought some relative peace and quiet afforded by the darkness. Shady-looking men and women hung around the bus shelters and street corners. Hookers struggled to appear as if they were not trolling for customers.

After walking a block, he jogged again to establish his guise as a fitness buff out for a nighttime run. When the police on foot patrol barely noticed him as he passed, he concluded that a jogging suit made an excellent disguise for a fugitive. He just needed to keep jogging so they wouldn't get a good look at his face.

All the scenarios Matt considered as he headed for the river could quickly go south because of the unknown. If he was being asked to commit a crime, he'd need to rely on his improvisation skills to succeed. Improvising the blues on his bass was one thing. But acting quickly in a life-or-death situation would strain his abilities to their limits. He knew that kind of adrenaline rush all too well, having taken part in four different gunfights in the past year in which people died. Yet tonight's rush also generated eagerness and positive energy because this was a high-risk, high-reward job with a five-thousand-dollar payoff—*if* tonight was for real. He could almost smell the unique inky tang of a stack of crisp new bills. Once he got the money, he'd buy his new identity and start over somewhere far from

Minnesota and its accompanying mental and physical baggage. Then and only then would he have a chance to ease his conscience.

All afternoon and evening, he'd asked himself if he could kill another person for money. To rationalize his decision, he equated tonight with going to war. He'd gotten that reasoning from Hypo and Hawk. They'd talked about the killing they'd done for the U.S. military and CIA. A few evil people needed to die to ensure the survival of hundreds of thousands of innocent ones. The government condoned killing the enemy, and—assuming this job was what he anticipated—drug dealers were the enemy. One less drug dealer in the world was a good thing, right?

After trying but failing to do the right thing so many times, Matt was sick of being noble and virtuous. In the past year, the only rewards nobility had earned him were a mangled body, a tortured mind, and dead friends. *Fuck the greater good. Tonight's for me and nobody else.*

At Washington Avenue, he turned right and headed to Third Avenue. The night was cool even for April, but he was sweating from his two-block jogs alternating with one-block walks to catch his breath. The condominium he'd lived in for almost ten years was nearby. His lease had expired last year, and Matt wondered what had become of its contents. He hoped his attorney, John Maxwell, had taken the initiative and arranged to store those assets. If not, all Matt owned was likely stuck in some anonymous warehouse or had been sold at auction. Damn, he might have lost his extensive vinyl LP collection forever. Besides his instruments, they were his most valuable possession because he'd bought many duplicate copies of some of the greatest albums and never removed the plastic wrap. Mint condition. Some were quite rare or had historical significance. Another possible casualty of his war with Smythe.

With a few minutes left to reach his post, Matt started across the walkway on the south side of the gently curving bridge that spanned the Mississippi River. When he got to the center, he stopped and admired the view.

On the east side of the river was the modern bustle of the St. Anthony Main neighborhood. Downriver was Lock and Dam No. 1, paralleling St. Anthony Falls—the birthplace of Minneapolis. Next was the iconic Stone Arch Bridge. Farther downriver were I-35W and Dinkytown. Partially visible around a river bend were the lights of the massive University of Minnesota campuses—East and West Banks. To the west rose the downtown Minneapolis skyline. Although there were no contenders for the world's tallest skyscrapers, all had been built after 1972 when the city's first—and still tallest—legitimate skyscraper, the IDS Tower, was erected. What the newer towers lacked in height, they made up for with style and distinction. On this clear, starlit night, the illuminated cityscape was impressive. Yes, Minneapolis was a legitimate big city, and Matt was playing hardball with real-life, big-time drug dealers.

Checking his watch, he returned to the downtown side of the river and found the lamppost at Third Avenue and First Street. It stood next to the end of a short chain-link fence blocking a steep drop-off to West River Road Parkway, which ran below the bridge. He stood nonchalantly at first, trying to look as if he was resting from his jog, stretching a bit as he examined the lamppost. Sure enough, a white envelope was stuck to the concrete base on the side, hidden from street view. Faking another stretch, he reached down and grabbed the envelope, then opened it and read the instructions.

"Seriously?" he asked the trees behind the fence. *Is this a practical joke?* Stifling a laugh, he raised his head and glanced up at the night sky. He reread the note to make sure he'd read it correctly. Then he said again, with no emotion, "Seriously."

Reflexively, he spun and looked around for some sort of setup or ambush. Seeing nothing unusual and hearing nothing but traffic noise and the faint roar of St. Anthony Falls, he relaxed. A buzz of excitement charged through his body. His intuition told him this was real. If Queenie was being honest with him, the payoff was minutes away. He reread the lengthy instructions, folded the envelope, pulled off a shoe, and slipped the envelope inside his sock so it rested under the sole of his foot. Then he put the shoe back on, checked his watch, and stepped into the cover of an alcove created by the fence near the corner of the bridge. His earlier excitement was now mixed with fear and flashes of violent memories from last year.

Chapter 27

After two drinks, Double Tap Taylor looked and sounded looser and paid increased attention to Keisha. Hondo had one drink early, then switched to club soda. A minor problem, but Queenie's primary focus was to get Taylor soused.

Victor's phone rang again. He answered, listened, said, "Thanks," and rang off. Again, he flashed a thumbs-up to Queenie under the table.

"Something wrong, Victor?" asked Taylor with suspicion in his voice.

Victor waved nonchalantly. "Nah, man, I put a serious bet on a basketball game." He pointed to his phone. "My man givin' me updates."

Taylor arched his eyebrows. "Basketball this late?"

Victor nodded. "Out west. Can't say the teams. Dude out there got himself a system. He swore me to secrecy. If this pans out, Queenie might expand into some sports betting."

Queenie turned toward Taylor. "I'm always open to new profit channels, Tyrone. I'm sure an astute businessman such as yourself also thinks about diversifying, right?"

Taylor's eyes bounced back and forth on his hosts. "Gamblin', huh? Yeah, I guess that could work. Mafia boys had a profit machine runnin' numbers and shit like that back in the day. Why not us tappin' into a little NBA action?"

Queenie said, "Let me freshen your drink, Tyrone." She got the bartender's attention and pointed at Taylor. The bartender nodded and prepared another spiked Chivas and soda.

"Thanksss." Taylor appeared to struggle with focusing his eyes and his brain. "Ya sure I can't buy a round?"

Queenie shook her head. "Your money's no good here, Mister Taylor." The *Mister* was an added suck-up to her soon-to-be-former business partner.

Taylor beamed, put his arm around Keisha, and surreptitiously tried to cop a feel.

She smiled and gently but firmly moved his hand to her shoulder. "Later, baby. After you're done talking business."

Queenie sensed Victor's stare and turned enough to see his slight nod. All systems were *go* for the Double Tap Takedown. She'd worn a low-cut blouse which showed a tastefully erotic amount of cleavage, so when she leaned toward Taylor, his eyes widened with lust. With a suggestive tone, she said, "Why don't we take this party to the next level at my place? We can finalize our merger and celebrate with my best product."

All pairs of eyes except Victor's lit up in anticipation. He smiled conspiratorially at Queenie, who stood and assumed the regal bearing that had earned her the nickname. Victor paid the check, and the group ambled outside. Stopping next to Victor's car, Queenie breathed deeply and said, "Tyrone, let's drive to the Third Avenue bridge but then walk across. We can talk privately about some things."

Taylor swayed. His expression showed confused surprise. "Why you wanna walk?"

"Why not? It's a beautiful spring evening." She caressed his arm and lowered her voice. "And people in our positions need to stay healthy and get some exercise, right?"

She nodded. Victor and Cara nodded. They all smiled. Taylor got the hint and half-nodded, his head lolling up and down. "Shhhure, why not?"

With the look of a worried security expert—which he was by default—Hondo said, "You sure about this, boss?"

Queenie held up her hand. "Tyrone, I live right across the river. We'll take Hondo and Victor along as bodyguards, and we can put the cars on opposite sides of the bridge as lookouts for trouble. But I walk through St. Anthony Main regularly and never have security issues."

"Easy for you to say, lady," Taylor said. "You a rich white woman. I got two strikes against me already, seeing's how I'm a black brother."

"Then we'll bring Cara and Keisha along for the walk. Safety in numbers. A cozy group of friends out for a moonlight stroll. Best of all, you and I can admire a huge piece of our newly combined territories." Queenie ran her hand up and down his arm, maintaining eye contact.

"Hey, thasss right. Our *combined* turf."

She gave herself a mental pat on the back for subtly implying there could be more to the Queenie-Double T partnership than business. Much more.

Taylor opened the car door, gestured for Queenie to get in, and said, "In 'at case, let's us go for a lil ol' walk an' talk some big ol' business."

Chapter 28

When a dark-blue Cadillac slowed and pulled to the curb where First Street South intersects Third Avenue South, Matt ducked into the shadows of the alcove next to the bridge where he'd been waiting. Victor exited from the front passenger seat. Queenie and Cara emerged from the back seat.

Moments later, another large sedan pulled up behind the Caddy. A linebacker-sized man got out of the front passenger seat. Another man and a woman stepped from the back seat. That man was Matt's "assignment." The driver of the second car pulled away and drove across the Third Avenue Bridge. Victor's car and driver stayed at the corner with the motor running. The group of six began walking across the bridge toward St. Anthony Main.

Matt mentally rehearsed Victor's instructions one final time. The last line of the note now in his shoe was Victor's promise to pay him $5,000 if he succeeded. The note also said Victor would "take care of the body-guard," whatever that meant. Promises, promises. Only as strong as the integrity of the promisor. After all, he was trusting these criminals to honor their end of the deal.

Suddenly filled with self-loathing, Matt suppressed his guilt by reassuring himself his target was another lowlife who deserved to die. It would be no different from killing the four other lowlifes in the past year who had deserved their fates. Summoning his sight-reading abilities, he put his brain into the gear that optimized quick data intake, instant analysis, and decisive action. A split second of reaction time might be the difference between success and failure. For a surreal moment, he wondered what his obituary would say if he ended up dead tonight. Something like: *Once a world-class musician, Lanier's downfall was rapid as he spiraled out of control, became a serial killer, and ended up homeless on the streets of Minneapolis before authorities dredged up his bullet-riddled corpse from the Mississippi River.*

Matt breathed deep, trying to calm his shaking body. He hadn't been this nervous or afraid since the start of the gun battle on Big Island in the Boundary Waters. What focused his resolve was the chance to regain a semblance of his old life. True, he might fail, might even die. But the risk was worth it if he could escape the life he was stuck in now, battling the double whammy of Smythe's hit man and the police wanting to kill or capture him.

Then the Cadillac's headlights flashed off and on in his peripheral vision. *Showtime!* Stepping from the shadows, Matt jogged toward the walkers. They were the only pedestrians on the south side of the bridge. A few late-night bikers pedaled in both directions in the bike lanes. Car traffic was sparse. When Matt was about one hundred yards behind the group, they stopped and turned to admire the cityscape. Queenie and Matt's target stood alone. The others were in a group about twenty feet from them. That was Matt's cue.

He sped up, closing the gap. They were chatting and laughing, but Matt heard only his breathing and his heartbeat pounding in his ears. When he was thirty yards away, a car pulled alongside him and slowed to match his pace. The driver honked several times. Queenie's group turned toward the sound. Matt hesitated, annoyed that his stealth approach had been exposed. The front passenger window lowered to reveal a shadowy profile.

A male voice hollered, "Hey, Jazzman. The fuck you doin,' joggin' on a damn bridge at all hours o' the night? Trainin' for the damn Street People Olympics?"

Hypo!? Matt stopped, unsure of what to do. The car stopped next to him. Hypo dangled his silver flask out the window. Matt's already raw nerves tingled. This couldn't be good for either him or Queenie, having a witness who called him by his nickname.

The back window of the car glided downward. Hawk's face appeared. With casual aplomb, he said, "Good evening, Jazzman."

What the hell? Matt whipped his gaze from Hawk back to Victor. Even in the low light of the bridge lampposts, Victor's eyes were shooting fireballs at him. Queenie held her composure. The others in the group seemed bewildered and curious.

Matt looked back and forth between Hypo and Queenie. Fear and nervousness were replaced by confusion. Even his sight-reading skills couldn't correctly assess this situation. In a sharp stage whisper, he said, "What're you two doing here?"

"Savin' yo' stupid white ass," Hypo said under his breath, sounding royally pissed off.

"Please get in the car, Matt," said Hawk in a soft but commanding voice.

Matt looked at Victor, who reached into his jacket with his right hand. The other bodyguard made the same motion. Both men moved to shield their bosses from sight and attack. Game over, at least for tonight. With a palms-up shrug, Matt smiled feebly at Victor and said, "My drunken friends need me to show them how to get to a private club I told them about."

Hawk opened his door and slid over. Matt ducked into the back seat behind Hypo. The driver sped away. Matt got his second surprise in less than a minute when the driver glanced over his shoulder and made eye contact.

With a hint of sarcasm in his voice, Ben Nowitzki said, "Matt Lanier, we meet again."

Chapter 29

After Nowitzki had crossed the river to Southeast Minneapolis, Matt calmed his frantic nerves enough to say, "What the hell is going on, Hawk?"

"It's all good, my friend," Hawk said, patting Matt's knee. "You're safer now than you've been in a long time."

Matt fought the urge to lunge at Nowitzki and choke him to death. If he thought he could do so without causing a crash, he would. His next impulse was to open the door and jump out of the moving vehicle, then run and hide in the bowels of downtown. "Safer?" he exclaimed. "This man's been trying to kill me for three months."

Nowitzki said, "That was true until a few days ago, when I received new information about you from several reputable sources."

"What sources?" Matt said, still fighting to control his conflicting urges.

"Let's call them friends. That'll protect them as well as me."

"What the hell are *you* worried about?"

"Seriously?" Nowitzki asked as he turned onto the Hennepin Avenue bridge and headed downtown. "If Smythe hears about this, guess who takes your place on his hit list?"

"The last time we met, you said you weren't in danger from him, even though you screwed up."

"Circumstances changed."

Hypo turned around from the front seat. "What say we go someplace safe and discuss what to do? If Queenie's pissed off, she might come after us with a small army."

"I know a spot," Nowitzki said. They were near the intersection of Hennepin Avenue and Twelfth Street. Two minutes later, he pulled into a parking space at the Minneapolis Sculpture Garden, part of the Walker Art Center west of Loring Park.

"Why here?" Matt asked, still unsure of Nowitzki's motives. For that matter, he was now uncertain of Hawk's and Hypo's allegiance and motives too.

Nowitzki said, "It's free, open late, and we won't look suspicious wandering around admiring the sculptures."

They got out and strolled toward the garden entrance. A few couples wandered about or sat on benches near some sculptures. Matt shivered and thrust his hands into his pockets, wondering why he'd never considered bringing women here for some romance back in his college days. Except for the nearby hum of freeway traffic, the Sculpture Garden was a pleasant urban oasis. After finding a quiet corner with no one else in sight, the group stopped and stood in a loose circle.

"Okay, Lanier," Nowitzki said. "Now that we've all caught our breath, how about a proper introduction to your friends? All we had time for was Ben, Hawk, and Hypo." He said *Hypo* with a question in his tone, much like Matt had initially reacted when he and Hypo first met, as if he'd misheard the name.

Matt looked at his friends for permission. After they nodded, Matt pointed to Hawk. "Ben Nowitzki, this is Norman Peltier." He gestured toward Hypo. "And this is Kenny Carrillo."

"Thanks," Nowitzki said. "I always like to know the names of the people I work with."

"Yeah, yeah," Matt said, not bothering to hide his frustration. "Let's get down to business. Now would be a peachy time for an explanation, guys. You just messed up a perfect chance for me to get my life back on track."

Hawk snorted. "I hardly think committing murder is any man's first choice for rebuilding his broken life."

"Yeah," Hypo added. "Wise up, you stupid mofo."

"Setting aside Lanier's stupidity," Nowitzki said, "I'll start by saying I had a change of heart."

"About what?" Matt asked.

"I believe you didn't blow up your father's house and kill the cop."

The statement hit Matt so hard he took a step back to steady himself. "How? Why?"

"I also believe you didn't murder anyone else, either. Justifiable homicide? Probably. You acted in self-defense when you were cornered by Smythe's operatives."

Matt's head spun with mixed emotions: relief, surprise, hope, suspicion. The big question was why a hired gun would abruptly switch sides and give up a huge payday. Then a more immediate question came to him. "How the hell did you track me down? I didn't tell anyone about tonight."

"It's pretty amazing," Nowitzki said. "But first, how well do you know these two?"

"Hypo, a couple months. Hawk, a couple weeks."

"Do you trust them?"

"*Pfft!* A hell of a lot more than I trust you."

"If we all work together to stop Smythe, would you trust them with your life?"

Matt eyed Hawk, the Army war hero and PTSD counselor. Then he studied Hypo, a hero in his own right for risking his life to help take down the most wanted terrorist in the world. Despite their brief friendships, Matt felt closer to them than almost any of his other friends, past or present. They'd taken a considerable risk to help him twenty minutes earlier when he'd been willing to kill—or die—for a few thousand dollars. He had no doubt he'd lay his life on the line for either friend. He returned his gaze to Nowitzki and said, "Yes."

"Good," Nowitzki said. "Because I'm looking for redemption after returning from the dark side. I realized I care more about the truth than the money. I can't kill simply because a rich prick wants someone dead and will pay to make it happen." His knowing look wasn't lost on Matt.

Two men strolled around the corner arm-in-arm and stopped nearby to admire a sculpture. Nowitzki motioned for the others to follow him. They walked past the Spoonbridge and Cherry sculpture to another deserted corner of the garden.

"I need to ask Hawk a question in private," Matt said.

"Of course," Nowitzki said with a shrug.

After leading Hawk back to a small alcove they'd passed some twenty yards back, Matt spoke softly. "I respect your quick-read ability on people, but two months ago, this guy was willing to kill me for money. Six figures. I need your complete assurance he's on my side—*our* side. If he still intends to kill me, he may kill you and Hypo if you get in his way."

Hawk clamped his hand on Matt's shoulder and stared into his eyes. "I can't do that, Matt. Very little in life is absolute."

"Okay, then. He asked me if I'd trust you and Hypo with *my* life. Would you trust *him* with *your* life?"

Gazing past Matt, Hawk furrowed his brow and worked his jaw in a ruminating motion. Then he re-engaged Matt's eyes. "If two men the caliber of you and Hypo were on my team, then yes, I would."

Matt studied Hawk's face for sincerity, for conviction. What he saw was his usual impassivity. But his voice had been decisively confident. Matt's choice was clear: Despite his distrust of Nowitzki, he'd be a fool not to seize this moment and take the fight to Smythe. "Fair enough," he said. "Thanks."

When they rejoined the others, Matt addressed Nowitzki. "Back to how you found me tonight."

"After I processed what I learned in the last few days," Nowitzki said. "I went to Hawk's to talk to you, but you'd already left for the Diamond. I leveled with them about our past history, then convinced them I can help you beat the rap *and* put Smythe in jail."

Hypo tilted his head toward Nowitzki. "He seems legit for a former cop. Hawk made a judgment call, and he's never been wrong in all the years I've known him. He's on another level as far as reading folks."

"I'm starting to believe it," Matt said, looking at Hawk with increased admiration. The man was a freaking human polygraph. Minutes after sitting down and talking with someone, he could accurately discern bullshit from the right stuff.

Hawk said, "After that little Russian Roulette display in front of my place the other night, Hypo and I discussed the matter. We concluded you were wading into shit that would smell way worse than you imagined. But we were certainly surprised when Nowitzki said he saw you that night too.

After he correctly deduced you were going to do Queenie Delacroix's dirty work, he convinced us we needed to find you ASAP. So Hypo mobilized his street army."

Matt frowned and narrowed his eyes. "Street army?"

Hawk said, "You probably noticed this young man knows *lots* of people."

Matt shot Hypo a wry grin. "He might be too outgoing for his own good."

Nowitzki jerked his thumb in Hypo's direction. "According to Hawk, this guy has more connections than a Hollywood gossip columnist."

"So what? They don't know me."

"You didn't notice anyone watching you between the Diamond to the bus terminal to Nicollet Mall and down to the bridge?"

"I passed hundreds of people tonight. They were all a blur."

Hypo picked up the narrative. "You and I have decent crowds when we perform, right?"

"Yeah, but not enough paying customers to offset a chance to make five grand in one night."

"Lots of street folks show up when we perform because they've got nothing else to do. You haven't been around long enough to recognize or get to know them as well as I do."

Matt tried to remember faces he'd seen more than once at their gigs. Not counting the bald guy from Peavey Plaza, a few came to mind: those with bright or wild-looking clothes or hair; the psychotics and/or addicts; people with large or small bodies; attractive women; obnoxious louts. "I guess I've seen a few more than once."

Hypo said, "What you don't know is that a dozen or so spread the word and show up almost every place we play. I've known most of them for a couple years. Enough of them own cell phones, so if I text a few about one of our gigs, they'll tell another ten or fifteen folks each. They don't crowd around us because they don't want to scare away the people with money. So they hang to the side, around the corners, in the shadows. But they listen and still enjoy the music. Tonight, we texted or called everyone on my contacts list and said you were in trouble. Each one of them contacted their friends. It was a big urban phone tree. I even sent a photo of you so they'd know who to look for. When one of them spotted you, they called Hawk or me, and we guided the rest of them in that general direction. The toughest part was when you started jogging. Not that you were sprinting, but most of these folks aren't exactly in shape."

"I told them to check outside the Diamond first," Nowitzki said. "Figured you might be there again."

"That was a smart call," Hypo said. "A lot of my homies hang out down there at night because it's packed with rich folks who feel guilty about partying when poor homeless people, especially women, are sitting in doorways shaking tin cups and holding up cardboard signs asking for a dollar. One of the few places where panhandling is profitable."

"Bottom line," Nowitzki said, "no one followed you for long because they handed you off to someone else within a block or two. Even an expert CIA operative like Hypo would've been easy to tail. We used my car as command central and drove to where you'd last been seen. Caught up to you in the nick of time, about a hundred yards across the bridge. We followed slowly until we recognized Queenie and her group. Hawk figured things out first and told me to floor it."

Matt ran a hand through his hair. "I had no idea."

Hypo said, "There's a lot of things you have no idea about concerning the street, my friend."

"I see that now."

Hypo lowered his chin and narrowed his eyes. "Guess who did a huge chunk of the word spreading tonight?"

"Who?"

"The woman with the daughter in Loring Park after our first Peavey Plaza gig. Celia."

Matt recoiled with surprise. "But neither of us knew her before then. And we only gave her a few bucks. Why should—"

Hypo cut him off with a raised hand. "After you left, I gave her another five, walked with her to the store, made sure she bought some nutritious food for her and her daughter, Ella. Ten bucks is nothing to a normal person with a job and a house and food on the table. But to street people like Celia, ten bucks from two guys who look like they only have eleven between them is a sign from God. She couldn't stop talking about us not wanting anything in return. Said it was the nicest thing anyone had done for her since she'd been on the street. I got her cell number. Told her I'd keep in touch. I like to make my homies believe someone cares about them, even if that someone's a broken-down ex-CIA agent."

For the first time since he'd returned to Minneapolis, Matt began to understand the point of view of those experiencing homelessness. He still saw himself as an outsider—someone who'd soon fix his personal problems and return to his earlier life as a successful musician. Most of Hypo's and Hawk's friends and acquaintances were going to be lifers—or at least long-term victims. And the mental grind of month after month of despair made it all the harder to stay positive and work to get out of the gutter.

Thoroughly chastened by his naïveté, Matt said, "Your people are amazing. I wish I could thank them all."

"Do it when you get the chance," Hypo said.

Not only was Matt impressed with Hypo's street connections, but he also was impressed that so many strangers with their own problems took the time to help Hawk and Hypo find a fellow street person. Then reality hit him. *I am a street person.* "Okay, I'll admit you all saved me, but I'm still broke and on the run." He glanced at Nowitzki. "Having you on my side barely improves my odds of surviving, let alone winning. What do we do now?"

"I know someone who might get interested in your case *real* fast," Nowitzki said. "I'll give her a call, see what she thinks. But let's drop off your friends first. We might ask for their help later, but the less involved they are with you going forward, the safer they'll be."

"I'm good with that," Matt said. "I don't even want Queenie to learn their names."

Hawk and Hypo exchanged glances. Hawk said, "We'll help you in any way possible, my friend. Neither of us fears death if we go to war for the right reason. Going to war for you is a damn good reason to fight."

Humbled, Matt lowered his head. "I appreciate it, guys." Then he looked up, smiled hopefully, and said, "Let's go home."

Chapter 30

The foursome stopped at the bus depot so Matt could retrieve his clothes from the locker, then proceeded to the alley behind Hawk's apartment, where Hawk and Hypo got out and went inside. Nowitzki then drove around to the front and parked where he and Matt could see Hawk's bedroom. Matt relaxed when the bedroom light flicked *on-off-on*. That was the prearranged signal telling them their friends were safely inside. They waited on the street for another thirty minutes in case Queenie was planning some sort of retribution for what happened on the bridge.

Satisfied that an attack wasn't imminent, Nowitzki said, "You can stay with me tonight. I'll call my friend in the morning, and we'll kick this investigation of Smythe into gear."

He drove to his motel and parked. They got out, looking left and right for anyone tailing them. Nowitzki opened his trunk, pulled out a large case, closed the trunk, and unlocked his room door. They slipped inside. Nowitzki secured the knob lock and deadbolt while Matt scanned the accommodations.

The Sleep Tite Motor Hotel was a one-story, mid-twentieth-century mom-and-pop operation, so amenities like high-tech security and thick towels—even thick walls—were lacking. But it beat sleeping in Nowitzki's car or on the streets. The room had two queen beds with slightly concave mattresses, a small flat-screen TV sitting on a dark-brown dresser, and a mini fridge next to the dresser. Matt sat on a rickety chair at a rickety desk near the window.

Nowitzki slid the large case under one bed, presumably his, and said, "I don't like leaving my weapons and other gear in the car, especially in a low-rent district."

"Makes sense," Matt said. Seeing the weapons case under the bed implied that Nowitzki was in for the night and might be serious about wanting to help him. After all, if Nowitzki still intended to kill him, wouldn't he have driven Matt to a remote location and put a bullet through his head instead of inviting him to stay with him at the motel? He began to believe Nowitzki truly wanted to help him take down Smythe. But he needed more answers before he was convinced. Weary from the evening's extreme tension and stress, he slumped in the chair and asked, "Why the change of heart? The last time we met, you tried to kill me. Kinda hard to forget that ever happened."

In the silence before Nowitzki replied, they heard a couple next door having sex. The headboard rhythmically thumped against the shared wall. The woman moaned, then squealed with either delight or pain. The thumping resumed.

Red-faced at the neighbors' intrusion into their conversation, Nowitzki said, "Simple. I've done more research on Smythe and Millennium Four. Found almost nothing about the conspiracy, but Smythe certainly is a shady character, to say the least. More importantly, several good, honest folks in Straight River convinced me you're telling the truth."

"Who?"

"They're safer if you don't know. I don't want the body count in Straight River to get any higher. If necessary, I'll tell you later."

"Right," Matt said in grudging agreement. No doubt one person Nowitzki had interviewed was Betty Myrick. It was hard not to believe her when she sang Matt's praises to the world.

Matt asked, "How'd you track me from Castle Danger to here?"

Nowitzki said. "Unlike Hypo's homies, I'm a trained detective. And I'm damn good too. I have a feel for my targets, kind of like Hawk has for detecting character. I easily tracked you to Minneapolis, figuring you'd be in the low-rent district because you're broke. I made the rounds of all the places poor people might congregate: soup kitchens, shelters, free clinics, street corners. Showed your picture around. The fact that you play guitar on the street trimmed the candidates from hundreds to a handful. Went pretty fast from there."

"It was that easy?" Matt said, aghast. He thought he'd hidden well. But he was coming from the viewpoint of thinking if he avoided middle-class society—his old life—he'd remain anonymous no matter what he did. Nowitzki kept on impressing him, which caused Matt to feel even luckier that he'd prevailed in their first encounter in Castle Danger.

The couple in the next room started round two of their lovemaking. The men heard faint slaps of flesh on flesh along with sharp cries of "Oww," and "Yeah, baby," and "Oh God, it hurts so *good*." Nowitzki chuckled. This time, Matt's face flushed with embarrassment.

"Um, yeah," Nowitzki said, glancing at the thin wall between them and the rutting couple. "You're not a career criminal or spy. Being on the run is still new for you. You don't know how hard it is to drop off the map, even if you avoid all technology. I got a hit from a soup kitchen pastor who mentioned your guitar. Then I ran across Hypo. Hard to forget him. Then a guy mentioned Hypo was promoting your Target Center gig. I went there, hid, and waited. You had some sort of panic attack, right? Saw you go down from the street below the skyway. When you packed up and left, I tracked you to the men's shelter, then to Hawk's."

"That was days ago," Matt said. "What were you waiting for?"

Nowitzki stiffened. "I wanted to be a hundred percent sure."

Matt shook his head. "You are one hard-to-figure cat, Nowitzki. In the music world, you'd be the smart-ass piano player in the ensemble who changes key in the middle of his solo just to keep the rest of the band on their toes."

Nowitzki gave him a blank look. "All I can play is 'Chopsticks,' so I'll take your word."

The rutting couple had either stopped after a successful conclusion to their passion play or collapsed from exhaustion. Matt glanced at the shared wall and said, "What do we do now?"

"We could give them a rousing ovation," Nowitzki said, "but chances are we'd get an invitation to make it a foursome."

Matt shuddered. "Not even remotely funny. I meant, how do we stop Smythe?"

"We sleep. We eat breakfast. I call my friend. She owes me a big favor. It's payback time."

"Payback for what?"

Shrugging his shoulders, Nowitzki said, "The first year we worked together, I saved her life."

Chapter 31

Nowitzki treated Matt to breakfast at a nearby diner. Matt accepted because he had less than fifty dollars to his name. He kept it light: a bacon-and-egg breakfast sandwich and coffee. Nowitzki had a bigger appetite and no charity-case guilt. He ordered eggs Benedict, hash browns, fresh fruit, and coffee.

They ate in silence until Matt asked, "Tell me about the friend you're going to call."

Nowitzki swallowed and wiped his mouth with a paper napkin. "I was her first partner at the Minneapolis Police Department. Showed her the ropes. She was good too, except for one rookie mistake she made. We stopped a guy in his car for an outstanding warrant. Arrested him, had him spread-eagled against the car. She frisked him but was only looking for a firearm. Turns out he had a switchblade stashed in his sock. He fell down like he was having a seizure. She knelt to help him. I turned around just as he popped the blade on the knife. She froze. He lunged at her. The point of the blade was heading for her throat. I dove at him like a soccer goalie dives for a ball." Nowitzki held up his hand to show a long scar on his palm. "Made the save."

"Wow," Matt said.

"When she saw the knife stuck in my palm, she unfroze." He laughed. "Almost beat the poor bastard to death. MPD made an inquiry through Internal Affairs, but the guy's rap sheet was longer than my arm, including a voluntary manslaughter conviction. I got a commendation; she got an official reprimand. Releasing her anger that one time was helpful because she never forgot the lesson. From then on, she became a model officer. A few years later, she left for the FBI."

"The *what*?" Matt said. The instinct to flee shot through his nervous system. "Hold on a damn—"

Nowitzki jabbed his fork upward to interrupt. "Trust me.."

Matt looked around to see if the other diners were eavesdropping. He lowered his voice to a harsh whisper. "I thought your friend was a beat cop or fellow private eye. An FBI agent is a serious law enforcement officer. I'm not ready to talk to them."

Nowitzki speared a cube of cantaloupe. "We can use the local LEOs and Bureau of Criminal Apprehension for the in-state killings. However, because you dug up an interstate conspiracy, which is a federal crime, the Feds have to take the lead."

Even with his limited knowledge of levels of law enforcement, Matt suspected Nowitzki was right. "If I turn myself in, they could easily say, 'Hey, here's a ten-most-wanted suspect in a slam-dunk case. Let's bust him and call it a day. Who cares about an alleged conspiracy?'"

Nowitzki leveled a glare at him. "Okay, Lanier, let's get something straight. I'm trusting you as much as I'm asking you to trust me. We're the only people who know I'm guilty of attempted murder, and I want to keep it that way. Do you think there's any chance I'd drag the FBI into this if I thought you'd crumble and squeal on *me* just to cut a leniency deal?"

Matt's face grew warm as he struggled to answer honestly. "I don't know. I—"

"Remember," Nowitzki said, "I can hang you out to dry anytime I want. Like it or not, we're in this together. Play your cards right, and we can get Smythe and clear your name. You can repay me by never telling anyone what happened in Castle Danger. But if I think for one second you'll betray me, I'll feed you to the wolves and disappear. Unlike you, I've got money, an escape plan, and access to a new identity."

Nowitzki shoved a forkful of hash browns into his mouth and sat back without taking his eyes off Matt. The stare down lasted until he swallowed. "I'm not stupid," he said. "I'll lay the groundwork of your story, but I won't mention your name. After you get a sense of her character, you can share your evidence if you're comfortable. But if you're not ..."

Matt filled in the blank. "Then I can kiss my ass goodbye."

Nowitzki tapped his nose. "You were willing to kill for your last chance at freedom. Willing to die for it too. I'm offering you a greater chance to succeed. But I can't guarantee the FBI brass will listen to you. That's why we're calling my friend first. She'll give us a read on how interested they might be in your story. If you're right about Smythe, this could be a blockbuster case that would boost a lot of careers."

Matt stared at the crumbs on his plate. The weight of this decision pressed down on him like his metaphorical two-hundred-pound backpack. Despite having slept well last night, he was tired. Tired of running. Tired of not trusting anyone. Tired of being afraid. Tired of being tired. He breathed in and out slowly. "Sorry I doubted you. From now on, I'm all in."

Tight-lipped, Nowitzki nodded. "It's still a long shot. But if we can get buy-in from the FBI, we can pull this off."

They finished their meal and returned to the motel. Nowitzki pulled out his phone and called Special Agent Regina Irving on her cell phone. After exchanging pleasantries with her, he put his phone in speaker mode.

"I've got something important to tell you that will interest the entire Minneapolis Field Office."

"Oh, really?" she asked.

"And Reggie," he added, "I gotta remind you that if this turns out well, you'll have paid your debt to me."

Irving said, "You said that a dozen times when we worked together, and it's never happened." Her gravelly voice had a Melissa Etheridge quality, with a hint of an accent from the east. *Pennsylvania?*

Matt swallowed hard and tried to stay calm. He was about to tell his story to someone who held the key to his future.

Nowitzki said, "I'm calling because I've got a lead for you from someone you may have heard of in a professional capacity."

"Sorry, Ben, I just woke up," Irving said. "And as you know, I'm not a morning person. Still waitin' on my damn coffee to get brewed. I'll need some help here."

"No names yet, but he's on your Ten Most Wanted list."

"Bullshit."

"And he can lead you to someone I'll bet the Bureau has been watching for a while."

"How the hell ..." she said, trailing off into a mumble.

"Long story, Reggie," Nowitzki said. "If you're at all interested, I'll explain. Then I'll tell you what we want. But it doesn't include arresting my client."

Irving said, "*Aaand* here it comes."

"Seriously," Nowitzki said, "I'm convinced he was set up. No one knows more about his case than I do because I'm also sure *who* set him up. If I'm right on both counts—and I am—you'll be in line to make the biggest bust of your career."

"You do understand it's my constitutional duty to arrest him if he's a wanted man."

"But you won't, because if he has any doubts about this, he'll disappear. He's managed to avoid capture for a long time. I did some serious begging to convince him to talk to you. Unless you're hot on his ass and not telling me, you won't find him unless he screws up."

"This is the kind of stuff that gives me nightmares, Ben. Except I know this isn't a nightmare because I smell coffee, and I *never* smell anything when I'm asleep."

"I know this is from left field, but I called because you've got the brains and common sense to understand."

"Please give me something to pique my interest," she said. "All I'm hearing right now is a bucketful of mystery babble."

"Fair enough," Nowitzki said. "Here's something concrete. A man calling himself Jones hired me to find this guy." Nowitzki then explained how he first got involved without admitting Jones had hired him to kill Matt.

"This is where it gets interesting," Nowitzki said, glancing at Matt. "During my investigation, I learned one key piece of information and the real reason I was hired."

Irving said, "Don't keep me in suspense, Benny boy."

"Jones's real name is Leland Smythe."

A long pause ensued. Matt sensed Irving recognized the name.

"He got a motive?" she asked.

"A nationwide conspiracy he wants to keep under wraps."

"A *nationwide* conspiracy." Her tone was one of disbelief.

Nowitzki said, "Minnesota-to-Texas national, anyway. An illegal land grab of small farms adjacent to Interstate 35. That's why we need the FBI. My client can explain."

Matt coughed, more to calm his nerves than clear his throat. This was the moment he feared more than anything other than being killed. "Um, should I disguise my voice?" he whispered, unsure how sophisticated FBI technology was in tracking voices during random, spontaneous phone calls.

"No," said Nowitzki. "She's on her personal phone. Besides, if they believe us, you'll have to tell them your name."

Matt wasn't thrilled about that eventuality, but he'd committed to seeing this through. "Okay, here goes. It began more than a year ago. I was back in my hometown, settling my father's estate after he died. A week later, my father's neighbor died from an apparent suicide. His widow insisted the manner of death was wrong. Her husband wouldn't have committed suicide because that would invalidate a big life insurance policy they bought on the husband a year earlier. She asked me to help her prove he *didn't* commit suicide."

"I'm still listening." Irving said, sounding disinterested.

"I started asking around and heard about some suspicious real estate transactions involving area farms. My father had also been suspicious of those deals and conducted some research. He didn't trust one local realtor working for a shell corporation. Long story short, Smythe owns that corporation and dozens of others in Minnesota, Iowa, and Missouri. All those companies were lowball buying or stealing land from small farmers who owned property along I-35. Killing or injuring farmers too, if that made it easier to get the land. Our farm was one of the first Smythe tried to buy in the county. My father died because he suspected something fishy and wouldn't sell. Soon after that, Smythe discovered that I knew this information and tried to kill me ... on five separate occasions."

At this point, he imagined Irving was thinking, *this guy sounds like another nutcase.*

"Hmm," Irving said with heightened impatience. "I'm interested now, but without more details from your boy here—names, dates, documentation—you're wasting my time."

When Matt hesitated, Nowitzki gave him a sincere look and said, "Reggie's one of the good ones. She's tough, but she plays fair. I'm sure she'll see this like I do and back you. But you gotta take that leap of faith."

"You sound damned confident about that, Nowitzki," Irving said.

"Only because you've been a Fibbie for less than five years," he said. "Anything longer than that, and you guys turn into robots."

"Ha, ha," she said dryly. "But Ben's right, sir. This is a confidential, off-the-record conversation until you say it's official."

After a deep sigh, Matt said, "Okay. In the space of several weeks, Smythe's men tried to run me over, blow up my dad's house with me in it, and shoot me on three different occasions."

During the ensuing silence, he imagined Irving frantically looking at her computer files of the FBI's Ten Most Wanted list and making the immediate connection that he was *the* Matt Lanier.

Nowitzki stared at Matt, probably wondering if he might crack and screw up their agreement. Matt gave him a reassuring nod. By now, he didn't care if she figured out his identity. He'd started down the ski slope of truth and decided the best, least painful way to get to the bottom was in a straight line.

"My name is Matthew Lanier. I was accused of killing officer Steven Sandvik in the explosion at my dad's. That's why I've been on the run for a year. I didn't kill Sandvik, although I killed two men who tried to kill me. But I only killed them in self-defense."

Nowitzki's nod and slight smile were reassuring. After Irving digested those revelations, she spoke. "So, Matthew Lanier, you claim you're innocent of all the charges against you other than justifiable homicide?"

"Yes."

"Why not run to the authorities after the first attempt on your life?"

"I tried, but the local cops wouldn't believe me. Not even a friend on the force believed me until it was too late. He ended up dead, along with almost every other witness who could help me prove my case. So I ran and hid. I intended to regroup and find a way to stop Smythe, but that hasn't worked out the way I'd hoped. If five men from little old Straight River ended up dead from suspicious causes—and many others were cheated out of their farms—then the total destruction Smythe has caused could be mind-boggling."

Irving said, "So you say. But because Big Ben believes you, you're coming clean?"

Matt shot an irritated glare at Nowitzki. What little energy he had left drained away as he realized he was past the point of safely backing out of Nowitzki's plan. "He didn't give me a choice. He says he has additional evidence that backs up my story. I've been hiding for a year because my evidence is circumstantial, and my corroborating witnesses to the killings are all dead. He claims his information is solid. If it is, this is my one and only chance to clear my name."

"Let me get this straight," Irving said. "You believe you have enough information to take Smythe down for this alleged conspiracy, along with a bucketful of murders and assorted real estate transaction wrongdoings?"

"I do. But without corroboration or proof that he owns those shell corporations, screwed dozens of farmers out of their land, and ordered those murders, it's all a paranoid delusion on my part. That's Smythe's genius. He hides behind so many layers of secrecy and protection that he can plausibly deny every accusation. And I doubt he leaves much of a paper trail."

"With all due respect, the FBI never met a paper trail we couldn't uncover."

"That's why I called you, Reggie," Nowitzki said. "Between my discoveries, Lanier's data, and some corroborating character witnesses, there's enough probable cause to investigate. I came to you because the MPD would laugh in my face, then tell me to go fuck myself."

Irving said, "Good point. You royally screwed your reputation before you left."

"Right. All I'm asking is for you to check his data, listen to the witnesses, and go from there. I'm confident we can prove Lanier's innocence and nail the murderous bastard."

Irving hesitated before saying, "Our white-collar division has long suspected Smythe of some shady shit. But as you say, he's damn clever. Every time we get close, some politician steps in and runs interference. Plus, his lawyers make sharks seem like minnows."

"So, what do you say?" Nowitzki asked. "I'll keep Lanier out of danger until you check everything out, then go where the info takes you. If the FBI can't crack this conspiracy or won't take the case, I'll turn him loose."

"What about protective custody?" Irving asked.

Matt shook his head. "I won't let you hide me in any sort of jail where someone who knows Smythe might recognize me. His network almost certainly includes jailhouse snitches and crooked cops. He had the Straight River police chief in his pocket. If his network is that extensive, there's better than even odds he'll find out where you're hiding me."

"How about this?" Nowitzki said. "I'll take charge of him. If Lanier bolts or does something stupid, it's my ass, not yours."

Irving said, "So, I'm supposed to trust a disgraced former cop—who's now a marginal private dick at best—with a wanted serial killer?"

"Reggie, baby," Nowitzki said, cracking a huge grin and sounding like a sleazy Hollywood agent, "it's no wonder you're on the short list for promotion. Your perception of the issues rises so far above the average Special Agent. Remember, this is off the record, and you can still pretend this is all hypothetical. You heard a plausible story from a credible anonymous caller that connects Smythe with some major crimes. You ask your boss if you can follow the lead for a few days. But if you don't do it our way, we'll both go to our graves denying this chat ever took place."

The two men stared at each other as they waited for Irving to respond. Matt's pulse was beating at a quick-march tempo. After an excruciatingly long silence, they heard Irving's exaggerated sigh. She said, "I'll see what I can do."

Chapter 32

Whatever Special Agent Irving did when she told them, "I'll see what I can do," happened at lightning speed because she called an hour later. Matt and Nowitzki were chilling in the motel room. Matt was on his bed, watching a chatty morning network television news program. Nowitzki was sitting at the desk, streaming *Jeopardy!* on his laptop. He was playing along, firing off responses in a soft tone so Matt could still hear the TV. After she identified herself, Nowitzki put his phone on *speaker*. Matt slid to the edge of his bed so he could hear better.

"My boss was reluctant to buy my hypothetical proposal," Irving said. "He wants solid evidence. He also wants another white-collar crime specialist to be present. She'll have more insight into the conspiracy angle."

"We're amenable to that," Nowitzki said after Matt gave him a confirming nod.

"Can we do another phone meeting?" Matt said.

After an exasperated sigh, Irving said, "Mr. Lanier, we need to hear your story in detail. We'll want to ask questions. And frankly, we want to size you up in person, evaluate your believability and overall character."

"What about a video conference?" Nowitzki said.

Irving hesitated. "That's acceptable. But we want to see *all* of your documentation. We'll have a lot of questions."

"I don't have it with me," Matt said. "But I can get it soon."

"How soon?"

"I need to call my lawyer."

Nowitzki's eyebrows shot skyward. He mouthed, "You have a lawyer?"

"Mr. Lanier," Irving said, "you aren't under arrest. You don't need a lawyer to talk to us."

"He's holding my documentation," Matt said. "He also knows how to contact the young man who helped me crack the conspiracy."

Again, Nowitzki did the eyebrow thing.

"Call us back after you talk to your lawyer," Irving said, "and we'll set up a time. We can use any online video-conferencing app you prefer."

"I'll set up a Zoom meeting," Nowitzki said. "We'll get back to you ASAP."

They ended the call. Nowitzki leaned back in his chair and crossed his arms. "A lawyer and a *partner*? You've been holding out on me."

Matt stared him down. "To protect them. Smythe knows the name of my partner but not his location. He also knows I have a lawyer, but not his name or location. The two of them are too valuable to put at risk. They've got evidence and access to documents in that cloud thing."

Nowitzki chuckled. "Man, you are a techno virgin, aren't you?"

Matt shrugged. "Can't be an expert on everything. Music was tough enough to master. Didn't have time for much else. Will the Feds know our location?"

"Not unless we tell them or they figure out my IP address and find us from that." He noticed Matt's puzzled look. "Don't ask. Not important for you. I know how to hide us."

Still hesitant about sharing this information, Matt stared out the window and drummed an intricate quick-time marching rhythm on his thighs. "Can we do this video meeting from anywhere?"

"Wherever there's an internet connection."

"Can I ask my lawyer to be present during the call?"

"Irving said you don't need one."

"For moral support, maybe some advice if he thinks I'm telling too much too soon or otherwise screwing things up."

"Sure. He doesn't even need to identify himself."

At that moment, Matt decided that if he survived this mess, he'd bone up on computers and cell phones and the latest technology. Zach Perez's computer expertise had helped make a compelling case against Smythe. Cell phone communication between Hypo and his street friends had probably saved his life on the Third Avenue bridge. Video conferencing would allow him to tell his story without getting double-crossed by the Feds.

"Okay," Matt said. "I'll call him and see if we can set up a meeting. He's semi-retired, so he might be available later today."

"Fine. What's his name?"

"You'll find out when we get there."

Nowitzki frowned. "Still in protection mode, eh?"

"Yeah."

"Don't want to put anyone else in danger. I understand. Getting shot at is no fun. Even though I was a cop, I'm a chicken at heart."

"You ever take one for the team?"

"Flesh wound. A through-and-through in my calf during a car chase and subsequent shootout. Bled like a stuck pig but only felt like the worst bee sting in the world. You?"

Matt shook his head. "A few bullets whizzed past me too close for comfort Up North. However, I gotta believe getting blown up is worse. Lots of stitches, a concussion, broken ribs, mangled hand." He wiggled his injured fingers. "Still not one hundred percent."

"Let's hope those are the last war wounds we ever get."

"I can live with that," Matt said, then called John Maxwell with Nowitzki's phone. The attorney was thrilled and relieved to hear from him, and Matt immediately asked about Zach.

"He's doing quite well," Maxwell replied. "Hasn't missed a single check-in."

"Great to hear, Max. I'm calling because I have a spark of hope that I can end this business with Smythe and clear my name with the police."

"Really?"

"Yes, but I'll need your help as my attorney and Zach as my data expert. Call him and have him send you the research data he hid for me. I also want him to figure out how to play Flannery's recorded confession to the FBI via a video computer conference."

"FBI? How did they get involved?"

"I have a new ally who knows an agent. Through her, he thinks he can persuade the FBI to investigate Smythe and Millennium Four. They want to do a video conference, talk to me, see my data, and probably hear the Flannery confession. Can we hold the meeting in your office today?"

A brief silence ensued as Maxwell presumably checked his calendar. "How does two o'clock sound?"

"Perfect. Thanks, Max." He ended the call and faced Nowitzki. "We're set for two o'clock. Let Irving know so she can prepare."

"Right," Nowitzki said. He made the call and scheduled the meeting.

Matt borrowed a notepad from Nowitzki and jotted down his thoughts about what to tell the FBI. Nowitzki left to gas up his car and get some snacks and sundries since he now expected to stay in town for several more days than he'd initially estimated.

An hour later, Nowitzki returned. "How about some lunch? My treat."

"You already picked up the breakfast tab," Matt said. "I can pay for my own."

Nowitzki waved him off. "Save your money. I'll add it to your bill when this is over."

For a split second, Matt thought he was serious. But Nowitzki's grin dispelled that thought. "Thanks," Matt said. "If I offered to pay, we'd stop at Aldi for some off-brand peanut butter and a loaf of Wonder Bread."

"Yummy," Nowitzki said, deadpanning. "Tough to pass that up."

They got in his Taurus and drove to a neighborhood joint. Nowitzki swore it wasn't a cop hangout even though he used to bring dates here back when he *was* a cop. "Fabulous burgers. Blow-your-mind sweet potato fries. Super crispy."

Matt began salivating as soon as they entered the place. He inhaled the smoky, greasy, oniony aroma deep into his lungs. Between food-shelf products, soup-kitchen fare, and low-budget meals at Hawk's, he hadn't enjoyed a high-quality meal since eating at the Halcyon months ago.

They found a table in the back corner of the place. The nearest patrons were well out of earshot if Matt and Nowitzki talked softly. Matt chose the seat facing the door. Ever since the abandoned job for Queenie, an underlying tension had built up in his body about being seen, heard, or followed. Along with two burger platters with sweet potato fries, Nowitzki ordered beer for both of them. Another small luxury Matt hadn't savored since the Halcyon. After the server had taken their order and left, the men suffered through an uncomfortable silence. Their beers arrived, and Matt took a long swig of his. As the cold, bubbly brew slid down his throat, some of his tension dissipated.

"I forgot until now," he said, "but thanks for plucking me off the bridge last night."

"It was the right thing to do," Nowitzki said with a nod of acknowledgment. "Although I'm not sure your presence there was the wisest career move."

"Stress does that to a man. I've been slowly going crazy for the past few months. Thinking I had the balls to yell at a total stranger, 'You hooked my sister on drugs and killed her!' and then shove him off a bridge was proof of that."

Nowitzki leaned back in his chair, easing into a wry grin. "You were going to say *that*?"

"Victor's final instructions word for word. I saved the note."

"I'd like to see it. But I guess it wouldn't be admissible in court as proof of Queenie trying to kill the guy. Did they tell you who your target was?"

Matt shook his head. "Just said it was the shorter of the two men with them. Glad it wasn't the tall one. He looked like an ex-football player."

"You get a good look at the target?"

"Nah, the bodyguards blocked him off fast."

When their food arrived, both men ate in silence for several bites. Nowitzki squirted mustard on his pile of fries. Matt winced at the sight, then focused on his ketchup-dipped fries. Nowitzki's change of heart about killing him came to mind, and he wanted more answers. "Who'd you talk to in Straight River?"

Nowitzki frowned. "I guess it won't hurt to tell you. Betty Myrick and Amy Swanson."

Matt had forgotten about Amy. "What did Amy tell you?"

"Told me about Witt beating up her and her husband. The fake rape. Dave's wild-ass guess about where you were hiding. Witt taking off immediately after that. Your last conversation with her."

"That's everything," Matt said, nodding grimly. He'd told her to stay quiet for her own protection. If Nowitzki had coerced her or somehow forced her to talk ... He calmed his growing alarm and asked, "How'd you get her to share that information?"

"She volunteered after I gained a modicum of trust," Nowitzki said matter-of-factly. "Said she wasn't afraid of Smythe because her life was meaningless without her husband."

Matt sagged in his seat, agonizing over the pain Amy must have endured since being widowed at such an early age—thanks to him. So many people had suffered since he went on his foolish little crusade to stop Smythe. Anger welled up in his body. "The damn fool was beaten to a pulp," he said. "Should've stayed in the hospital. But somehow, he talked Clay Gebhardt into bringing him along to help me up on Big Island. The big dumb lug."

"Dave didn't know the rape was faked," Nowitzki said in a calming tone. "You'd have done the same thing if a troglodyte like Witt assaulted your wife. Any man worthy of a good woman would've done that. Blame it on Witt and Smythe and stop beating yourself up."

He was right, of course. Matt sat up and sipped his beer. "Sorry. More stress."

Witt and his work as Smythe's lead goon triggered a question in Matt's mind. "How easy is it to get payroll information, employee records, and other data from a business?"

"Depends," Nowitzki said. "If you convince the boss it'll help solve a crime—pretty easy. Otherwise, you jump through the hoops and convince a judge to issue a search warrant."

"That requires probable cause, right?"

Nowitzki nodded as he stuffed a mustard-drenched fry into his mouth.

Matt said, "I'll bet my young friend could hack into Smythe Properties' computer system, but committing a crime to solve a crime doesn't make a lot of sense, does it?"

"Nope," Nowitzki said after taking a sip of his beer. They ate in silence until their food was gone. Nowitzki checked his watch. "Almost time to go."

"Right." Matt drained his beer while Nowitzki paid the check. His thoughts returned to Zach. Was there *any* conceivable way to keep the kid from getting involved with trying to nail Smythe's hide to the wall?

Chapter 33

Chilly drizzle began falling while Matt and Nowitzki ate lunch, so the drive down I-35 to Straight River was punctuated by the rhythmic *slap-slap* of the windshield wipers on Nowitzki's car. Matt played air double bass—pretending to finger the notes for an intricate etude he'd practiced a hundred times and could never forget. Nowitzki seemed pensive but held his lips in a tight horizontal line. He repeatedly glanced out the windows and checked the mirrors. His knuckles were white on the steering wheel.

"Something on your mind?" Matt asked.

"Huh? Oh, nothing. Just doubting our ability to pull this off and put Smythe on ice."

Matt let out a *chuff* between his lips. "Is that all? I thought you were thinking about asking Special Agent Irving for a date. You two sounded pretty chummy on the phone."

"What? *No.* We were partners at MPD. That's all. I mean, we got along well, but it was strictly work-related." He turned to give Matt a disdainful scowl. "Unlike someone else in this car who's done a lousy job of separating business from pleasure when it comes to women."

"What're you talking about? I never—"

Nowitzki cut him off with a raised finger. "You talked your ex-wife into joining your little mystery investigation last year." He raised a second finger. "You got personally involved with your boss, Allyson Clifford, up in Castle Danger. That's enough evidence for me."

Nowitzki had a point. Matt might have given up on Smythe if he hadn't run into Diane at the Dakota Jazz Club and asked for her help. As for Allyson, he would've liked a relationship with her. Unfortunately, events moved much too fast in Castle Danger, and he'd still been mourning Diane's death. He would've kept their relationship professional if Allyson's husband hadn't shown up. After that, Matt did what needed doing to save her and her son, then left.

With a softer tone, Nowitzki said, "I don't fault you for either situation. Allyson's an absolute stunner. I was tempted to ask her out the first time I saw her. Sorry if I assumed too much. But I was there when she read your goodbye note. I'll never forget the look on her face. She was totally crushed that you left. When I was a cop, I told a few women that their husbands or boyfriends had died. They all had a certain look. Devastation. Allyson had that look."

Matt snapped his head around to stare at Nowitzki. His insides churned with a mix of disbelief, hope, and remorse for making what now seemed to be a poor decision to leave Castle Danger. "You're not just saying that?"

"Why would I encourage my competition? I'm simply telling you the truth as I saw it." He focused on passing a semitrailer through the road spray, then said, "I did plenty of research on Diane, and I always wondered why you two got divorced. She was a looker and smart enough to handle you, so I figured you were a good pair."

Matt shook his head. "Wasn't my idea."

"You cheat on her?"

"Hell, no," Matt snapped. "Wouldn't have found anyone better than her, and I knew it."

"So why then?"

"Daddy thought she was slumming with the likes of me. She was on the fast track to a high-powered legal career. Lowly musicians were only worth a polite *thank you* for entertaining the rich snobs in the mansion at the end of the soirée."

"Hmm," Nowitzki said, "my research on you didn't take me that far. Who's daddy?"

"Edward Blake, beloved father and esteemed Minnesota Court of Appeals judge."

Nowitzki did a double take. "*That* Edward Blake?"

"Yeah. So?" Matt said nonchalantly. "Just another anonymous judge as far as most people are concerned."

"I guess you haven't heard. The honorable Edward Blake is now on the state *Supreme* Court."

Matt did his own double take and gaped at Nowitzki.

"He's also on a fast track to becoming chief justice."

"When the hell did this happen?"

"About nine months ago."

Matt did a quick calculation. Only a few months after Diane died. A dull ache grew in the pit of his stomach.

Nowitzki said, "Don't you read newspapers these days?"

"Only the ones I fish out of trash cans on the street. Besides, Supreme Court business isn't everyday news. Why is he fast-tracked?"

"Media says it's because he was chief of the Appellate Court. Knows how to be in charge. It's funny though. Turnover on the Supreme Court has been higher than usual this year. A couple of early retirements came out of the blue. Blake's now in the middle of the seniority list too. Gives him more street cred with the Governor when the current chief justice retires."

"Shit," was all Matt could think to say.

"Something wrong?" Nowitzki asked.

"Nothing on the surface, but my gut tells me differently." The dull ache had intensified. Matt thought back on the adversarial relationship he'd had with his former father-in-law. In public, Blake was the doting father, proud of his daughter and her husband, whom he often called a *musical genius*. But Matt always heard a slight annoyance and edginess in those two words.

In private, Blake was cold and distant, barely masking his disapproval of his only child's choice of husband. He'd made it crystal clear that he had big plans for Diane and that Matt was a liability to her career. Fortunately, Diane never saw it her father's way until she made the leap from public defender to working in the state Attorney General's office. After it became obvious that Diane was a rising star there, Edward relentlessly pressed her to divorce Matt. Diane had shared only bits and pieces of her conversations with her father, so Matt never knew the whole story. He sensed that her family obligations and the image her father wanted to project to the world of a legal dynasty would always take precedence over true love. Especially since Diane would be the only one to represent the fourth generation of Blake lawyers. And so Matt was left in the dust, albeit with a generous divorce settlement that tacitly obligated him to keep his mouth shut about who called the shots regarding Diane's career.

Chapter 34

When they arrived in Straight River, Nowitzki passed Maxwell's office, drove around several blocks making random turns, then parked in front of the beautifully restored Victorian house on Main Street. It was a short walk to the county courthouse for the firm's lawyers.

Satisfied they hadn't been followed, Nowitzki said, "Okay, let's go in."

The men exited the car. Feeling exposed and vulnerable to an attack from Smythe's unknown, unseen gun for hire, Matt led the way as they hurriedly entered the empty foyer of the house.

Maxwell appeared from his office down a short hallway. Smiling, he said, "Welcome home, Matt."

"Great to see you again, Max." Being in Maxwell's benign, grandfatherly presence slowed Matt's heart rate. He introduced Nowitzki. The two men exchanged greetings and shook hands, then Maxwell led them to his office.

The classic lawyer décor hadn't changed since Matt's last visit a year ago: dark wood, massive partner desk, vintage brass banker's lamp with a green glass lampshade. Diplomas, tasteful oil paintings, civic and philanthropic citations, and plaques adorned the walls.

After his guests sat in the upholstered client chairs, Maxwell eased into his oversized leather executive chair with a groan. Now in his late sixties, years of desk work and a sedentary lifestyle had slowed him down. His silver-white hair was trimmed short around a modest bald spot. With craggy features and a disarming smile, Maxwell could switch roles easily in court, going from a gentle father figure to an imposing, tough-talking legal shark before witnesses knew what had hit them.

Maxwell had been a rising star in his youth—one of the firm's youngest partners—and he'd rapidly ascended to managing partner. Because of retirements and deaths, only three lawyers, a paralegal, and an office manager remained. Maxwell now worked one or two days a week on selected cases. He occupied the plum office on the first floor, close to the reception area. The other two partners and the paralegal worked on the second floor.

"Down to business," Maxwell said. "You mentioned a videoconference with the FBI."

"Yes," Matt said. "Did you connect with Zach?" He glanced at Nowitzki, whose poker face was inscrutable.

"I did," Maxwell said. "By the way, he's had no trouble from Smythe since last year."

"That's great," Matt said. He'd made a deal with Smythe that Zach wouldn't be harmed, provided they both kept silent about Millennium Four. It was the best deal he could make at the time. Now, with Nowitzki, Hawk, and Hypo also on his side, he was ready to resume his crusade, more confident than ever he could keep Zach safe. "Did he send you the recording?"

Maxwell tapped his computer terminal. "Cued up and ready to play."

Nowitzki glanced at Matt. "What kind of recording?"

"Audio from the Boundary Waters incident," Matt said. He shot a hesitant look at Maxwell. "Should we play it for him now or wait for the FBI meeting?"

"Wait," Maxwell replied. "We'll go slow at first. Make sure they're interested before we show all our cards."

Nowitzki pursed his lips, obviously annoyed at not being privy to all Matt's evidence before he shared it with the FBI.

"Shall we make the call and set up the conference?" Maxwell asked. "Even though I'm semi-retired, I don't have all day."

"Sure, Max. Sorry." He'd forgotten that one of Maxwell's strong points was not wasting time, words, or resources on any sort of case.

Nowitzki called Special Agent Irving and told her to prepare for the video meeting on her end. Then he extracted his laptop from its case and turned it on. Maxwell gave him the password for the firm's secure internet access. After typing and clicking for thirty seconds, Nowitzki said, "We're good to go."

Maxwell stood. "In the interest of security, sit in front of my door, so they won't get a clue to your location from the identifiable items on my walls. I'll stay out of sight for now."

Nowitzki seemed impressed. "I like your choice of legal counsel, Lanier. Damn sharp for an old guy."

Maxwell gave him his grandfatherly smile.

Nowitzki positioned the laptop's camera so the six-panel mahogany door was in the background behind Matt and him, then clicked a screen icon. The image flickered to life, revealing two female agents sitting in front of a black wall. Each woman wore navy-blue slacks and blazers over white crew neck T-shirts. Matt estimated both women were in their early thirties. Irving introduced herself and Special Agent Juanita Zamora, a specialist in white-collar crime.

Irving possessed a decent figure and wore her straightened black hair in that bob style where the ends curl forward under the ears. Her square jaw and high forehead eyes suggested intelligence and toughness.

Zamora was pretty but not strikingly so—wide, dark-brown eyes; full lips; turned-up nose; a pixie haircut with her mahogany hair parted on one side and swept across her high forehead. Shorter and slighter than Irving, her physique was lean and athletic. Matt guessed she'd been a competitive swimmer or runner in her school days, someone who still worked out daily. He also noticed Nowitzki checking her out with more than casual scrutiny.

Matt's throat tightened, and he swallowed with difficulty. This was a moment he'd not dared imagine during the last harrowing, stressful twelve months. He summoned his powers of concentration and attentiveness to prepare for explaining events clearly and discerning if the agents were buying his story. He wanted to believe this interview would be the first step in his redemption. But he steeled himself to the possibility it could send him on the run forever if the FBI didn't take up the case against Smythe.

Irving explained she'd checked with her boss, Special Agent in Charge Phil Ebner, who grudgingly allowed her to hear Matt's story and follow-up if necessary. Ebner had emphasized the need for hard evidence of a conspiracy before wasting the FBI's time and money on an investigation. Then Irving informed them she would record the meeting.

Her statement heightened Matt's concern that the FBI would trace him through this video conference. He gave Nowitzki a concerned look.

Nowitzki noticed, leaned toward him, and whispered, "Don't worry. I hooked up a VPN."

"A what?"

"Virtual Private Network. It messes up any tracking they might try to do by electronically hiding our location. I don't fully trust them."

Matt nodded and relaxed a bit. He massaged his fingers and tapped out a hard rock beat with his feet that mimicked his heartbeat and resembled the iconic *stomp-stomp-clap, stomp-stomp-clap* of Queen's megahit "We Will Rock You."

"Okay, let's start," Nowitzki said. "I'll briefly share my perspective. Let me speak non-stop so you get the complete synopsis. Then you can ask questions. After that, Matt will provide the details of his involvement with Smythe and his conspiracy. Any problems with the agenda?"

The agents shook their heads.

Nowitzki projected a take-charge attitude Matt found comforting despite Irving's earlier mention of Nowitzki being a disgraced cop. That characterization initially raised concerns about the shady PI who had once tried to kill him but now wanted to help. Maybe Nowitzki *was* a good guy at heart. After all, money had a way of corrupting otherwise honest, trustworthy people. Hell, Matt considered himself a good, honest person, but he'd been willing to sell out for a measly five grand. Nowitzki passed up a six-figure payday.

Nowitzki asked Irving and Zamora, "Did you both read the files on this case?"

"Only a quick scan so far," Irving said. "All police, coroner, and newspaper accounts in the Twin Cities, Duluth, and Ely. Even the *Straight River Press*. Gotta say they don't paint a pretty picture of your boy."

"I had the same impression," Nowitzki replied. "The knee-jerk assumption is either a cunning serial killer or mentally deranged man who went off the deep end. But as we all know, the rich and powerful often conceal truth and facts by using bribery, fraud, blackmail, and violence. Throw in well-connected politicians, and a false narrative is even easier to write.

Lanier's story is quite unbelievable unless you understand that most of his witnesses are dead."

Deftly omitting his original reason for tracking down Matt, Nowitzki summarized being hired by his anonymous client with the promise of a finder's fee if he succeeded. He then itemized the charges against Matt: first-degree murder for killing a Straight River policeman last year; killing two men in the Boundary Waters Canoe Area Wilderness; killing two more men at the hospital in Ely a few hours after he'd inexplicably brought them there for treatment of their gunshot wounds; shooting to death his ex-wife and a man to whom she'd recently been romantically linked and who also happened to be the Governor's chief of staff. When Nowitzki finished, Zamora jumped on his glossing over how and why he was hired to find Matt.

"You decided to look for a serial killer by yourself even though the state and local police were all over this case?" Her voice was reminiscent of the lower range of a viola. Subtle and rich.

Nowitzki nodded. "Correct. Except he's an *alleged* serial killer."

Zamora suppressed a scowl. "How long did it take?"

"I started several months ago."

That was true. However, Nowitzki didn't mention he'd actually found Matt twice. The first time, Matt had overpowered him and escaped.

"What made you think he'd be in Minneapolis?" Zamora asked. "He could've been anywhere in the world. And even with a ton of manpower and technology, the FBI can take years to find a suspected criminal. But you found him in a few months. *By yourself.*"

Zamora had unwittingly given Nowitzki an out. "My client believed Lanier was still in Minnesota. I did my research, made a few educated guesses, and wore out a lot of shoe leather. Sure, I got lucky. But luck equals preparation combined with opportunity, right?"

Zamora sat back with a look of dissatisfaction.

Irving cleared her throat. "You said *most* of the witnesses are dead. Do you intend to present any living witnesses to us?"

Nowitzki said, "That's Lanier's decision. He'll answer when it's his turn to talk."

Looking disgruntled, Irving then said, "Why do you believe Lanier is innocent of this long list of homicides?"

"Character references," Nowitzki said. "Lanier had some issues growing up. But he showed no signs of being a psychopath or sociopath. The key is what happened in Straight River that got him suspicious about Smythe. I talked to several folks who provided crucial details about crimes in the county that Lanier did not commit. His father was one of the victims."

"Patricide happens," Irving said. "Why do character references and hearsay clear him?"

"They don't," Nowitzki said. "But he found out a neighbor's autopsy was altered by the county coroner because the local police chief black-mailed her."

Matt suppressed a double take. Michael Flannery, the police chief, had confessed that fact to him in the Boundary Waters. Nowitzki could've known only by talking to the coroner, Dr. Anne Vincent, and persuading her to reveal that fact. For the first time that morning, Matt felt optimistic that he and Nowitzki could convince the FBI to investigate.

The agents exchanged surprised glances. Zamora checked her notes. "Which autopsy?"

"Helmer Myrick's," Nowitzki said. "A second autopsy was also falsi-fied."

"Pertaining to Lanier's case?" Irving asked.

"Lanier's father."

Matt spun in his chair to gawk at Nowitzki. "What?"

"Flannery told her to omit reference to a skull fracture inflicted by someone powerful enough to throw your father against the silo wall."

"Oh, God," Matt said, anguish in his voice. His father must have seen Witt coming up the silo ladder for him. He'd have been confused at first, then scared out of his mind. He pictured the hulking Witt grabbing his helpless father by the collar, slamming him against the metal wall of the silo, then tossing him into the fifty-foot pile of corn below like a rag doll. A wave of nausea grew in his stomach. He forced it down with several hard swallows.

"I'll let Matt take it from here," Nowitzki said. "He can explain everything—at least *his* version of everything. And you can pick apart his story as much as you need to."

The agents looked at Matt. He glanced at Maxwell, who'd been sitting quietly with a bemused expression on his face. Maxwell nodded reassuringly. Matt dried his sweaty palms on his jeans and shifted in his chair. *Where to begin? How to begin? From the beginning, I guess.*

After a nervous cough, he said, "Early last year, I was a normal guy. Middle-class lifestyle, divorced, distinguished career, some money in the bank. A modest version of the American Dream. Then my father died. I went home to settle his estate. While I was there, Dad's long-time neighbor, Helmer Myrick, was found hanging by his neck in his barn. His widow, Betty, insisted he never would've killed himself for two reasons. First, he was a God-fearing man who believed suicide was a sin. Second, he'd taken out a life insurance policy the year before to guarantee a farm machinery loan. The plan was to pay off the loan with the proceeds from his crop sales. Helmer was in poor health, so the Myricks bought the insurance in case he died before planting the crop. It was intended to provide for Betty so she wouldn't lose the farm."

Special Agent Irving interjected. "You ever hear of insurance fraud? Happens all the time."

Matt shook his head. "Uh-uh. Not Betty Myrick. She's the most honest, morally upright person I've ever met. She stepped in as a mother figure after my mother died from cancer. Betty helped me get my shit together before I went too far down the juvenile delinquent path. In my book, that act of love alone puts her on the short list for sainthood when she dies."

The agents exchanged dubious glances.

Matt tensed. "Betty asked me to check with the police and coroner in case there'd been a mistake or misunderstanding. It certainly looked like suicide, but now that we know the police chief blackmailed the coroner, the suicide was obviously staged. Then I found some documents my father had compiled about suspicious farm sales and did more research. He had a crazy theory about why these deals were happening. Something to do with a North American Superhighway."

Zamora blurted out, "A *what*?"

"A gigantic corridor that would expand upon the current Interstate 35. From Duluth to the Texas-Mexico border. Not just multiple vehicle lanes in each direction, but dedicated truck lanes, high-speed railroads, and space for power, water, natural gas, and oil pipelines. There'd be intersecting terminals and interchanges every thirty to fifty miles where trucks or trains could branch off or have their cargo offloaded to local or regional carriers for distribution."

"Sounds pretty futuristic to me," Irving said.

"Mega-freeways already exist in major cities," Matt said. "This expands on that concept. The obvious goal is more efficiency and lower cost to move goods and people around. But the ultimate goal is strategic in a geopolitical sense. That's where Smythe comes in."

"*Finally*," Nowitzki said. He'd been looking bored for most of Matt's story.

Zamora flicked her hand up to ask a question. "You believe he's the head of a group that's planning this superhighway?"

"Yeah," Matt said. "The group is called Millennium Four. If Smythe was using legal means to buy the land, I wouldn't be in this mess. But I know without a doubt that the man who tried to kill me three times worked for Smythe. I saw him once in Smythe's office. Then I got a glimpse of him when he tried to run me over with his SUV. I'm pretty sure he's the one who staged the explosion that destroyed my father's house, killed the cop, and put me in the hospital. At our last encounter, we exchanged gunshots at close range. He missed. I didn't."

The mention of the brief, bloody shootout activated panic in Matt's mind. Horrific visions of blood and thunderous echoes of gunshots swirled around his brain. But now that he knew how Witt had so callously, nonchalantly killed his father, he was almost glad he'd fired those extra shots at Witt's corpse. He inhaled deeply, trying to steady his trembling body.

Maxwell noticed and spoke for the first time since the start of the video-conference. "Matt, are you okay? Do you need some water?"

"Who else is there?" Irving demanded.

"I'm okay," Matt said to Maxwell. "Give me a minute."

Maxwell spoke louder but stayed off camera. "I'm Mr. Lanier's attorney, but I wish to remain anonymous for the time being."

Zamora opened her mouth to protest, but Irving put her hand on Zamora's arm. "I see," Irving said. "We don't intend to arrest or charge Mr. Lanier with any crimes at this point. Do you understand this meeting is strictly informational?"

"I do," Maxwell said. "Just remember to Mirandize him if you do manage to arrest him."

"I know the law, counselor," Irving said in a sharp-edged tone.

"I'm sure you do," Maxwell said. He sat back with a smirk and nodded at Matt.

Irving said, "Take your time, Mr. Lanier. We're in no hurry."

"Back to the conspiracy," Zamora said. "What led you to that discovery?"

Matt nodded and massaged his jaw with his good hand. He summarized his suspicions about Smythe's shell companies hiding his farm purchases. The common thread was that almost all land sales adjacent to I-35 had a suspicious element about them: the sudden death of an owner, an unexpected bankruptcy, or a loan foreclosure. That's when Matt had hired Zach Perez. Together they uncovered dozens of suspicious transactions in Minnesota, Iowa, and Missouri. Soon after, they decoded the missing link. All the names of the shell companies contained a variation of the word *green*. The controlling corporation was called Saxony Partners. Once they'd discovered that fact, a conspiracy was the logical conclusion.

Zamora said, "What about the shootout at Thompson Hill Rest Area between you and Steven Crossley? Do you think he was connected to Smythe?"

"Absolutely," Matt said. "My ex-wife dated Crossley for months until a week or two before she died. She heard him talking to Smythe over the phone on multiple occasions. She dismissed it as a high-ranking government official discussing legal business with Minnesota's richest real estate developer. When I shared my suspicions with her, she immediately deduced that Crossley had been helping Smythe by bringing political pressure to bear when needed. Covert pressure, of course, but undeniable."

Zamora said, "That raises the question *why*."

"If building a superhighway is going to happen, federal and state governments will be key players in funding and planning. Smythe's going after hundreds of small farms now so he can sell them *en masse* to the feds at sweetheart-deal prices. He expects to net billions in profits from those sales. But imagine if all those farmers got advance notice that a superhighway was going to be built on their land. Each farmer would either sue the government to leave their land alone or envision a major financial windfall and set an exorbitant selling price. With all those delays and inflated costs, the project would be scrapped."

Irving said, "Wouldn't the corporate landowners be tempted to do the same thing?"

Matt shrugged. "Some might be willing to sell a chunk of their land. Most would be forced into cooperating because tax and political pressure could easily be applied. Better to play their game than resist and be destroyed."

Zamora said, "You have a point, Mr. Lanier. I've seen it many times in my white-collar crime work. It's always about money and power."

"But we still need concrete evidence," Irving said. "Can you give us anything we can take to our boss?"

Matt said, "Since everyone involved in the gunfights is dead, I can't prove self-defense. However, two friends will affirm that I told them the same story I'm telling you."

"That's all well and good," Irving said, "but I'm not sure it's enough. Is there anything else you can give us?"

Matt's throat tightened. She was asking for his hole card—Zach Perez. If he gave them Maxwell first, maybe he wouldn't need Zach's corroboration. He glanced at Nowitzki, who had noticed he was conflicted.

"My lawyer has hard copies of my research," Matt said, "and a detailed account of what happened to me. My key evidence is a recording I made after the Boundary Waters shootout. Flannery confessed his connection with Smythe to me and Clay Gebhardt."

"Video?" Zamora asked.

"Audio. But Gebhardt's voice is on the tape too. And you might be able to find some notes or data he collected as a police officer when he was pursuing leads on Charlie Witt."

"That recording might be enough for us to continue," Irving said. "Can we hear it?"

Matt looked at Maxwell for reassurance. Maxwell nodded and moved his hand to his computer keyboard.

Nowitzki said, "Do it, Lanier. You gotta take that final leap of faith."

Matt massaged his injured fingers. He'd wanted this for almost a year, but he'd wanted Clay Gebhardt at his side when it happened. Sure, he was worried about his safety. But now he had a real chance to obtain justice for the dead friends and family lost during his attempts to stop Smythe. Quietly, somberly, he said, "Play the recording, Max."

Chapter 35

Special Agents Irving and Zamora sat in the office of their boss, Special Agent in Charge (SPAC) of the Minneapolis Field Office (MFO) Phil Ebner. The women exchanged nervous glances as Ebner read the transcript of Lanier's tape-recorded conversation between himself, Straight River Police Chief Michael Flannery, and Sergeant Clayton Gebhardt. Before meeting with Ebner, they'd discussed the odds of being allowed to pursue what could be a volatile, high-profile case. On the surface, it was a long shot. But they'd agreed that Lanier was believable and telling the truth. The hard part would be persuading Ebner to authorize an investigation—official or unofficial.

Ebner was a block of a man, above average in height, late fifties, with a jowly face and meaty hands. He favored three-piece suits and silk ties and liked to complain about the FBI's more relaxed dress code compared with what he called "the old days." Irving thought he looked like Jackie Gleason. Zamora had told her he resembled Paul Sorvino. But any celebrity resemblance faded when Ebner spoke. He had a thick southern accent, slightly tempered by his long tenure at the MFO after stints at the Omaha and Milwaukee Field Offices.

After tossing the transcript on his desk, Ebner looked at Irving. "Let's give a listen."

"Sure," Irving said and clicked *play* on her laptop. The three agents listened again through the entire tape, some twenty minutes long.

After it ended, Ebner said, "Go back to the part where Gebhardt asks Flannery about why Smythe told him all the conspiracy details."

Irving clicked backward on the timeline, found the right spot in the recording, and hit *play*.

GEBHARDT: You're a small-town police chief. Why the hell would Smythe tell you all these secret details?

FLANNERY: I didn't know until a few days ago. Once Smythe decided Witt needed my help to kill you, I demanded a damn good reason to put not only my career, but also my life on the line.

GEBHARDT: You're willing to obstruct justice and commit murder, all for a better job?

FLANNERY: Not just a job, a significant law enforcement position. Chief of police in Minneapolis. Chicago after that.

LANIER: Did Witt kill my father?

FLANNERY: Yes.

LANIER: How?

FLANNERY: Witt opened the silo hatch late one night, then waited in the woods until Ray noticed it early the next morning. He knew no one else was around at that time and figured Ray would climb up himself to close the hatch. Once Ray started climbing, Witt came out, forced him to the top at gunpoint, and pushed him in. The corn did the rest.

LANIER: Did Hibbert kill Myrick and make it look like a suicide?

FLANNERY: Hell, no. (coughing sound) Myrick had a heart attack.

LANIER: Why did the autopsy confirm suicide?

FLANNERY: Witt was at the Eagles Club that night keeping an eye on Hibbert. Myrick collapsed and died in the parking lot. Witt called Smythe for instructions. Smythe knew about the bank loan and their insurance policy. When Betty went bankrupt, Smythe planned to take her farm for pennies on the dollar. Smythe told Witt and Hibbert to drive Myrick's body back to his farm and string him up. He told me to blackmail Dr. Vincent and force her to falsify the autopsy results.

LANIER: What happened to Hibbert?

FLANNERY: I didn't ask, but Witt left town for a few days. I'm pretty sure he tossed Hibbert off that cliff in the Black Hills.

"That's enough," Ebner said, pushing back from his desk and staring out his window.

Irving pressed *stop* and glanced at Zamora. Her raised eyebrows and pursed lips implied she hoped Ebner would give them the go-ahead to open an official investigation.

"Did the sound tech verify this was unedited?" Ebner asked, looking at his agents.

"Yes," Irving said.

"And the background noise—the wind, the birds, the squirrel or chipmunk that was caterwauling in the first few minutes—that was all real?"

Zamora said, "We obviously need to obtain the physical tape and the recorder to confirm its authenticity. But my first impression of Lanier is that he's not so deluded that he'd go to these extreme lengths to concoct this crazy-ass story. If he's out to get Smythe for no good reason, this is stalking in the first degree. Plus, he's got verified physical wounds from his alleged encounters with Smythe's men. Also, Nowitzki told us privately after the video conference that two of Lanier's friends claim he has PTSD."

"Hmm," Ebner said, furrowing his brow. "Let's say we make a case against Smythe. Go to trial. Put Lanier on the witness stand. What if he freaks out? Goes into a shell or a trance? Withers under a few minutes of pressure from the defense attorney?"

"A definite possibility," Irving said. She was far less gung ho on this case than Zamora, but still wanted to support her. "But the tape is solid evidence. And we should be able to find *some* dirt on Smythe. There's always a weak link, right? Someone cracks under pressure and rats him out. Or he made a mistake somewhere, and we find it. A loophole. An incriminating document."

"I can't imagine the tape holding up in court," Ebner said. "I reckon the defense'll claim Lanier and Gebhardt were pointing pistols at Flannery's head during the entire interview."

Zamora said, "But now we can check records and other data from everyone connected with the case who was killed. Even this Hibbert character. The local police didn't have any reason to check because they didn't know what to look for. They had no idea a conspiracy was the common denominator surrounding all the deaths."

"True," Ebner said. "But our big problem is we're bound by law to arrest Lanier on suspicion of murdering that cop in the explosion."

Zamora looked at Irving, frustration showing in her eyes. The tension between both women and Ebner was thick. They'd foreseen Ebner's objections and hesitation as they prepared for this meeting. They'd also discussed putting their careers on the line with this long-shot case. They enjoyed living and working in Minneapolis for the FBI. What they didn't enjoy was working for Ebner. And they knew he didn't want them working for him because they were women in what he saw as a male-only profession. Compounding that friction was Ebner's planned retirement in three years. He didn't want to do anything stupid like authorizing an investigation that might embarrass the Bureau and push him out the door prematurely. The Rule of 85 was a powerful motivator to not screw up.

On the other hand, Irving and Zamora had much to gain and little to lose by working this case. If they backed off, they'd remain near the bottom of the MFO pecking order for the next few years until Ebner retired. But breaking this case would shoot them up to the top of the list and open the door for promotions and better assignments. They'd decided to gamble.

Irving said, "Sir, what if Juanita and I work this case off the record? Give us one computer tech to help us obtain records we think may be helpful. If nothing comes of it, we drop it. If we get any incriminating evidence, you tell Washington we got a confidential tip and want to do a full investigation. If they give us the okay, we give Lanier immunity in exchange for his testimony."

Irving scanned Ebner's face for a reaction. He'd steepled his fingertips together and rested his chin on his thumbs. Otherwise, he showed no emotion. She said, "This could be your big chance to get rid of us."

His eyes widened at her presumption, but he said nothing.

"If we fuck up, you can either transfer us to the hinterlands or fire us for insubordination."

He dropped his hands into his lap, narrowed his eyes, and leaned back in his chair. "That rascal's been on the Bureau's radar for years. Nailing him would be a terrific way to close my career."

Gotcha! Irving thought. She knew that the idea of a career-capping score was important to Ebner. That, along with his typical male ego and bureaucrat's penchant for shifting responsibility and avoiding blame whenever possible, played perfectly into their gamble.

"We shouldn't have a problem swearing Lanier and his friends to secrecy," Zamora said. "Lanier's been running for more than a year. Any shred of hope we can give him will guarantee he'll keep himself and his friends quiet."

Irving nodded in agreement. But she worried about Nowitzki. His rep as a Minneapolis cop had been that of a hot dog, a showoff, someone who craved the spotlight and aspired to be the superstar. She would still trust him with her life in a dangerous situation, but years had passed since that trust had been tested. Something was missing from the story he'd given her about tracking down Lanier. Was Nowitzki still vulnerable to being bribed? If so, this time it might be to sell out either her, Zamora, or Lanier himself.

"Reggie?" Zamora asked.

"Oh, yeah, sorry," Irving said. "I was concentrating on something." She looked at Ebner. "If you give us the go-ahead, we'll start our investigation today."

"Y'all realize you believe a man who's a suspected *cop* killer, don't you?"

"The explosion?" Irving said. "The police and fire department reports both concluded it was a remote detonation. Anyone within range could have triggered the blast. It's hard to believe Lanier would stand twenty feet from the house, almost get himself blown up, then still be able to hide the detonator and electronics before the authorities arrived."

Ebner fiddled with a pen on his desk, tapping the tip against his writing blotter. "What about all the shootings?"

"He admitted pulling the trigger in those gunfights," Zamora said, "but that doesn't prove or even suggest premeditation."

"He grew up country," Ebner said, "and country folk think differently than city folk. Might be he got pissed off about the house explosion and his father dying, and he wanted revenge." His eyebrows flicked upward, contemplating the possibility.

"Lanier doesn't strike us as vengeful," Zamora said. She glanced at Irving, who nodded.

"Give us a couple of days, sir," Irving said. Right or wrong, she wanted to work on a case that might achieve actual justice and prevent further loss of lives and livelihoods.

Ebner had a smug yet somehow also concerned expression on his face. He pointed a finger at them, pistol style. "I can't give y'all any tech support. You can use the FBI databases, but otherwise, use your personal computers. Also, I don't want to see any notes, documents, or anything related to the case in this office unless and until y'all give me something ironclad against Smythe. And this conversation never happened. Is that clear?"

"Yes, sir," the women said in unison. They exchanged their own glances of concern. He'd called their bluff. This officially *unauthorized* case would play out one of two ways: fast-tracked careers or no careers at all.

Chapter 36

Matt, Hypo, and Hawk were eating breakfast the following morning when Hawk's phone rang. He answered, listened, said, "Yeah, he's here," and handed the phone to Matt. "Your PI friend."

Matt took the phone, set down his coffee cup, and said, "What's up?"

"The FBI's on board … unofficially."

"What do you mean *unofficially*?"

Hypo and Hawk stopped chewing and leaned forward.

"Irving and Zamora are in," Nowitzki said, "but if things go south, their boss will deny any knowledge of their activities."

Matt sighed. "I guess it's better than nothing. What's our next move?"

"Put me on speaker first."

Matt pressed the appropriate button, then set the phone on the table. "Go ahead."

"They want to meet all three of you in person."

"Where?" Matt said.

"A secure site that's safe for all of us."

"And where the hell might that be?" Hypo asked. He cracked a grin at Hawk, who pressed his lips into a shape that barely qualified as a smile.

"Zamora's house," Nowitzki said. "Irving says she's a security freak, so the place is about as safe as the Situation Room in the White House."

"Won't do it," Matt said with all the finality he could muster. "They're obligated to arrest me if they get the chance."

"But this is an off-the-record meeting. They're doing this as private citizens."

"Forget it, Nowitzki. I'll do all the virtual meetings they want."

"But—"

"Virtual only. Not negotiable."

During the long silence that followed, Matt regarded Hypo and Hawk. Their expressions implied they were comfortable meeting the FBI in person. *Screw 'em if they're on Nowitzki's side. They're not risking jail time or worse.*

Nowitzki exaggerated a sigh. "Fine. Virtual it is. But can *I* meet with them in person? I want to pursue a lead, and a federal agent will come in handy for getting faster cooperation."

"Do whatever *you* want. But if someone sticks a gun to your head and forces you to lead them to me, I'll kill you." Matt hoped he sounded sufficiently menacing, but he knew that Nowitzki knew it was mostly hyperbole.

"Irving still owes me until we get you off the hook, so she'll cooperate."

"Okay," Matt said. "I'll trust you, although I'm still struggling with why I should."

"Can I come over there to set up the video meeting? Irving wants to move fast on this."

Matt looked at his host.

Hawk saluted him with his coffee cup. "Anything to help."

Nowitzki said, "I'll be there in twenty minutes."

Thirty minutes later, the four men sat on one side of Hawk's kitchen table, focused on Nowitzki's laptop. On-screen, Irving and Zamora sat in what looked like someone's living room. They both wore jeans and T-shirts instead of the FBI uniform they'd worn yesterday.

"We worked until early this morning reviewing Lanier's case," Irving said. "The FBI information is restricted, but we can tell you Smythe has been on our radar for years. We've been searching for income tax irregularities because his legal team is highly skilled at camouflaging the true finances of Smythe Properties."

"I noticed that too when I was with the MPD," Nowitzki said. "Some detectives looked into commercial real estate transactions downtown. One seller claimed a big-shot developer bribed three different appraisers to lowball the property value so he could save a million bucks on the deal. When we talked to the appraisers, they denied being bribed. But one of them had this look in his eyes I'll never forget. Fear combined with shame. The guy could barely make eye contact. Like he wanted to speak up but didn't for a reason worse than admitting he took a bribe."

Hypo asked, "Like he was a pervert, and the developer literally caught him with his pants down?"

Nowitzki nodded and crinkled a corner of his mouth. "My gut told me he was blackmailed. I can imagine Smythe pulling shit like that."

Matt asked, "How easy is it to access data on Smythe's employees?"

"Tough unless a crime has been committed," Zamora said. "Law enforcement can always ask nicely, but the owner has every right to refuse. Why?"

"Charlie Witt *must've* been on Smythe's payroll," Matt said. "He drove a new Mercedes Benz SUV, had access to weapons and explosives, and spent plenty of time hanging around Straight River while I was there. Then he and Flannery came after me in a brand-new canoe and gear with guns blazing. Trying to kill me became a full-time job for him. No one does that on their own dime without a good reason. I'd never seen Witt before I met him in Smythe's office, so there wasn't any personal animosity between us."

"Matt," Irving said, "you hinted at receiving some outside help to uncover Millennium Four last year. Some computer searches, correct?"

Matt tensed. He had to mention Zach eventually, but still hated the idea of involving the kid again after almost getting him killed last year. "Yes," he said. "Why?"

"Despite having a small army of cyber specialists, we can't use FBI computers other than to access our various databases. But tracking Witt's financial situation will be much easier online."

"Go on."

"Would your helper be willing to do some *unofficial* research for us?"

Matt looked at his friends. Nowitzki surreptitiously ogled Zamora, which he'd been doing throughout most of the meeting. Hypo gave him a non-committal shrug. Hawk folded his arms and tucked his chin down. His eyes shone as though they were glowing from within. For an instant, Matt believed the old Army Sergeant was telepathically sending him some advice, and he was pretty sure what it would be.

His stomach churned with indecision. He didn't want to put Zach into a dangerous situation. But Zach's talent was the reason they'd gotten this close to stopping Smythe. And with at least some FBI protection, the risk might be small enough to manage. After running his fingers through his hair and exhaling through puffed-out cheeks, Matt said, "I'll give him a call."

"Heck yeah, I'm in," Zach said without hesitation when Matt called and asked if he'd do some more computer work on Smythe and Millennium Four to help the FBI. "Things were okay for the first few months after you left. I called Maxwell every week and never noticed anything suspicious. But the constant worry about waking up every day and wondering if that was the day Smythe would kill me was dragging me down. I got depressed and struggled with school. Couldn't stop imagining what it would feel like to get shot or strangled or pushed off a bridge. So if I can help end this mess, I'm all in, *amigo*."

Matt arched his eyebrows and looked at his friends. "Well, then ... great."

"And the F-B-freakin'-I. How awesome is that?"

Matt hadn't thought someone would be so eager to work with a federal agency. *The innocence of youth?* "Don't get too excited, kid. It's not as if they'll give you a gun and a badge. Your work will be strictly off-the-record."

"Still, it's valuable experience. Like an internship. If I do well, there might be a job offer down the road."

Matt chuckled. *Definitely the innocence of youth.* He said, "One step at a time, *amigo*."

"Yeah, yeah, I get it. So what do they want me to do?"

"Come to Hawk's place first. Our command HQ. We don't want to know where you live. That way, if the worst happens ..."

Silence. Then Zach said, "Thanks. I appreciate it."

"And it goes without saying, you need to give us your best spy impersonation and tell no one where you're going or what you're doing. Is that possible?"

"Yeah, I've got my own place again. It's not much, but I'm working more hours on campus and got a generous scholarship for my last year, so I can afford the rent."

Matt gave him Hawk's address. Within an hour, Zach knocked on the front door. When Matt let him in, Zach gasped, wide-eyed. The last time they'd seen each other, Matt was clean-shaven, had short hair, and wore fresh, clean clothes. Now his clothes were worn and stained, and his shaggy hair and beard, leaner physique, and haggard eyes had probably aged him twenty years in Zach's eyes. Then he shocked Matt by giving him a tight, heartfelt bear hug.

"When you called," Zach said, "I thought Smythe might be playing a trick, like he'd hired someone who sounded like you to draw me out. I needed to see you to believe you're still alive."

Matt returned the hug. "I'm so glad you're safe. That's been my constant worry for a year."

Zach waved him off. "I'm good. Been working out a little. Took a self-defense class." He cracked a grin. "I actually have a bulge in my biceps now."

Matt laughed and led him into the kitchen, where he made the introductions, both in-person to the men and virtually to the women. Hawk brought out snacks and bottled water and refilled the coffee pot.

Zach's eyes widened when he saw Special Agent Zamora through the laptop screen, as if he were surprised to meet a Latina federal agent. After accepting a water, Zach said, "What exactly do you want me to do?"

Special Agent Irving explained the unofficial nature of their investigation and how the FBI computers and experts were off-limits until they'd found solid evidence to open an official investigation.

"That's cool," Zach said. "Sounds pretty much like what I did for Matt."

Irving looked at the camera intently. "Except we're asking you to work on the edge of legality here. Nothing we can't explain away to our boss. At the same time, we don't want any internal FBI records of this work."

"Okay," Zach said and glanced at Matt. Apprehension showed in his eyes. This hacking would be several degrees more consequential than his discreet hacking into the Minneapolis city website to erase a few traffic tickets, something he'd casually mentioned to Matt last spring that "proved" his hacker qualifications.

Matt said, "While we were waiting for you to get here, we generated a playbook of steps to try. The first few are relatively safe and easy. If those don't pan out, we go to the next step, and the next, and so on. The risk of getting found out increases as we go. The goal is to find conclusive evidence that links Smythe to either Witt, Flannery, or Crossley."

Zach nodded, looked at Matt, then at the others. He seemed to notice Hypo's missing fingers for the first time, but he suppressed whatever visceral reaction he may have had. His gaze lingered on the FBI agents. Pursing his lips, Zach said, "So this is real—and serious."

Matt put his hand on Zach's shoulder and squeezed. "This is my last shot, kid. We've all got a small part to play in a big script. Everyone here believes in me now, not just you and Maxwell. I've got a real chance to take the bastard down. I don't know why they give a shit about me. Maybe they don't. Maybe all they give a shit about is putting a major-league crook behind bars. The fact that we all came together in such an unpredictable way gives me more faith than I've had since before my mother died."

Hawk cleared his throat. Even seated, he had a quiet, commanding presence that surpassed everyone else's. "I can't speak for the others, Matt, but I give a shit about you because you seek the truth, and you want to live an honorable, moral life with integrity and honesty. No one can fake those qualities, at least not with me. You're worth helping, and if stopping Smythe helps you find peace, then I'm all in."

Everyone went silent until Zach said, "I'm here because you saved my ass after things got out of control. I owe you my life, even though you're the one who first put me at risk. I was naïve going in, but not now. I've thought about this for a year. I decided there's more to life than money, a job, and living well. You gotta have a reason to live. Might as well do good, help people, because if no one helped each other, we'd have anarchy. And you're a cool dude too."

Zamora sat back and folded her arms. "That's all heartwarming—all violins and touchy-feely, but I'm working on a career. I intend to bust a hell of a lot more crooks bigger than Smythe in the future. So far, all we have is a convincing story that may or may not be true. So until we get some solid evidence, I'm stuck working with a bunch of amateurs and has-beens." She glanced at Hawk and Hypo. "Nothing personal, guys." Looking at Nowitzki with a frosty glare, she added, "And I did my homework on you too. I wasn't impressed."

Zamora had always seemed more suspicious of them than Irving had been. But this was the first time she'd hinted at less than a complete buy-in of this investigation.

Irving said, "Please remember that JZ and I are gambling with our careers, our livelihoods. If this blows up in our faces, you all go on your merry way—except for Lanier, of course. We could be demoted, put on the invisible shit list of agents who'll never move up the ranks, or get fired."

"Look," Matt said. "I realize everyone in the room is taking a risk for me. It's still early in the game. Let's go one step at a time and see what happens." He focused on Irving and Zamora. "Allow Zach to do his magic for a day or two. And I have a few ideas I'd like to pursue. After that, if the FBI thinks we can't get this to an official investigation, you can bail out. I'll thank you for trying and keep plugging away on my own. No one owes me anything. You're simply honorable people who still believe in truth and justice."

Hypo turned on his street persona. "My man speakin' the truth, brothas and sistas. He talkin' dyin'. We talkin' 'bout nothin' nearly as bad." As quick as he'd turned it on, he turned it off. "I'm in because nothing worse can happen to me than what happened in Afghanistan. Even though I'm ex-CIA, my mama hardwired me to fight for the underdog. Matt's the biggest underdog I've ever known. He's got every cop in the state looking for him, and one of the most powerful men outside of the federal government is trying to kill him. Not quite as big as tracking down bin Laden, but a helluva challenge."

After glancing sidelong at Irving, Zamora cocked an eyebrow at Hypo. "Who *are* you?"

He chuckled—three short staccato bursts. As he primped his short curly hair, he said, "Only my hairdresser knows for sure."

Zamora's expression showed puzzlement and frustration.

Hawk said, "Trust me, Special Agent Zamora. In the battle we're going into, you definitely want this man on your side."

"That's my problem," she said. "I've never had good luck trusting strangers."

Chapter 37

Smythe tapped the number into his burner phone keypad and waited. After three rings and a disinterested "Hello" on the other end, he said, "This is Jones. Your two weeks are up. Did you fulfill your end of the contract?"

Nowitzki was silent for several seconds before saying, "No."

Ever since Nowitzki's earlier call, Smythe had suspected something was amiss. The delay between Nowitzki's first failure to kill Lanier and his request to try again was suspicious. Why hadn't he immediately gotten back on Lanier's trail? The longer he waited, the harder it would be to find him. Plus, Nowitzki's failed career as a cop and his mediocre private investigator business suggested someone desperate enough to concoct any sort of scam for easy money. Nowitzki had quickly found Lanier on the North Shore, so his tracking skills were adequate. What disappointed Smythe and raised his suspicions was Nowitzki's questionable ability and willingness to kill.

"You've failed twice," Smythe said. "And both times, you seemed so confident. The last time we spoke, you all but guaranteed success."

"Desperate men can be resourceful."

"*My* experience is that desperate men make lots of mistakes."

"The world's a big place, Jones. Lots of places for someone to hide."

"Regardless, I'm disappointed. I trust you'll honor our deal by keeping your mouth shut about this matter and skulking back whence you came."

"A deal's a deal."

"If you don't, I'll remind you that your future will be quite bleak. Moribund, actually."

"Understood."

Smythe feigned a smile so he could force some cheeriness into his voice. "Of course, if you give me any intelligence you've collected regarding this case, you'll at least have a future."

"Even though that wasn't in our contract, it's a moot point. I hit a dead end."

"Did you now?"

"My leads were bogus. Mistaken identity."

Smythe maintained his forced cheer. "Perhaps you should find another line of work."

After a long silence, Nowitzki said, "Anything else?"

When the second man in the small office gave Smythe a thumbs-up, Smythe said, "No. Goodbye."

After ending the call, he spoke to the Smythe Properties technician who'd successfully triangulated Nowitzki's location from his cell phone. "Well done. The test worked perfectly. You may leave."

After the tech departed, Smythe faced the third man in the room, Ivan Volkov, who'd been observing the technician during the call. Volkov said, "According to the map, he's in Northeast Minneapolis. It's late, so we'll assume he's staying in a motel or with a friend."

Smythe opened the dossier he'd compiled on Nowitzki late last year and handed Volkov a photo of the man and a slip of paper containing the license plate number of Nowitzki's car. As Volkov studied the documents, Smythe said, "He drives a gray Ford Taurus with this license plate number. Take two men, find him, watch his car, and follow him wherever he goes. Report back on any of his stops, even if he only buys gas or fast food."

Volkov said, "Yes, sir," and headed for the door.

Before Volkov opened the door, Smythe said, "Call me as soon as you find him."

Chapter 38

Matt and Zach were at Zach's apartment the next day, working on the cyber angles of accessing data that might show Charlie Witt's employment history with Smythe Properties. Zach had insisted on using his place because his computer setup was state-of-the-art fast and powerful. No doubt he wanted to show it off virtually to Special Agent Irving too. *Never hurts to lay the groundwork for a potential job interview.* After establishing another video chat connection, Zach gave Irving the thirty-second explanation of his machine's power and capabilities. To Matt, he said, "I've been researching Smythe since the day you left town. I'm obsessed with learning everything I can about him. Might give me a slight advantage in case he tries to kill me again."

Matt raised his eyebrows, surprised and concerned. He'd wanted Zach to live a normal life and not fear for his life every day. Knowing Zach had been so stressed the last twelve months raised his ire once again for Smythe's continued disruption of so many lives.

"What did you learn?" Irving asked.

"Not much. His personal cyber presence is almost nonexistent. But Smythe Properties is all over the internet and old-school media. They've made several big deals and are talking about a few more in the future that focus on urban redevelopment. I figure it's a public relations ploy. Hype all the new jobs he'll create in the building trades, more affordable housing units, all that stuff. He's been photographed at a lot of meetings, groundbreaking ceremonies, and social events."

Matt sensed Zach wasn't sharing everything he'd learned. He also suspected Zach of withholding some of his methods.

Irving narrowed her eyes. "So why are we here if all you've got is information anyone can read in the *Star Tribune* or a business magazine?"

Zach looked down and away. "It's just that …"

Matt said, "You won't get busted for what you've done so far or what you might do for us, kid. Trust me."

Glancing sidelong at Matt, Zach said, "I tried hacking Smythe Properties several times but got nowhere. I would've tried a social engineering hack, but I'm lousy at pretending I'm someone else."

"Social engineering?" Matt asked. He'd heard the term before, but wasn't sure what it meant.

Irving educated him. "Social engineering refers to hacking into a website by tricking someone into giving you information such as passwords and usernames. You can also trick them into opening attachments on emails the hacker has implanted with spyware or a computer virus."

Matt said, "Sounds risky."

"It can be," Zach said, "unless the hacker is a fast talker, and a convincing actor, and knows what to say in certain situations."

"If this backfires on us, will Smythe find out?"

"Depends on how security conscious he is. But I can prevent him from knowing *we're* doing the hacking."

"Making them nervous might give us an edge. If Smythe believes we're on offense, he's more likely to panic and make a mistake."

"Has he made any mistakes yet?" Irving asked.

Matt slumped his shoulders. "None that I ever noticed, other than using a lame common thread for his shell companies that we quickly deciphered. And his choice of Hibbert working on the farmers in Straight County was suspect too. But Hibbert might have begged his way in because he was desperate for money. Maybe if he had lived …"

That was the problem: Smythe was highly efficient at eliminating all liabilities—witnesses like Hibbert, Flannery, and Gebhardt, who all knew too much to be allowed to live. Especially Flannery. Even though his recorded confession might not hold up in court, it was more than enough to put Smythe away for a long time—maybe for life.

Nowitzki returned to Zach's apartment in midafternoon. He and Zamora had worked the Charlie Witt angle of the case for two days. He connected with Special Agent Irving via Zoom, then quickly updated her, Matt, and Zach. State motor vehicle records led them to Witt's last known address, an apartment in Hopkins, a western suburb not far from Smythe Properties.

Nowitzki said, "The superintendent said a moving van and crew showed up a few days after Witt died and cleaned out his apartment. We got the name of the movers, visited their office, and talked to the manager. With a persuasive flash of Zamora's creds, he gave us the address of the storage facility where the truck delivered its load."

"Did you find anything useful in his belongings?" Matt asked.

Nowitzki shook his head. "The storage compartment was empty."

Matt's mood soured. "Great. No chance of finding any old paycheck stubs or 401(k) statements from Smythe Properties."

"Hold on, Lanier," Nowitzki said. "Zamora and I aren't raw rookies, you know. We cornered the storage facility owner and had an unofficial chat with him. He remembered the day another truck showed up and emptied Witt's storage garage."

"And the truck had *Smythe Properties* printed on the sides?"

"Not quite. But the manager remembers checking the monthly billing spreadsheet at the end of that month and noticed that the rent for Witt's storage space had been paid for by none other than Saxony Partners."

Matt almost sprang out of his chair with excitement.

Irving said, "Smythe's shell corporation, right?"

"Yep," Nowitzki said. "We got a solid connection to Smythe Properties. It doesn't prove Witt was an employee, but this isn't a coincidence."

"We gotta follow that lead," Matt said. "But how?" He turned to his computer expert. "Any ideas, Zach?"

"As a matter of fact …" Zach said. "My obsession this past year led me to learn his organizational structure and who the key players are. That led me to a friend of a friend who knows someone in tech support."

"So call your friend and ask for a small favor," Matt said, suddenly impatient. "Have them check on a former employee named Witt."

Zach shook his head. "That might've worked fifty years ago. Today, most records are confidential. Any breach of an employee's privacy rights can lead to a lawsuit."

After seeing a nod of confirmation from Irving, Matt said, "Okay, can we sneak in?"

Zach said, "If we can work a little social engineering phone scam on the tech support guy ..." He fidgeted with his hands as he glanced at Irving.

"This is where it gets dicey," Irving said. "Scamming him to get a password is one thing. But if you use it to gain access to the Smythe Properties computer system, Zamora and I can't be connected in any way. What you'll be attempting is illegal."

"Ah." Matt mentally slapped his forehead. "So if *we* break into Smythe's system without your knowledge, what do we do with any information we find?"

"We can't advise you on that either. But I assume you'll know what to do."

Nowitzki said, "I got it covered, Reggie."

"With that," Irving said, "I'll leave you three to your business and brief JZ about this conversation. Good luck." She closed her video connection, and silence filled Zach's apartment.

"Now that she's gone," Nowitzki said, "will you excuse us, Zach? I need to talk to Matt alone."

Zach glanced at Matt—who had no idea why Nowitzki wanted to talk in private—then quickly said, "Sure. I'll go to the can."

"Thanks," Nowitzki said.

"What's up?" Matt said after Zach was out of earshot.

"Smythe called me the other night," Nowitzki said softly. "Reminded me my contract was up. He's never called me before other than when he first hired me. My bullshit radar lit up like a spotlight. He was talking like he didn't think I had tried hard enough to kill you. He might've traced my location by triangulating my cell phone."

"If he succeeded, he could have found you, right?"

Nowitzki nodded. "He knows my car and license plate number, so I went to a rental car company and got some new wheels. Then I parked my car in a nearby strip mall. We should be safe for the time being, but we're dealing with a master crook. The sooner we bust him, the better."

"Thanks for telling me," Matt said, feeling his energy and optimism wane. "As if this entire operation wasn't tough enough, the son of a bitch keeps finding ways to make it tougher."

"Tell me about it," Nowitzki said. He summoned Zach back to the room, clapped his hands once, and warily eyed his host. "Okay, techie whiz kid, how do we do this phone scam?"

Zach said, "I set up a spoof website for this job. Then I set up a phone number that resembles other numbers used by Smythe Properties. All company phones have the same prefix, and the company's big enough that no one can know all the phone numbers. We'll call tech support from our spoof number. Then we say we need to get into the fake site to help close a deal because a wealthy client wants the salesman to research a competitor. Something like that. I don't know if that's the best scenario."

Matt sat up in his chair. "So the tech guy checks the spoof website, thinking you're a legitimate employee, and when he types in the password you give him for the fake site, you what?"

"Gain access to *his* computer. Which means we gain access to the entire Smythe Properties computer system."

"Whoa," Nowitzki said. "You think you can pull it off that easily?"

Zach shook his head. "*I* can't." He pointed at Matt. "But *he* can."

"Me?" Matt exclaimed. "Why me?"

"Because I suck at thinking fast on my feet. We can't predict what the techie will say, so we gotta go with the flow. In other words, *improvise*."

Matt's eyebrows involuntarily shot upward. "Oh. Right." But it had been a long time since he'd improvised anything, let alone in a life or death situation like this. "Man, I dunno. My improv chops are pretty damn rusty."

Zach shook his head. "I listened to a lot of your jazz music in the last year. I also checked with some guys at the University of Minnesota's School of Music. Some said you're one of the best jazz bassists in the country."

"They lie," Matt said. "There are hundreds of brilliant jazz musicians on all instruments. But no one ever hears about them because—well, because it's jazz and hardly anyone listens to it."

"I'm with the whiz kid here, Lanier," Nowitzki said. "You've been a pro for decades. You don't lose that skill in a year. Sure, you might be rusty, but we have the advantage of practicing several different conversations and preparing for all possibilities."

"But I don't know shit about being a salesman."

"Worst case," Zach said, "the guy gets suspicious and hangs up. If he checks the phone number, he'll get a voice mail prompt with your voice on it. If he gets extra suspicious and tries to trace the phone, he'll hit a dead end because it's a burner." Zach noticed Matt's questioning look and explained. "A throwaway phone for short-term use. I'll either remove the sim card, or we'll turn the phone off and toss it in a dumpster."

"Oh," Matt said, then faced Nowitzki. "You ever done something like this before?"

Nowitzki shrugged. "Smythe used burner phones when I was tracking you. At least that's what he said. He gave me a new number to call each time, so I believed him."

Matt did a drumroll with his fingers on his thighs and studied the worn carpet. Doubt and hopefulness fought a brief battle in his mind. "Okay, I'm ready to try this."

Smiles from Zach and Nowitzki boosted his confidence. Zach certainly knew what he was doing. And Nowitzki had plenty of street smarts. If either of them smelled something fishy, they'd undoubtedly tell him to cut the call before disaster struck.

Over the next hour, they worked out a basic script of what Matt would say, along with possible responses from the Smythe Properties tech support person. Zach had dealt with dozens of computer techs over his young computing career and had done lots of tech support for friends and family, so he played the practice role of the company techie. Nowitzki schooled Matt on some real estate basics he'd learned after inheriting the duplex in Duluth, where he grew up. After his mother died, Nowitzki learned to manage the other unit and knew about property taxes, mortgages, loan rates, and closing costs.

Matt practiced pretending to be a new hire in the company, trying to close a big deal with a customer. That part was easy enough, but he worried about being asked questions concerning specific people in the company—mainly his direct supervisor or someone with whom everyone was familiar.

At the end of the hour, all three were convinced of Matt's ability to improvise the role of a sales rep. Their final ace in the hole was that Smythe Properties was large enough to have several tech support personnel. If the friend of Zach's friend didn't fall for their story, they'd simply redial the tech support number until they got a different person on the line.

"Ready when you are," Zach said. "The fake website is live. You've got the password and several script outlines, and the timing is good. The shift change starts in ten minutes, so whoever we talk to will be motivated to clear this request before they leave."

Nowitzki said, "The phone'll be on speaker. We'll listen and help if you get stuck."

Matt looked from Zach to Nowitzki and back to Zach. Each had confidently noncommittal expressions. Matt said, "I guess it's time to mess with a millionaire."

Chapter 39

Their first two attempts to find a compliant person in tech support were quickly aborted when the responders asked for Matt's full name, department, and immediate supervisor—details Zach hadn't thought would be necessary. After Zach flashed the throat-cutting sign with his hand, Matt said, "Oops, sorry. Thought I dialed accounting," and clicked off.

The third time, if not the charm, at least started out more promising.

"Tech support. Baumgartner. How can I help you?"

Matt focused his concentration as if he'd just stepped on stage with his old trio for a big performance. *Improvise! You got this, Matty.* Speaking rapidly, he forced mild panic into his voice, hoping to convey a sense of urgency and gloss over his identity and position. "Yeah, hi, this is Johnson up in the commercial department. I'm desperate, and I've got an *enormous* problem that might get me fired if I don't fix it fast."

"What kind of problem?" Baumgartner asked. He had a get-to-the-point voice, a rapid-fire staccato monotone reminiscent of a snare drummer tapping out various rhythms.

"Well, Mister Bomb—um, Boom—um, you got a first name?"

"Justin."

"Much better. So here's the deal, Justin. I'm new. A week on the job. Still having trouble learning the computer system. Boss Lady's working on a major deal with a big-name client. But the client is a first-class asshole. Know what I mean? She can't stand him, but hey, this sale will make her year, she says. The client wants some fancy-pants data from a certain website. Boss Lady told me to get it for Mr. Asshole Client because—get this—she's got a hot date with her husband and doesn't want to be late. Typical management, right? Dump the crap work on the new guy."

"Okayyy," said Justin. "But what do you need help with?"

"It's this computer system, you know? I learned on Macs at my old job, so I figured no problem. But *nooo*. This place uses PCs. It's like learning English but then being expected to know how to speak Portuguese. *Comprendo?*"

"What's your name again?"

"Well, maybe not Portuguese, but German for sure."

"Who'd you say your boss is?"

"Stupid PCs. If this company wasn't so tight with its budget, we'd all use Macs, and I'd be in line for a bonus. What I really need is a tutorial so I can figure out this damn website and all the other websites Boss Lady'll send me to for work."

"A *tutorial*?"

"I figure a half hour. I know I don't sound like it, but I'm a quick learner."

"Izzat so?" Justin sounded more annoyed by the minute.

"Oh yeah, especially if you show me some screenshots. I'm a visual learner. Forty-five minutes tops." Matt thought he heard Justin slapping his forehead.

Zach gave him a *thumbs up*. Nowitzki stifled a laugh.

"What's the *specific* problem?" Justin's voice now had an impatient edge.

"The specific problem is the client's an asshole."

"We've established that. What's your technical issue?"

"Oh, right. Jeez, it's close to quitting time for you, huh? Wanna get out of the ol' cubie and breathe some fresh air, not stare at a computer screen and four walls."

"As a matter of fact ..."

Matt's heart raced. His old music improvisation energy flowed through his body. He switched to sympathy mode. "Sorry, man. My bad. Shouldn't have asked for so much help this late. Even though I get to stay here till freakin' midnight working on this deal, there's no sense in making you stay late. Tell you what. Can you at least get me into this damn website? I'll muddle through from there."

"Sure. What's the website?"

"I could do stuff like this on my Mac like falling off a bicycle, you know. But on the PC? Sheesh and double shit."

"The *website*?"

"If I tried my password once, I tried a million times. Always get this stupid four-oh-four message."

"A standard error message."

"Then I figure the password needs uppercase letters, or numbers that *look* like letters, or *symbols* that look like letters. I try every variation I can think of. A million combinations. So far, I'm batting a nifty little oh-for-the-game."

"Look, just give me the website address and your password. I'll see if I can log on, okay? Then you can get your project done by eleven o'clock instead of midnight. Sound good to you?"

By now, Matt imagined Justin's teeth were grinding hard enough to make cornmeal, and his knuckles were white as he gripped his mouse or edge of the desk or chair arm.

"Sorry for the play-by-play, dude. It's just that my job's hanging by a loose wire. If I botch this, Boss Lady'll tell me to hit the stones, you know. Unemployment City here I come."

"The website and password, *please*."

"Oh, sure. You got a pad and pencil?"

Justin's exaggerated sigh *whooshed* through the speakerphone. "Go ahead."

Matt gave him the information.

Justin clicked away at his keyboard, then said, "Okay, I'm into the site."

"Huh? So fast? How'd you do that, my man?"

"I typed the password into the blank where it says *password*, then clicked on the icon that says *open*."

"Well, I'll be damned. Let me try now." On cue, Zach tapped his keyboard as if he were entering a password. When Zach stopped, Matt said,

"Heyyy, it works! Fantastic. I don't know what you did, Justin, but you saved my ass. I owe you lunch, my man."

"Forget it," Justin said, sounding tired and exasperated. "Just doing my job."

"Thanks a—"

The connection went dead.

Matt leaned back and looked at Zach, who focused on his computer screen and typed and clicked. Seconds later, his wide grin told Matt and Nowitzki all they needed to know. He said, "Smythe Properties' internal website is at your service, gents."

"Great. Get in there and start digging."

Zach closed his laptop lid. "Not now, *amigo*. We need to wait until Justin goes home. He's a techie, so he probably has a way to know if someone is using his connection while he's there. Then we'll have until tomorrow morning to use his access. But depending on their security, we could get busted anyway."

Matt said, "Busted as in they come here and arrest us?"

"Nah," Zach said. "They'd just notice some unusual activity—unauthorized access into certain accounts, especially if we get into employee files. I'll work fast to minimize the danger."

"What can we do to help?" Nowitzki asked.

"Make some coffee. I might not find anything for hours. And when I'm on a hacking roll, I go through a *lot* of chocolate."

"What kind of chocolate?" Matt asked.

"Double chocolate chip cookies are great. I'm also into seventy-percent dark chocolate. But if you can't find any, a few Snickers bars will do."

Matt and Nowitzki exchanged bemused looks.

"I'll go," Nowitzki said. "Any grocery stores close by?"

Zach gave him the location of the nearest grocery store and a list of his favorite cookies and dark chocolate bars. Matt suggested Nowitzki get some food and drink for all of them in case tonight turned into tomorrow morning before they had any results. Zach's place was woefully short of food on the shelves, but had a surplus of used takeout containers and pizza boxes.

After Nowitzki left, Matt turned to Zach. "You know what we need, right?"

"Info on Witt. Anything that looks like payments, communications, or other transactions between Smythe Properties and shell companies like Saxony Partners or the other local shells we found last year."

"Right." Matt glanced at the time on Zach's monitor. "I'll make the coffee if you show me where it is."

Surprisingly, Zach had a newer-looking coffeemaker and an assortment of gourmet beans and flavored coffee. He told Matt what to make, then Matt set about preparing a whole pot. His body ached with anticipation of having Zach dig into Smythe's internal website and find every piece of incriminating evidence they could that would help put Smythe away for life or longer. He paced and massaged his injured fingers while listening to the coffee percolate and Zach typing and clicking to prepare for the hoped-for information grab. What they were about to do was illegal and might get all three of them arrested. Still, the risk would be worth taking if they could supply any incriminating evidence to Special Agents Irving and Zamora.

Nowitzki eventually returned with two plastic bags. One was stuffed with several boxes of cookies and various chocolate bars. The other contained sandwiches from a neighborhood sandwich shop Nowitzki had patronized when he was a Minneapolis cop. He passed a sandwich to Matt and unwrapped one for himself. Zach grabbed a dark chocolate bar, broke it into individual squares, and laid them on a plate. Matt poured three cups of coffee, set one in front of Zach, and said, "I'm done waiting, kid. Get after it."

Zach popped a chocolate square into his mouth. "Me, too. Here goes."

Yes, they had waited long enough. Zach was no doubt thinking in terms of the minutes since they'd concluded their social engineering gambit. Matt's frame of reference was a *year* of waiting since he first tried to bring the Millennium Four conspiracy to the attention of the authorities. And that year had been so overloaded with danger, violence, anguish, and loss that it seemed more like a lifetime.

Chapter 40

While Zach labored into the wee hours digging through Smythe Properties' financial and employment records, Matt and Nowitzki used their meager computer skills to search for new farm sales along Interstate 35 from Minnesota to Missouri. Finding any shell companies in one or more of those states would bolster any conspiracy charges that might be filed. Zach supplied the original list of green-related company names he and Matt had compiled last year. But soon after starting to check the activities of those companies, Matt noticed something that crushed his optimism.

"They're gone," he said flatly.

Nowitzki gave him a quizzical look. "What do you mean, gone?"

"I've checked for deals by all the companies we discovered last year when we uncovered the Millennium Four conspiracy. Not only are there no new deals, but the old deals Zach and I found aren't listed under them anymore, either."

"How can that be?"

Matt said, "We've got a problem, Zach."

Zach stopped typing and looked at them. "What's up?"

Matt explained the missing companies and deals.

"I'll bet Smythe changed the names," Zach said. "Either that or he closed them down and organized new shell corporations."

"My gut tells me he's got some other keyword," Matt said. "He impressed me as a stickler for detail, precision, and organization, like a military general. He sees this as a war game. Winning the war means closing all the deals he can in the next few years while the political forces line up to make the I-35 superhighway a done deal with the feds."

"What keyword then?" Nowitzki asked.

They brainstormed some ideas for a while. Then Matt said to Zach, "Have you checked to see if Saxony Partners is still an entity?"

"I did," Zach said. "It's not."

"What happened?"

"It liquidated."

"What about the land it owned?"

Zach shrugged. "No idea."

"Okay," Matt said. "Confirm this for me, Ben, but there's got to be a record of Saxony selling its holdings to another person or entity, right?"

Nowitzki nodded. "Sure. All real estate transactions have to be recorded by the county for tax roll purposes."

"That's what I thought. Zach, you have a new project."

Zach had already turned back to his computer. "On it, boss."

Within an hour, Zach had traced the original Saxony Partners purchases to another company—Springfield Holdings, LLC.

"Any significance in using an *S-word* for the name?" Matt asked.

Nowitzki looked thoughtful, then said, "On *Jeopardy!* I learned that Springfield's the second most common city name in the nation. He might be going for nondescript."

"Which means his other shell corporations might also be nondescript," Matt said.

"Could be," Nowitzki said. "Or he could go in another direction alto-gether."

Matt pursed his lips. "Might be better to focus on finding records of Witt working for Smythe. That's a lot more finite. Either Zach finds him, or he doesn't."

"I agree," Nowitzki said. He turned to Zach. "Back to work, kid."

Zach nodded and resumed his search. Speed was essential because of the risk of the hack being discovered. If that happened, Smythe's technicians might track their location or, at a minimum, disconnect them permanent-ly. Matt refilled Zach's coffee cup and opened another dark chocolate bar. He and Nowitzki returned to searching for real estate deals—just in case.

Another hour passed. The coffee pot was empty. All that remained of the sandwiches were crumbs and wrappers. Half the chocolate was history.

With a huge sigh, Zach sat back in his chair and swiveled to face his friends. "I searched everywhere I could think and didn't find anyone named *Witt* or anything close to *Witt.*"

Silence hung over the room until Matt said, "I'm not surprised."

"I copied everything I looked at," Zach said. "But check it yourself. I might've missed something." He yawned. "I haven't pulled an all-nighter in a while."

Matt said, "Print out all your data, then take a break." When Zach started that task, Matt turned to Nowitzki. "You any good at deciphering data?"

"I doubt it," Nowitzki said.

"Close enough. Take half of what Zach gives us and start hunting."

While Zach slept, Matt and Ben scanned dozens of pages of employment data, salaries, accounts payable and receivable, schedules, performance appraisals, and anything else to do with personnel at Smythe Properties. After they'd each looked at the entire pile of papers, both stood and stretched. Matt drained his coffee, cold now. Nowitzki did an overall body shake to get his blood flowing.

"I'm going outside to get some air," Matt said. He glanced at the clock on Zach's computer screen. Almost four a.m. He hadn't been up that late in years. Early in his career, he'd attended numerous all-night jam sessions at local clubs that let the featured band and their friends stay and play until whenever. This wasn't quite the same, though. A lack of mental stimulation had dulled his wits. He went downstairs and outside to the front yard of the building. The stars still shone in the cloudless sky. Faint hints of daylight showed in the east.

After a couple of cleansing breaths and some muscle stretches, Matt's alertness improved. Despite being confident Witt had been a Smythe employee, a thorough look at the company's records for the last three years had yielded no such connection. *Why not?*

His thoughts returned to all-night jam sessions. Forming his trio. Getting the word out to club owners that they were available for a reasonable price. The first year, gigs were all about exposure and attracting fans who would come and listen no matter where the group performed. He remembered being put off by the business side of the music. Negotiating contracts, paying his drummer and piano player, filling out tax forms . . .

"That's it!" Matt said out loud and scurried back inside. Once there, he shouted down the hallway, "Wake up, Zach."

"What?" Zach said from his bedroom in a half-groaning tone.

"Get back into Smythe Properties."

"It's a lot riskier the second time, dude."

"This should only take a minute," Matt said. "All I need is one set of data."

"Okay," Zach said as he staggered into the room and woke his laptop from its *sleep* mode.

Matt faced Nowitzki. "Big companies never do everything in-house, right?"

"In-house?" Nowitzki asked.

"Certain jobs that aren't needed every day are cheaper if the company hires an independent contractor. A company specializing in jobs such as window washing or exterior maintenance or groundskeeping or HVAC repairs."

"What are you getting at?"

"Witt's primary job was security, which he was doing when I first met him in Smythe's office. That's a service that would be cheaper to obtain by hiring a security company. We need to look at all the independent contractors hired by Smythe Properties and find out if he hired outside security firms."

Nowitzki pursed his lips and nodded. "Good point."

Zach's urgent voice interrupted their momentary triumph. "Got a problem, boss. They know someone's hacking their site. It's taking me twice as long to navigate the pages."

Matt thought for a moment, then said, "Get me everything you can find on independent contractors who were paid by Smythe Properties in the past three years. Names, addresses, employees, sub-contractors, anything and everyone not directly employed by Smythe Properties."

"Okay," Zach said, "but what if they ID us?"

"What does that mean?"

"If they get my IP address, they'll trace my computer to here."

"We'll worry about that later. Work as fast as you can, kid."

"Got it."

"And print copies of everything you find even if you're not sure what you've got."

Matt and Ben stood behind Zach and monitored his activity. Sure enough, he found an accounting page that listed all the independent contractors Smythe Properties had hired in recent years. A quick scan only showed company names. No individuals were listed. Not surprising. It would make sense for Smythe to keep Witt's identity as hidden as possible. But since security services weren't cheap, chances were good that Witt's assignments included jobs other than trying to kill Matt and his allies. Smythe couldn't avoid showing those expenses unless he dared risk committing tax fraud.

"*Mierda!*" Zach said. He slumped back in his chair, a look of defeat on his face.

"What?" Matt and Nowitzki said simultaneously.

"I got closed out of the system."

"What does that mean?" Matt asked.

"Someone figured out I was hacking and blocked my access."

"Are we in immediate danger?"

Zach shook his head. "They only know someone hacked in. They don't know who."

"Still," Nowitzki said, "we'd better stop milking that cow."

Zach gave him a puzzled look, but Matt understood the phrase.

"You did good, kid," Matt said. "We'll do the best we can with what you dug up."

"I hope so," Zach said.

"Let's look at those ICs," Nowitzki said. "We might get lucky."

He and Matt picked up the independent contractor listings Zach had compiled. Fortunately, there were only four pages. They quickly eliminated companies that referred to their job in their company name. After crossing off several dozen, they were left with some thirty possibilities.

Matt circled the names he thought could be connected to Witt. Nowitzki did the same with his data. They ended up with ten possible ICs.

"Go to the Minnesota Secretary of State's website," Matt said to Zach, "and look up all these businesses to see if Witt is the owner. I doubt he'd be stupid enough to list his own name, but we might catch a break."

Nowitzki said, "If Witt was a licensed security man, or what they call a Protective Agent in Minnesota, there's a record of his licensure and required training."

Matt said, "Witt wasn't the kind of guy to follow the rules, so don't be surprised if you don't find anything. Or if he did have a license, it may have been a fake."

Zach said, "I've checked five now, and none look promising." He sat back and let the other two see his screen.

"Where'd you say Witt lived?" Matt said to Nowitzki.

"Hopkins."

"There," Matt said, pointing at the third entry. "Hopkins address."

"Yeah, but Witt's not the owner," Zach said.

"That's because the listed owner of Premier Security Services is none other than Springfield Holdings, LLC," Matt said triumphantly.

"Son of a bitch, we got 'em," Nowitzki said.

Matt knew from having registered his trio as a small business in Minnesota that records were available online through the state—for a fee. "Get those documents, Zach."

"Want me to hack into that database?"

"No. Not worth the risk. But I'm broke." He turned to Nowitzki. "Got a few bucks to spare so we can order the documents?"

"Hell, yeah," Nowitzki said. He pulled out his wallet and retrieved a credit card.

Within minutes, they had obtained all pertinent registration documents for Premier Security Services. Matt confirmed that, based on what Clay Gebhardt had told him before he died, Charlie Witt had changed his name from *Whitt* to *Witt* shortly after the company was established. Witt had made the name change to camouflage his criminal past. Charles *Arthur Whitt* had multiple violent convictions, including manslaughter. Charles

Allen Witt was a new person with no record of any sort. There was no doubt Smythe had set up this shell company to hide his criminal employee and the dirty work he was doing on behalf of Millennium Four.

"We need proof of payments from Smythe Properties to Premier Security Services before we have a case," Nowitzki said.

"Right," Matt said. "But Witt's been dead for a year. His business records were probably destroyed by Smythe after he cleaned out Witt's apartment. Where does that leave us?"

"Bank records," Nowitzki said. He turned toward Zach and arched his eyebrows. "Up for hacking a bank?"

With a glance at Matt, Zach said, "Probably won't work. Bank security is usually tighter than my Tio Pedro after Cinco de Mayo."

"So, we gotta go back into the company's files," Matt said with resignation in his voice. His injured fingers ached. Ratcheting up the risk might get them caught.

Nowitzki gestured with his hand. "Maybe this is enough for the Fibbies."

"You think?" Matt said.

"Witt had a criminal record. He was found shot to death in the Boundary Waters. Now that we've tangentially connected him to Smythe, he's definitely a person of interest to the Feds. We don't want to risk trouble with the law by doing more hacking than we've done. I'll call Zamora, get her opinion."

"Okay," Matt said, "but let's keep working other angles in case the FBI can't or won't act."

"I'm good with that." Nowitzki checked his watch. "I'll wait until sunrise to call her, so she won't tear me a new one over the phone."

Zach grinned and gave Matt a conspiratorial look. "Yeah, ask her out to breakfast and tell her then."

Matt chuckled.

Nowitzki's eyebrows shot upward. "What's that supposed to mean?"

"We can both tell you've got more than a professional interest in her," Matt said.

"It's that obvious?"

Matt and Zach nodded. Matt said, "You make any headway with her face-to-face in the past two days?"

Nowitzki pursed his lips. "Don't know, other than I don't think she's disgusted by me anymore."

"See?" Zach said. "You're halfway there."

Nowitzki scowled. "Back to business, gentlemen."

"Yeah, I'm beat," Matt said. He looked at Zach. "You mind if we crash on your furniture for a few hours?"

"Go for it," Zach said.

Chapter 41

After a four-hour nap, Matt awoke feeling surprisingly rested and refreshed. His brain felt as though it was back in gear for the first time in months. Zach had returned to his bedroom. Nowitzki appeared from around the corner of the small kitchenette, holding a cup of steaming liquid.

"Coffee's ready," he said. "I'm going to hit the shower, then call Zamora."

Matt yawned and stood. "Thanks." He also wanted a shower, but that could wait. "I need another video chat with Irving. Can you set it up first?"

"Sure," Nowitzki said. He called Irving, fired up his laptop, and set up the video meeting. Then he strolled toward the bathroom, whistling the *Final Jeopardy* time clock theme song.

As he poured coffee, Matt racked his brain for a grain of information he'd overlooked in Flannery's taped confession that might lead to a breakthrough. So much damning evidence, yet it was virtually useless right now. If only Gebhardt and Flannery had lived.

After Irving appeared on the screen and they'd exchanged greetings, Matt said, "Have you seen all the autopsy records related to my case?"

She glanced skyward, thinking. "Pretty sure. There were so many."

"At least four too many," he said, not trying to hide his bitterness. None of his friends, especially Diane, should have died because they helped him stay alive and out of jail. "Did any seem suspicious to you?"

"I'm not a forensic specialist, but no. All seemed accurate."

"Anything unusual about the crime scene investigations?"

"Those I'd have to study again. Especially the Boundary Waters shootout. Lots of shell casings, footprints, and other bits of evidence were probably missed."

"Yeah," Matt said. "Also, no survivors, no witnesses, no point in a thorough investigation."

"Since you were implicated shortly after that, the BCA stepped in. But the crime scene had already been compromised by scavengers. And they assumed you'd committed all the murders, including Flannery and Gebhardt at the hospital, so they looked at everything through that lens."

Matt nodded. "Of course. What about Crossley and Blake at Thompson Hill Rest Area?"

Irving gave him an annoyed look. "*Again*, I'd have to re-examine the evidence."

"Will you?"

"Now?"

"Yes, it may be crucial."

"What're you driving at, Lanier?"

A seed of an idea took hold in Matt's mind. "Maybe nothing, but I'd like to know what they concluded and compare it to my recollections of events."

Irving shrugged. "Okay, if you think it might help." She pulled out her cell phone, dialed a number, and muted her connection. A minute later, she ended her call and unmuted herself. "My technician at the MFO is emailing all the autopsy reports related to your case to me. Give me your email address, and I'll send them to you."

"Thanks," Matt said. He roused Zach from sleep and had him send Irving his email address.

Within seconds, Zach's inbox had a new message. He busied himself opening the attachments while Irving did the same on her end.

Matt's apprehension grew. He'd never viewed autopsy photos. And even though he'd seen the lifeless bodies of Witt, Swanson, Crossley, and Diane after those gunfights, those moments were so surreal, so dreamlike. Seeing photos of each person lying on a stainless-steel examining table would be far too real and confirm they were most certainly dead. His heart sped up.

He couldn't keep his knee from bouncing up and down. Brief flashbacks of the lifeless faces ricocheted around his brain, blurring the table full of computers in his actual field of vision. His fingers and toes tingled. His mouth dried up. Swallowing took effort. Gunshots from a year ago echoed in his memory. He wiped a palmful of sweat from his face. As the walls of Zach's apartment closed in around him, a jolt of nervous energy urged him to run—anywhere. *Just run and don't stop.*

"You okay?" A voice broke through the haze of his visions.

Matt raised his head. Zach had a look of concern on his face.

"What's wrong, Lanier?" Irving asked.

"Flashbacks," Matt said. "I need some air." He bolted out of the room, down the stairs, and out into the front yard of the apartment building. He'd traveled only a hundred feet, but he was gasping as if he'd run a mile at full speed. The dizziness started. He went to one knee. Violent memories built up like a tsunami about to make landfall. Panic infused him, and he collapsed into the fetal position.

Thompson Hill Rest Area. Duluth, Minnesota. Midnight. Matt sits in his truck, exhausted, anxious, eager. Diane's Lexus appears. Her lights flash to acknowledge his headlight signal. Her car approaches. Matt's heart leaps with relief and joy. But it's not her. Crossley fires his pistol at him from the driver's window. Matt dives to safety in the truck. Bullets whiz and thump into the vehicle inches from him. He recovers. Fires back. Fifteen shots from Crossley. Five from Matt. The last shot from Crossley. Different sound. Matt floats out of his body and hovers over the scene. He watches himself hold Diane one last time, kiss her one last time, caress her hair one last time.

Dead silence. How did Crossley know she was meeting him here? He has killed again. His worst nightmare has come true. And now it's a nightmare of a nightmare. All his senses are amplified. The sound is deafening. The blood glows electric red. Night becomes day under a blinding white light that gives him a headache. He almost enjoyed killing Crossley. Is this his new identity? Will he kill more people? Enjoy it more? Once again, Smythe,

the puppet master, hovers above the entire scene, always untouchable. Matt's brain feels as if it's being sliced in half by the anguish of trying to make the correct decision: run or surrender. His headache grows. He's endured the pain for a year. Moments before he believes his head will explode from pain and pressure and give him peace, he wakes.

Matt sat up, shivering with fright and feeling damp grass through his clothes. He refocused on the buildings, the trees, and the stars. The fresh April air calmed his mind, and the cool breeze evaporated the sweat on his exposed skin. He stood, rested his hands on his knees, and took slow, deep breaths. Damn it, he'd done so well the past few weeks managing his PTSD symptoms. Now, despite having a legitimate chance to end this nightmare, he'd again spiraled down to the depths of despair he'd last endured the night before he met Hawk.

"This is stupid," he said to the grass as his heartbeat slowed down. "Get your shit together, Matty. You owe it to so many people to stop that bastard."

He owed his best effort to the memory of Diane, whom he never should have approached for help. Even if chance or fate or bad luck had made them run into each other at the Dakota Jazz Club and Restaurant last March, he should've kept his fat mouth shut. Should've asked someone else for help to uncover Smythe's role pulling Hibbert and Flannery's puppet strings in Straight River.

Matt returned to Zach's apartment and faced Irving on the computer screen. "I'm okay," he said. "Just a minor meltdown."

She still looked concerned. "Tell me what you're searching for, and I'll help."

He nodded and told Zach to display the autopsy photos of Witt and Swanson onto a separate laptop screen so he could maintain visual contact with Irving. Gritting his teeth, Matt locked his eyes on the screen. Those were the most gruesome photos to see because both had multiple gunshot wounds. He was curiously fascinated by the job his bullets had done on

Witt's face. He remembered seeing nothing but blood. However, the photo of Witt after the autopsy showed him cleaned up, no blood, with four holes in his head: two in the forehead, one where his nose used to be, one in the chin. Even dead, Witt's expression was the permanent scowl Matt remembered from the hit-and-run attempt and the frozen split-second before each had pulled their respective triggers on rifles aimed at the other.

Matt briefly glanced at Dave Swanson's bullet-riddled body, then closed his eyes to fight back the tears. The big dumb lug should've stayed home with Amy instead of joining Clay for their ill-fated rescue attempt in the Boundary Waters. Swanny had come to avenge Amy's honor because he believed Witt had raped her. Gebhardt's reason was professional pride. And a rescue it was. Without his friends, he would have died. He was outgunned and trapped on an island with no escape route. He'd naïvely thought he could get the drop on a police chief and a hired killer. In hindsight, he'd been foolish to think his plan could work. For that foolishness, two friends had paid the ultimate price.

After composing himself, Matt said to Irving, "Was anything useful found in Swanson's or Witt's personal effects at the scene?"

"Swanson's wallet, cell phone, keys, and some chewing tobacco," she replied. "Witt had a fake driver's license that turned out to be a dead end. There was also a satellite phone we couldn't trace to an owner and a credit card with the same fake name as the driver's license. Otherwise, just clothes and all the camping gear left behind."

"Right," Matt said. "How about the Thompson Hill Rest Area scene?"

Zach pulled up the autopsy photos while Irving did the same on her end. Diane's expression in death was calm and restful. Matt presumed she'd died instantly from her gunshot wound to the temple. Crossley had a neutral expression that didn't mask his smug nature. The guy's *GQ* looks were a perfect match for his superior-chauvinist-pig persona. Matt admired his shooting handiwork—an almost wild shot that had nailed Crossley square in the forehead. Crossley had deserved to die solely because he'd raised a hand against Diane, which—again—never would have happened had Matt not imposed on her for help.

Matt asked Irving and Zach to move on to the crime scene photos: Diane's shot-up Lexus, broken windows and windshield, glass fragments on the parking lot pavement, blood spatters, and shell casings. As he viewed the photos of the shell casings, Matt counted them silently. Fifteen shots from Crossley's weapon. Five from Matt's Glock 17. He remembered the exchange of gunfire as easily as he memorized a complicated bass line: two shots from Crossley; silence; three shots from Crossley; silence; three shots from Crossley; silence; three more shots from Crossley; silence; one shot from Crossley. Then Matt counterattacked: two wild, rage-filled shots; two shots from Crossley; three more from Matt actually aimed at Crossley; two seconds of silence; then the solo shot from Crossley that stood out in his memory. But *why* did that shot stand out? Was it the time delay before the last shot? Was it louder or softer than the other nineteen? Were there other noises in the immediate area that had influenced his hearing? Or was the nagging ache in his head and stomach caused by something else?

As Zach reached the photo of the last shell casing, Matt abruptly blurted out, "Stop!"

"What?" Zach said with mild alarm in his voice.

"Something wrong?" Irving asked.

"The last shell casing is *inside* the Lexus," Matt said, his voice quavering. "In the back seat."

"Correct," Irving said.

"All the others would've been on the parking lot pavement, right? Or maybe in Crossley's lap or the front seat. I saw a few near my truck and some near the driver's door of the Lexus."

Irving mulled over the question. "Not necessarily. Shell casings don't eject in predictable patterns."

"Yet most of the casings near the Lexus are on the hood and near the front fender. That implies most of the ejections were to the right of the fired weapon."

"Well, yeah, but—"

"If that last shot was fired at me, could the shell casing have ricocheted into the back seat of the car, especially if Crossley's head and torso blocked most of that access?"

"It's possible. We can't be sure without an eyewitness. What're you getting at?"

"So the odds of the shell casing ejected after a shot fired out the driver's window are extremely low?"

"Quite low, but not impossible." Irving gave him a puzzled look.

Matt's insides revved like an outboard motor at full throttle, and a sudden spike of energized understanding surged through his brain. "Flip to Diane's autopsy report."

Zach and Irving did so, and Matt scanned down to the cause-of-death line: *Gunshot wound to the left side of the head.*

"Anything unusual in the autopsy?" Matt asked, hesitant to know but hoping for something helpful.

Irving said, "The only thing I saw was that Diane's blood showed she'd been heavily sedated."

Matt silently thanked Crossley for knocking her out before she was shot. She wouldn't have been terrified in those final minutes. Wouldn't have suffered. "What about gunshot residue?"

Irving gave him a sour look. "Hold on." She scrolled through her computer and studied her screen. "Nothing other than trace amounts that drifted through the interior while Crossley was firing his weapon."

"And the size of the entry and exit wound?"

"Consistent with a nine-millimeter slug."

"What was Crossley's weapon?"

Irving studied her screen. "Shell casings were all nines. Cops at the scene noted it was a Beretta 92 nine mil." She stared back at Matt before saying, "What're you getting at, Lanier?"

"Something's not right. I can't prove it. I just know it." His seed of an idea now had some fertilizer. The autopsies and crime scene reports were too perfect, except for the random pattern of shell casings being ejected from semi-automatic pistols. Fourteen shell casings out of fifteen ejected from Crossley's gun had ended up outside Diane's Lexus on the asphalt. Logical because Crossley, a right-handed shooter, had been shooting at *him.* Most of those shells had ejected to the right, toward the front of the car. The fifteenth had ended up inside the car in the back seat. A left ejection that also traveled a great distance backward from Crossley's weapon. What were the odds of that happening? Matt snapped out of his trance of concentration, but decided it would be best not to tell Irving of his next step.

"There's no point in wasting your time with my gut feeling, Special Agent Irving. I still think connecting Witt to Smythe is our best bet."

With a shrug, Irving said, "Okay. Keep me posted," and then signed off.

When Nowitzki reappeared after his shower, he had dressed, but his hair was still wet. Smiling, he waggled his phone. "Zamora thinks the Feds can dig into Witt and Smythe Properties."

Matt gaped. "Seriously? That's fantastic."

Nowitzki held up a warning finger. "She also said we need more documentation. Smythe can plead ignorance of Witt's extracurricular activities because the independent contractor relationship doesn't prove he specifically endorsed or ordered Witt's activities."

"That's fine," Matt said, "because I've got an idea that might break everything open for us."

Although that connection was his best hope, it might not be enough. Not if Smythe lawyered up and threw legal double-talk and stalling tactics at a prosecutor. Nailing a crooked mastermind had to be a one-hundred-percent slam dunk. If it wasn't, Matt would probably end up dead. His bubbling insides suggested he might be creeping toward ninety-nine percent. He stood abruptly, wanting to race to his next destination. But to do that, he needed a car.

Turning to Nowitzki, Matt said, "We need to talk with Hypo and Hawk."

"About what?" Nowitzki asked.

"I'll explain while you drive."

Chapter 42

"Of course we'll help," Hypo said after he and Hawk had listened to Matt's rudimentary plan to exploit Smythe's one apparent mistake to date. They were in Hawk's apartment, sitting around the kitchen table, along with Zach and Nowitzki. Hawk was putting together a batch of Matt's chicken salad for an impromptu lunch.

"We have some weapons," Matt said. "I mean, Nowitzki has a few pieces. However, I worry about those guns being traced to you. I don't think we'll need to fire them, but Smythe has always found a way to stay one step ahead of me. I thought about that bastard every day for the last year and how he seemed to know what I would do before I did it. I was always reacting in panic to an unexpected situation. Now it's our turn to make him panic."

Hawk set down a bowl of chicken salad, a loaf of bread, and lettuce, tomatoes, and mayonnaise for garnish. Zach and Nowitzki began making sandwiches.

"If this is a nighttime operation, stealth and silence are our allies," Hawk said. "Guns have their place, of course, but Hypo and I still remember most of what we learned about hand-to-hand combat in the military. And I keep my old service revolver ready to fire. Never hurts to have protection in a big city."

Hypo nodded in agreement. "We have other tools we use for self-defense around here that won't get you in as much trouble with the law as a handgun can."

"Okay," Matt said, huffing out a sigh. "We only want to capture whoever Smythe sends after me so we can verify their connection. I don't want to shoot someone and have them die before we force them to talk."

Hypo said, "Because you want to do this at night, Matt, communication will be tough without shouting. Can't do hand signals or get visual cues. How're you going to work around that?"

Nowitzki interjected. "I can help. I have a PI colleague in St. Paul who owns some miniature communication devices similar to what the Secret Service uses when they're protecting the president in public. I'll call and see if he can lend them to me."

"You think they'll help?" Matt asked.

"No one's gotten through to a sitting president since Reagan got shot back in the eighties. They'll help."

Matt pursed his lips and nodded. "Make the call."

Nowitzki called his colleague. He was out of town and wouldn't arrive home until that evening, but he was willing to lend his devices to Nowitzki.

That meant Matt's plan would be delayed one day. Worth the wait to ensure better communication, but he dreaded having so much time to reconsider his plan. His gut churned with indecision. Three new friends wanted to help him on the front line. He wanted this mess to end, but he didn't want anyone else to die. Still, he respected his friends and knew they wouldn't boast of their training and fighting skills if it wasn't true. They all knew the risks. The wild card would be how Smythe or his soldiers reacted to Matt's provocation.

Early the next morning, Nowitzki returned to Hawk's apartment with his weapons and the miniature communication devices—wireless transceivers with small battery packs that clipped onto a belt or waistband. An earbud the size of a hearing aid fit into the ear and provided clear sound. A small plastic extension curved down toward the user's mouth and had a microphone secured in the tip. Matt likened them to the headsets singers used to hear themselves onstage instead of relying on large monitors and handheld microphones. The men would communicate as if they were on a four-way conference call.

After Nowitzki gave them a thorough tutorial, they practiced talking back and forth outside, each about one hundred yards away from the others. The sound quality was crystal clear and static-free.

They spent the rest of the morning studying a house in the St. Paul suburb of White Bear Lake on Google Maps, reviewing and refining Matt's plan. By noon, they were ready to start. However, activating the plan today required that the first step, a simple phone call, be successful. Nowitzki tapped the number into his cell phone, then clicked on *speaker* mode.

After two rings, a woman's voice said, "Good afternoon, Arrowhead Medical."

Nowitzki said, "May I please speak to Dr. Ramsey?"

They heard a click, silence, another click, and then a terse, "Ramsey."

"Hi, Dr. Ramsey, this is Ben Nowitzki, the private investigator. I've consulted with you on a few cases in the past."

"You a big guy?" Ramsey asked. "Likes *Jeopardy!?* Drinks Grain Belt Nordeast beer?"

"The one and only."

"Sure, I remember you, Ben. What can I do for you?"

"I'd like to drop in this afternoon and ask you about an autopsy you did last year."

"Which autopsy?"

Nowitzki put a modest amount of hesitation in his tone. "Um, I'd rather not say over the phone. High-profile case, my client is paranoid about security."

Ramsey was silent for several beats. "I'd prefer to know now so I can refresh my memory."

"Please, Doc. He's paying me a boatload of money to guarantee his privacy."

"Well, I suppose. But I'm pretty busy this afternoon. What time?"

"Any time after three," Nowitzki said. "I just need five or ten minutes."

They heard rustling paper. "Okay. I can delay a meeting if you promise to keep it quick."

"Scout's honor. Thanks, Doc." Nowitzki ended the call.

Matt nodded and looked at Hawk. "You and Hypo good to go?"

"We'll be ready," Hawk said implacably. Noticing Matt massaging his left hand, he said, "It's a sound plan. We'll make it work—unless Smythe sends a small army."

"Got a ways to go before you hit CIA level," Hypo said through a crooked grin. "Of course, those guys had unlimited funds to work with too. So, dollar for dollar, not bad."

Matt took little satisfaction from the fact that his friends approved of his cobbled-together plan. Murphy's law usually found a way into any situation where some factors couldn't be controlled. In the past year, he'd analyzed every move and countermove Smythe had made to stop him. He'd started a new chess game against Smythe, only this time he tried to think five moves ahead rather than two.

Nowitzki drove and Matt rode shotgun as they headed for Duluth. Silence reigned until they reached the open road after the merger between I-35E and I-35W near Forest Lake. Nowitzki set his cruise control to seventy-nine m.p.h. and dropped one hand from the steering wheel.

"I don't mind helping you," he said, glancing at Matt. "But I know this guy well enough to know he's got an impeccable reputation. I can't imagine he'd take a bribe from anyone."

"Bribe, maybe not," Matt said. "Blackmail, possibly. Two autopsies were falsified by a well-respected coroner in Straight River. If that's how Smythe operates, he's probably bribed or blackmailed several other coroners and medical examiners from here to Missouri to cover up murders that were officially classified as accidents or suicides. Last year, Zach and I found records of several deaths that happened too conveniently mere weeks before a shell company of Smythe's swooped in to buy the property. Unless something else falls into our laps, either this or connecting Witt to Smythe with the employment angle is our best shot to nail the bastard."

Nowitzki glanced out his side window. "Okay, then. But think about alternatives if this angle's a bust."

"You don't know Smythe as well as I do," Matt said. "I think about him every day, what he did to me, my father, my friends, my ex-wife, and all the other farmers whose lives he's either damaged or destroyed. He's ruthless and has unlimited funds. What stuck with me is how quickly Gebhardt and Flannery were killed after I dropped them off at the Ely hospital. I doubt he has a man in Ely because that's outside the I-35 sphere of business for him. But Duluth is the northern terminus of the freeway. I killed his right-hand man and my ex-wife in Duluth. It makes sense that he checked out the county Medical Examiner for a weakness."

Nowitzki asked, "What if he recognizes you and calls the cops?"

"I doubt that'll happen. Besides, I've got enough persuasion to give me time to read his face, his reactions, his tone of voice." Matt patted the jacket pocket holding his Browning 9mm—courtesy of Nowitzki. "You said the security in his building isn't too tight, right?"

"Ramsey only works part time for the county. Today he's in his office—a regular physicians' group renting one floor of a five-story building. Last time I was there, they only had security cameras in the main lobby."

Chapter 43

At 3:15, Matt strode into a newer-looking stone-and-glass building in the Kenwood neighborhood of Duluth, near the University of Minnesota Duluth campus. He took the stairs to the third-floor suite of Ramsey's physicians' group. The lobby décor was modern yet modest, typical of a professional setting.

A woman sitting behind a waist-high laminated counter smiled robotically as she looked up and said, "May I help you?"

"Yes," Matt said, "Ben Nowitzki to see Dr. Ramsey."

Her smile sagged into a disdainful frown as she focused on the stranger with the frayed, stained clothes, shaggy beard, and Twins cap pulled low on his forehead. "Is he expecting you?"

"I called earlier. He agreed to give me a few minutes of his time after three."

"Umm," she said and glanced hesitantly over her shoulder. "Let me see if he's in."

To reassure her that he meant no harm, Matt said, "Sorry about my appearance. I'm a private eye. I came here straight from tracking a client's husband and didn't have time to clean up. She suspects he's cheating on her, so I followed him to work. He's a carpenter. I had to blend in with the crowd at a workingman's bar over in Superior."

Her eyes flashed with relief. "Oh, I see. I wondered about your clothes."

"Just between you and me," he said, giving her a conspiratorial wink, "the wife was right. He was drinking with a woman who looked barely legal."

"Really?" she said in a gossipy tone. "Aren't wives always right about their cheating husbands?"

"Thank God for that. Those two-timers keep me in business."

Matt eyed her as she picked up the phone's handset. If she pressed an extension button, he was safe. However, if she tapped in 911 or a full-length phone number, he'd have a problem.

She pressed one button, waited, announced Ben Nowitzki, listened, and hung up. "Go right in," she said, pointing to a hallway. "Second door on the left."

"Thanks." He walked down the hallway to the second door, knocked, waited for a second, and entered.

Dr. Dean Ramsey stood from behind his desk and said, "Good to see you again, Ben. It's been—"

He froze, staring at Matt with narrowed eyes, trying to remember what Ben Nowitzki looked like from their last meeting. Before Ramsey could say more, Matt closed the door to prevent the receptionist from hearing.

"You're not Ben," Ramsey said, confusion tensing his face.

"I apologize for the ruse, Dr. Ramsey, but I need to speak to you in the utmost confidence. My life's at stake. After this meeting, yours may also be at risk."

"Who *are* you?" Ramsey demanded. "Where's Ben?" His strong tenor voice had a mellow trombone timbre that fit his appearance: white, sixty-ish, with a short, solid build and gray hair around his temples. An everyman countenance that exuded professionalism.

"You don't need to know my name. And Nowitzki's whereabouts aren't your concern."

"Well, then, I'm sorry, but this meeting is over."

Matt shook his head. "This meeting is over when *I* say it's over."

Ramsey stiffened. "I agreed to meet Ben Nowitzki, not some vagrant off the street. Do you even know him? Have you harmed him in any way?"

"Our relationship and his health are none of your business. When I'm done here, you're free to call him and discuss the matter."

"You've got a lot of nerve barging in here under false pretenses. I—"

Matt thrust his hand up to cut him off. He set his jaw and lowered his voice. "Listen carefully, Ramsey," he said, pulling his pistol from his pocket so Ramsey could see the grip. "I'm here for information about an autopsy, and I'm not leaving without it."

Ramsey's gaze dropped to the weapon. Eyes wide, he focused on Matt. "Is that a threat?"

"No. It's a sign of my sincerity about the danger I'm in. If you're innocent, you have nothing to fear from me. If you're guilty, you'll have a much bigger problem because the man who pulled you into this case hates loose ends. As soon as I leave, you may become a loose end. If you do, he'll erase you like a student who erases the wrong answer on a test."

Ramsey swallowed hard and sat in his chair. "Very well. Ask your questions."

Matt sat in an armchair in front of Ramsey's desk. "You performed the autopsy on Diane Blake and Steven Crossley last April, correct?"

Ramsey's pause was a beat too long. "That's still an open murder investigation." His tone became strident. "I can't divulge any information."

He focused harder on Matt's face as if staring intently would help him identify his visitor. His knuckles were white from gripping the arms of his chair.

"If I were you," Matt said, "I'd worry less about legal ramifications and more about staying alive." He leaned forward and locked eyes with Ramsey's. "But if it lessens your legal concerns, we'll call my questions hypothetical."

"Hypothetical?"

"Was Diane killed by a bullet fired from the gun of Matt Lanier, the alleged killer?"

"That's my conclusion."

"You ever consider the possibility of suicide?"

"*Suicide*? Where'd you get *that* idea?"

Matt willed his hearing and vision to catch every nuance of Ramsey's reaction to his questions. "The papers said it was a love triangle between Blake, Crossley, and Lanier, right?"

Ramsey faced Matt straight on, as someone would if they were telling the truth. But his eyeballs quivered, never coming to rest. "The evidence was clear. Lanier killed them both."

Matt was now positive Ramsey's reputation was far from lily-white—it was gray and getting darker. "Humor me, okay?"

"I really need to run in a few minutes."

"What if Diane Blake was torn between two lovers, like the old song? She loves them both equally but for different reasons. Maybe Crossley drives her there to meet Lanier and talk things out. But she doesn't know they have guns. They argue over who deserves her more, start shooting, and her worst fears kick in. Crossley's mortally wounded. Maybe Lanier's wounded too. No one knows because he left immediately and has never been found. She decides that she caused this fight and does the noble thing, because she can't live without either of them. So she grabs Crossley's pistol and turns it on herself."

Ramsey's nervous laugh was rife with tension. "Seriously?"

"No, *hypothetically*. Remember?" Matt feigned a thoughtful expression and spoke as if he were thinking aloud. "Maybe Diane's family didn't want the public to know their precious superstar lawyer was weak enough to kill herself. Her father was recently appointed to the Minnesota Supreme Court. That might not have happened if a family scandal got splashed across the media."

"I'm aware of that," Ramsey said. "But your story is so preposterous I won't dignify it with a response."

"I dunno, Doc," Matt said through a humorless smile. "I gotta believe it's pretty easy to retouch the crime-scene or autopsy photos to hide the gunshot residue on Diane's temple. And it only takes a few seconds to wipe fingerprints off a gun. Makes me wonder what the going rate is for turning a distraught woman's suicide into her tragic murder by a scumbag musician." Keeping his voice nonchalant, which was in complete opposition to his roiling insides, he said, "Is it possible that *someone* on your *team* was blackmailed?"

The ensuing silence was all the confirmation Matt needed. His skin prickled with excitement that he'd guessed correctly about the falsified autopsy.

"Now look here," Ramsey finally said. "Implying that I or any other member of my team would take a bribe is reprehensible. If you continue this campaign of innuendo and allegations, I'll have no recourse other than to take legal action."

"I'm sorry to hear that," Matt said. "Because my next step is to visit Justice Blake and request an independent autopsy by a forensic pathologist of his choice."

"You must excuse me," Ramsey said. "I'm late for a meeting. But I assure you Diane Blake's autopsy is true and accurate. No one was bribed."

Matt leveled one last stare at Ramsey, reading the fear and confusion in his eyes. "If you ever grow a pair, Ramsey, call Nowitzki. If you call soon enough, we might prevent you from getting killed."

"Please leave," Ramsey said, pointing toward the door. "I can't tell you anything more."

The way Ramsey said *can't* stuck in Matt's mind like the dissonance of an out-of-tune guitar string. Ramsey didn't stress the word to emphasize the illegality of sharing autopsy information with a stranger. His emphasis was laden with fear.

As he stood to leave, Matt said, "You had your chance, Doctor. I strongly suggest you watch your back from now on."

Nowitzki was leaning against his car when Matt exited the building. Upon seeing Matt's subtle nod, Nowitzki's lips formed a tight smile. "How did it go?"

Matt opened the passenger door and got in. "Let's leave in case Ramsey's watching."

Nowitzki got behind the wheel, started the car, then pulled out of the parking lot and headed down the hill toward the freeway. "Okay, Lanier. Talk."

"I asked him if he thought Diane could have killed herself with Crossley's gun."

Nowitzki's head jerked right in a small double take. "Why?"

"To keep him off balance. He would've guessed my identity if I'd asked him if Crossley could have shot her, because I'm the only person with a vested interest in the answer. I bought us some extra time to prepare."

"I thought we allowed for plenty of time to get back to the Cities."

"Normally, I'd say yes, but we're dealing with a master tactician who always thinks two moves ahead."

"How did Ramsey react? He's on the hot seat now even if he doesn't know Smythe is his blackmailer."

"He was almost shaking with fear, so I'm sure he'll call either Smythe or his man in Duluth. I'll bet he's dialing right now." Matt looked at Nowitzki. "How're you doing? When Smythe finds out I used your name to get in to see Ramsey, he'll put you on his hit list too."

Nowitzki waved him off. "Occupational hazard. I'd rather sleep well at night, so I'll take my chances."

"Thanks. I appreciate it."

After Nowitzki turned off London Road onto the beginning stretch of I-35, he said, "Why're you so sure Smythe or a hit man will show up at Blake's?"

"I'm trying to think like the man. If he finds out someone asked to have Diane's corpse exhumed for an independent autopsy, he'll act fast to prevent that. And if he does nothing, we can still ask Blake for help. Smythe'll be screwed no matter what."

"Good point," Nowitzki said. "If Blake agrees to exhume his daughter's body, we win. If he doesn't, we know he's probably under Smythe's thumb too."

"If Blake wants to keep his precious Supreme Court seat, he'll do anything to protect it—even if it means believing we can keep him out of trouble. He's a pompous ass with an ego the size of a hot-air balloon, but he's also a law-and-order type. When I knew him, he was as fair and impartial as any judge. Strict moral compass. Unless he's changed, he'll do the right thing."

"Trouble is," Nowitzki said, "you haven't spoken to him for years. People do change over time."

"It's a chance I have to take."

"One more question. What if the police show up instead of a hit man?"

"They won't."

"Because?"

"Smythe knows you're on my side now. He can't be sure you won't break your deal and rat him out on the hit angle or that you convinced someone in authority to believe me, which you did. Plus, he won't take the chance that I'll sing like an Italian tenor before he can have me killed in jail."

Nowitzki shot him a sideways glance. "You sound pretty confident."

"I'm not. But I trust my instincts. If the cops show up, we'll regroup and change our plans."

"Okay then," Nowitzki said. "Ready for step two?"

Matt's chest was tight. The scars he'd gotten during his various battles to stay alive in the past year tingled as if to suggest more war wounds were imminent. "Call Hawk and Hypo. Tell them to get into position."

"You call 'em," Nowitzki said and handed him his phone. "I don't want to get pulled over for distracted driving."

Chapter 44

"Please repeat that," Smythe said, gripping the phone as if to crush it like a paper cup. He glanced at his door to make sure it was closed so his assistant, Mary, couldn't eavesdrop.

The caller, Walker—his fixer in the Duluth area—said, "A man claiming to be Ben Nowitzki just left Dr. Dean Ramsey's office. He asked about Diane Blake's autopsy."

Smythe flattened the burner phone against his suit coat and cursed as loud as he dared without Mary hearing him. "Son of a *bitch*. I'll kill him with my own hands." After calming himself, he put the phone back to his ear. "Did Ramsey describe the man?"

"Shabbily dressed," Walker said. "Shaggy, light-brown hair, scruffy beard, six feet tall, medium build but lean. He also said the guy had a wild expression, like he was a little crazy."

Nowitzki's hair was dark brown, and he was far from lean, mean, and wild-looking. Sure, he'd developed a tough-cop aura from years of working for the MPD. But in all other respects, he resembled a regular middle-class guy. After ruling out Nowitzki, Smythe was convinced of the stranger's identity. With his mind whirling, he said, "Thank you. Keep an eye on Ramsey. If he behaves unusually in any way, call me at once."

"Yes, sir," Walker said and clicked off.

Smythe picked up a second burner phone and dialed a number. When the connection went through, he said, "Top priority, Mr. Volkov. Drop everything. I need you to intercept the musician and the private eye, probably tonight. You have about two hours to prepare. Take both as quietly as possible and dispose of them in the usual manner."

"Yes, sir," Volkov said. "But two hours is pretty short notice."

"Damn it, I know. Find a way to make it happen." Now that he'd thought about the situation for a minute, he decided on a slight alteration in strategy. "If there's any chance they might elude you, take them both out on the spot and retreat to the safe house."

After a pregnant pause, Volkov said, "Are you sure? We've never done that before."

Smythe clenched his jaw and controlled the anger in his voice. "Don't *ever* question my commands."

"Sorry," Volkov said. "Just double-checking I heard correctly."

"I've never been more certain about an assignment. My success—and your paycheck—depends on these men being silenced as soon as possible ... *permanently*."

"Consider it done, sir."

Smythe gave him Edward Blake's address and clicked off. He wished he could have had the pleasure of slamming an old-fashioned phone receiver back into its cradle. However, he refrained from throwing the burner phone against the wall.

Chapter 45

Minnesota Supreme Court Associate Justice Edward Blake and his wife Pamela lived in a mid-century modern house on the shore of White Bear Lake in the upscale St. Paul suburb of the same name. The one-story structure with a walkout lower level sprawled parallel to the lake. If the house had been built in the 1990s or later, it would have been dubbed a McMansion. It was built on a rectangular one-acre lot and set back one hundred feet from the street. A well-manicured back lawn sloped down to a ten-foot-wide sand beach that ran along the entire shoreline. Large evergreen hedgerows on the north and south ends of the lot separated the Blake homestead from its neighbors. A small grove of maples and elms twenty yards deep spanned the hedgerows and isolated the house from the street. The final defense was the waist-high fieldstone walls on either side of the driveway running parallel to the road. Although the Blake estate was not impenetrable, not a fortress with a moat, not part of a gated community, it gave the impression of being highly secure. Anyone loitering near the property would eventually be questioned by locals or reported to the police for suspicious activity.

That's why Hawk and Hypo sat in Hawk's old Chevy Malibu, well down the street from the property. They were waiting for dusk before taking their positions. The pair had a clear view of the approach to the house from both directions. So far, they'd seen no suspicious activity.

Each man wore dark clothing. Nowitzki had outfitted them with some of his high-tech surveillance equipment. Besides the wireless ear-bud-and-microphone communication system, he'd given them night-vision scopes with video capability, and small, powerful Maglite flashlights. Hawk, ever the old vet, was packing his Army-issue Beretta M9. Hypo was content with a menacing KA-BAR tactical knife along with his street smarts and CIA training.

"When're we expecting Matt and Ben again?" Hypo asked as he focused on the oncoming vehicle and pedestrian traffic.

Hawk checked his watch. He'd been monitoring traffic behind them using all three car mirrors. "Another hour. We'll get in place in about thirty minutes."

"I sure hope Matt knows what he's doing. If the cops stop us before he shows, we're in big trouble carrying this much hardware."

"Got your cable ties?"

Hypo patted his jacket pocket. "Sure do. You?"

Hawk patted his black denim jacket pocket and nodded. "Flashlight?"

"Check."

"Night vision scope?"

"Check."

"What's in the fanny pack around your waist?"

A sinister grin crept across Hypo's lips. "A little persuader in case we need answers from someone who doesn't want to talk." He took a nip from his flask, then held it toward Hawk. "Want some?"

"I'm good," Hawk said. "You ever gonna tell Matt what's in your flask?"

"Nah, I like to keep him guessing. Let him believe the worst." He shifted in his seat. "You nervous?"

Hawk shook his head. "Just clearing my head and running through my pre-battle checklist."

"It's been a while since I saw any action," Hypo said. "I think I'll be okay, but if shots are fired ..."

Hawk patted him on the knee. "I had a long break between frontline tours because of my wounds. When I went back into action, I had the same doubt. But at go-time, my training kicked in, and my sole concern was protecting my soldiers. You'll be fine once the action starts."

"Hope so," Hypo said, then focused on the street. "Car coming."

A dark SUV approached from the north. Trees on the west side of the road blocked the setting sun, so they didn't see the driver until the car was almost upon them. Hawk pretended to stare at his cell phone while Hypo studied the man from the relative cover of the passenger's seat.

"He's a contender," Hypo said after the SUV passed. "Going slow enough to indicate he's not familiar with the area and looking for an address. He was glancing back and forth, taking in the entire scene."

"Wanna bet he's our man?" Hawk said as he watched the SUV disappear in the driver's side mirror.

"All I have in my pocket is bus money, dude."

"That's okay. We'll just bet our professional pride. I say *yes*."

"Then it's a tie because I say *yes* too."

"A second pass'll confirm."

They waited five minutes. Then Hawk said, "Vehicle approaching from the south."

Ducking low to make their car appear empty, they heard the vehicle slow as it approached them. It stopped, idling next to them for a long, tense moment. Hawk braced for action, but then the vehicle drove away.

Hypo peered over the dashboard enough to see the rear end of the same SUV that had passed them earlier. He said, "We have a winner."

Hawk checked his watch. "A bit earlier than I'd prefer, but we can get into place now."

After they tested their communication devices and adjusted the volumes, Hawk drove through the neighborhood. He circled back to Blake's property from the north so it would be on his right as he approached. When Hawk stopped his car near the hedgerow, Hypo stepped out, did a graceful half-barrel roll over the fieldstone wall, and ducked out of sight. Hawk drove forward to the next cross street and parked halfway up the block—far enough away to avoid suspicion or recognition by the SUV driver. After turning off the ignition, he clicked on his transmitter.

"You in place?" he said softly.

"Roger that," Hypo said.

"I'll be there in two. Keep me apprised."

"Copy."

Hawk strolled to the intersection, crossed over to Blake's side of the street, and ambled toward the stone wall. He barely moved his head, but his eyes were scoping all one hundred eighty degrees in front of him. Twilight was imminent, so his face was obscured from any neighbors who might glance out a window. To his left, the last remnants of sunshine glistened on the lake. The sky was mostly clear. The crescent Moon was low in the eastern sky. The only ambient light other than indoor light leaking through windows was the yellow-orange glow of a streetlight fifty yards north of Blake's property.

Ten feet from the south end of the stone wall, he heard a vehicle approaching from behind. A second later, he heard Hypo say, "Civilian on your six."

Hawk stopped and pulled out his cell phone, pretending to answer it. The car that passed was indeed a civilian—a woman driving a minivan. After the van disappeared down the block, Hawk pocketed his cell phone. He reached the stone wall in three strides and did his own barrel roll over the barrier. With a good twenty years on Hypo, plus a few dozen extra pounds and less natural grace, Hawk landed clumsily on his lead hand. It buckled, and he tumbled into one tree with a thud that bruised his spine as well as his ego.

Righting himself, he settled into the corner of the yard where the wall met the hedge. He had a relatively clear view of Blake's house, driveway, and the south side of the front yard. Hypo's vantage point covered the north side. Anyone sneaking onto Blake's property from the street, even under cover of darkness, would be seen easily by one of them.

"Nice maneuver, old man," Hypo said through his mic.

"Try this again in twenty years and see how well you do it, punk," Hawk said. "Any activity?"

"Nope. Matt said Blake's due home from the golf course between seven and eight."

Hawk pulled the Beretta from his pocket and checked that the magazine was securely in place with a bullet in the chamber. He felt for the night vision scope, flashlight, and cable ties in his other pockets. Heart pounding, even after he'd had time to recover from his clumsy gymnastics, his adrenaline started pumping despite the lack of activity on the grounds. It *had* been a long time since his last combat action. Yet, the pre-fight jitters were as intense as they had been when he faced the prospect of fighting a horde of Iraqi guerrillas armed to the teeth and rabid with hatred for American soldiers.

He took a deep breath and focused on happy memories of childhood, particularly harvesting wild rice on his reservation. He'd come a long way since then, but sometimes wondered if leaving the rez had been the best move for him. He made a rough estimate of how many veterans he'd helped to overcome or at least successfully manage their PTSD. Could he have helped more people in different ways on his own reservation? If he hadn't gone to war and experienced the trauma firsthand, then probably not.

Nevertheless, the past was the past. Tonight, he had this battle to fight, maybe his last. But it was for an honorable reason, to help a brave, torment-ed man. A man battling extreme odds trying to stop a rich, powerful man who embodied all that was evil about the American system: greed, power, corruption, violence, oppression, and exploitation of the less fortunate no matter their race, creed, or color.

Chapter 46

At Matt's direction, Nowitzki parked his Taurus on a side street two blocks from Blake's home. Matt pulled a gear bag from the back seat. From it, they each took a pistol, a small Maglite, some cable ties, and a night-vision scope. Both men then set up their communication devices.

"I'll check in with the H-boys," Nowitzki said, activating his microphone. "Hawk, this is Ben. We're two blocks away. Give us a status report."

"We spied a possible perp before we took positions," Hawk said. "Single driver in a navy-blue SUV. Blake came home ten minutes ago. No apparent passenger. House lights are on. No one else entered from the street. We've checked the backyard every ten minutes. Nothing unusual."

"Copy that," Ben said. "We'll sit tight for a few minutes."

Hypo said, "What if our target *isn't* waiting here for Matt? Are you a hundred percent sure Smythe will send someone?"

Matt said, "I know him. He'll act. This is a golden chance for him to get rid of me."

"Do you really know him, though?" Nowitzki asked. "You met him once and talked to him a few times. Hardly qualifies as intimate knowledge of the man."

Matt could not—*would* not—acknowledge the possibility of a no-show. He wanted to end his nightmare, and he wanted to end it tonight. He faced Nowitzki.

"I've replayed and analyzed everything he's done to me, my father, my friends, and everyone else he's hurt, a thousand times. He hides behind layers of protection, but that doesn't mean he hasn't revealed himself. I finally figured him out. Ever since Witt tried to run me over, Smythe has worked off the presumption I'm a clueless yet incredibly lucky amateur in a panic. My chat with the medical examiner sent a signal to Smythe that I'm messing up his plans again. He'll believe I naïvely mentioned going to Blake for help and won't expect any opposition when I get there. But now we're ready, and I'm *not* in a panic. He'll send someone tonight. All we don't know is *who, how many,* and *how.*"

"Pfft," Matt said. "In that case, this'll be a cakewalk." Having the unknowns pointed out to him drove home the craziness of his plan and the low odds of its success. But it's the best he could under the circumstances.

Nowitzki started to speak, but Hypo's voice over their mics cut him off. "Vehicle approaching from the south. Truck or van. Slowing in front of Blake's. Opposite side of the street. Stopped."

"How many in the cab?" Matt asked.

Hypo said, "Driver only."

"Any markings?" Nowitzki asked.

"North Suburban Plumbing and Heating," Hawk said.

"Anyone ever heard of them?" Matt asked.

No one replied.

"Looks legit," Hypo said. "But there might be a squad of stormtroopers in the back. Happened to me on a mission in the Middle East."

"Is there a phone number printed on the side of the van?" Matt asked.

"Yeah," Hypo said.

Nowitzki pulled out his phone. "Give it to me. I'll call to see if the company's legit."

Hypo recited the number. Nowitzki dialed and waited. Then he held the phone out so Matt could listen. A recorded message thanked them for calling but stated the office was closed now. They were instructed to leave a message or call back during regular business hours or call an emergency number to summon the on-call plumber.

"Sounds genuine," Nowitzki said.

"My gut says *no,*" Matt said. "Can you get onto the internet from here?"

Nowitzki hit some buttons on his phone and studied the screen. "Yeah, I've got a connection. Why?"

"Look them up. See if they have a website, social media presence, or anything else."

Two minutes later, Nowitzki clicked off his phone. "No website or social media. I looked up the phone number in a reverse directory. Hit a dead end. I'll bet it's a burner. Nice catch."

"Jackpot," Hypo said, a little too excitedly. "Let's take 'em out."

"Not so fast," Nowitzki said. "We don't want to storm the van without being absolutely sure. If we move in now, anyone who's inside will lawyer up, maybe claim they were playing an elaborate prank on a friend. We need to catch them in the act. Let's wait for the smoking gun."

Matt flinched and glared at Nowitzki. "How about two seconds *before* the smoking gun?"

"Oh, all right. If you insist."

The four waited in silence for the van or its driver to move. Matt massaged his left hand and silently relived his solo performance with the University of Minnesota Symphony as a college senior: Koussevitzky's Double Bass Concerto, Opus 3. Why that performance memory popped into his head at that instant puzzled him. He let the memories of his nearly virtuosic performance, the synergy with the orchestra, and his sense of relief after he'd finished, wash over him like calming music therapy.

Hypo's voice jarred him back to the present. "Plumber started the van."

"Is he leaving?" Matt asked.

A second later, Hypo said, "Affirmative."

"*What*? Do we have the wrong guy?"

"Don't know," Hawk said. "Stay alert."

They waited five minutes. Hypo and Hawk reported no one walked past. No one drove past. No one stepped out of a house or car. No sounds other than night animals. No movement other than leaves in the breeze and bats swooping and swirling above the treetops.

Matt said, "He's waiting for me to make the first move. He wants the cover afforded by Blake's property, so let's oblige him."

Nowitzki said, "Remember, we gotta be ready for any weapons the hit man might use. The logical choice is to get the drop on you and put a gun to your head. But he might use a baseball bat, knife, Taser, hypodermic needle, chloroform on a rag, tranquilizer dart."

"Get outta town, bro," Hypo said in his street voice. "*Tranquilizer* darts? How cool that be? Why didn't we think of that shit?"

"You a descendant of a dart-blowing tribe in Africa, Hypo?" Hawk asked in a tone as dry as Matt's mouth.

"Take a lot more testicular fortitude, blow a dart from twenty feet than shoot a damn arrow from fifty yards, Chief Not-so-Funny."

"At least—"

"Guys," Matt said, cutting them off. "Can we *please* focus on the job?"

"Right. Sorry," Hypo said in his normal voice.

"Agreed," said Hawk.

"Time to force the issue," Matt said. He opened his door and stepped out. "I'm moving in."

"This is it, gents," Nowitzki said. "Be ready for anything." To Matt, he said, "I'll be thirty seconds behind you."

Matt flashed a thumbs up and set out for Blake's driveway. The night was balmy for mid-spring—maybe sixty degrees. Already damp with nervous sweat, Matt sucked in the humid air. He walked deliberately. Not fast. Not slow. Just a man out for an evening stroll in his neighborhood. He wanted to swivel his head full circle to look for an attack coming from an adjacent property. He limited himself to slight glances from side to side, straining to catch all motion in his periphery.

Half a block from Blake's, the thought leaped into his brain that the plumbing van driver might be a lookout. Had the real hit man positioned himself on Blake's property *before* Hawk and Hypo had arrived? Matt stopped and risked a quick look with his night-vision scope. He saw nothing, not even the top of Hawk's or Hypo's head jutting above the fieldstone walls. Smythe had barely two hours to prepare for an attack. Hawk and Hypo had been staking out the location for almost ninety minutes. Thirty minutes couldn't have been enough time to put someone in place. He dismissed that notion as impossible.

Matt then focused on the surrounding sounds. A chorus of tree frogs croaked and trilled and chirped in the background. A light breeze ruffled the early budding leaves. In the far distance, he heard the hum of a motorboat on White Bear Lake. The prime Minnesota fishing season wouldn't start for another few weeks, but someone might have been angling for panfish, which were always in season. Or it could be a pleasure boat out for a night cruise. The motor sounded closer now. He peered through the foliage toward the lake, trying to see the navigation lights required for boating after dark. As Matt reached Blake's driveway, Blake's house blocked his view of the lake and muffled the motor sound.

After a quick glance all around, he strode between the fieldstone walls and started up the driveway to the house. Lights illuminated the living room and front hall. He'd visited the place with Diane on dozens of occasions during their marriage and knew the floor plan well. The living room occupied the entire south end of the house and had windows on all three sides. The dining room, kitchen, and guest bedrooms faced the street. The den, family room, and master suite faced the lake. A three-car garage and an adjacent workshop covered the north end.

Blake was a consummate creature of habit. On Wednesday afternoons during golf season, he played eighteen at the White Bear Yacht Club course, followed by drinks and dinner with his foursome—usually other judges and lawyers. The WBYC wasn't the most prestigious course in the area, but it was highly regarded among golf aficionados. That's the way Blake liked it—a top-ranked course that flew under the radar. After dinner, he went home, had a nightcap or two, perhaps caught up on paperwork, watched the ten o'clock news, and turned in. The odds were good that at this hour on this Wednesday night, he was enjoying a scotch in his den.

When Matt was twenty feet from the front door, a faint noise behind him caught his attention. Owl? Raccoon? He spun around, looked toward the street for movement, listened for a sound other than the tree frogs or rustling leaves. The motorboat he'd heard earlier had either stopped or was out of earshot. Seeing and hearing nothing unusual, he turned toward the door again. Then he heard Hawk's voice in his earbud.

"Man on the move near where the van was parked. Heading toward Blake's driveway."

Damn! After the plumbing van had first appeared, no one expected the hit man to show up on foot. Had he walked from blocks away, creeping through backyards and climbing over fences? Did that mean he would try to kill Matt and then escape on foot? That didn't fit Smythe's pattern of surreptitious killings that couldn't be traced or appeared to be accidents.

Matt resumed walking. "I'm almost at the front door."

Hawk said, "He's twenty yards behind you."

"I'm one block away," Nowitzki said, "you know what to do, H-boys." His heavy breathing suggested he was jogging.

Two simultaneous replies of "Roger" sounded in Matt's earbuds. He stepped toward the front door, looking for movement and listening for sound inside. Adrenaline energized him, and he took a deep, stabilizing breath.

If Blake was in the den, he wouldn't hear as much as he would have from the living room. But any commotion louder than a fistfight would arouse his attention, which Matt wanted to avoid if possible. If Blake had also imbibed a few post-golf beers, the odds increased he wouldn't hear any outside noise. With any luck, he might doze off soon and be dead to the world.

The wild card was Pamela Blake. She was a descendant of an old-money dynasty that had made the family fortune in the timber industry back in the late 1800s. Edward and Pamela weren't terribly in love. Theirs was a marriage of convenience and prestige. Therefore, her routine on Wednesday during golf season was to make herself scarce. When Matt had known her, that meant she'd go to dinner with girlfriends at an upscale restaurant, then take in a movie or a concert followed by a nightcap at a nearby cocktail lounge. Hawk and Hypo had reported no sightings of Pamela either coming or going. Hopefully, she'd be a non-factor tonight.

Matt reached the front step and waited impatiently for the hit man to arrive. He glanced right toward the north hedgerow where Hypo should be hiding, then left toward the south hedgerow where Hawk should be lurking. He pretended to ring the doorbell, waited five seconds, and pretended to ring again.

"Holy shit," Hawk said. "The plumbing van just turned into the driveway."

Chapter 47

Matt turned to see a man pointing a weapon at his midsection. He was as tall as Matt but, judging by his silhouette, outweighed him by thirty or forty pounds.

"Don't even think of moving," the man said in a menacing tone.

"Van's halfway to the house," Hawk said into Matt's earbud. "You almost here, Ben?"

"Ten seconds," Nowitzki huffed.

The van came to a quick, silent stop near the gunman. The sliding side door opened, but no interior light went on.

"Get in," the gunman said, gesturing with his weapon. It didn't resemble any pistol Matt had ever seen.

"No," Matt said, standing tall, steeling himself for a bullet or an attack. If he died right there, he knew his allies would overpower the gunman and carry on his fight against Smythe.

"*Get. In.*"

"*Fuck. You.*" Matt said. "And if Smythe's listening, fuck you too, Smythe."

A beam of red light clicked on from the tip of the gunman's weapon, pointing at Matt's chest. He reflexively turned and ducked as the gunman pulled the trigger. The weapon emitted a short popping sound. Pain similar to a bee sting slammed into Matt's arm. He grabbed the stinger and pulled. The needle-like barb of a Taser wire popped out, hurting more than it had hurt going in. Then he realized he hadn't gone into complete body spasms because the other barb had missed. He used that one-second surprise to dive at the gunman, aiming low as the man raised his arm to strike Matt with the discharged Taser. Matt made a textbook tackle around the man's waist, doubling him over and negating the force of the blow on his back. They tumbled to the fieldstone sidewalk. Matt's weight knocked the wind out of the gunman, but Matt's forearms were pinned under his assailant's back. Matt rolled them both sideways as he scrambled to gain the advantage. He wondered why the driver hadn't shot him, fired another Taser, or cracked him on the head with a blackjack.

He got his answer when, from outside the driver's window, Hawk barked out, "Freeze."

From behind the back right fender of the van, Nowitzki pointed his pistol at the gunman and yelled, "Give it up, asshole."

Hawk said to the driver, "Hands on the wheel, pal."

Matt stood, grabbed the first gunman by the collar, and yanked him to his feet. "Turn around and put your hands on the van."

The man's scowl was visible in the faint light from Blake's living room, but he slowly complied. Matt patted him down, pulled a pistol from the man's shoulder holster, and jammed it into his waistband. Hawk shoved the driver into the back of the van. He and Nowitzki stood guard as Matt secured the men's hands behind their backs with cable ties.

He'd imagined success in this mission, dreamed about this day. The day he'd outwit Smythe. The day his year-long nightmare would end. Bubbling with optimism, he turned toward the house and said, "Time to talk to Blake."

"Not so fast," a voice commanded from the front of the van.

Matt spun toward the sound and found himself staring at the barrel of a .50 caliber Desert Eagle. The owner's head and weapon hand were visible. The rest of him was protected by the van's hood. Matt's optimism popped like a balloon. *Shit! Smythe played me again.*

Nowitzki glanced at Matt as though he was willing to make a move on the new opponent. But the man would probably shoot two of them before the third could get off a rushed shot. *Where the hell is Hypo?*

As if he'd read Matt's mind, Hypo's voice sounded in his earbud. "Heard a man on the dock. Went to head him off, but he got up here too fast. Don't worry, Jazzman. I got your back."

"Don't try anything, Ben," Matt said. "You either, Hawk." Both men complied by dropping their weapons onto the van's floor and raising their hands.

Smythe's "backup" backup plan instantly became clear: send reinforcements in from the lake. That was the motorboat Matt had heard minutes earlier. He balled his fists and stifled a scream of frustration. Could Hypo possibly bail them out? If Smythe sent in a fourth man as double insurance, it would be game over.

The new gunman stepped out from behind the van. He pointed to the back end and said, "Lanier, over there."

Matt stepped to the end of the van and turned to face him. The new guy produced a knife and slid over to slice the cable tie restraining the first gunman, who retrieved his pistol and trained it on Matt as the new guy freed the driver's wrists. Then the driver used cable ties to secure Hawk and Nowitzki by the wrists.

"Time for our boat ride," the original gunman said. He was obviously the one in charge, the hit man. His accomplices nodded, devilish grins on their faces. Hit Man picked up his Taser and reloaded. He turned to the driver. "Watch these two until we come back."

"They have a boat at the dock," Hypo said to Matt through his mic. "Walk slow."

Matt had no clue about Hypo's plan, but he took his cue from Hypo's instruction and stalled for time. "Even if you kill me," he said, "you won't get away with it. Blake's expecting me. I called him earlier. If I don't show, he'll get suspicious and call the cops."

"Nice try," Hit Man said. "Blake's phone has been tapped for a year. You never called him." He nodded toward the backyard. "Now shut up and move your ass."

For emphasis, he poked Matt in the ribs with the Taser and shoved him toward the backyard. One accomplice walked beside Hit Man holding two pistols. Matt took slow steps, pushing back against the weapon in his side. As they rounded the corner of the garage, the lake came into view. Two boat lifts sheltered by cloth tarps—each about half the length of Blake's dock—sat on either side of the T-shaped structure. One held a pontoon boat. The other sheltered a runabout powered by a large outboard motor. Moored some twenty feet off the end of the dock, a twenty-foot, single-masted sailboat bobbed on the rippling water.

Matt recognized the flotilla from his last visit years ago, but he saw little more than their silhouettes in the dim light of the crescent moon and house lights dotting the lake's far shore. Nearing the water, he saw the outline of another boat bobbing at the end of the dock. As Matt got closer, he recognized it as a standard fishing boat and motor with a canoe tied to its stern. Hit Man's contingency plan came into focus: Put Matt in the canoe. Tow him to the center of the enormous lake. Zap him with the Taser. Capsize the canoe. Prevent him from swimming to shore. Watch him either drown or die of hypothermia. Elapsed time, fifteen minutes. Twenty max. Another perfect accidental death that would, in fact, be murder.

To delay a few seconds, Matt feigned a stumble, staggered, and dropped to his knees. *Come on, Hypo. Do something.*

Hit Man grabbed him by the collar and yanked upward, hard. "Get up, asshole."

"Hey," Matt said, almost hissing, putting extra irritation in his voice. "In case you didn't notice, I'm walking blind here." *Anytime, Hypo.*

Matt resumed walking and took his first step onto the aluminum dock. It squeaked under his weight and flexed slightly. He turned and said again, "You'll never get away with this."

"Keep walking."

Hypo's voice finally sounded in Matt's earbud. "Stop at the *T*. When you hear me coming and they turn, grab one and dive left into the water. I'll take the other and go right."

Matt slowed even more to make sure Hypo had plenty of time. He got another shove in the back from Hit Man. During that last forty feet, he calculated the approximate temperature of the water: late April, cold winter preceding, deeper-than-average lake, ice out maybe two weeks ago. Drawing on past experience swimming here with Diane, he estimated the temperature in the shallows was fifty degrees. He'd swum in Solitude Lake in the Boundary Waters last year until it iced over and was used to water much colder. But someone with no expectation of the shock he'd experience in the cold would panic, gasp in pain and surprise, and become disoriented trying to claw to the surface and get out.

After reaching the *T* in the dock, Matt stopped, turned, and took a step back to the edge, ready to use it for leverage against his enemy. He looked toward shore but couldn't see Hypo. So, as a confirming signal to his ally, he said loudly, "What now?"

Before Hit Man could speak, Hypo's footsteps pounded across the aluminum in an uneven, two-toned *clang*. He was yelling gibberish in an eerie, high-pitched voice. The two goons turned toward the commotion. Matt grabbed the barrel of Hit Man's Taser, yanked him off balance, locked his arm around the man's neck, gulped air, and tumbled them both into the lake.

At impact, the icy water sent a jolt of pain through Matt's body. He resisted the urge to open his mouth and scream. As expected, Hit Man bellowed a bubbly yelp of shock that lasted a second before he choked on a mouthful of water. Matt held on tight, stayed parallel to the bottom, not allowing Hit Man to find his footing and stand up. He torqued Hit Man's wrist as hard as he could, heard an underwater groan, then felt the Taser slip from Hit Man's grip. The man flailed and struggled, thrashing so hard he almost escaped. Matt found the sandy bottom with his feet, regripped his captive with both arms, and rolled on top of him. He surfaced and managed a quick gulp of air before putting all his weight on his prey and forcing him down. Hit Man struggled for a few seconds, then his thrashing slowed. All the rage and frustration Matt had repressed for a year awoke with a vengeance. He desperately wanted to hold Hit Man underwater until the life drained from him, air bubble by air bubble. But he resisted the temptation. He needed this guy alive. Needed him to incriminate Smythe. He hoped he would be the missing piece of the puzzle that would end the death, destruction, and despair that had fucked over Matt's life for twelve nightmarish months.

Hit Man kicked his feet one last time, then went limp. Anticipating a ruse, Matt surfaced again, gulped air, and found his footing, staying crouched in the waist-deep water so Hit Man couldn't breathe. He replayed their last few seconds on the dock, listening with his memory for how much air Hit Man took in before going under.

Hearing splashing and thrashing near the other end of the dock, Matt turned and saw Hypo standing in the water with his man in a choke hold. Hypo saw him and said, "You okay, J-man?"

Matt nodded. "Yeah. You?"

"Yeah, but I'm freezing my ass off. How do we get out of here and not lose these two?"

Matt let his man come up for air. Hit Man gasped and coughed, sucking air into his lungs as fast as he could. He wasn't faking. Matt regripped, squatted, and bench-pressed the guy onto the dock. Then he scrambled up and on top of him, letting his full weight constrain the sputtering, gasping prisoner.

"Bring your guy over here," Matt said.

Hypo did so. Matt grabbed the guy's collar and helped Hypo manhandle him onto the dock. Hypo climbed up, pulled out two cable ties, and bound the two men's hands behind their backs. Each man had been in the lake for less than a minute, but they'd need to get warm soon to restore their motor skills and coordination. Hypo was already shivering. Matt's shivers had subsided. He figured pure adrenaline shielded him from the negative effects of his ice bath.

"What the hell did you yell when you ran down the dock?"

Hypo grinned, his white teeth glowing in the moonlight. "A little Pashto battle cry I picked up in Pakistan."

"Jesus H. Christ! You sounded like you were demonically possessed. Nearly gave me a heart attack, you crazy spy."

"Sorry about that. But it threw them off long enough for me to engage."

"Whatever works, I guess." Matt looked at the house. "Let's pat these guys down, then deal with the driver."

Each assailant's primary weapons had ended up in the lake, but both had a small revolver in ankle holsters and switchblades in their pockets. Hypo confiscated them and handed a pistol to Matt. He said, "What if they come around enough to start yelling?"

Matt thought for a moment and asked for a knife. "Cut off a piece of their clothing and stuff it in their mouths." It took them a minute to gag each man. Matt gestured toward the driveway. "Got a plan?"

"Our transmitters are shot," Hypo said, pointing to his earbuds. "We can't warn the guys, so let's divide and conquer. Haven't heard the van's engine start. I'm guessing the driver's job is to wait until these losers return."

Seeing no activity in the house, Matt presumed Blake was unaware of the scuffle on the dock. But the driver might have heard Hypo's war cry and the splashing. He could be hiding, ready to ambush them both. A greater concern was the welfare of Hawk and Nowitzki. They might be seen as expendable by the Hit Man, who might have told the driver to kill them silently while he waited.

"Split up," Matt said, pointing to the north side of the house. "I'll go straight. Signal me with your flashlight in the trees when you're ready to move. I'll distract the driver. You come in from the passenger side. Have a pistol ready, but shoot only if you have no other choice."

Hypo nodded, grim-faced. "Roger that. See you in sixty seconds."

Chapter 48

Matt crept toward the garage, keeping low so his silhouette wouldn't show against the moonlit lake. Had the driver called in reinforcements? Would Smythe want Matt dead at all costs if the initial plan to stage his death as an accident failed? If Matt's survival was at stake, he'd shoot to kill. Better if he or one of his allies survived to tell his story and keep fighting than to have them all die because of his overcautiousness.

At the side of the garage, Matt raised his pistol and strained to see any motion at the front corner. No one appeared, so he continued forward. At the corner, he peered around at the van and saw the shadow of the driver at the wheel. Not quite in a position to see Hypo's signal, he darted toward the hedgerow and the protection of a tree trunk that barely concealed half his torso. His inner metronome had ticked off fifty-five seconds. He watched and listened for the faintest movement or sound.

When Hypo's Maglite beam hit a tree across the yard, Matt clicked on his Maglite and pointed at the driver. In a commanding tone just loud enough to carry twenty feet, he said, "Police. Freeze!"

The driver's head jerked toward the noise and the light. "Don't shoot! Don't shoot!"

"Hands up," Matt said from behind the tree. The driver winced and shielded his eyes.

Hypo sprinted to the van's passenger side with his light shining at the driver. From the passenger window, he said, "One stupid move, and you're dead."

"I'm raising my hands," the driver said as he slowly raised his hands. "Please don't shoot."

Matt sprang forward, opened the driver's door, and leveled his pistol at the man's head. "Get out."

"Yeah, yeah. Whatever you say. Just don't shoot me."

After the driver got out, Hypo circled the van and bound the man's hands with a cable tie behind his back. They hustled him around to the sliding door and opened it.

"About time you showed up," Hawk said with no hint of impatience. "We were getting bored. You get them?"

"They're tied up at the dock," Matt said. "You two okay?"

Both said, "Fine."

Hypo used his knife to cut their restraints. They slid out of the van, rubbing their wrists.

Matt found Hawk and Nowitzki's pistols in the front seat and handed them to their owners. "Watch the driver. If he opens his mouth, stuff a rag in it. We'll retrieve the other two."

Matt and Hypo returned to the dock, dragged the soaking wet, shivering thugs to their feet, then led them back to the van. So far, Blake had shown no sign of being alerted to the noise outside. Maybe he was on his third scotch rocks and down for the count.

Once the three assailants were settled in the back of the van, Matt said to Nowitzki, "Time to get your laptop."

"I'll be back in five," Nowitzki said. He took off for his car, where he'd securely stored his laptop with copies of the compiled evidence and testimony Matt had shared with the FBI.

"Crank up the heat, Hawk," Matt said. "Hypo, get in back with me and these losers."

Hawk complied, and a weak stream of heat wafted through the van. Matt and Hypo climbed into the cargo area, closed the door, and studied their prisoners. The driver was wide-eyed with fear. The two from the dock shivered and avoided eye contact, humiliated for being outsmarted. In no mood to waste time, Matt eyed each man with laser-like intensity before speaking.

"Talk fast and don't lie. I know you work for Smythe. I know he wants you to kill me. You tell me what I want to know; I'll let you live. If you don't, well, you're the least of my worries. And believe me, I've got a lot of worries. If killing you is the only way for me to survive, I won't hesitate for a nanosecond. Your choice: Take your chances and hope for a light sentence for being accessories to conspiracy, or die."

Each man shot sideways glances at the other two, probably wondering if one or all should cooperate or if Smythe would kill them for failing their assignment. Hit Man finally spoke.

"I have no idea who this Smythe guy is." His defiant stare seemed forced.

Matt detected a slight accent—Russian or Polish—and said, "What's your name?"

"We're three plumbers who got called to a job, pulled into the wrong driveway, and got jumped by four lowlifes who tried to drown me and my apprentice."

Anger rolled from Matt's toes to his fingertips. He made a fist, using all his willpower to hold back a sucker punch to Hit Man's nose. "One box of generic tools hardly qualifies as a well-equipped plumbing van. More importantly, since when do plumbers carry semiautomatic weapons and Tasers?"

"Lotta dangerous neighborhoods. A guy's gotta be careful."

One of Hit Man's buddies smirked.

"*This* is a dangerous neighborhood?" Matt asked.

"Didn't think so until tonight. But we work in a lot of dicey areas. Besides, look at what happened to us in this *safe* neighborhood. You gonna rob us now? Steal our van? Who do *you* work for?"

Silence.

"Okay, 'nuf o' this bullshit," Hypo said in his street voice. "My man askin' you questions. Ain't polite to diss him. So I'm gonna ask you my *own* way." He locked stares with each man to drive his point home. Then he held up his right hand and wiggled its three fingers. "See this? Bet you wonderin' how the brotha lost them fingers." He thrust his prosthetic left foot forward. "Bet you wonderin' how the brotha lost this too. Any guesses?"

Hypo waited a long moment for an answer Matt knew wouldn't come.

"You probably thinkin' I'm one dumbass mofo keeps losin' body parts. Maybe got careless with a table saw in shop class. Or I'm a crackhead who got high and messed with some cherry bombs I shouldn't have messed with."

The prisoners had sullen expressions, like teens sitting in the principal's office after getting busted for bullying a nerdy kid.

"Wasn't nothin' like that. I lost 'em with somethin' look like *this* bad boy."

From the fanny pack around his waist, Hypo pulled out a large metal tool—pruning shears with heavy-duty saw teeth instead of scissor blades. Their captives' eyes widened in unison when he worked the mechanism. The teeth made an unnerving metallic rasp. *Snip.* His gleaming smile and wide-eyed manic look were more unsettling than the tool.

"Funny thing is, I lost 'em while servin' my country in the Middle East. Al Qaeda *loves* tools like this. The nastier, the better for them crazies. With this, they can torture a fella *slooow*." Hypo worked the pruning shears three times, emphasizing the downstroke. Once for each prisoner, inches from their noses. Then he lowered his voice and seemed to fade back to his past in a haunted tone. "They started with my foot. One toe at a time. Wasn't so bad 'cause a brotha can still walk decent with no toes. And shoes cover up the ugly. Mofos don't much care for anesthetic, neither. 'Specially when they question a spy. After five questions and no answers, they cut off the rest of my foot."

Matt forced down images of his own foot minus five toes, bleeding profusely, wondering how bad the pain would be, how easily he would have cracked.

"The interrogator figured I was a challenge, so they skipped my other foot and started on my fingers. Fingernails first. Ripped 'em off with pliers. They make you watch too. Grab your head, hold it in place, even pry your damn eyes open. Let you think about it for a day, watchin' your fingertip bleed, throbbin' like hell. But fingernails grow back, so you still got some hope. A day or two later, they talk to you again. Give 'em a jive answer they don't like or don't believe and *snip!* They hack off a joint at the knuckle.

Those mothers ain't *never* growin' back. One per day." He worked the shears six times. "Six cuts, six days."

The prisoners' faces were ashen. Their sullen looks had turned to wild-eyed fear.

"Fingernail and three joints, times two fingers, add up to eight interrogations. By then, if you still sane, you beggin' to die."

Matt's face flushed as detailed images burst into his brain of Hypo strapped down, being interrogated by ruthless, sadistic enemies.

"But you know what?" Hypo said. "I love this country so much, and I hated what that SOB bin Laden did to us on nine-eleven, that I never told them nothin' except my name, rank, and serial number."

The prisoners' expressions were of utter incomprehension.

"So dis how it's going down, you stupid dickheads. You tell my man the truth; you keep your fingers. He give me any kind of stink eye he don't believe you; I start snippin'." He raised the shears and worked the mechanism again. *Snip.* "Only one question." *Snip.* "Who." . . . *Snip* . . . "Goes." . . . *Snip* . . . "First?" *Snip.*

He leered at each one, letting them see the crazed sincerity in his eyes. There was no doubt Hypo would follow through on his threat. After everything he'd been through, Matt didn't care about sparing them severe pain if that benevolence might cost him his freedom.

The driver, whose eyes were still bugged out from Hypo's story and the menacing shears, blurted, "Damn it, Volkov, I didn't sign up for this shit. I'm just driving the fucking van. I don't know anything about anyone named Smythe, and I sure as shit don't want to lose my fingers for five hundred bucks!"

That explained why the driver was an easy takedown: Smythe had scrambled for bodies. Maybe his army of crooks wasn't as big as Matt had imagined. Matt faced the man to whom the driver had spoken—the hitman. "Volkov, huh? Do *you* work for Leland Smythe?"

The motor purred, and the heater *whooshed*. Despite being cold and wet, Matt ignored his discomfort. The only motion was Hawk turning to watch Volkov.

Volkov swallowed hard, his gaze fixed on the pruning shears. "Yes."

Matt resisted the urge to leap into the air and do a classic fist pump, followed by a triumphant shout. Instead, he smiled grimly, as if that answer only compounded his problem. "For how long?"

"A year."

"Do you work for Smythe Properties?"

"No."

"Premier Security Services?"

Appearing surprised that Matt knew the name of his company, Volkov nodded.

"But you mostly work for Smythe."

"Yes."

"Doing what?"

"Strong-arm stuff. Persuasion, you might say."

"Let me guess. Mostly farmers along I-35."

Volkov glared defiantly at him.

Hypo worked the pruning shears. *Snip.*

"Yes!"

"What's your territory?"

Volkov hesitated, then said, "Southern Minnesota, most of Iowa. Here to Des Moines."

"Do you also deliver bribe money?"

Volkov nodded.

"How many people has Smythe blackmailed in your territory?"

Volkov hesitated as if he were counting.

Feeling sudden pressure to get this evening over with, Matt slammed the inside wall of the van with his palm. "How many?"

"I don't know," Volkov said, desperation in his voice. His gaze darted back and forth from his captors to the pruning shears. "Maybe ten."

"How many people have you killed?"

"Now, hold on," Volkov said. "You're starting to sound like judge, jury, and executioner. I got my rights. I want a lawyer."

Hawk chuckled. "My friend, think of this van as a tiny, independent nation. We answer to no one. You have no rights unless we say you have rights. So quit bitching and answer his questions."

Surprised by Hawk's outburst, Matt suppressed a smile and looked at Volkov. "I'll throw you a bone and rephrase my question. How many accidents like the one you had planned for me have you arranged?"

"Some," he admitted.

"Give me a number," Matt said through clenched teeth.

Hypo did a *snip-snip* an inch from Volkov's nose.

"Five!" Volkov said. "You'd have been six. You were his top priority. You and the other guy."

"Nowitzki?"

"Yeah."

As if on cue, Nowitzki slid open the van door. "Got the laptop."

"Good," Matt said. "I've got enough to work with from this guy. But I need you with me when I talk with Blake."

"Sure thing. You ready?"

An innocent question with significant implications, not to mention risks. Matt would be asking a father to exhume his daughter's body for a second autopsy. When Blake asked why he should cooperate, Matt's claim that Crossley had shot Diane would probably be met with a derisive snort and a question about Matt's sanity. Why does the wanted man, accused of murder, think he can get cooperation from a supreme court justice just because he has a hunch that the biggest real estate tycoon in the state blackmailed a medical examiner into falsifying his daughter's autopsy?

Then again, Blake might turn him down cold. Refuse to see him for personal reasons. Blake resented Matt because he believed Matt had had some kind of hold on his daughter while they were together. That influence dulled her judgment and put her fast-track legal career in jeopardy. Old-fashioned elitist snobbery, plain and simple. In Blake's eyes, social standing, reputation, knowing the right people from the right families—and making alliances with those families—trumped love every time.

A third possibility was Blake had witnessed tonight's activities on his property and called the police. There was no time to waste. All or nothing or die trying. With forced confidence, Matt said, "I'm ready."

Chapter 49

Matt rang Blake's doorbell twice, then knocked hard, a five-beat cadence that would be heard throughout the house. His heart thumped in his chest. The dryness in his mouth contrasted with his soaked clothing. He shivered, eager to get inside and warm up before meeting his fate.

Eventually, faint footsteps sounded inside. The outside light flashed on. The solid mahogany inner door swung open into the backlit foyer. Seeing no one, Matt opened the glass storm door and stepped in. Nowitzki followed.

"You've got a hell of a lot of nerve coming here," Edward Blake said as he stepped from the darkness, holding a shotgun aimed at Matt's chest. "If I shoot you dead right now, I'm well within my rights."

"Lovely to see you again too, Edward," Matt said with no cheer in his voice.

"I guess that music career of yours hasn't worked out so well, eh?"

Matt ignored the cheap shot that restarted the battle of wills and wits, a hallmark of their rocky relationship.

In the eleven years since their last encounter, Matt's former father-in-law had added twenty years of age and twenty pounds of weight. His once-solid, medium-sized frame sagged under the weight and pressure of a high-powered career. His square jaw was now rounded by fleshy jowls. Bags under his eyes highlighted the deep creases in his face. His thick, dark hair had gone wispy and gray. The only part of his face that didn't show extreme age was his bright-white teeth. Too perfect to be natural for a sixty-something who *wasn't* a movie star or other celebrity.

Blake was a fourth-generation lawyer whose ancestors had slowly amassed a respectable estate, with each generation more than doubling that fortune. He'd risen to the top of his profession, mostly on talent. He'd also forged friendships and connections with the Twin Cities elites. As much as any judge could be, Edward Blake was a player in Minnesota's political scene.

"Smythe called me at my club," Blake said. "Told me to expect some trouble from you. Laid it all out. He had a plan to remove you before you could get to my door. But he also warned me that you had cleverly evaded him for more than a year. In the event you reached this point, he told me to deal with you in any way I choose. I prefer the home-invasion angle. So neat and tidy. And who on earth would ever question the word of a state supreme court justice?"

"So he got to you too," Matt said, disappointed but not surprised.

Blake waved his shotgun at Nowitzki. "This your friend Nowitzki?"

Matt said, "I came here believing you loved Diane more than you loved your career. Thought I had a chance to convince you of my innocence. Boy, was I wrong."

"I loved Diane more than you ever did," Blake said, raising the barrel of the shotgun to point at Matt's face. "I did everything I could to make her life perfect."

Matt shook his head, but remained focused on Blake's trigger finger. "You did everything you could to make her life perfect for *you*."

"What's wrong with being the best? With the résumé I was building for her, Diane could've been on the national political stage in ten years. Could've been the first female president."

"She didn't want that," Matt countered. "The happiest I ever saw her was early in her career as a public defender. She'd finish a sixty-hour week, come home, crash on the sofa, and tell me about all the people she helped in meaningful ways. She was making the world a better place, one person at a time. And when Monday rolled around, she was recharged and ready to do it all again."

"Hah," Blake scoffed. "The equivalent of rearranging deck chairs on the *Titanic*. All those losers would stay losers no matter how many hours she worked. Breaking barriers in national politics, bringing sweeping reforms to the entire nation, *that's* worth striving for."

"For you, maybe. Not for Diane. She obeyed you because she was a dutiful daughter who was pressured by her family legacy."

Blake's eyes softened. "It's all moot though, isn't it?"

Matt met his gaze.

"Because you killed her," Blake said.

"Did Smythe bother to tell you why he called tonight?"

"What difference does it make? You're a wanted killer."

"Think about this, Edward. How could Smythe have known I was coming here? I swear on Diane's memory, I didn't talk to him."

"Why should I believe you? You're a common criminal."

"He's not a mind reader. The only people who knew I'd come here were my friends. And they're loyal to a fault."

"That's not what I heard about Nowitzki."

"I changed sides," Nowitzki said, glaring at Blake. "Decided to do the right thing instead of the profitable thing."

"Oh really?" Blake said and literally looked down his nose at Nowitzki. "And how's that working out for you so far, chump?" He snorted, then gestured at Matt with his shotgun barrel. "You're one trigger pull away from going down with your foolish friend here."

Matt raised his hands. "We're armed, Edward, but we won't use our weapons on you."

"We *won't*?" Nowitzki said, shooting a quick glance at Matt before returning his focus to the shotgun.

Matt shook his head. "Did it ever occur to you that Smythe has eyes and ears all over the state? He's committed so many crimes, he has to cover his ass twenty different ways."

"The opinion of a desperate criminal," Blake said. "Leland Smythe is a savvy businessman and a friend who has generously donated to my campaigns."

"Get real," Matt said. "Judges at all levels in this state can fund their campaigns with piggy bank change. All it takes is a postcard sent out a week before the election reminding voters you're still alive. As long as you haven't raped or murdered anyone, you'll get reelected."

Nowitzki said to Matt, "I think what he means is that Smythe bought him the supreme court seat. I followed the story in the news last year." He turned to Blake. "Without him, you'd still be on the court of appeals."

Blake stiffened.

Matt said, "I'll chalk up your lack of comprehension to all the scotch you've had tonight, Edward. You can't hold your liquor as well as you could in the old days."

"He said you'd be gunning for me," Blake said. "You killed my daughter, and now you want to kill her old man."

Matt laughed out loud. "I get it now. You don't *want* to know the truth. You want to wallow in grief. Blame me for fucking up your grand plans for your precious daughter." He injected a whiny smarm into the phrase *precious daughter*.

Blake tensed his grip on the shotgun. "Watch your damn mouth, punk. You have no right to talk about her that way."

"Listen carefully," Matt said, ignoring the shotgun barrel pointed at his torso. "*Think* carefully. Smythe was tipped off by the medical examiner who performed the autopsies on Diane and Crossley, Dr. Dean Ramsey."

"How do you—" Blake broke off, seeming to realize the answer to his question.

Matt nodded. "I went to see him today. Nowitzki said he's a reputable man. Stellar career. Highly respected in the medical community. However, he nearly freaked out when I questioned Diane's autopsy results. Because of his rep, I never thought he would take a bribe. But there's another way to get someone to lie. Care to guess?"

Blake's focus was on the wall over Matt's shoulder. No doubt he was imagining his daughter's body being carved up on a stainless-steel autopsy table.

Matt said, "Blackmail. After our visit this afternoon, Ramsey panicked, contacted Smythe, and said someone pretending to be Nowitzki asked about the Blake-Crossley case. He worried that if he *didn't* inform Smythe about me, his terrible secret would come out, and his career would implode. Blackmail also worked against the Straight River M.E. It's probably worked several times in other small towns to cover up suspicious deaths."

Stepping forward until his chest was inches from the shotgun barrel, Matt continued. "My *father* was Smythe's victim. I initially believed his death was accidental. But the real autopsy proved Smythe's goon murdered him. My neighbor almost lost everything because of a blackmailed coroner. Diane and two of my best friends died because of Smythe. See the pattern, Edward? He uses people to get what he wants. He's using you right now. If you pull the trigger, you're the one who lives with it, not him. Self-defense? Doesn't matter. A supreme court associate justice shoots and kills his former son-in-law in his house. How's that gonna look on your family legacy?"

Blake wavered. He swallowed hard. "How do you know he blackmailed Ramsey?"

"He said the bullet that killed Diane was from my gun. But I know with ninety-nine percent certainty that Crossley killed her. Ramsey probably doctored the photo of the gunshot wound to eliminate the gunpowder stippling and burn marks from a point-blank shot. He probably lied about the angle of the entrance wound. He dismissed the fact that only one shell casing out of fifteen ejected by Crossley's pistol was inside the car. The last shot. The shot that killed Diane."

Blake reacted as if he'd never considered the possibility that someone other than Matt killed his daughter. He *wanted* to believe it because he'd detested Matt from the day they met.

"I know this is a shock, Edward," Matt said. "What I'm asking you to do is difficult. Believe me, I wanted to find another way. But I've been running from Smythe for more than a year. This is the first tiny chink I've found in his armor. With your help, I can *prove* Crossley killed Diane. I *never* would've killed her. I didn't even know she was in the passenger seat until after the shooting stopped. I thought she was driving alone, like we'd discussed earlier over the phone. But then someone else started shooting at me from the driver's seat. I fought back against *Crossley* in self-defense. At that moment, I never imagined he'd bring her along when he tried to kill me."

Blake's knitted brow showed confusion. "But she and Crossley were going to marry," he said. "Steven even asked for my blessing a week before she died."

"*What?*" Matt said, mouth agape. "That's impossible. Diane and I had been speaking for several weeks before she died. She confessed she broke up with that bastard because he'd gotten violent with her. That was only days before Crossley killed her."

Blake's face reddened. "No. He was going to *marry* her."

"Why would Diane lie? If she and Crossley were destined to be the next great power couple from Minnesota, she would've told me he treated her like a queen."

"Crossley was always the perfect gentleman. They'd come out here, and we'd have relaxing afternoons on the boat, delightful dinners. He seemed perfect for Diane."

"Hah-hah!" Nowitzki's guffaw caught Blake's attention.

"What's so funny?" Blake demanded.

"You got Eddie Haskelled."

Blake's blank stare showed no comprehension of the phrase.

"Eddie Haskell," Nowitzki said. "The two-faced suck-up from *Leave it to Beaver* who was a perfect gentleman in front of Beaver's parents but a wise-ass bully to Beaver." Nowitzki shook his head. "And to think I was going to vote for you in the next election. I dunno, man. Not so good if a supreme court justice can't tell when someone's feeding them a trough full of bullshit."

When Blake's expression didn't change, Matt said, "For Christ's sake, Edward. Wake up. Crossley manipulated you for the sole purpose of getting to Diane. He didn't love her. He only used her to advance his career. He knew the Blake pedigree. Knew you'd push her to keep climbing the political ladder. Above all else, he knew she'd be the obedient daughter."

Doubt showed in Blake's eyes.

"Here's the kicker," Matt said. "Because she'd broken up with him, Diane became the enemy. Smythe probably ordered Crossley to kidnap her and bring her to the rest area in Duluth. Crossley planned to kill me there, then drive to a remote location, kill her, and dump her body. But when he didn't kill me and I mortally wounded him, he couldn't let her live. Diane had to die because she knew too much."

Keeping the shotgun leveled at Matt, Blake rubbed his face with one hand. He was cracking under the pressure of doubt Matt had planted in his mind. Matt pressed his advantage.

"I've got nothing to lose, Edward. Smythe ruined my life, but I'm still alive. Diane and many others are dead because of what he's trying to do. Crossley was an equal partner, but in the end, Smythe didn't need him either. Even if you kill me and claim self-defense against an intruder, Smythe will discard you at the first sign you're not all in with him."

Blake's face tightened, and he looked away.

"He's got you by the short hairs. When he needs a favor, say, a case ruling or even a well-timed phone call from you to someone important to him, you'll do what he asks or else. He's too powerful. This conspiracy is national. I'll bet he's got dozens of U.S. senators and representatives in his pocket. Major corporations. A billionaires' club like you can't imagine. The sad part is, Smythe sees this as a gigantic game. He doesn't care how it *ends*. All he cares about is that *he's* the first one to cash out of this Ponzi scheme."

"What the hell are you talking about?" Blake demanded.

Matt and Nowitzki exchanged puzzled glances.

"You don't know about Millennium Four?"

Blake shook his head.

Matt said, "I have a taped confession that Smythe is the head of a conspiracy called Millennium Four." He explained the North American Superhighway concept and M4's goals as briefly as he could, then said, "Its members have killed many people and ruined dozens of farmers and their families. Some of those people died because I tried to stop the conspiracy. Smythe wants the success of Millennium Four to be his legacy. But he doesn't care if the goal is ultimately reached. It's a game of who can suck the most money out of innocent farmers *and* eventually the federal government without getting caught."

Blake scoffed. "Sounds like a fairy tale to me. How do you prove something so ludicrous?"

"That's why we focused on Diane's autopsy. It's the weakest link."

"You want me to dig my daughter's body out of the ground and have it re-poked, re-prodded, treated like a piece of meat again?"

Matt lowered his head. "It's the only way. Please, Edward. Listen to the recording before you decide."

Blake lowered his shotgun. His eyes were full of fatigue and confusion. "I need a drink."

"Good idea," Nowitzki said, sounding relieved that death wasn't imminent.

Blake led them to his wet bar at one end of the spacious dining room. After leaning his shotgun against the wall, he fixed a scotch for himself and motioned for Matt and Nowitzki to help themselves. Matt declined. Nowitzki poured himself two fingers of bourbon.

Blake took a sip, paused, swallowed, winced, and said, "Play the recording."

Nowitzki opened the laptop, opened the file containing Flannery's confession, and hit *play*. They listened in silence. Matt relived the conversation as if he were back on the island, standing in the cold, clean air, shaking with fear, rage, and disbelief that he'd been forced to fight to the death and take a man's life. By the time the recording had finished, Blake's glass was empty.

Elbows on knees, Blake regarded Matt with a sidelong glance. "Sounds authentic. I couldn't hear any obvious cuts or splices. I'm no expert, but you'd have to go to extraordinary lengths to produce a recording that long and make it seem real."

"It's authentic," Matt said. "I brought the tape recorder with me to record what went down from my perspective because I didn't know if I'd survive. Gebhardt and I didn't plan to record any conversations until the shooting was over. Then we figured it couldn't hurt, since he and Flannery were both wounded. Better to get something before they passed out, or worse. Turns out, that's the only thing besides me that survived the battle."

"I had no idea Smythe is behind this, this—"

"No one else does, either, besides my friends outside."

"I watched you being marched down to my dock and the ensuing scuffle. Gotta say that looked real."

"They were going to drown me. Capsize the canoe. Stage an *accident*. Classic Smythe."

Blake sat back and stared at his former son-in-law. "I never liked you, Matt. Mainly because I was raised to believe entertainers were second-class citizens. It was ingrained in my cultural upbringing. The band playing for the party or wedding or corporate shindig was expendable. People with a single talent who anonymously added atmosphere to an event."

"I know," Matt said. "I played a lot of those gigs in high school and college."

"We went to the symphony to see and be seen," Blake added. "Social status and all."

Matt nodded. He couldn't argue. Rich snobs like Blake had paid his salary as an orchestra member. Most of the elite class didn't particularly appreciate the talent of the musicians or composers.

"Diane always defended you," Blake said. "She tried to get me to understand your drive, your discipline, your incredible talent. Even up to the end. She called last March, mentioned she'd seen you at a club, said you were the same old Matt but seemed to have gotten better musically. Years more experience, I suppose."

Matt's heart fluttered, then ached. Diane had been one of the few from the privileged class who enjoyed his musical genres—jazz and classical—and appreciated the years of dedication, study, and practice required to become a top-level performer. If she'd been in the room at that moment, he'd have given her a long hug, a tender kiss, and a sweet "I love you."

Blake swirled the ice in his glass. "The one trait I give you credit for is honesty. You never tried to suck up to me with an ulterior motive. You stood your ground when I gave you shit. I was tough on Diane's boyfriends because I wanted them to understand that our family was part of the package. You get my daughter; you get the entire Blake family going back four generations. They all crumbled fast when they realized that. You didn't. I admired you for that. But I never let you forget I was part of the deal. It eventually got to be too much for Diane. We argued about you a lot. In the end, I suppose I won, if you can call the result we're facing today a victory."

Blake stared at the floor. Nowitzki drained his bourbon.

Matt cleared his throat. "It's time to decide, Edward. Either request an exhumation or …"

Blake looked up. "Or what?"

Matt chuffed out a breath of air. "I don't know. You're my last hope. Either call the cops or shoot me and put me out of my misery."

Blake pondered his request over for a minute, then checked his watch. "Hmm, it's a bit late, but I think a supreme court justice can cut through the red tape and order an exhumation."

Matt's jaw dropped. "Seriously?"

"Your story is hard to believe, but I want to find out for myself. Pamela and I raised Diane to strive for a high moral code. Higher than mine, I'm ashamed to say. She'd have wanted the truth to be known. I swear to God I thought Crossley was the right man for her. If she'd told me he'd even said a cross word to her, I would have killed him with my bare hands."

Fighting back tears of joy and relief, Matt said, "I-I'm speechless, Edward. Thank you."

Nowitzki patted Matt's shoulder. "Congratulations." To Blake, he said, "I've got a contact in the FBI who'll handle the case once we get a definitive autopsy that proves Crossley killed your daughter. Of course, she'll want to speak to you before taking action against Smythe."

Blake nodded and went to the kitchen to make a phone call. Upon returning to the dining room, he said, "It'll happen tomorrow. Exhumation in the morning, examination in the afternoon by the best independent forensic pathologist in the state."

Both Matt's and Nowitzki's eyebrows shot upward. Rank definitely had its privileges.

Chapter 50

When Matt and Nowitzki came out of Blake's house, Hypo and Hawk were standing next to the open sliding door of the van. Their prisoners were sprawled in the cargo hold, looking sullen and defeated.

"What did Blake say?" Hawk asked.

"He agreed to exhume Diane's body," Matt said. "Now, let's hope my hunch is right."

"What are the odds?" Hypo asked.

Matt sighed. "I dunno. My hearing has never let me down. But I *was* fighting for my life. I replayed that shootout hundreds of times. It was like listening to a CD. Exactly the same every time. My one worry is that Crossley's last shot missed Diane. He had to be close to dead by then. If that's true, then *my* bullet killed her."

"Even so," Nowitzki said, "it's pretty hard to miss from point-blank range."

Matt forced down the gruesome image of Crossley pressing the barrel of his gun to Diane's temple and firing. But he was as sure as he could be about Crossley being her killer.

"What's our next step?" Hawk asked.

Nowitzki said, "I'll call Reggie Irving. We might be able to haul these losers down to the Minneapolis Field Office tonight."

Nowitzki stepped away to make the call. Matt realized he was still wet from his little swim in the lake. He focused on Hypo. "You warming up?"

"Not bad," Hypo said. "The van's heater helped. Glad this didn't go down last month."

Matt chuckled. "If it had, we would've become human icebergs floating across the lake."

Hypo took a sip from his flask, then offered it to Matt. "Funny how going for a swim makes me thirsty. Want some?"

"Been a long night. I could use a belt." Matt put the flask to his lips and braced for the sting of brandy or gin or schnapps or whatever Hypo's beverage of choice was. But as he tipped and swigged, the sting of straight liquor was absent. He swallowed and shot his friend a wry grin. Hypo's bright smile gleamed in the dim light. Matt feigned indignation. "*Water?* Who walks around with *water* in a hip flask?"

"At least one person," Hypo said.

"Care to explain?"

"Not really, but you're my friend, so I will."

"It's an interesting story," Hawk interjected.

"When Al Qaeda captured me, they had other torture methods besides lopping off fingers and toes. They saved those for when their first-line torture methods didn't work. No food or water was a biggie. They figured everyone would eventually talk if it meant getting a crust of bread or a cup of water."

"Nice guys," Matt said.

"They starved me for a week. I must have a slow metabolism because it didn't bother me too much. But no water? Whoa. *That* was different. After three days in a windowless cell in the brutal Pakistan summer, I was freaking out. Lucky for me, I passed out before I could trade them information for a cup of water. They must have been worried I'd die on them without spilling CIA secrets, so they gave me water and switched to the amputations. I never want to experience that level of thirst again. So I haul this flask around and take a sip of water every few hours to reassure myself I won't die of thirst today."

"I see," Matt said, remembering the few times he'd been truly parched and could think only about getting some water into his system as fast as possible. *Three days?* He couldn't remember going any longer than three or four *hours* without water when he was awake. Once again, hearing of

Hypo's suffering knocked Matt's self-pity for a loop for thinking his own PTSD was such an extreme case.

Nowitzki returned, stuffing his phone into his pocket. "Irving will meet me at the MFO. I'll drive the van. Hypo, you ride shotgun. Hawk, follow me in your car and take Hypo home when we get there." He tossed his keys to Matt. "Take my car back to Hawk's place. We'll drop these sorry excuses for assassins off at the MFO, talk to Irving, and confirm that the FBI now has reason to investigate. Then I'll call you, Matt. Let's wait until after the autopsy before you turn yourself in."

Grim-faced, Matt nodded. The possibility still existed that the FBI wouldn't believe them and arrest Matt outright with no chance of any sort of protective custody. If Volkov and the other two clammed up under threat of death from Smythe, then Matt's best chance for success, other than persuading the FBI to investigate Witt's employment connection to Smythe, was Diane's new autopsy.

Chapter 51

At Hawk's place the next night, Nowitzki was regaling Matt, Hypo, and Hawk with tales of some of his more interesting MPD cases. Interrupted by a phone call to his cell, Nowitzki answered and almost immediately offered his phone to Matt. "It's for you."

Matt raised his eyebrows and mouthed, *Who?*

"Blake."

The autopsy results. Matt tensed, flushing with trepidation. If he'd been mistaken about his bullet not killing Diane, then his quest was over. He swallowed hard and took the phone.

"Yes, Edward?"

"I owe you an apology," Blake said with a hint of remorse.

"Apology for what?"

"Crossley killed my daughter, not you. I apologize for believing you were her killer."

Matt was glad he was sitting on the living room sofa because his knees would have buckled if he'd been standing. He pumped his fist and smiled at Nowitzki, who returned the gestures.

"Thank you," Matt told Blake. "What was the proof?"

"Simple, yet easy to gloss over. Crossley's weapon fired different bullets than yours. Both were nine-millimeter. The bullet that killed Diane was a *jacketed* hollow point. The bullet in *his* head, from your weapon, was a *plain* hollow point. Smythe ordered the M.E. to alter Diane's autopsy just the way you suggested they might."

Matt pressed his eyes closed, holding back tears of ... relief? Closure? Sorrow? Vindication? He'd been right. Guessed right. Not precisely, but close enough to persuade Blake to find out for sure. In the end, it didn't matter. Diane was dead, and he'd been partly responsible. His voice quavered. "I owe you an apology for getting Diane involved in my mess. If I'd known *any* sort of trouble would result from me digging into Smythe's activities, I'd have walked away from her that night in the club."

Blake cleared his throat. "You couldn't have known events would have snowballed so badly. Can't change the past. What do you want me to do now?"

Aware of the conversation's track, Nowitzki had already written Regina Irving's phone number on a piece of paper and held it for Matt to see.

"Call this number," Matt said. After reciting it, he said, "Special Agent Regina Irving of the Minneapolis FBI. She'll tell her boss, and they'll begin an investigation into Smythe Properties. We already smoothed over the incident at your house last night, so we'll keep you out of the spotlight as much as possible. If any reporters ask, tell them I called you and convinced you to exhume Diane's body. Nothing more."

"I may still lose my seat on the court," Blake said.

"I'm sorry if it happens, but you did a noble thing. The whole conspiracy has probably killed dozens and ruined hundreds. You helped me put a stop to it."

"Maybe someday I'll sit down with you and listen to how you unraveled this scheme."

"I'd like that," Matt said. "I'll buy because you may need a few drinks to believe my story."

"I'll hold you to it," Blake said, chuckling.

They ended the call. Smiling, Matt tossed the phone to Nowitzki. "Take me to the FBI."

An hour later, Matt and Nowitzki met with Special Agents Irving and Zamora in a windowless conference room at the FBI's Minneapolis Field Office. Stomach churning, heart pounding, Matt couldn't help wondering if Smythe was still somehow playing him, and he'd end up rotting in prison for life—or worse. He dictated a statement that took an hour, then

Special Agent in Charge Ebner joined the group. He, Zamora, and Irving interviewed him for several more hours.

Ebner was tough, grilling Matt on the tiniest details of his written statement. He probably suspected Matt of fabricating this bizarre story to cover his ass and stay out of jail. But Ebner couldn't deny the fact that a state supreme court justice had gone to bat for an accused cop killer. Matt stuck to the facts and kept his explanations detailed, yet straightforward.

Tie loosened, shirtsleeves rolled up, with a cold cup of coffee sitting next to a yellow legal pad filled with several pages of notes, Ebner finally caved. He tossed his pen onto the table.

"Well, I'm satisfied. Craziest story I've heard in my thirty-year career. But I reckon we have enough to issue search warrants for Smythe's home and businesses. The statements from the thugs you captured at Justice Blake's home corroborate your version of that incident. Volkov admitted he works for Premier Securities and does what he called 'special projects' for Smythe. That plus Witt's connection with Smythe through Premier gives us probable cause to reopen the Boundary Waters homicide investigation."

"Thank you, sir," Matt said with a heavy sigh. He'd been as tight as a coiled, compressed spring during the entire interview, so he slumped in his seat and tried to relax his body.

Irving and Zamora leaned back in their chairs with expressions of anticipation. They would undoubtedly focus their attention on arranging for and executing the warrants.

Matt glanced at Ebner. "What's next? Do you arrest me?"

"Normally, yes," Ebner said, "since you're accused of murder. But I respect your concern that Smythe may have jailhouse snitches who might hurt you while you're locked up. Especially now that I know he had such high-level people working with him."

"What're you going to do with me?"

"I have a suggestion," Irving said. "We could bend the rules and put him in the Victim Assistance Program."

Ebner narrowed his eyes and lowered his chin. "The man's admitted to *killing* two men. How does that make him a *victim*?"

Zamora said, "Self-defense. With no surviving witnesses, it's a fifty-fifty call."

Irving said, "Lanier claims Smythe tried to have him killed six times to date. Seven, if we believe he didn't blow up his own farmhouse."

Ebner furrowed his brow. "The blast that killed the local cop, right?"

Irving nodded. "The Straight River Fire Chief concluded the house exploded because someone loosened the gas main, then detonated the blast remotely when the inside light switched on. Anyone could've pressed the button. With our new evidence on Witt, I'll bet we can convince the Straight County Attorney to rescind the warrant on Lanier. Especially now that Smythe is under suspicion for all the conspiracy-related charges."

Ebner tilted his head back, a look of comprehension beginning to grow on his face. "Go after the bigger fish."

Irving said, "Lanier sustained multiple injuries in the blast, which certainly qualifies him as a victim of a crime. Drop the charge. He's no longer a suspect."

Ebner rocked slowly in his chair. "Where we gonna stash him? Can't let him run around hog wild because if this all goes to Hell-in-a-handbasket, I'm screwed." He swiveled to face his agents. "And you two are out of a job."

His sour expression and burning stare unnerved Matt, who figured Zamora and Irving were feeling twice the pressure he felt. Matt said, "I'm done running. I'll stay wherever you put me."

Nowitzki shot a sidelong glance at Zamora and coughed. "He could stay with Special Agent Zamora. I understand her place is quite secure."

Zamora shot a pissed-off look at Irving, who she guessed had told Nowitzki about her home fortress. "But I'm at work most of the time."

Nowitzki's eyes brightened. "What if I stay there too, as a bodyguard?"

Matt suppressed a grin. *Ol' Ben's making his move.*

Zamora looked to Ebner for guidance—or perhaps a good reason to veto that suggestion.

Ebner sighed, looking as if *he* didn't want to decide the matter. "Since this is all unofficial, I'll leave the decision to you, Zamora."

Zamora shifted in her chair, a resigned expression growing on her face. "Yeah, I guess." She wagged a finger at Matt and Nowitzki. "But you two clean up after yourselves, understand? Don't think for one second you're staying in a hotel. Not a B and B. Not even a crappy man cave."

Both men nodded vigorously.

Ebner stood. "Okay, then. Zamora, take 'em home and set 'em up. Irving, get warrants for Smythe Properties, Smythe's personal residence, all computer records, Premier Security Service, and every shell corporation even remotely connected to him. I'll call the Straight County Attorney and ask her to rescind Lanier's arrest warrant."

As the group stood and headed toward the door, Ebner said, "All y'all listen up. No one discusses the case with anyone other than me or the computer techs involved. If we screw this up and Smythe gets off, the MFO may cease to exist."

Chapter 52

Juanita Zamora's house in the Bryn Mawr neighborhood west of down-town Minneapolis was indeed an urban fortress. After buying the Arts and Crafts-style house a few years ago, she'd installed iron bars on the basement windows; motion-sensitive lights around the outside; solid-steel front and back doors; and had wired all the windows to a silent alarm system. A security control panel mounted on a kitchen wall near the back door coordinated all facets and could be armed or disarmed by entering a numeric code. If anyone was foolish enough to attempt a break-in, they'd either meet their worst nightmare in Zamora, or the police would arrive within minutes. After briefing her guests on all this, she assigned Matt to her upstairs guest room, Nowitzki to the living room sofa, then went to bed.

She was gone before the men awoke the next morning. But they found hot coffee in the pot and a note explaining breakfast options. By ten o'clock, Matt and Nowitzki were bored, restless, and lounging on the sofa, watching television. All they could do was wait for the FBI to do their job.

"You think the search warrants will be executed today or later?" Matt asked, not understanding that part of the legal process.

"Depends," Nowitzki replied. "Case like this, I hope they move fast. Smythe probably figured something was wrong while we were talking to Blake the other night. We confiscated the thugs' phones so they couldn't tell him anything. And Blake not calling the police was huge because Smythe can't find out what went down through a spy in the department."

Matt extended a finger upward. "What if Smythe called Blake after we left his house? I knew Blake pretty well when we were in-laws, but I'm not convinced he could stonewall Smythe. What if that's the warning bell?

What if he activated a doomsday self-destruct button and vaporized his computer records?"

Nowitzki wrinkled his brow. "I doubt he's that sophisticated. And if he doesn't know what the FBI is looking for, he can't be sure he's destroying the right files."

Nowitzki's ringing phone cut off their discussion. He tapped a button and put the phone to his ear. "Nowitzki." After listening for ten seconds, a smile crept across his face. He glanced at Matt and said, "I'll tell him."

"Tell me what?"

Nowitzki clicked off his phone with a flourish. "The Fibbies just hit Smythe Properties."

"And?"

"The preliminary search found Witt's history with Smythe through Premier Securities."

Triumphant energy coursed through Matt's veins. All the accumulated stress and tension of the past year poured out through every pore in his body. He felt lighter, as if the pressure that had weighed him down over the past year was escaping through his skin. "Did they bust his pathetic, slimy ass?"

"He wasn't at work."

"Too bad," Matt said. "What about Smythe's personal computers and documents?"

"The second team of agents will be at his house anytime now to search the place."

"Do you think they'll arrest him there?"

"If he's home, I sure as hell hope so. Of course, he could be flying to a deserted island with a suitcase full of cash instead."

Matt thought for a minute, then set his jaw. "I want to be there for the bust."

Nowitzki recoiled and screwed his mouth sideways. Then he chuckled. "I don't think so. Feds are sticklers for procedure. And that doesn't include civilians."

"Maybe Zamora can let you be there, and I'll hide in your back seat."

"I doubt it. She doesn't seem interested enough in me to do me a favor."

"Nah," Matt said, waving him off. "She's hiding behind the tough-agent persona. Probably doesn't want a social life to interfere with her career."

"You think?"

"It's a hunch. I've seen her shoot a few ogles at you when you weren't looking. And I *know* you scored some brownie points when Irving explained you saved her life back in the day."

"I dunno," he said, exhaling slowly. "If she ever finds out about Castle Danger ..."

"I'll take that secret to my grave," Matt said. "All Allyson knows is you did something wrong and wound up tied to a chair in her kitchen. She didn't say anything to the sheriff, did she?"

Nowitzki shook his head. "Not then or ever, because I never had a follow-up visit from said sheriff." He looked at the ceiling, pensive. "My alibi was, I saw a flickering light from the cabin fire through the trees, went to investigate, and got jumped by a stranger—you—who tied me up in her kitchen. She said the stranger was her temporary chef, Matt *Johnson*. The sheriff bought her story that Johnson saved her and her son and then disappeared before she got home."

Matt digested that statement. The FBI had known his name for two weeks and hadn't once asked him about the two dead men in Castle Danger. Turning back to Nowitzki, he said, "You have nothing to worry about. Allyson and her friends will never betray us." He paused. "I assume Smythe paid you in cash?"

"Yeah," Nowitzki said. "I conjured up some fake clients to account for a few large bank deposits, but I kept most of it in my home safe."

"So call Zamora," Matt said. "If they raid Smythe's place, tell her we'll sit in her back seat and watch from there, so she won't get in trouble."

"All right," Nowitzki said, shrugging in surrender. "But don't get your hopes up."

"Hey, if she says *yes*, let's pack a lunch, make a day of it."

Nowitzki rolled his gaze heavenward as he pulled out his phone. "Crazy musicians."

Zamora turned them down flat. "No way. Not gonna happen," she said over speakerphone. "Totally against protocol. Besides, Lanier's got to appear in court to get his murder warrant rescinded before he can show his face in public."

Matt figured as much, but the urge to see Smythe do a perp walk was powerful. He'd hoped against hope to get a small measure of satisfaction from seeing the great and powerful tycoon humiliated on his home turf.

"Thanks anyway, Special Agent Zamora," Matt said.

Nowitzki clicked off and pocketed his phone. "When's your court date?"

"Couple of days."

"Need a ride down to Straight River?"

"Thanks, I'd appreciate it."

Chapter 53

Two days later, Nowitzki and Maxwell escorted Matt into the Straight County Courthouse. For the first time in a year, Matt didn't fear being recognized. He'd shaved his beard and borrowed money from Nowitzki to get a haircut. Maxwell had put Matt's belongings into storage after his condo lease expired last year, so Matt stopped by the facility on the way to court and found one of his white dress shirts, a suit, and a tie, then changed clothes in Maxwell's office.

Inside, his eyes took several seconds to adjust to the dim lighting after the bright sunshine outside. As he looked around, still nervous about appearing as his true self in public, he was taken aback when he recognized the woman sitting on a lobby bench.

"Amy!" he said. "What are you doing here?"

Amy Swanson smiled, stood, and hugged him. "To get justice for David, and you, and Clay, and everyone around here who was harmed by Witt and that bastard Smythe. I gave a statement to the county attorney, so I'm here in case she has questions about my testimony."

"So wonderful to see you," he said, extending his arms to give her a once-over. "You look good, considering …"

She lowered her head. "It was tough for a long time. After you told me Dave died helping you, I blamed you. Hated you at times. But the pain has dulled. I want to believe doing this will give me some closure."

Maxwell greeted Amy with a polite handshake. Then his attention was diverted to activity over Matt's shoulder.

Matt turned to see Special Agents Irving and Zamora escorting Smythe into the courthouse lobby. Behind him stood three men in expensive suits sporting hundred-dollar-haircuts and leather briefcases. Smythe looked the same as he had a year ago. Medium height, medium build, impeccably dressed, military bearing, steely eyes. The urge to flee was surpassed only by the desire to lunge at Smythe and choke the life out of him.

Through ventriloquist lips, Nowitzki softly said, "Easy there, big fella."

Matt steadied himself with a deep breath and a concerted effort to keep his feet anchored to the floor. If his eyes had been laser-capable, his glare would have vaporized Smythe in seconds.

Smythe met his glare with the haughty sneer Matt remembered from their initial meeting. A look that implied obvious superiority. A look that suggested contempt for all but a few lucky elites. A look that implied showing up in court escorted by two federal agents was a massive waste of time.

Scanning Matt from head to toe as if he were deciding whether to bother acknowledging his presence, Smythe said, "We meet again, Mr. Lanier."

Matt locked eyes with Smythe's. He would *not* blink first. "What a coincidence, Smythe. I figured the next time I saw you would be in Hell."

"A formality," he said, nodding his head toward the judge's bench. "A simple misunderstanding with one of my alleged former independent contractors." The emphasis Smythe put on *alleged* was subtle yet undeniable.

"Remember our last conversation?" Matt said, resisting the urge to blink, let alone look away. "We discussed chess in the context of our situation. I called it a stalemate. We could each make as many moves as we wanted, but neither of us had a winning advantage."

Smythe shrugged but maintained eye contact. "The only conversation we've had was a year ago. You conned your way into my office by impersonating a business associate. I called security when I realized you were unbalanced and dangerous."

Matt ignored Smythe's posturing. "Instead of continuing the stalemate, I started a new game. The fun part is, I didn't tell you."

"As I said, unbalanced and dangerous. You're rambling, talking nonsense, like many of the desperate, unbalanced people who try to get a piece of me."

"I'm here to see the judge about the warrant you ordered Flannery to put out on me for blowing up my father's house and killing Officer Sandvik.

You're here to answer for Witt's assorted crimes in the county on behalf of Millennium Four. I'd hardly call that a misunderstanding."

Smythe finally broke eye contact and glanced at his attorneys.

"And there's also the matter of Witt murdering my father." Matt focused on the side of Smythe's face, wishing again for a laser-powered glare.

"I'm done here," Smythe said to his legal team. "May we proceed with this kangaroo court business?"

He took a step to go around Matt. Matt sidestepped and blocked his way. Smythe's eyes flared, and his jaw muscles tensed.

"Our new chess match is in the endgame stage," Matt said. "And I'm winning. You couldn't buy the silence of one man, and your choice of Witt as your muscle was flawed. Turns out he wasn't very good at his job."

Smythe maintained his calm façade. "As I understand the law, your penalty for murdering the police officer will be rather severe. Life without parole, possibly death."

Matt turned toward Maxwell, who motioned him to enter the courtroom. Inside, they sat at the defense table. Nowitzki and Amy Swanson sat behind them. The rest of the people involved took seats in the gallery. Smythe and his group sat in the last row, looking bored.

Maxwell leaned over and spoke softly. "The FBI went into high gear after you got Edward Blake's cooperation. All your research and data—along with Flannery's recorded confession and evidence of blackmailing the two coroners—triggered a search of Witt's activities. Amy gave a statement saying Witt assaulted her and Dave in their barn, and she identified him from his Premier Securities ID photo. Witt was also foolish enough to use his credit card on enough purchases to show he's been here on multiple occasions. Best of all, the feds placed him in Rapid City the day Hibbert died. They verified Clay Gebhardt's trip out there to persuade a young prostitute to file assault charges against Witt after an incident that occurred in a motel later that same day."

Matt sat back, suddenly lightheaded, and ran his fingers through his hair. *I'm not crazy. People who aren't dead actually believe my story.* Twelve months ago, he and Zach fought alone against the system. Now the FBI, a state supreme court justice, and many others were on his side. "I can't believe this day has come, Max. I thought about it constantly. Dreamed about it. But as time passed, it seemed less likely to happen."

Maxwell patted Matt's knee. "The truth usually finds a way to the surface, son."

When the Honorable Rosalind Koch entered the courtroom, everyone stood, then sat when commanded. The bailiff called Matt's case. Maxwell did his thing for twenty minutes, depositing file after file with the court clerk and citing all the facts about the explosion that destroyed Matt's father's farmhouse. The pivotal point of the case was a sworn statement from Dr. Anne Vincent that Chief Flannery had blackmailed her into falsifying the autopsy results of Helmer Myrick and Matt's father. This cast enough doubt on Flannery's warrant request for Matt's arrest as a suspect that the county attorney couldn't dismiss the charge fast enough.

The proceeding was blurred and muffled, as if Matt were looking and listening through a frost-coated window. Maxwell nudged him and gestured for him to stand and face the judge. On wobbly legs, Matt stood and braced his hands on the defense table.

"Mr. Lanier," Judge Koch began, "in light of the evidence presented today and the agreement by the county attorney that the warrant for your arrest was fraudulently requested, I hereby dismiss the first-degree murder charge against you for the death of Officer Steven Sandvik."

After the murmur of surprise running through the courtroom had subsided, Koch continued. "Nevertheless, you are, at minimum, a person of interest connected to the next case on my docket. Therefore, I order you to remain in the state until such time as the court summons you for questioning. Additionally, Mr. Maxwell has agreed to post a $50,000 bond guaranteeing you will turn yourself in if charges are filed against you in the future. Do you understand?"

With a dry mouth, through lips that felt thick and numb, Matt said, "Yes, Your Honor."

After Judge Koch instructed her bailiff to call the next case and people moved into and out of the room, Matt shook Maxwell's hand. "I can't thank you enough for believing in me, Max. But I can't allow you to put up that kind of money on my behalf."

Maxwell waved him off. "I'm a rich old widower. How else should I spend my money? I know you won't betray my trust. Your folks raised a good, honest man with brains and integrity. Not even this whole bizarre odyssey you've been on for the past year could change that. Plus, my gut tells me you won't be charged. I'm only *lending* the money to the county for a few months."

As Matt and Maxwell walked up the aisle to leave, Smythe and his team walked toward the defense table. Matt made eye contact with his adversary and stopped on the right side of the aisle. As Smythe passed, again with that snobbish, haughty sneer on his face, Matt quietly said, "Checkmate."

Chapter 54

After the murder charge was dropped, Matt regained control of his assets. As the sole heir to his father's estate, he received the insurance payout for the destroyed house. That plus six hundred acres of prime Minnesota farmland comprised a substantial nest egg. Maxwell had converted the farm-related equipment and vehicles to cash and put the money into an escrow account. That fund would've paid Matt's legal expenses if he'd stood trial for Sandvik's murder. Matt hadn't been this flush since before Diane divorced him and took half their joint assets more than a decade earlier. Using his credit card again to buy necessities without fear of being tracked became one of life's simple pleasures. He'd taken so much for granted before Millennium Four encroached on his life.

For convenience, until Smythe's expected trial was over—and much to Zamora's relief—Matt moved back in with Hawk and Hypo, and Nowitzki returned to Duluth. To keep his mind clear, his fingers nimble, and to relieve some of the stress of waiting, Matt bought a decent guitar and amp so he and Hypo could play some street gigs. No longer afraid to show his face in public, he regained the joy of making music he'd always known before Smythe entered his life. Playing guitar also eased his PTSD symptoms, especially the nightmares.

After Edward Blake called in a high-level favor, the FBI worked at an accelerated pace until they could present a solid case to a grand jury. One catalyst was the collected digital evidence connecting Smythe and Witt and documenting all the shell companies. Testimony from the blackmailed medical examiners ensured Smythe would face extortion, blackmail, and murder charges under the Racketeer Influenced and Corrupt Organizations Act (RICO). Then, if the subsequent jury trial resulted in even one guilty verdict for first-degree murder, Smythe would face decades in prison.

A week after Matt's court appearance in Straight River, a federal grand jury convened in Minneapolis to consider an indictment. Matt was the first witness. His testimony began with his initial inquiries back in Straight River more than a year earlier into Smythe's shell company, Saxony Partners. Data obtained from Smythe's personal computer through the FBI warrants proved especially incriminating. It included details of dozens of land purchases he'd already closed, as well as deals on which he'd been working before his arrest.

Matt recounted the harrowing weeks, starting when Witt tried to run him down with his SUV, through the shooting of Diane and Crossley in Duluth and his subsequent decision to flee and hide in the Boundary Waters. When asked what he'd done after coming out of the wilderness, he simply said, "I was broke, feared for my life, and needed to survive anonymously. So I worked my way to Minneapolis and lived on the streets. There I met Ben Nowitzki, who believed my story and contacted the FBI."

Neither the U.S. attorney nor the jurors pressed him on those missing few months. They only questioned his sanity for choosing to live primitively in one of the harshest winter environments in the nation. Matt admitted he thought himself crazy on many days, but trusted his survival skills well enough to justify the risk.

When Nowitzki testified, he chose his words carefully, using lies of omission when he could do so safely. Still, he convinced the jury that his initial involvement was merely getting hired by Smythe to find Lanier, learning that Smythe might be the real criminal, then finding Lanier and contacting the FBI.

Zach was understandably nervous when he testified, stumbling over several answers. But once he began talking about computer details and technology, he found his groove and answered clearly and confidently. Blake was somber and dignified. Maxwell, Zamora, Irving, and the blackmailed medical examiners were all professional and poised. An indictment seemed inevitable, but Matt tamped down his excitement in case a disaster occurred.

The grand jury took only two weeks to indict Smythe on multiple counts of conspiracy, fraud, blackmail, and murder. When informed of the indictment, Smythe's attorneys raised holy hell, protesting that their client was the victim of a witch hunt because of his wealth and notoriety. It was a feeble attempt to try the case in the court of public opinion because most of Smythe's business acquaintances and employees detested him. Numerous responses from Smythe's enemies that showed zero sympathy for the man appeared in the local media.

To further aggravate Smythe, but primarily to get the trial over with as soon as possible and not dwell on the circumstances of his daughter's death, Edward Blake called the U.S. Attorney assigned to the case—a former protégé—with instructions to go to trial as soon as possible. Thanks to Blake's rank and privilege, the jury trial began four months after the first warrants had been executed. The whole mess would still take many months, but not the year or more typical of high-profile cases.

Wearing a gray suit, blue shirt, and navy tie adorned with musical notes, Matt watched intently from the front row of the gallery when the trial began. Smythe appeared with his usual small army of briefcase-toting lawyers. Other than responding to the judge when required, he remained silent except for a few whispers to his lead attorney. Matt studied Smythe's composure, admired his stoic bearing, wondered what the bastard was thinking and feeling as his empire crumbled.

Matt was the first witness for the prosecution. He answered the questions with the same casual confidence he'd shown with the grand jury. He augmented his testimony with charts, graphs, diagrams, and copies of everything he and Zach had discovered. There were also maps of his Boundary Waters outpost on Big Island in Crystal Lake, where the five-man shootout took place. Matt felt thankful that his testimony took all day, so he'd have a night to steel himself for the defense's inevitable verbal slicing and dicing during cross-examination.

At 9:00 a.m. the following day, defense attorney Thomas Holland stood at the lectern, dressed neck to foot in Brooks Brothers and radiating an imperious air.

"Mr. Lanier," he began, "let's discuss your personal history dating back to March of last year. It's a fact your father and a long-time neighbor died within weeks of each other. It's a fact you narrowly survived a hit-and-run attempt. It's a fact you almost lost your life when your father's house exploded. It's a fact Straight River police officer Scott Sandvik perished in the blast. It's a fact you sustained a concussion and other severe injuries. It's a fact two of your childhood friends suffered violent deaths."

"Your Honor, I object," said U.S. District Attorney Gerald Dow.

"On what grounds?" Judge Walter Williams asked.

"While Mr. Holland has demonstrated an excellent command of the facts concerning this case, he has yet to ask a question of my client."

"Your Honor," Holland said. "May I explain?"

Williams nodded.

"I'm providing relevant information so the jury will understand the context and reason for my question."

"Objection overruled," Williams said.

Holland turned away from Williams, smirked at Dow, then faced Matt again. "Each of these traumas alone is incredibly stressful. Pile one atop another atop the others, and the strongest individual would incur unbearable mental and emotional suffering. It's a fact that yesterday you stated, under oath, that you suffer from post-traumatic stress disorder, commonly known as PTSD. Isn't it possible, perhaps probable, that your outlandish story—accusing my client of ordering dozens of criminally heinous acts, including murder—is a complete figment of your PTSD-induced state of mind?"

"No," Matt said flatly.

"Here are more facts. You admitted to participating in at least two separate gun battles and killing no fewer than two people in those bloody incidents—Charles Witt and Steven Crossley. In the last gun battle, you witnessed the violent death of your ex-wife. Didn't those events add *more* stress to your mind, rendering it *less* stable than before?"

Matt summoned all the self-control he could muster to appear unfazed by the flood of memories and bloody images Holland had sparked with his comments. Dow had briefed him that his mental competence would be the focal point of Smythe's defense. Still, he'd never publicly been accused of being crazy, and it stung. Slowly, calmly, but emphatically, he said, "No. I was fighting for my life in those gun battles. I was as focused and clear-headed as I've ever been."

Holland feigned surprise. "My understanding of war and violence is that most participants remember being anything but focused and clear-headed. Do you have battle-tested experts who will support your claim?"

"No," Matt said. "It's *my* experience. Just because others had different reactions doesn't make mine invalid."

Holland continued, point by point, dissecting every violent incident by asking, "Is it possible you could have set it up this way?" Then he laid out bizarre examples of what a crazed madman might do to stage a violent scene in such a way that it would *appear* to be a case of self-defense, but was actually premeditated murder.

Matt emphatically answered "No" to each bogus scenario but grew tenser with each question. Holland grilled him for another two hours, mainly about his real estate research, then about how he'd *coerced* Edward Blake into agreeing to exhume his daughter's body.

At the end of the day, Matt felt more physically exhausted than mentally exhausted. Telling the truth under oath with so many lives and livelihoods on the line had been incredibly stressful. After returning to Hawk's, he ate dinner, then slept for a solid ten hours.

The rest of the trial was a blur of testimony, cross-examination, one expert after the other countering claims from the opposing side, and an increasing number of objections from the defense.

Each side's closing arguments differed little from their opening statements. Dow made a cogent plea for the jurors to believe Matt's story—unbelievable on the surface—because sometimes, just sometimes, truth is indeed stranger than fiction. He also emphasized the indisputable fact that Witt had worked for Smythe on behalf of Smythe Properties; the paper trail of bribe money sent to dozens of individuals through many of Smythe's shell companies; the phone records of Smythe's many burner phones showing calls to Witt, Volkov, and others; the many bankers and loan officers who were extorted into calling in farm loans to put certain farmers in a financial bind that would force them into bankruptcy or lead to foreclosure.

On the twenty-fourth day of the trial, the jury went into deliberations. Matt and his legal team went to lunch at a nearby restaurant in case the jury reached a swift verdict. Gerald Dow told him that if the jury didn't decide today, they'd probably take several more days before reaching a verdict. Because Matt's improbable story required a leap of faith, a prolonged deliberation implied more doubt in the juror's minds. The bottom line? *Swift* meant *positive*.

Distracted, Matt ate heartily but tasted little. He ran his testimony through his mind, looking for weak spots that would give the jury a reason to acquit Smythe. Reasonable doubt was subjective, which meant all twelve jurors needed to be convinced his story was true. If any of them believed a man who'd been through Matt's trauma in the past year wasn't a reliable, believable witness, then the mountain of factual evidence against Smythe would be meaningless.

The group whiled away another hour at the restaurant without hearing anything. Matt went for a walk around the block outside the courthouse after Dow promised to send someone to find him if the jury reached a verdict that day. On his tenth lap, Matt noticed one of Dow's assistants hustling toward him. His heartbeat sped up as the woman approached.

"Jury reached a verdict," she said in a neutral tone.

Swift means positive ... unless it's not. He nodded grimly and followed her, bounding up the courthouse steps two at a time. He entered and took a seat behind Maxwell. In due course, all participants arrived, the jury filed in, and everyone sat in silent anticipation. Matt's pulse pounded in his ears. His breaths were quick and shallow. The moment for which he'd fought so hard over the past year and a half was imminent. In the next few minutes, twelve strangers would decide his future.

A guilty verdict meant redemption for him and the resumption of a normal life. Not guilty meant watching over his shoulder twenty-four seven for retribution. Smythe was the type who held grudges and always got revenge thanks to his money and power. He'd ensure Matt suffered one way or the other—a quick, violent death that couldn't be traced or years of mental harassment and torture that could make his life impossible. Guilty verdict or not, bringing the Millennium Four conspiracy to the public's attention meant Smythe's dream project would never happen—at least not the version where Smythe realized billions in personal gain.

Feeling dizzy, Matt took slow, deep breaths and tilted back to stare at the ceiling. Then the judge entered. On the bailiff's commands, everyone rose and then sat. The judge spoke. The jury forewoman spoke. Inside Matt's head, the roar of giant waves crashing on a rocky shore obscured the words. Maxwell grabbed his arm. Matt emerged from his daze. He looked at his lawyer, his friend. Maxwell beamed. Shook his hand. Dow and his legal team were also smiling.

Searching Maxwell's eyes, Matt asked, "What'd she say?"

"Guilty on all counts," Maxwell said, his voice cracking. "They'll appeal, but I can't imagine they'll win. You *nailed* the bastard."

Chapter 55

The dam of pent-up emotions Matt had built and fortified for more than a year gave way to a tsunami of relief. He broke down, sobbing with feelings of joy, vindication, justice being served, the triumph of truth, and belief in the system.

Maxwell let him cry, patting him on the back as he chatted with Dow. After wiping the tears from his face with the handkerchief Maxwell handed him, Matt stood and beheld his friends and allies: Hypo, Hawk, Ben, Zach, Max, a beaming Betty Myrick, even Amy Swanson, whose cheeks were also tear-stained.

"Thank you all," he said in a shaky voice. "Thank you." No other words could express his immense gratitude. He stepped toward Nowitzki, the catalyst for his triumph, and embraced him. "Thanks for believing me, doing the right thing, doing your job well, and getting *all* the facts."

Nowitzki clapped him on the back. "I had to know the truth. Couldn't live with myself if I'd stayed with Smythe but later found out I was part of so much evil. I like to believe there's still a place in Heaven for me despite my errant ways."

Matt let go and stood back. "I'm hoping I haven't blown my chance either. My sin list is a lot longer than yours."

Flashing a sly grin, Nowitzki said, "If you insist."

As the group filed out of the courtroom, Matt spied Victor in the last row of the gallery. Wearing a suit and tie, he looked every bit the part of a successful businessman rather than a drug queen's bodyguard and second in command. Victor rose and timed his walk to meet Matt at the door to the courthouse lobby. Matt's pulse rose as he gauged the likelihood of Victor trying to kill him for bailing out on the bridge. If Victor intended to try something here and now, it would be up close and personal, like a knife to the gut or lethal injection of poison. Fortunately, several deputies were stationed in the lobby as a deterrent to those who might try to harm anyone in the building.

Matt said to the others, "I'll catch up with you," then turned to face Victor. "I'm surprised to see you again, especially in a courtroom."

Victor shrugged. "Not my idea. My boss's."

"She's been following the trial?" Matt asked, bracing for an attack.

"The entire *state's* following the trial, man. I'm only delivering a message from her."

"What's the message?"

Victor glanced around to make sure no one was within earshot, then leaned in and lowered his voice. "Her words, Jazzman: You fucked up my plans on the bridge big-time, Mr. Gorilla Balls. For some reason, I let you live. But if you ever cross my path again, Victor gets to make that call."

Matt digested the comment and studied Victor's face. Victor nodded with a look that implied, "Shoot first, don't bother with questions." Suddenly weak in the knees, Matt replied, "Tell Queenie thanks and goodbye forever."

Victor narrowed his eyes, cracked the slightest of smiles, and left.

That evening, Matt treated his friends to a celebration party at a restaurant near Orchestra Hall. Maxwell insisted on buying Champagne for the group: Matt, Nowitzki, Hawk, Hypo, and Zach. When the glasses were filled, Maxwell raised his and said, "Gentlemen, a toast."

Everyone raised their glass and faced Max.

"To Matt, who persevered and ultimately prevailed in the face of daunting odds. When others would have ignored the wrong being done to those he cared about—his friends and neighbors, his father, and Diane—Matt fought to ensure they all received justice."

"To Matt," the group said as one. They clinked glasses all around and sipped.

The dinner was festive and cordial. The food was delicious. Matt bought two bottles of one of his favorite wines for the entire party, a great Oregon pinot noir as good as the best French Burgundies. At one point, the restaurant's background music system played Prince's unforgettably infectious dance tune, "1999." Ironic, Matt thought, because the lyrics described a party signifying the end of something, while his party was celebrating the start of his renewed life as a normal human. After the main course, but before dessert, Matt gestured to Zach to accompany him to a quiet end of the bar.

Once there, Zach said, "What's up, *amigo*?"

"Um." Matt hesitated. He wanted to get the words right. "It's just ..." He cleared his throat. "This is tough to say, but I need to say it."

"Go ahead," Zach said. His puzzled expression showed he didn't suspect what was coming.

"Okay, here goes," Matt said. "I am incredibly sorry I dragged you into this mess. I almost got you killed more than once, and I selfishly used you to get what I wanted. You were a major help last year when we cracked Smythe's shell-company code word. When I was in Castle Danger, your computer savvy was the key reason I found Vossler and stopped him. When I came to Minneapolis, the last thing I wanted to do was bring you into the Smythe battle again. But once Nowitzki and the FBI came into the picture, I had to because we finally had a real chance of beating the bastard. Nevertheless, until the guilty verdict came down, I was terrified I'd screw up big-time and get you killed. That would've hurt me almost as much as it hurt to lose Diane."

Zach reddened and looked away, clearly surprised at Matt's words. "Hey, it's cool, man. After you left last year, I knew I could handle myself. I was actually hoping you'd find a way to get back on Smythe's ass and bring me into the fight." He looked up and made eye contact. "Believe me. You don't need to apologize."

Matt did, which offered him a bit of comfort. "Okay, we're square on that point. But I still want to pay you back for all you've done. You really are a superstar on computers."

Zach raised a hand and shook his head. "The experience was payback enough. Not often a pimply-faced college geek gets some *genuine* real-world experience."

Matt dug into his pocket and pulled out a business card. Handing it to Zach, he said, "Special Agent Irving was impressed with you, especially after I bragged about the computer work you did for me last year."

Zach took the card and studied it.

"Bottom line, she thinks you might be a good fit for the FBI's cyber-crimes division. Anytime you're ready, call her. She'll set up a job interview with the right person."

Mouth agape, Zach said, "Seriously?"

"Scout's honor."

"*Madre de Dios!*" Zach lunged at Matt and wrapped him in a bear hug so tight he had difficulty breathing. "Thank you so much."

Matt teasingly pushed him away, and they returned to their table.

After the group finished dessert, Maxwell announced he was heading home before it got too dark. Zach asked for a ride home. The others in the group stood to shake their hands.

"Thanks again, kid," Matt said, giving Zach a gentler hug than the last one.

"It was one hell of an adventure, *amigo*," Zach said. He waved Irving's business card. "I'll call her tomorrow."

"Good luck," Matt said. "Let me know how it goes." To Maxwell, he said, "Send me a bill for your work, and do *not* lowball me."

"The hell I will," Maxwell said. "This was a year's worth of *pro bono* work."

Matt's jaw dropped. "Seriously?"

Maxwell solemnly raised his hand. "Attorney's honor."

After Maxwell and Zach left, Hawk and Hypo headed for the restaurant's bar to get a nightcap. Matt and Nowitzki sat alone at the table. Matt sipped the last of the wine he'd been drinking.

Nowitzki eyed him curiously, then said, "So what's next for the luckiest man in the state?"

Matt lifted his gaze and thought. "Find a place to live. Get a job that offers group health insurance." He wiggled his damaged fingers. "I'd like to get these fixed, but I'll have to do some research to see if some brilliant surgeon can fully restore my dexterity."

"I was talking more about immediately, like taking a little vacation ... Up North?"

Matt eyed him, aware of the implication that *Up North* specifically meant Castle Danger. With a conspirator's smile, he said, "No comment."

Nowitzki's eyebrows arched. Grinning, he hoisted his beer. "Uh-*huh*."

Forcing down an oncoming blush, Matt switched topics. "What about you?"

"Think I'll double down on my private investigator business. Buy some ads, talk to a reporter friend I have at the *Duluth News Tribune*, persuade him to write an article about how my investigative skills helped to stop this big conspiracy."

"Yeah. About that." Matt reached into his pocket and pulled out a check made out to Nowitzki. Handing it to him, he said, "For your service and expenses babysitting me. I estimated everything, then added twenty-five percent to make sure it was enough."

Nowitzki regarded the check with raised brows and an approving expression. "Far too much, but thank you. I'll put the excess into my ad budget."

Hawk and Hypo wandered back from the bar. Each held a brandy snifter containing a clear brown liquid. "Don't worry, J-man," Hypo said. "It's cognac, but not top-shelf."

"Doesn't matter," Matt said. "You two are definitely worth top-shelf hooch."

Nowitzki checked his watch. "Gonna hit the road, fellas. Want to get home by midnight if I can." He stood and faced them. "It's been a singular adventure, gentlemen. Something for your memoirs. But if you're ever in Duluth ..."

He tossed three business cards on the table, shook their hands, and sauntered out the door.

Hawk drove Matt and Hypo back to his place for Matt's last night. Matt slept well, then ate a breakfast of eggs, bacon, toast, and coffee that his host prepared the next morning.

"Help you pack?" Hypo said after they'd finished eating and cleared the dishes.

Matt laughed. "Sure. I've got so much gear. One whole backpack."

"Then you'll need a supervisor." Hypo's toothy grin lit up the kitchen.

In their bedroom, Matt pulled his backpack from under the bed and began transferring clothes from the dresser to the pack.

Hypo sat on his bed and leaned against the headboard. "What's next for the dragon slayer?"

Matt shook his head. "I'm done with that line of work. Right now, today, I'll rent a car, do some traveling until I figure things out. After that, get back into normal life."

"Going anyplace special?"

Afraid to admit where he most wanted to go, Matt said, "I'll just pick a direction and drive."

"Need someone to ride shotgun?" Hypo's eyes glinted with hope. It reminded Matt of Nowitzki's knowing look last night.

Matt stopped packing and faced his friend. "It'd be a hoot and a half," he said, "But maybe another time. I'll keep in touch."

Hypo cast his gaze downward. "Yeah, sure."

"No, seriously. Let's plan something for later, a real buddies road trip—after I get my shit together. Right now, I need some alone time."

"No worries, brother. I know how you feel. When I was done with the CIA, I floated around the country like a balloon on the breeze. It ran out of air one September here in Minneapolis. I liked the fall weather and decided to stay for a few days. I was walking around downtown, absorbing the vibe, when I ran into Hawk working his magic with a group of vets in a little park. We got to talking, and I'm still here ten years later."

"I sure hope you can add me to your list of success stories. You two pulled me back from the precipice. I owe you more than I can ever repay."

Hypo wagged a finger. "Just don't hire a drummer for your street gigs until you call me."

Matt clapped him on the shoulder. "You'll forever be my first call."

When he'd finished packing, Matt walked with Hypo to the kitchen to say goodbye and thanks to Hawk. He removed two more checks from his pocket and handed one to Hawk. Using his given name for this somber moment, he said, "Norman Peltier, this is for back rent, food, and hazard pay. Thank you." Hawk's eyes bulged when he comprehended the amount. Anticipating a protest, Matt quickly added, "If it's too much, put it toward your PTSD ministry. Your clients deserve it. And speaking of PTSD, I'm going to buy a smartphone and learn how to use it. Can I call you if my symptoms resurface?"

"Of course," Hawk said. "Traumatic memories never completely disappear, so relapses under pressure are common. And you know where to find me if you need a face-to-face chat."

Matt nodded, smiled, gave Hawk a thumbs-up. "I'll remember that."

He then handed the second check to Hypo, who put his palm on his forehead, looking shocked and surprised when he saw the amount. "Kenny Carrillo, this is also for hazard pay and, well, just because you're you. A true brother-from-another-mother if ever one existed. Keep on making music and sharing your unique gifts with those who need you, my man."

Both men thanked him profusely. Matt downplayed his gifts as more than fair since he had a large inheritance and wanted to spread the wealth. Then all three stood in awkward silence. Hawk sniffed. Hypo toed the floor with his prosthetic foot.

Matt cleared his throat, struggling to hold his emotions together one last time. "There's no way of knowing what the future holds," he said. "But no matter where our paths take us, you'll always be a part of my life in spirit, if not in person."

After hearty hugs and sincere handshakes, Matt walked out the door a free man in all ways for the first time in his life. No family, no job, no debt, no place to live, no obligations. Most importantly, no one trying to arrest or kill him. Utter loneliness filled his body as he adjusted his backpack and headed for the rental car office on the south end of downtown.

Chapter 56

In the nerve-wracking seconds after he knocked on the door of the Halcyon Bar & Grill one sunny Monday morning a few weeks later, Matt's feelings zigzagged from panic and dread to excitement and anticipation. He briefly considered leaving, but he couldn't postpone this meeting any longer. Whatever happened, he wanted closure.

Allyson Clifford opened the door, recognized him, and froze. Her hand went to her mouth. "Matt?"

Much like what he'd noticed during their first meeting, beauty, poise, and sensuality radiated from her like sunshine. She wore faded jeans, a white T-shirt, and a royal blue hoodie. Her long brown hair was tied in a loose ponytail, and she wore no makeup—not that she needed any. Multiple emotions slammed into overdrive: love, apprehension, worry, fear of rejection. She hadn't leaped into his arms and kissed him passionately. Hadn't even smiled. But neither had she frowned or demanded he leave.

Afraid to say anything else until he could get a better feel for her reaction, he simply said, "Hello, Allyson."

She glanced over his shoulder, presumably to see if he'd come with someone else. "Why're you here?"

"It's complicated. ... Well, not really. Just hard to say."

Allyson wiped her palms on her hips and gave him an apologetic look. "Some hostess I am. You came all this way to see me, and I just stand here. Coffee's still hot. Please come in."

She stepped back and let him enter, and they walked toward the bar.

Sweat prickled the back of his neck as he worried about how she'd react to what he wanted to say. "How are you?"

"Fine thanks. You look well."

He nodded. "How's Josh?"

A prideful smile grew on her face. "Terrific. He just started third grade and loves his teacher."

"I'm glad. I'd sure like to see him."

"Maybe later. He gets home from school around four."

"Ah." Matt didn't dare presume she'd let him stay long enough to say hi to Josh, so he kept silent and settled onto a barstool. She walked behind the bar, poured two coffees, and gave him one. However, she remained behind the bar. *A physical barrier between us.* He sipped his coffee, then looked at the seating area near the fireplace. He'd hoped for a warmer welcome—perhaps an invitation to sit in comfortable chairs and have a casual conversation about the rest of his life.

She set her coffee down and braced her palms on the bar. "Before you say anything, I know about Smythe's conviction. Based on what I read in the paper, I hope he rots in prison for the rest of his life. And I know you were cleared of the murder charge. That's huge, and I'm happy for you. But your life was still turned upside down. You still have a violent past. The love of your life is still dead." She raised her thumb, index finger, and middle finger, respectively, as she ticked off those facts. "Any *one* of those pieces of baggage needs an industrial-sized handcart to schlep it around. You need a U-Haul trailer for yours."

Matt's insides dropped hard and heavy as if an anvil were crushing them. Her next sentence would be something like, "You're a nice guy, but ..." spoken with a sad, hopeful, regretful smile on her face.

He raised his hands, palms out, to prevent her from speaking further. He'd spent a week wandering around the Rocky Mountains, staying in isolated motels, spending his time hiking, stargazing, and soul searching. Upon returning home, he knew what he wanted from his life. During the drive up to Castle Danger, he'd perfected the speech that would explain all his feelings to her. Now his brain whirled as he tried to remember any piece of it. But the right words, the *perfect* words, wouldn't come.

Instead, he blurted out, "I love you."

His face flared hot. *Shit, shit, shit! Where the hell did that come from?* Other than a slight drop in her jaw, Allyson maintained her attentive expression. "Wait, I didn't mean it," he said, his brain unable to control his mouth. "I mean, I do love you. But I prepared this big fancy speech that was supposed to lead up to 'I love you.'"

He tensed, consciously relaxed with a deep breath, and exhaled. "What I meant is, I'm *in love* with you. Crazy in love with you. I've thought about you every day since I left. And it's not my PTSD talking. I'm not desperate for a relationship just to have one. I'm not playing on your gratefulness for saving you and Josh. I have no ulterior motive. But I've been through hell and back more than a few times in the last year. That focused my priorities like a laser."

Her cheeks flushed. She put her hand on his hand. "I'm flattered and surprised beyond words, but I—"

"I don't expect a reciprocal confession. But I don't have time to waste wondering about *what-ifs*. I'm more decisive with my life and more selfish too."

"But you *do* want to know my feelings, don't you?"

"Of course. But don't say anything until you're sure." He stared at the coffee in his cup. "Ever since I left last winter, my biggest desire was for us to start from square one as if we hadn't been thrown together by fate. As if we'd met normally—not under violent, life-or-death circumstances. But when I thought you were going to let me down gently just now, all the words evaporated except 'I love you.'"

She cocked her head. One corner of her mouth curled upward. "You sure know how to put a girl on the spot."

He slapped his forehead. "Oh, God, you're seeing someone else! How did I miss that?"

"No, no, no," she blurted. "There's no one else." She rolled her gaze upward. "I'm officially confused by this conversation." Then, furrowing her brows, she crossed her arms and said, "What do you want from me?"

"Go on one date with me. Dinner and a movie, a hike in the woods, a picnic at Gooseberry Falls, whatever you want. We'll ignore our past and try to pretend we don't have a strong physical attraction—*yet*."

She opened her mouth to protest, but he cut her off. "We do, and we both know it."

"Okay, we do." She gave him a playfully sullen look.

"After one date, you decide if I'm worth a second date. We go one step at a time. If we're not meant to be, I'll leave, and we'll go on with our lives knowing we gave it a shot."

She pondered his proposition, staring through the window at Lake Superior, a sparkling blue-gray thanks to the mid-morning sun sneaking through fluffy clouds. She broke into a warm smile, flashing her perfect white teeth. "I accept your ground rules, Mr. Lanier. You've got yourself a date."

He expelled the breath he'd been holding. "Great, thank you." Unwilling to risk instant rejection for a lame date suggestion, he said, "What would you like to do?"

Allyson tilted her head, glanced at her dining room, then met his gaze. "Ever been to Naniboujou Lodge?"

Matt's face grew hot. Was her idea of a date an overnight stay in a remote lakeshore lodge? Noticing his beet-red face in the bar's mirror, he stammered out a shaky, "Umm, no."

Allyson waved her hand dismissively. "Mind out of the gutter, Lanier." She smiled wistfully. "I've never been there. I hear the food's excellent, and I'd like to spy on my competition."

Matt huffed out a relieved sigh. "Ohhh, right. Dinner."

"Actually, I was thinking lunch. Today."

He recoiled and raised his eyebrows. "Today?"

"The Halcyon's closed. Naniboujou's open, and it's close enough to drive up for lunch. Might as well find out now if we can do this square-one thingy."

"I'm a bit road weary. Not sure I brought my A game for dating purposes."

"Freshen up at my house. Take a quick nap if you want. I'll finish here, then get ready. But I want the old-fashioned, gentleman drives, opens doors, pays for the meal, horn to tail."

"Say what?"

"It's an old Colorado saying. Lots of ranchers where I grew up. When they send cattle to the slaughterhouse, every part of a steer gets used.

Nothing is wasted from the horn to the tail. I want the full date treatment from horn to tail."

"How western of you," was all he could manage.

"So?" She looked at him with wide eyes and a hopeful expression.

"I'm in. I hope I remember how to be a gentleman."

"Good." She smiled. A knee-buckler. A heart-warmer. "You've got an hour to jog your memory."

Chapter 57

Naniboujou Lodge's cathedral-like dining room—adorned with a bright, beautifully painted ceiling and walls inspired by Cree Indian designs—was surprisingly intimate. Matt and Allyson had one corner to themselves. They enjoyed the lake view and quiet conversation without intrusions by misbehaving children or boisterous groups. Their discussion ranged from childhoods, likes and interests outside their current professions, travel, family, friends, and other topics typical of first dates. The difficulty was not to slip into a discussion of their shared history. Matt tried to speak as if none of his recent traumatic past had happened. He occasionally slipped, as did she. His toughest challenge was to avoid talking about Diane. But he didn't dwell on her any more than Allyson stumbled when she tried not to mention Vossler.

Driving her home, Matt relished his feeling of contentment. As luck would have it, the local independent radio station, WTIP, was playing Eva Cassidy's impeccable rendition of "At Last," a soul classic made famous by Etta James. He silently sang along with Eva. Love might or might not come along after this date with Allyson, but for the first time in years, his lonely days were over for the time being.

The day was a classic late-summer North-Shore day—a few fluffy clouds, light breeze, sixty degrees. They mainly drove in silence, enjoying the scenery. Matt pointed out parks, motels, restaurants, and sights he'd visited in his many travels to the area. Allyson filled him in on businesses that had changed hands or closed, as well as the general vibe of North Shore residents in the five-plus years she'd lived in Castle Danger. He tried to gauge her overall impression of their date, but she deftly used her acting skills to keep him in suspense.

When they arrived at the Halcyon, Allyson unlocked the door, led him in, and closed the door behind them. This was decision time. She'd either say the date had gone well or give him the "You're a nice guy, but..." speech.

Instead, she grasped his shoulders and kissed him firmly, tenderly, on the lips.

His shock quickly changed to comprehension. He pressed into her, wrapped his arms around her waist, and let out a low moan. Arousal coursed through his body. She held the kiss for several seconds, came up for air, then kissed him again, this time teasing him with her tongue. At first, he reciprocated tentatively. He didn't want to get too revved up if this was only a goodbye pity kiss. After several more seconds of intense kissing, she pulled back and gazed into his eyes. He stared into hers, searching for a hint that her feelings were real. Allyson was a few inches shorter than Matt, so their bodies fit together well in a standing position. Chest to chest. Pelvis to pelvis. It was an easy leap to imagine them horizontal and naked in her bed ... or on the Halcyon's bar top.

"Well," she said after a gentle sigh, "*that* was everything I'd hoped for and a little more." To punctuate her statement, she pressed her hips forward into his, then headed for the bar. "Shall we discuss a second date?"

The mischievous sparkle in her eye intrigued him. Eager to extend this day as long as possible, he said, "Sure."

She reached up to the top shelf behind the bar and pulled down the iconic bottle Matt immediately recognized as Louis XIII Cognac. Removing the stopper, she said, "Today is worth the good stuff."

His intuition that she was attracted to him had been correct. But what now? He had no place to live, no job, no immediate plans. He'd postponed those decisions until he knew whether she wanted to attempt a relationship. Suppose he wanted a long-term relationship with her. In that case, he'd be starting from the bottom—a man with minimal prospects, albeit a sizeable inheritance, hoping to win the hand of one of the most beautiful, charming, competent women he'd ever known.

Allyson poured generous splashes of the cognac into two snifters and walked toward the fireplace seating area. Matt followed, taking in the view of her from behind with the lust of a man now entitled to think of her as a sexual being. She flipped the switch for the gas fireplace and settled into one of the comfortable upholstered chairs facing the flame. He sat in the adjacent chair. They clinked glasses and simultaneously grinned.

"To the future," Matt said, trying to keep the questioning tone out of his voice.

"To the future," Allyson said.

After they'd each taken a sip, he said, "So ... you wanted to discuss a second date?"

Nodding, she said, "Yes. If you *don't* ask me out again, you are quite possibly the stupidest man who ever lived."

Matt blurted out, "How about dinner and a movie tonight?"

She giggled at his desperate tone. "You're one smart cowboy, Lanier. However, ..."

Her hesitation set him slightly on edge. "What's wrong?"

She waved a dismissive hand. "I want to wait until Josh comes home and see if he approves of his mother dating a former fugitive."

She was serious. Her son was part of the package. Matt would need to accept Josh, and Josh would need to tolerate Matt in his mother's life. "Oh, yeah, Josh, sure. I understand. I can wait."

He massaged his left hand and stared out the picture window at Lake Superior. A fatherless young boy could react to a new man in his mother's life in multiple ways, positive or negative. Matt couldn't imagine how Josh felt after he'd left without saying goodbye, without explaining why. He steeled himself for a veto from a nine-year-old.

"I hope he'll be okay with us," Allyson said. "But he's harder to read now than when he was five." She stood. "Let's finish our drinks and go to the house. He'll be home from school in twenty minutes."

As they sat in her kitchen, sipping glasses of lemonade, dread enveloped Matt. What if Josh *wasn't* glad to see him? What if he resented Matt for leaving so abruptly last winter? What if he'd been scarred by the trauma of running for his life, then being kidnapped and drugged by his own father? Lacking any knowledge of child psychology, Matt didn't know what to expect.

Allyson noticed his worried expression. "Relax, ya' big chicken," she said. "Josh was shaken by the entire experience, but we discussed it often, especially about his father being killed. I haven't told him why *you* pulled the trigger. He needs to be older to understand that. And I showed him the note you left me—the one where you said you'd come back someday."

"I felt like a coward," Matt said. "I figured it was better to run and regroup rather than stay here and take my chances with the sheriff."

She leaned over and took his hand gently in hers. "It took me a while to accept your leaving too, but I knew deep in my heart you'd keep your promise and come back someday."

Presently they heard the rumble of the school bus in the Halcyon parking lot. Matt stood next to the table. Allyson opened the back door. Josh's footsteps grew louder as he scampered the fifty yards between the Halcyon and the house.

As Josh reached the stoop, Allyson said, "How was your day, sweetie?"

"Okay, I guess," he said as he shrugged off his backpack and hugged and kissed her.

"I have a surprise for you, Joshie." She turned so Josh could see into the kitchen.

Matt stepped forward, palms sweaty, mouth dry, smiling tentatively. Josh recognized him immediately, then backed up a step, his mouth as wide open as his eyes. Matt's heart leaped into his throat. Josh glanced at his mother. The love in her eyes was as deep as her smile was luminous.

"Matt!" Josh sprinted forward and clamped his arms around Matt's waist.

"Hi, buddy," Matt said, trying to keep his voice from cracking. He hugged Josh as tight as he dared without causing pain. "It's great to see you. I missed you so much."

Josh's beaming smile and Allyson's approving nod, with tears trickling down her cheeks, told Matt all he needed to know. He'd found a new home, a starting point for the rest of his new life. His Halcyon dream had come true ... at last.

Thank you to the outstanding beta readers who helped me improve this book in a huge way: Roberta Edwards, Dave Hanna, Carol Hoepner, Dennis Koch, John Loch, Kay Norbury, Erin Ramsey, Allan Schwartz, and Glenda Thompson. Each of them contributed valuable critiques and comments.

Thanks also to my outstanding cover designer, Carl Graves of Extended Imagery.com. *Dangerous Straits* is the third cover he's created for me. As far as I'm concerned, Carl hit a home run each time. D.J. Schuette of Critical Eye Editorial and Publishing Services kept me from taking the story on a flight of fancy in the outline phase of the project that would have been a supreme challenge to land. Then he did another fine job of copyediting the actual storyline. Ray Riethmeier did the proofreading. Any typos that snuck past his sharp eyes are my fault, not his.

I stayed motivated by all the fans of my previous books who frequently asked, "So, when's the next book coming out?" It's hard to give up when so many people believe in your storytelling ability even when you have one of those "bad author days" when you worked on the book for months and months and feel like quitting because you "know" it stinks.

Motivation also came in the form of pastries and coffee. Thanks to all the locally owned coffee shops I patronized in southern Minnesota who provided sustenance, caffeine, and a comfortable place in a corner of their shops where an author could turn a jumble of a thousand ideas and a hundred thousand words into a coherent story that people will want to read.

Thank you for reading *Dangerous Straits*. If you enjoyed it, please tell your friends and family who love to read. Also, consider writing a *brief* online review of the book on your favorite book website. Word-of-mouth advertising and online reviews are the keys to success for most authors. We don't have the advantage of national advertising campaigns, book tours, and other publicity that big publishers provide to their bestselling authors. Here are some popular online review websites for you to consider:

www.goodreads.com *(my personal favorite)*
www.barnesandnoble.com
www.bookbub.com
www.amazon.com

Simply go to your preferred website, type "Dangerous Straits" into the search box, and follow the prompts to write your review. Some websites may require you to sign up before posting reviews. Please follow me at **chrisnorbury.com** for news about upcoming events and future projects.

Sincerely,
Chris Norbury

Chris Norbury is the un-gainfully employed, non-bestselling author of four novels. Each book has earned various book awards most people have never heard about and probably won't remember, anyway. His Matt Lanier thriller series stars a musician hero who stumbles upon a violent, powerful conspiracy that ruins his life and nearly kills him because he's too brilliantly stubborn to let the bad guys win.

His newest book—*Little Mountain, Big Trouble*—is a middle-grade adventure novel inspired by his experiences as a volunteer with Big Brothers Big Sisters for twenty years.

Chris grew up in the Twin Cities where he earned a B.S. in Music Education at Minnesota. He's had careers as a public-school band director, financial planner, wine consultant, and day trader before taking up the challenge of being an author. He belongs to the Twin Cities and national chapters of Sisters in Crime and the Alliance of Independent Authors.

He lives in southern Minnesota with his wife, Sandra. For bizarre reasons even *he* can't understand, he's a lifelong golf addict. Another passion is canoeing in Minnesota's Boundary Waters Canoe Area Wilderness. He's taken dozens of canoe trips there, plus several other river trips over the decades. Many have been solo adventures.

After publishing his first book in 2016, Chris began donating a portion of all his book sales to Big Brothers Big Sisters of Southern MN. For more information, visit chrisnorbury.com.

www.ingramcontent.com/pod-product-compliance
Lightning Source LLC
Chambersburg PA
CBHW020123310726
48970CB00006B/1703